NIGHT SHADE

NIGHT SHADE

AUTUMN WOODS

PAN BOOKS

First published 2025 by Slowburn
an imprint of Zando

First published in the UK 2025 by Pan Books
an imprint of Pan Macmillan
The Smithson, 6 Briset Street, London EC1M 5NR
EU representative: Macmillan Publishers Ireland Ltd, 1st Floor,
The Liffey Trust Centre, 117–126 Sheriff Street Upper,
Dublin 1 D01 YC43
Associated companies throughout the world

ISBN 978-1-0350-8400-5

Pan Macmillan does not have any control over, or any responsibility for, any author or
third-party websites (including, without limitation, URLs, emails and QR codes)
referred to in or on this book.

9 8 7 6 5 4 3 2 1

A CIP catalogue record for this book is available from the British Library.

Text design by Neuwirth & Associates, Inc.

Typeset in Adobe Caslon Pro
Printed and bound by CPI Group (UK) Ltd, Croydon CR0 4YY

MIX
Paper | Supporting
responsible forestry
FSC® C116313

Visit **www.panmacmillan.com** to read more about all our books
and to buy them.

Do you ever feel like you're being watched?

Anything in excess is a poison.
—Theodore Levitt

NIGHT SHADE

AUTHOR'S NOTE

THANK YOU SO much for picking up *Nightshade*.

This book is intended for an audience aged eighteen+, and contains themes of murder, depression, bereavement, drowning, suicidal thoughts, declining health of a parent, and violence, as well as sexual content.

You should be aware that this book forms the first half of a duet, and that Ophelia and Alex's story will be completed in a second book.

ANONYMOUS

Annalise was mine. My sweet solace. My English rose. I loved her with a fire all-consuming, a burning from within. She was mine, and always should've been mine.

My love for her was a disease, and disease knows no boundaries. It knows no laws and no repentance. It doesn't care who belongs to who; it'll sever branches from a family tree without thought.

And this disease, it crawled its way into my soul and sat there, rotting and festering in the cage that *he* built for it. That was, until it ate its way out through the bars and into every vein, muscle, and bone in my body. Until all that was left was the monster he always told her I'd turn out to be.

It was supposed to be me and Annalise until the end of time. She'd leave it all behind and hold my bleeding heart in her hand until the cracks started to fuse.

But she chose *him*. Annalise and the girl, they both chose him.

PROLOGUE

Annalise was my treasure. The prize I never deserved. And even with my fingertips outstretched, she was always just out of reach. And do you know what our ancestors did with treasures they couldn't make use of?

They buried them.

So I did.

And Annalise remains as she should have always been—forever mine.

Chapter 1

OPHELIA

The week my father was killed, I promised him I'd never set foot at Sorrowsong University.

I made him a lot of promises, from the boring and ordinary, to the abstract and emotional. That I wouldn't leave my bedroom light on, that I'd follow all my dreams. That I wouldn't shower for too long, that I'd always love myself.

Standing here represents the final domino falling in a long streak of letting him down.

The gates of the university stare back at me, the wrought iron twisting into a snarl, daring me to take one more step. The gulls above my head take their mournful cries with them, wise enough to fly away from the castle built into the valley before me.

A shudder racks my spine as a thick fog rolls in over the tarn to my left, the sun struggling to rise behind an overcast sky. Despite the weather, I can still make out the script beneath the university's crest.

Scientia potentia est. Knowledge is power.

My snort comes out as a white smudge in the bitter air. It's not a surprising motto for a university. Sorrowsong just doesn't mean it like the other universities do. They're not referring to cures for cancer or faster ways to get to the moon; they're talking about blackmail. Manila folders exchanged in shadowy alleys, and business deals conducted underground.

Sorrowsong is where the wealthiest of the world's men and women are sculpted into little clones of their corrupt parents, and the air around me reeks of wasted potential.

The duffel bag containing my worldly possessions huffs an anxious sigh when I drop it at my feet to rub the sore indents it has left on my shoulders. Through the howl of the wind and the oddly comforting patter of rain against leaves, I can hear the distant buzz of other new students making their way across the drawbridge and into the facade of the castle. I'm already running late, but as the gates creak open via some invisible control, I can't quite will myself to walk through them.

A depressing truth gnaws at the back of my mind. I don't even want to be here.

But I have no choice.

I've not been blessed with forks in the road; I've not stood in the center of a crossroads and carefully selected my path. Life has funneled me to these ornate black gates. Now it's up to me to walk through them.

There are two girls living inside me: the one clinging onto her final shred of hope, and the one that wants to burn the world down. One tugs me backward, the other forward.

My feet don't move.

2

A loud car horn shocks me out of my internal debate, my shadow appearing over the roughened terrain before me. I whirl around to face two bright lights in the driving rain, drawing closer by the second. Frozen in place by panic, I shut my eyes, bracing for the impact.

But it never comes, just the squeak of brakes and the gentle kiss of cool metal against my thighs. I pop an eyelid, my gaze connecting with an…angel? A woman cloaked in silver, bending down before me.

The Spirit of Ecstasy.

The figurine is delicate, almost apologetic, unlike the rest of the classic Rolls-Royce Phantom, which is about an inch from crushing me into the muddy trail beneath my feet. The haze of the rain in the headlights leaves the driver anonymous, but the deep, angry voice that wafts from the window raises the hairs on the back of my neck.

"What in the ever-loving fuck do you think you're doing? Are you *trying* to get killed?"

Am I? Maybe I am. I can't deny that my efforts to cross train lines and get crumpets out of toasters have been increasingly sloppy lately.

"What am *I* doing? What do you think *you're* doing barreling down a narrow lane in fog like this?" I shout back, hauling my sodden body and bags out of the road with an unceremonious squelch.

The black Phantom creeps forward a little, so the wing mirrors fall in line with my shivering form. I stoop to see the driver, one trembling hand keeping the rain out of my eyes.

My stomach flips at the sight of him, a warning sign flashing somewhere in the distance.

3

The man behind the wheel does nothing to slow my thundering heartbeat. On the one hand, he looks like he could've been plucked from a boardroom on Wall Street earlier this morning. With a shirt as crisp as the air around me and a jawline just as sharp, he taps out a text on his phone as if nearly killing me was just another inconvenience in his day.

But as I study him closer, there are faults in the investment banker image I'd invented for him. Black ink spills from beneath his rolled-up shirt sleeves. Vines, flowers, and ravens waltz along the defined muscles of two powerful forearms, another bird's wing peeks through the opening at the top of his shirt. His dark hair is disheveled, cutting across his forehead in tousled waves. He looks a little older than me.

Unease prickles the back of my neck, and I'm paralyzed momentarily by a pair of intense green eyes that morph from irritated to curious as he finishes whatever it is he's doing, chucks the phone in the center console, and turns his attention to my bedraggled appearance.

Silence unravels between us, his head dipping a fraction to see even more of me. Under the somber lighting of the storm, he looks ethereal.

Something deep in my chest screams at me to *run*.

His eyes shift from me to the gloomy pathway ahead, before turning to regard me again. The curiosity in his eyes has been masked with an emotion that makes me take an involuntary step back.

"Rather die than go in?" he asks, an easy grin spreading across his face. The smooth baritone of his voice unsettles me; it doesn't match his aura or the wicked look in his eye. I can't quite place his accent.

I pull a lock of hair from where it has plastered itself to my lips, eyeing him warily. "Something like that."

4

With two fingers, he shifts the car into reverse. "I'll back up. I can make it look like an accident. You'd be the third one I have done today."

I'd smile if my face wasn't frozen in place by the biting wind. "Marvelous. If you could just throw me off the drawbridge when you're done."

"I heard the fish needed feeding." His immaculate shirt strains over his broad chest as he leans away from me to unlock the passenger door, but I don't miss the Patek Philippe hugging his wrist as he lazily drapes it over the driver-side window. "Hop in."

Amid the scent of marshlands and a forest swathed in rain, a wave of leather and smoke engulfs me. Every inch of this man screams *old money*, the very type that my mother and father made me swear I'd avoid. Grief rears its ugly head at the back of my mind, and the slap of my bag against my back as I swing it over my shoulder knocks enough sense into me to walk away.

But a green gaze and an arrogant smile soon catch up with me, impatient fingers drumming on the door of the car. "What's wrong, fish food? Scared of my driving?"

My boots skid to a halt in the mud as I swivel around to face him. "Is there a reason you're desperate to get an innocent girl into your car in the middle of nowhere?"

"Innocent," he repeats the word. Tests it. Lets it linger heavy between us, waiting for me to crumble under the weight of my small white lie. I breathe out a curse and wave my goodbye, but the engine purrs and the car jerks forward, lurching to a halt across my path. With my exit route blocked, my eyes dart to the woods on either side of the rugged track.

Bad things lurk in the Solemn Woods, Ophelia. Never go there.

Bad things lurk in luxury cars, too, Mama, but you're not here to help me now.

Turning my back to the stranger, I trudge my way around the bonnet, scowling at every rock, puddle, and twig that I pass. The sound of a car door opening sends my stomach plummeting to my feet. I glance over my shoulder and panic. My new friend unfolds his giant form and slinks out of the car with the grace of a panther.

I should've chosen the forest.

Over six feet of well-honed muscle strides toward me, each movement fluid and calculated, and instinctively I reach for the penknife in my pocket. Two black boots halt, toe-to-toe with mine and I feel his hot breath tickle my ear.

"Just out of interest, where would you stab me?"

I keep my voice steady, but my heart flutters uncomfortably. I don't bother asking him how he knew. He looks like the sort of man that fate itself would bow to. "In the voice box, probably. Seems it'll be the only way to get you to shut up."

His laugh, as warm and thick as honey, dulls the sting of the cold on my skin. Before I can react, four fingers slide beneath the strap of my bag and swiftly toss it onto the back seat of the car. My fists clench in my jacket pockets.

"Give that back."

"Get in the car."

"I'll just walk."

He bites his lip to stifle a smile, and butterflies dance in my lower stomach. I swear, they don't make men who look like this where I grew up. "And what does that make me? A glorified luggage service?"

"It makes you a thief."

"I'd rather be a kidnapper," he replies, gesturing to the passenger-side door.

I start to walk toward the castle, but something stops me. My phone is in that bag. Through the tinted window, my glare lands on the lucky key ring from my dad swinging from the handle, and I know the battle is lost. I'd rather lose my pride than that little piece of him.

I let out an insult just loud enough for him to hear and slip into the front seat, letting my wet hair soak the cream leather. I grimace at the state of my boots, stomping the mud off on the tan carpet at my feet.

A dark eyebrow arches in my direction as he slips into the seat beside me. "What's next? Spit in the glove box?"

I drag my gaze to his. "No, shit on the dashboard."

Another laugh, louder this time and lethally attractive. He flicks a few buttons and the leather beneath my thighs begins to warm, quiet piano filtering out of the speakers. It's comfortable, but I don't let myself relax. Something about him seems like an elastic band just waiting to snap.

"I just feel like there has to be a middle step there, fish food. Shit on the dashboard is extreme, you could at least…"

"Pee in the cup holder?" He hasn't driven yet. This was a mistake. This won't look good for me in the newspapers. *Girl dies in remote Scottish valley after blindly climbing into a complete stranger's car.*

He throws up a hand while the other one shifts the gear stick into first. "Exactly. Everyone is so terribly quick to jump to extremes these days." The car still stationary, he glances back over at me, running his eyes over my disheveled outfit and tattered bag. "Are you cosplaying Oliver Twist?"

"Fuck off." I scan his ridiculously overdressed attire. All he's missing is a top hat and a cane. "Would that make you the Artful Dodger?"

I catch his sly grin in the corner of my eye. "Clever and charming?"

"No, just irritating." I reach for the door handle to leave, but he holds up two hands in surrender and slowly peels the car forward. His demeanor may be easy, but something about him feels off. Something hides in those green eyes that is neither humor nor annoyance. Something deeper. Something darker, *hungrier*.

A sketchbook peeks out of the passenger door pocket. My fingers itch to touch it, to get a glimpse inside a mind that is not my own.

"Don't."

"I'm not gonna judge your Mickey Mouse fan art."

He snorts, eyes fixed on the road as he veers us round a fallen log. "More of a Minnie man myself."

"What *is* in there?"

The sparkle in his eye is frightening. "Drawings of all my previous victims."

Welp. I guess it's my fault for getting in the car. "Divorced, beheaded, died?"

He flashes me a wolfish smile, neither warm nor comforting. "Then divorced, then beheaded again. With any luck, you just might survive."

Terrific.

The car glides effortlessly over the bumpy pathway up to the campus. It's my first real chance to take it all in. Gargoyles weep tears of rain as we pass them, each one more anguished than the last. A spiked iron fence borders the Solemn Woods, but it wouldn't stop you going in if you wanted to.

I don't want to.

A shudder rolls down my spine, and for the first time since the seven-hour train journey and three-hour coach ride, it hits me how isolated it is up here.

Looming above us is Sorrowsong Castle, a centuries-old fortress embedded into the mountainside. Thick stone walls rise into turrets, proudly holding the tiled roof aloft against a charcoal sky. The landscape has been battered and broken by the elements, but the castle stands tall and intact above the river, tarn, and thick forest at its feet. Gray rain pelts gray stone and gray tree trunks. It's like whoever made the world ran out of paint by the time they got here. Even the grass is a muted shade of green.

A sinking feeling churns my stomach and I pull my phone from the puddle at the bottom of my bag. *No service*. It's not like I have any contacts, anyway, but it still worsens the nausea in my gut.

Three years. I just have to survive three years, and then I'll never set foot in this place again.

One large hand lazily hangs over the steering wheel, the other tapping on his thigh as he breaks the uncomfortable silence. "You haven't told me your name, fish food."

"And you haven't told me yours."

He veers off the uneven track so suddenly that I slap a clammy palm against the cold glass of the window. The car swings into one of two spaces decorated with gold plaques that very clearly say *Chancellor,* and my new friend—who I sincerely doubt is the chancellor—kills the engine. "Alex. My name is Alex."

Alex. Something about him seems familiar. A warning light flashes somewhere in my mind, but it's too blurry for me to read the caption. There's a reason my hand hasn't left the knife in my pocket; I just need to work out what it is.

The groan of the engine and the crunch of twigs beneath tires are quiet now, only the soft patter of rain on the windshield keeping us company. His eyes lazily take me in properly for the first time, lingering on the sliver of wet shirt beneath my jacket for a beat. They coast back up to mine, a seductive smile tipping the corner of his mouth up as he pulls a cigarette from a metal box on the dashboard. He tucks it between his lips and the flame of his lighter makes the mischief in his eyes burn brighter. "Maybe Oliver Twist was a *little* harsh."

I tug the hem of my skirt down slightly and gather my duffel and tote bag, my breaths constrained by the thick tension in the car. With a mumbled goodbye and eyes looking anywhere but at him, I leave Alex and break into a jog toward the castle gates. I feel his stare burning the back of my head, but I don't entertain it.

I am not here to fool around with criminally attractive men. I am here for two reasons and two reasons alone: to graduate from the only university on this planet that had a place for me, and to find out why my parents died a mile away from where we are parked.

Chapter 2

OPHELIA

The planks of the drawbridge sound unnervingly hollow as I hurry across them, like something is rotting beneath their smooth facade, eager to drag me under. No time to dwell; I haul my aching limbs and overfilled bag into the impressive Grand Hall.

It's odd to think I've never set foot inside, given I'd lived nearby for most of my childhood. My parents never crawled their way out of our council estate, but despite a decade of working here and an offer of a staff cottage on the grounds, they never took me here. My father went to great lengths to make sure that not one single day of my childhood was spent between these walls, even if it meant nights apart and long commutes.

I never understood why. There's drama here, but mostly between the children of rival families. They'd leave an outsider alone. Or maybe that's wishful thinking.

The hall is empty, but there's a diminishing buzz in the air like it was full of life just moments before. Overhead, a chandelier sways slightly, the polished crystals tinkling quietly as the wind slips through gaps between roof tiles. The mosaic under my feet depicts the school's crest in subdued shades of white and brown, but my focus is snatched by the centerpiece of the room.

The painting opposite me must be fifteen feet tall, occupying a vast panel of wall between two spiral staircases. The woman in the artwork is dirty and dusty, slumped over on a rock in a desolate landscape. Tears and fresh blood glisten on her hollow cheeks, yet beneath greasy strands of blonde hair, her lips form a manic smile. The colors are dull, as if the painting itself is suffering under years of neglect, but the four objects in her hand are as vibrant as if they were painted this morning. It doesn't take a genius to work out what they are; they're plastered on all the banners hanging from the turrets.

Hemlock, Nightshade, Cortinar, and Snakeroot. Four deadly plants. The four houses of Sorrowsong University. What university has *houses*? It's straight out of a creepy fantasy book.

My eyes flick back up to the chilling smile on her face as I become aware of another presence beside me.

"Beautiful, isn't it?"

The older gentleman who appears to my left exudes a classic sort of handsomeness that defies his years. Dressed immaculately in a tailcoat, the shade of red so dark that it sucks the glow from the rest of his graying skin, he seems like a memory from a past era; a ghost trapped in the castle that might've accidentally stumbled upon the wrong century. The handlebar mustache on his top lip should look ridiculous, but it only adds to the whole Victorian undertaker look he has going on.

The vast expanse of the Grand Hall doesn't seem so spacious now, his presence so large that I half wonder if there will be enough air for both of us to keep breathing.

Unsettled, I cast my eyes back to the painting. Truthfully, I'm not sure that it *is* beautiful. I can't fathom why one would hang such a haunting painting over a room where people are supposed to dance, eat, study, and socialize.

"I suppose, if you like that sort of thing," I murmur, worried for some reason that the woman in the painting will hear me.

He sharpens his mustache between his middle finger and thumb, lost in his own reverie. "It's Achlys."

I meet his strangely dark eyes and shrug. "I've not heard of her."

"She's thought to be the personification of sorrow. When Lord MacArtain built this castle, his wife fell terribly ill before it was completed. Day by day, he watched the pink flush of life drain out of her until she was muted in shades of green and gray. Driven mad by his anticipatory grief, he claimed his wife was Achlys reborn." He lets out a weary sigh. "Such a sad soul she had, even in life. He swore he could hear her mournful wails tangled up in the wind, sweeping through the valleys when he could not sleep at night. He even said he could hear her quiet sobs underwater in the tarn. It's said she haunts the castle even today."

"Oh, excellent." I've probably already pissed off a ghost.

Sorrowsong. I suppose that name makes sense now. The story sends a chill into my bones that settles down and makes itself comfortable like it's here to stay a while. Love makes a fool of us all in the end. I've accepted a life alone. I *want* a life alone. If I'd hated my parents rather than loved them so fiercely that it burnt, my life would be a lot easier now.

I feel Achlys's stare on my cheek and turn to face her once more. She doesn't look sorrowful—perhaps in body, but not in spirit. She looks *evil*. "If she is supposed to represent sadness, why is she smiling?"

The man chuckles as if I've made a joke, the gold chain of his pocket watch slithering through his pale fingers. "Why indeed. And why did she provide Hera with poisonous flowers? Sad people are not always as deserving of our pity as they seem. Everyone has a limit at which they abandon their own morality, Ophelia Winters, even you."

My mind reels, scrambling to remember if I ever told this man my name. I didn't. I'm sure I didn't. His eerie words linger in the stale air between us, sinking into the back of my mind unbidden and unwelcome.

He claps his hands together abruptly and steps in front of me, watching me intently for a few seconds like he's reading a journal of my darkest thoughts and deepest desires. Does he see my rotting heart? Does he see the unfathomable rage that keeps it beating? I wonder if he finds it interesting, or if mine pales in comparison to the other monsters here.

"Jolly good. I have other endeavors to attend to. I hope you understand how very unheard of it is for the university to allow someone in out of charity, Ms. Winters. Don't fall behind the pack. It makes you easy prey."

"You'd expel me?" I choose to believe that's what he meant, rather than something more sinister. That's not an option. Not if I want to escape the eternal cycle of hopelessness I've been stuck in since I was seventeen.

A disconcerting smile wrinkles the translucent skin around his eyes as he backs away from me a few steps and tips his flat cap in my direction. He spins on the heel of his burgundy loafers and opens a door embedded in the painting that I would never have noticed before. "Worse things dwell in Sorrowsong than expulsion. Take the right staircase, second door on your left."

And with that, he is gone, leaving me stranded in the suffocating gloom of the hall. The hammering of my heart pounds in my ears, muffling the sound of ravens fluttering high above me in the rafters. A crow's cry echoes inside the gaping fireplace at the other end, spurring me faster toward the right set of stairs.

I don't like this room. Something about it feels ominous, making me keen to spend as little time here as possible. This place, that man, the painting—they all give me the creeps.

The offer of a paid-for course at Sorrowsong seemed an impossible stroke of good fortune, much too generous to turn down. Yet, as I hurry into yet another cobweb-ridden, barely lit corridor, a shiver runs down my spine and I wonder if I will pay a price far greater than money for my time here. But I have no other option, this is my last chance at life, my final resort.

The man in Achlys's Hall made one thing clear: one minor misstep and I'm done for.

If I'm to stay here, I need to excel.

The first door on the left is a huge double door, the gold sign illuminated by candlelight and the occasional flash of lighting as the storm rages on outside. *The Cortinar Halls.*

Between nervously staring out the window and daydreaming about any other life than my own, I did a little reading on the train. Your assignment to one of the houses, pointless as it may seem, hinges on the five-thousand-word essay you submit as part of your application. Cortinar House is renowned for its ruthless, logical approach to everything, molding clever creatives into society's most cutthroat businessmen and women. Many of the law and economics students end up there.

Hemlock House is for the strong and driven, those built with endurance who excel at physical challenges and tests of their sanity. It comprises an even blend of courses, but most of its students are on the sports teams.

Snakeroot House has spat out a long lineage of the world's finest surgeons. Many medical students find themselves there. It's just a shame most of them abandon patient care for a career exploiting the high demand for medicine by the time they turn thirty.

And then there's Nightshade. It boasts an endless list of famous alumni: CEOs, property tycoons, and investment bankers, alongside notorious serial killers, Mafia heirs, and famous hit men. There is a reason the Nightshade halls are the only dormitories excluded from the castle's central court of buildings. If the university's seventy-thousand-pound-per-year fee doesn't scare you off, its twisted reputation might. It seems students go missing or end up dead every year, and it's usually Nightshade to blame. If a degree from Sorrowsong wasn't like a golden ticket to Wall Street, I doubt anyone would dare set foot beyond the drawbridge.

I'm glad you'll never go to Sorrowsong, O. They live life by another rule book entirely.

My father's words linger in the shadows of my mind, where the memories of him and my mother lie. He'd often return from work weary, tired, and laden with stories of whatever heinous sins some of the students had committed that day: cars exploding at night, students left tied up in the woods, venomous snakes in pillowcases.

I've never been sure how much was true and how much was his overactive imagination.

Thankfully, I'll be in Hemlock. I think the only reason the chancellor let me in was my national ranking in swimming. My all-but-guaranteed place in Hemlock is the only reason I'm here.

"Oh good, you're late too. Is the welcoming talk this way?" A feminine voice, thickly accented, pulls me from my thoughts. A tall, tanned, leggy blonde in a stylish white shift dress pulls me into a warm hug like we've known each other for years. She smells like flowers and banknotes, like she knows what all the different-sized knives and forks are for. "Colette DuPont. So nice to meet you, and *so* nice to be here!"

"Uhh…" I adjust my bag on my shoulder and awkwardly shake her proffered hand. "Ophelia Winters, and I'm not sure. I'm as lost as you are."

She air-kisses my cheeks and squeals with delight like I've just said something incredible. *Terrifying.* "Such a beautiful name. What are you studying?"

"Psychology." Of the meager list of eight available courses at Sorrowsong, it was the only one I could stomach. "You?"

"Fine arts. My stepfather said he'll help me set up my own gallery once I graduate. He'd be *so* disappointed if he knew I was late on the first day. My driver was overly cautious on the roads." She picks up her Hermès bag, chatting away at me in an animated blend of English and French as we approach the second door on the left.

"Was it you I saw in the Rolls-Royce with Alex Corbeau-Green earlier? Would you introduce me?"

My feet skid to a halt outside the door. Colette's cheery anecdote about how Alex has a quarter of a million more Instagram followers than her is drowned out by a high-pitched ringing in my ears.

The world around me crumbles until I'm no longer standing in the corridor. I'm on my knees in front of the television in my parents' tiny kitchen, watching black smoke rise from damaged trees. I'm watching the hundredth call to my father go to voice mail and hitting the Call button all the same. I'm pulling the emergency cash from his safe and begging the taxi driver to drive faster.

And then I'm standing on the edge of it all, crawling under a yellow cordon and weaving through a sea of investigators, engineers, reporters, and firefighters. I'm staring at a sickening tangle of metal wrapped around a tree trunk, choking on black smoke, asking a god I never believed in why it was them and not me.

My memory of that day is messy, but one detail has been burned into the back of my retinas for four years. Amid the rubble, two words sat atop a charred splinter of metal buried in the earth: *Green Aviation.*

Perfectly manicured fingers click in front of my face. "Earth to Ophelia! I asked where your boots are from?"

I shake my head, casting the sound of my own screaming from my mind. Nausea churns my breakfast as I try to come to terms with the fact that one of *them* is here. Alex is the one person I never wanted to get friendly with, and I failed in the first hour. Never again. I let out a shaky exhale to quell the panic in my chest and pretend the world isn't swimming around me. "Um…I don't remember. Secondhand, I think."

Another giggle as we come to a halt in the hallway. "Cute *and* sustainable. I really need to do less shopping. This is the correct door, yes?"

I pause with bated breath, a mixture of nice, normal nerves and crippling existential dread washing over me. This is it. Run away or go inside. Be a regular person or be a Sorrowsong graduate. Play it safe, or...

Colette thrusts open the double doors and strides in with dazzling confidence and a titanium-white smile. The *tap-tap* of her heels echoes around the huge velvet banners hanging from the lofty ceiling. The room is almost as grand as Achlys's Hall, with rows of benches on either side and a long aisle leading up to a podium at the end. The impressive architecture suggests it was built as a chapel, but somehow I doubt it gets much use as one now.

"Sorry we're late!"

A hundred and fifty pairs of eyes land on us. Closest to me I recognize Mura Sayari, only because the nineteen-year-old super-model and Japanese technology heiress is on the front cover of the fashion magazine in my bag. I only bought it because they'd run out of crossword books at the bus station. I've unlocked ten new insecurities since I got on the coach: What is a hip dip? Why am I worried that I have one? I spent half the journey trying to work out if I have doe eyes or vixen eyes.

Clearly, my four years of wallowing in bed have left me a bit behind on the world.

Colette's glamorous entrance has well and truly shredded my plan for a subtle entrance. I cling to the hope that it can be recovered, but my legs refuse to move. I'm rooted in place by something—some*one*—casting a burning gaze that sears into my cheeks. My eyes are drawn upward by some irresistible force, and in the sea of faces, they land immediately on one. Time grinds to a stop, the ticking of the grandfather clock submerged in tar. I feel my face heat with an uncharacteristic rage.

So he's a new student, too.

A wicked grin appears on the face of Alex Corbeau-Green as he taps his watch twice and shakes his head at me. *So bad*, he mouths, his lips caressing each syllable in a way far too suggestive for what was once a chapel.

It might've been charming half an hour ago, but now that I know who he is, it's sickening. He's sitting with Nightshade. Of course he's in Nightshade; he'll fit right in. I shake my head, attempting to dispel the spell that seems to have woven its way through my brain. My teeth chatter as I drag my eyes away. I have definitely caught a cold.

The clearing of a throat reminds me once more that I am standing in the middle of the aisle, my clothes and bag creating a small puddle at my feet. The man I'd met in Achlys's Hall taps the podium impatiently with a wrinkled finger, his disapproving glare fixed on the two of us. It's nice not to be alone, at least. I think most of the male attention in the room is directed somewhere between the top of Colette's knees and the hem of her minidress. Except Alex's, but I ignore the way he stares at me.

"Colette DuPont. Your stepfather despises lateness. Take a seat with your classmates in Cortinar House."

"I know, Chancellor Carmichael, I'm so very sorry," she says, skipping off to slide onto a bench with a group of laughing girls it seems she already knows.

Did she just say *Chancellor*? Did I insult his painting choices to his face? Can I start today again and have another attempt? Preferably one that doesn't begin with me nearly getting run over by the spawn of Satan himself?

"And you, Ophelia. Go and join the rest of Nightshade."

I breathe a sigh of relief and flop onto the creaky bench to my left, pulling out my damp notebook to write down any snippets of wisdom I can gather from the welcome talk. Maybe I can get this day back on track.

When I look up and push the copper strands of hair from my eyes, everyone is still staring at me. Alex hooks a muscular arm over the back of the bench, twisting his intimidating form to get a better look at me. Glinting in his eyes is that same unnamed look that I saw in the car. Something between hunger and frustration, I think. It makes my skin prickle.

I look down to confirm that, no, my khaki top is not see-through enough that they can see my nipples, and look back up at the chancellor for a clue.

"Nightshade, Ms. Winters. Not Hemlock."

My ears ring. The thud of my heartbeat hits a little heavier in my throat. I glance at the sympathetic faces around me. They look…kind. Unassuming. Welcoming. *This* is where I belong. I've already made imaginary friendships with them. "There…there must've been a mistake."

There are a few snickers around the room, punctuated by a sympathetic gasp from Colette. Alex doesn't laugh, his gaze darkening on me as I sit like a lemon on the pew at the back of the room. The chancellor raps his knuckles on the podium twice. "Nightshade, Ophelia. *Now.*"

This cannot be happening. This is *not* happening. Maybe I did get run over by Alex, and this is some cruel punishment in the afterlife. Christ, all I did was steal a few things here and there. And maybe I slashed a tire or two. Or four. My point is, this punishment does not match the crime.

The girl beside me nudges me toward the edge of the bench and I walk to the other side of the hall under the weight of hundreds of eyes. I lower myself onto the farthest bench from Alex, waiting for the moment I wake up and discover this is a dream. A student in Snakeroot leans over and grins at me, popping his bubble gum in my face.

"They're gonna eat you alive in there."

Chapter 3

OPHELIA

Somewhere between the twentieth and thirtieth minute of Chancellor Carmichael's speech, my heart rate slows down just enough for me to actually listen. His voice, unwavering and cold, drones on about the legacy of the previous students here, what it truly means to be a Sorrowsong graduate, and how slips in academic performance will be severely punished.

"This institution is *not* struggling financially. Harsh as it may sound, I do not need all of you here. I will not mourn the loss of one, two, or even ten of you. If you do not prove to us the reasons you are here, then you will simply cease to be here."

His voice trails off, my focus firmly on the sports team sign-up sheets at the front of the room. There are four new places on the swim team available, and one of them is *mine*. I need it far more than most of these trust fund kids. It's the first rung on the ladder to *actually* graduating here.

23

As Carmichael finishes, he reminds us that we'll shortly be met by the Heads of Houses to be shown to our dormitories. Then, in a flash of silver-gray hair and well-tailored Brioni, he leaves behind a room charged with rivalry and ambition.

I make a beeline for the sports sign-up sheet on the pulpit at the front. When I flip to the swim team page, I'm pleased to see only a handful of names down.

I reach for the pen, but it freezes in midair, another hand gripping the opposite end. A familiar gold pinky ring glints back at me. *God, give me a break.* "Drop the pen."

"You're a real ray of sunshine, Ophelia. Anyone ever told you that?"

"Drop it."

Alex's face dips an inch closer to mine, green eyes alight with amusement. I'm close enough to smell his aftershave. Close enough to notice a small bruise decorating an old scar on his eyebrow. Close enough to see his playful mood fizzle out. "Not very good at making friends, huh?"

His remark brushes over a sensitive wound. I used to be good at making friends. Not so much nowadays. My finger tightens around the silver pen. It's petty. *I'm* petty. But I won't let that family take one more thing from me. "There isn't a sports team for being a spineless nepo baby."

He rakes his spare hand through his hair and flashes me a fake smile. I'm sure it works on most women. Not me. Not now that I know there's nothing but evil in his blood. "Carmichael's been ignoring my emails about adding *being a spineless nepo baby* to the syllabus for weeks."

"I'm serious."

24

He stifles a yawn, the heat of his skin reaching mine. "You know, I was going to sign up for rugby, but I'm suddenly remembering I'm actually a *really* good swimmer."

I edge closer, almost nose to nose. His pupils dilate, but I practically feel mine constrict with disgust. "Don't you dare. You'd never get in."

A muscle ticks in his jaw. "Yeah? And you sure looked athletic when you stood still and invited me to mow you over with my car earlier."

"I think anyone would consider ending it all if they had to face three years in present company."

He lets out a dark chuckle and releases the pen, his large hand curling my fingers around it. "We could re-create *Romeo and Juliet*."

No, no, no. I press the tip of the pen into the center of his muscular chest, rising and falling as hard as mine. I channel all my hatred, all my loathing for his family through the tiny but scorching point of contact between our bodies. "I see through your act, Alex. If you think I can't see that you're decaying from the inside out, you're sorely mistaken. Stay away from me and I'll return the favor."

I go to write my name for the swim team, but as the nib makes contact with the parchment, I catch the name at the very top of the list, written in different colored ink and messy handwriting. *Ophelia Winters.* I wipe my clammy palms on my skirt, uneasy. "Did you write this?"

Alex looms over my shoulder, the heat from his body thawing my frozen skin. "Looks like your bright and cheery disposition has earned you a secret admirer."

My patience wears to dust. "Did you do this or not?"

"You've not really given me anything to secretly admire."

It's a harmless prank, or even a favor, but just like my intuition with Alex in the car, there's a big, neon sign flashing the words *bad news* at the forefront of my mind. Even with my bag at my feet, the odd sensation of being watched has burdened me since the taxi dropped me off at the edge of Sorrowsong Valley and refused to come any nearer.

It doesn't make any sense, but I have a feeling I've made an enemy here already.

While Alex scribbles on the ivory paper, I turn on my heel and join the back of the small group of Nightshade students, staring at me as if I've grown a second head in the last two minutes. Alex joins the students at the front of the group with a casual bump of shoulders and a cold laugh that echoes around the chapel.

He settles into place beside a towering figure whose face is a maze of far more scars than one should have at our age. The two of them slip into easy Italian conversation that I can't understand, but when Alex mutters something under his breath, they both turn to stare at me for an uncomfortable minute until a beautiful, dark-haired woman beckons Nightshade out through the side doors.

I scoop up my bags and follow them, pausing at the doorway when the stained-glass window catches my attention. It isn't like the churches where I grew up. There is no biblical depiction in the window. It's Achlys, *again*, glowing in muted shades of green and brown. It seems I'll never escape her watchful eyes.

Without Achlys turning the tranquility into eerie silence, it would be peaceful here now that it's empty. Even the dust is still, suspended in time amid dull rays of sun.

"Do you dislike this artwork, too?"

I look up to follow the voice, Chancellor Carmichael looking down at me from the mezzanine above. A breeze of cold air licks the goose bumps on my arms, and I half wonder if this man is an apparition. I don't entertain his line of conversation. "I belong in Hemlock, sir. Surely you must see that."

"If you think there has been a mistake, you are more than welcome to report it to the board."

I drag a hand down my face, my sigh filtering through my fingers. It wouldn't matter if it didn't mean being so blatantly confronted with the cause of my parents' death every day. I glance back up and meet Carmichael's watchful gaze. I cannot get a hold on this man. I'm not sure if he's out to help me or break me. The gentle smile on his lips doesn't match the venom in his eyes.

"One of them will probably kill me."

He checks his pocket watch and snaps it shut, shattering the stillness in the chapel. "Disrupt or be disrupted, Ophelia. The choice is yours." He turns away from the wooden railing, but hovers there for a silent second. "I see you've made yourself known to Cain Green's son."

My stomach roils. "What about him?"

Carmichael doesn't turn around, but I can almost see the unsettling expression on his face. "I would be very careful around the Corbeau-Greens."

What? "Why? What do you know?" I take several steps back to see more of the balcony, but the chancellor is nowhere to be seen.

With Achlys's haunting sneer on my back, I hurry through the chapel door and into a gloomy tunnel. I'm lost in a creepy castle, but it's the least of my worries. What did Carmichael mean? If he knows something, is he just being cryptic to torture me?

The Corbeau-Greens played a heavy part in my parents' death, of that I am certain. Somehow, someday, I'll make that public knowledge. I'll bring their dynasty to its knees. I just need one final piece of proof.

FORTY-FIVE MINUTES INTO the most confusing campus tour in the history of campus tours, we're finally led out of the maze of poorly lit tunnels and hallways and into the courtyard to the north of the castle. Our tour guide, and the Head of Nightshade house, is a tall, Italian woman named Belladonna. She's wearing a sharp suit and black stilettos, navigating wonky staircases and cobbled paths with a deftness and lack of sprained ankles that I can only dream of.

She's in her fifth and final year of a medicine degree, and in her third year captaining the swim team. This means I need her to like me, and as she snaps her scarlet fingernails in the face of a student on his phone, I know it may be a challenge. A challenge Alex has no issues with, it seems. I watch Belladonna break her steely demeanor to bundle him into a rough hug, joining in step beside him and his friend.

The courtyard smells of rain and chimney smoke. The storm has calmed somewhat, but a biting wind still whips my drying hair around my face. I glance down at the map on my phone, which is even harder to make sense of than the castle itself. I've marked out the dining hall, two different libraries, a small student shop and pharmacy, and the psychology wing, but the rest looks like spaghetti at this point.

My phone flies from my hand abruptly as I'm pushed against the trunk of a beech tree by two of the other Nightshade students.

Judging by the deathly pale skin, black hair, and frosty blue eyes, I'd guess they're twins. My bag breaks most of the impact, but the air whooshes out of my lungs as two identical pairs of lips curl into menacing snarls. "Don't wanna be in Nightshade, huh?" says the guy, a hand around my throat.

My eyes flick back to the group moving farther and farther away. No one has noticed my absence. "Not particularly."

"Too good for us?" asks his sister, flicking her slick, black ponytail over her shoulder.

"I didn't say that," I manage, as her twin tightens his grip on my neck.

His eyes narrow and he releases me with a violent jerk. "Watch your step. Wouldn't want to fall into the lake, would you?" They both laugh, turning and sauntering off toward the group with a venomous look back in my direction.

Great. I'm zero days in and I've got a few bruised ribs and a bad reputation. I pick up my phone from the wet tile. If it's cracked any more than it already was, I can't tell.

A pretty, petite girl drops back from the group when she spots me. For the first time since I got here, I'm on the receiving end of a comforting smile. "Ignore Kirill and Sofia. They're just defensive because their father's territory in New York is receding faster than Principal Carmichael's hairline." She extends her hand to me. "I'm Divya."

Russian Mafia. That adds up. *Christ.* One day you're tearing a fifteen percent off fabric softener coupon out of a magazine and picking noodles out of your sink drain, the next, you're fighting for your life inside an Al Pacino movie.

I shake Divya's hand. "Ophelia. You're in Nightshade too?"

"Sadly. What sins did your parents commit to get you here?"

A sad laugh slips between my lips. "I'm still working that out. Yours?"

"My father has a monopoly on most of the insulin in India."

I grimace as we catch up with the others. "That's a bad one."

"Yup. Loves to drive up the prices for the hospitals. He actually studied medicine here, too."

It doesn't make sense. "I don't know why anyone bothers to come here."

"For the sun and sandy beaches, of course," she quips, before shaking her head. "It's well respected. I think most people here are trying to put as much distance between themselves and their messy home lives. We're all rich, and nothing turns families sour quite like money."

We stop in the center of the courtyard. The spire of the chapel looms behind us, thick stone walls dotted with arrow loops stand on each side. The space is sparse, lined with tiles that are a glossy shade of charcoal in the rain. It's the same muted palette of gray and brown as the rest of the castle, but there's the occasional tree or bench scattered around. I suppose if this valley ever managed to escape the perpetual storm that swirls overhead, it might be a nice place to sit.

We're led beneath the razor-sharp portcullis and out of the main castle grounds. From here, I can make out forested mountains and valleys as far as the eyes can see. The tops of pine trees pierce through a thick sheet of mist, straining to reach the heavy sky above. It's not yet midday, but it seems to be getting darker and darker out. I spare a thought for my vitamin D pills, abandoned in a cold, dusty cupboard back home where I didn't think I'd need them.

We approach a huge, Elizabethan-era manor house a few hundred yards away from the castle. I've seen it online a hundred times. *The Nightshade Halls.* Two deep purple banners fall from the top floor windows, embroidered with the Nightshade motto in gold thread. *Facilis descensus Averno.* I didn't really brush up on my Latin before coming here, but I'm sure it's something about death being the easy part.

As I stand in the drizzling rain and wonder why I didn't just take up a minimum wage job in the café in my parents' small town, Kirill engages in a fight with Alex's Italian friend. Nightshade is a sausage fest. *Fantastic.*

Cheers erupt from the group as Alex's friend pins the other one to the floor, and I'd be lying if I said I wasn't just a little glad.

I spin around, taking it all in. We're quite isolated over here. If something happened to me…I shudder. I was joking when I said I just have to survive three years, but it doesn't feel funny now. I gather my thoughts and square my shoulders. I'm in Scotland. It's the twenty-first century. *Laws exist.* No one is going to kill me, no one is going to die.

Belladonna swipes a black key card at the purple front door, informing us that the first-year residences are on the fourth floor of the mansion. The brass hinges creak open as though protesting my arrival as bitterly as I am. We file into a foyer dimly lit by candles on the wall, casting shadows on old portraits sitting in ornate gold frames. Faded patterned wallpaper sinks below wooden paneling, dotted with unlit sconces. It's like something from a horror movie. "What's wrong with the lightbulbs?"

Divya snorts beside me. "Power is terrible out here. There are lights, they just break every time there's a storm, which…"

"Is all the time. Brilliant." There's something eerie about this mansion. Even the rowdy ones at the front seem a little quieter. The hardwood floor creaks underfoot, illuminated by thin slivers of light that escape through swathes of rich red drapes.

Belladonna points out the door to the Nightshade library and I sneak a peek around. It's a scene straight out of a Brontë novel. Rows of classic books separate crimson chesterfield sofas and mahogany desks. Classic banker's table lamps cloak the dark room in a warm glow, turning the spiderwebs into threads of delicately spun copper. A bar sprawls across the northernmost wall, lined by bottles of whisky with the sort of price tags my parents and I would point and laugh at on the menu.

The next door in the foyer houses a gym so dark it's almost pitch black. Rows upon rows of weights sit at the base of floor-to-ceiling mirrors. The sharp smell of metal is jarring compared to the oddly reassuring musk of well-read books in the library. Belladonna states proudly that Nightshade gets the biggest gym, biggest bars, and least supervision.

There's another warmly lit bar in the eastern wing of the mansion, this one with dart boards, poker tables, and billiards. Polished brass beer taps sit atop a lacquered mahogany worktop, lined with upholstered bar stools. Other than the Sorrowsong sports memorabilia and the stain under the pool table that's almost definitely blood, it looks like every other pub. It's oddly comforting.

This house is like a maze, each dark corridor paving the way to one that looks the same. The handle on every heavy door is a flower crafted from brass. It's a deadly nightshade flower. The rational part of me knows they're metal, but I don't touch them. Who knows what poison lurks between these walls?

Belladonna swipes another key card in the foyer and leads us to a dark, spiraling stairwell. The stone steps are smooth and bowed slightly under the heavy weight of time. Even the walls seem heavy in a way I cannot explain. Like they're bursting with stories and secrets they cannot tell, aching to give way and crush anyone who dares stand between them.

Aside from the odd, overly rough shove and unintelligent insult, I'm largely left alone by my housemates. They haven't taken kindly to the fact that I wasn't stuck up Alex's ass in the chapel, but no one has stabbed me yet. It's a miracle I'm grateful for as we arrive at our halls of residence. There are sixteen rooms for the first years, four in each corridor.

I swipe my key card at the entrance to my hallway, stopping outside the room with the gold number four on the door. It'll be nice to have my own space. When the grief is all too much, I'll just hide in here all day. My sanctuary. I push the door handle down and step inside.

I'm pleasantly surprised. The room is large, far bigger than any room I've ever had before. Two generous single beds, two large wardrobes, and two bedside tables are arranged in a perfectly symmetrical layout. Except my desk has found its way over to the opposite side, the newly fashioned double desk already set up with makeup, skin care, notebooks, vodka bottles, and study material. *Is that a fucking knife on the bedside table?*

My idyllic dreams of roommate movie nights and female friendships wither away before me. Even my pillows are on the other bed, for heaven's sake. And pinned to my headboard is a strip of paper, torn from a page in a book.

When sorrows come, they come not single spies, but in battalions.

I know the *Hamlet* quote immediately. My mother named me after a character in the book, and my father sat by my feet at the end of the bed and read me the book more nights than I can count. It feels like my name at the top of the swim team register. It feels like Carmichael's strange tone in the chapel.

It feels like a threat.

"Hey, roomie." A Russian accent accompanies the sound of the bathroom door opening, and I swivel to face the source.

My stomach plummets fifty feet.

Chapter 4

OPHELIA

Sofia is my roommate.

Sofia, who tried to kill me about—I check my watch—forty minutes ago. In the poor lighting of our room, her lips curl into a snarl.

I suppose this is a nice ending to the day, in a poetic way. It fits perfectly with everything else that's happened. It would feel wrong if my day ended with a warm bath and a hot chocolate instead of an assassination attempt by my roommate.

She yawns, flopping onto the bed in her muddy boots and lying back on a pile of *both* of our pillows. "Didn't think you'd need the desk. I doubt you'll last around here. Lost your voice?"

"Why did you put that on my headboard?"

"It was there when I got here. The rest was all me."

I narrow my eyes at her, trying to decide if that's true. I choose not to believe her—choose not to believe I've found myself an anonymous stalker.

35

Sofia lights a cigarette, but I'm still frozen to the spot, my duffel dangling from my fist. I am *so* dead. My heart rate hits two hundred when I try to squash a moth. I couldn't kill this girl even with a ten-minute head start. I add a headstone to my shopping list, sandwiched between vitamin D pills and a copy of *Making Friends for Dummies*.

I opt for ignoring her, turning my back for one second to lock all my possessions in the wardrobe. When I spin around, I jump out of my skin. Her face is right there, an inch from mine. "Don't ignore me." Her breath tickles my lips, eyes manic.

I keep my inhale steady, eyes on hers. "I'm not ignoring you." *Small white lie.*

She steps back far enough for me to see the knife in her hand. "Find somewhere else to sleep tonight. I'm having someone over."

My sharp retort fizzles out on my tongue. I'm all for fighting it out, but not while one of us has a four-inch knife and the other has a two-pound coin and a melted Kit Kat. I pull my emotional support water bottle from my duffel, yank open the door, and storm out into the hallway.

An achingly familiar sense of loneliness washes over me. Growing up, Sorrowsong was at the very bottom of the universities I dreamed of attending, but circumstance has dragged me here and I'd hoped to at least get some good memories and friends out of it.

It sounds silly, but I'd imagined so many things with my roommate. Cozy evenings reading, nights out at parties, midnight cups of tea. Maybe she'd make me good at makeup, and I'd teach her how to do cryptic crosswords. Perhaps I'd finally open up to someone, and the isolation I've felt for so long would ease.

My eyes sting with tears. It's an overreaction, perhaps, but there's an ache in the pit of my stomach, a yearning to know what it is to have female friendships.

I brush the tears away before they touch my cheeks and remind myself of my real purpose here. I want justice, and I won't allow myself to break until it has been served.

WHEN I PULL myself together enough to wind my way down the staircase, most have abandoned moving into their rooms in favor of socializing in the communal areas on the ground floor.

Chatter about share prices and ski seasons is punctuated by the sound of corks popping and ice clinking in lowball glasses. I duck my head down, skirting around the edge of the spacious foyer in an effort to go unnoticed.

I have made it no farther than the first set of red velvet drapes when a large forearm shoots across to the wall, stopping me in my tracks. In the darkness, I recognize the short-haired Italian who's been glued to Alex's side all day. "What did the Ivanov twins say to you?"

His voice is so deep it takes me by surprise. American with a faint Italian accent, but it's rough and hoarse in comparison to Alex's buttery soft. "What?"

"Under the tree. What did they say?"

"You saw that?"

He nods, and I understand he's not in the mood for saying any more words than necessary. I huff out a small, disbelieving laugh. "Wow. Thanks for the rescue. They could've killed me."

His face hardens into a frown. "What did they say?"

"Nothing of consequence. They told me to watch my back. Divya said they're pissed because their father's territory is shrinking."

That earns me a gnarly smile. He mashes his bruised fist to his chest like some kind of tattooed gorilla. "Damn right, it is." He stops leaning against the wall, freeing up my escape route. "They probably think you're a spy. You hear one word from Sofia about anything at all, and you come right to me, yes?"

"I'm not sure what makes you think I'll be cuddling up with Sofia. And I won't spy for you. Doesn't really fit with my fly-under-the-radar agenda."

The cloudy expression on his face clears slightly. "The whole point of a spy is to fly under the radar. That's what they do."

"True," I say, through a laugh. He has a point. "But I have no intention of winding up dead in a Mafia war. Ophelia, by the way. Thanks for asking. Nice to meet you too." I veer past him toward the library, smiling to myself slightly as I hear him tell me he's going to get me a drink.

Maybe they're not *all* terrible.

The very second I cross the library threshold, I close the door behind me and lean against it, engulfed all of a sudden by a wave of exhaustion that weighs down my limbs.

This is all surreal.

On an inhale that smells like dusty books and cigar smoke, I curse the fact that my parents were taken from me. I curse the school that kicked me out before I had a chance to get back on track. I curse the endless list of universities that turned me down and funneled me toward this one.

Releasing my breath, I open my eyes and absorb the sight in front of me. It's *heaven*.

The warm air hums with the buzz of quiet chatter and glasses knocking against each other. I head straight for the shelf I'm looking for and take my favorite comfort read from between the faded spines, sinking down into a red wingback chair at the far end of the room.

The Great Gatsby. My father bought me my first copy for my fifteenth birthday, and I fell in love. I spent a whole summer lounging around in the garden beside my dad, each with a copy in our hands while my mother tidied the flowerbeds.

It was a simpler time. When summers were drenched in sunlight and the winters looked like cotton candy. Life felt manageable—*fun*, even. I had friends and hobbies. But like Gatsby's, my life has turned sour and lonely. Autumns fade into winters, which melt into springs, and through it all my mind remains stuck on the same rainy November day. I don't notice the changes in the world around me anymore.

The realization stops the words on the page wrapping me in a blanket like they usually do. It's hard to fly away in the twisted world of the rich and famous when I am imprisoned in it right now. Each sentence I read makes me sadder and sadder, and when I skip to the final few chapters, the words are blurred by my own tears.

"Bad first day?"

I bolt upright, an embarrassed blush heating my cheeks. Belladonna regards me with a cool expression, taking in my cheap outfit as she gracefully sinks down on the sofa opposite me. "I came here to look for Vin."

"Vin?"

"Vincenzo, my little brother. He was with you in the foyer."

"Oh. I don't know. The bar, maybe?" I suggest as she slips her blazer off her slim shoulders, leaving her in a white, satin camisole.

Her dark hair is thick and shiny, her gold jewelry immaculately styled. Even in the miserable gloom of Sorrowsong, a deep tan kisses her tattooed skin.

I think I'd like to *be* Belladonna when I grow up. "So, you guys are…?"

"Mafia. Our father is the one eating away at the Ivanovs' territory. Vin will take over from my father and Kirill will lead his side too."

I nod and pick at my tights, not sure what to say back to that. "And you?"

"My parents…work in government."

She narrows her eyes, waiting for me to say more. I don't. "Very coy."

Shit. I don't want to get on her wrong side. "I appreciate the company."

She humbles me with a glare as the door at the other end of the library creaks open, her brother sauntering through. "We're not friends. Don't get the wrong idea. Vinnie!"

Vincenzo looks up and shoots us a warm smile I suspect is reserved only for his sister. Alex is beside him, staring right at me like he's trying to get me to burst into flames. I sink a little farther into the chair as they approach. In a mansion of hundreds of rooms, of course he had to be here.

I'm determined never to speak to him again, not unless I have to.

Suddenly, I find myself craving peace and quiet, homesick for a home I no longer have. I try my hardest to tune out the world around me, reading the same sentence over and over in a bid to keep my emotions tethered.

"One of my favorites."

A husky voice makes me rapidly blink away the tears and I look up to see Alex and Vin sitting in the chairs around me. Vincenzo and Belladonna pour themselves a glass of red wine while Alex lazily swirls a glass of whisky, watching me intently.

He looks larger, more menacing in the soft shadows of the library, the broad line of his shoulders flexing as he rubs his jaw. He crosses his ankle over a muscular thigh. "Ophelia Winters," he drawls, slicing through the thick silence by making my name sound dirtier than it is. "We meet again."

"Can't you sit somewhere else?"

He smiles coldly, lips glistening slightly as he takes a sip of the amber liquid in the glass. He sits forward, moving his tanned face beneath a shard of light from the sconce on the wall. One intense green eye glows a brilliant shade of emerald. "Library's full. Tell me what your problem with me is. I thought we had a good thing going in the car."

Is he serious? Arrogant *and* ignorant. I whirl around and stare at the countless empty sofas behind me, my shoulders tensing with frustration. Pinching the bridge of my nose, I count to five on a slow exhale and turn back. I can't club him around the head with the book. When I bring the Corbeau-Greens down, it'll be with facts and figures, not violence and corruption. I won't sink to their level. I stand, tucking the book under my arm. "Well, it's been *delightful*."

"Come on, Ophelia. Have a drink." Vincenzo extends the wine bottle to me, baring his chipped front tooth to me in a cheery grin.

Alex narrows his eyes, leaning back in his seat once more. "You two know each other?"

"We just met," I say, leaning over to squeeze Vin's muscular shoulder. God, he's strong. I almost go back for another squeeze. "Find someone else to stroke your ego, Vincenzo."

His grin widens. "That's not what I'm hoping you'll stroke."

I flick up my middle finger as I walk away, but I'm trying not to smile. I like Vincenzo. "I'll stroke it with a cricket bat, if you're not careful."

His laughter echoes off my back as I round the bookshelves and out of sight, but I'm near enough to hear when he says, "Agree to disagree on this one, Alex. I quite like her."

FINDING ONE POSITIVE from the day, the late lunch served in the dining hall was delicious, even if I hadn't heard of half of the things on the menu. The food here looks straight out of a fancy restaurant, served in a dining hall that looks straight out of *Dracula*.

I ate with Divya, who seems to genuinely like me. We're going to watch a movie together later in the week. Hope swirls dangerously in my chest, but as I make the lonely walk across the gravel back to the Nightshade halls, every step nearer to my bedroom makes my stomach churn. *Any* other roommate would have been preferable. I have no idea how I'll last the year in a room with her.

Maybe not *any* other roommate. I think being in a confined space with Alex might actually be worse. I don't know if I can cope with being in the same building as him. My feelings toward him extend far beyond petty dislike and into burning hatred. His aloof attitude only makes it worse.

My feet come to a halt outside my bedroom door, and judging by the noises coming from the sliver of space beneath, Sofia is having a better evening than I am.

"Don't stop on my account," I chime, breezing past the tangle of limbs on *my* desk. I unlock my wardrobe and pull out the drawstring bag I'm looking for. "Although, if you wanted to migrate over to *your* desk, that would be great."

If I have to wipe a butt print off my desk tomorrow, it might be the very thing that tips me over the edge.

"What the *fuck*, Ophelia?"

I whirl to face her and her companion. It's Jaden Adeoye, the fifth son of some hotshot football manager. It's disappointing, really. He seemed nice in the dining hall. I'm not sure what he sees in the battle-axe he has pinned to the desk. "This is my room too. And I'm leaving, so…enjoy."

"I'll kill you when you sleep!" she screeches as I slam the door behind me.

I'll kill her first at this rate.

Stepping out of the Nightshade halls and into the murk of Sorrowsong Valley, I cast my eyes up to the blackened sky grumbling overhead. If I'm lucky, I'll get a swim in before the storm starts back up again. The swimming trials are at the end of the week, and lessons begin a few days after that, and I *need* to make the swim team to give Carmichael a good reason not to change his mind about letting me study here. Plus, a busy schedule might alleviate the hollow loneliness in my chest.

The winding path down to the tarn is shrouded by trees, blessing me with a reprieve from the biting wind. Near the top, I pass a group of students smoking under a tree, but it's otherwise deserted. In fact, there's not a soul to be seen or heard until I finally reach the water's edge, where a groundskeeper regards me warily, stopping what he is doing to lean on his shovel and stare. His face is

43

as weathered as the landscape around me, crumpled in a leathery frown.

"It's not safe to swim in the tarn," he says eventually, resuming his work while I change beneath a robe. "Swim in the loch, two miles that way." One callused finger points to an ominous-looking path carving its way into the woodlands beside me. The sort of path that people disappear on in the movies.

Two miles. It'll be dark by the time I get there, and that'll be even more dangerous. Hell no. I've seen *The Blair Witch Project*. "I'm just testing the water for a few minutes, but thank you." I place the robe on top of my bag, carefully folding my clothes beside it on the bank. It's not quite the tiny lake I swim in at home. Up close, the tarn is a yawning abyss of inky black water, churned by the icy wind.

I turn back to ask the groundskeeper how deep it is, but he's just a small figure halfway up the hill path, dragging the shovel behind him. *Great.*

I place my boots beside my clothes and tie my orange tow float to my waist, taking the first step into the water. It snatches my breath away, so cold it burns as it laps around my ankles. *Fucking Scotland.* Everything is either cold or wet—or both. By the time it sloshes at waist level, my breaths are shuddering, puffs of white air that vanish into the low fog around me. My hands sink first, then my arms and shoulders until I'm swimming lengths of the small lake, warmth finding its way into my muscles again.

There's something about swimming for me that just fixes everything. The stress, the grief, the worry, it all sits on the riverbank with my bags and shoes, patiently waiting for me to pick it back up again.

My mother used to take me to the local pool every Wednesday afternoon after school. We'd get into the water together and she'd turn face-up, stare at the moldy ceiling with a sigh, and say, *Isn't it lovely not to have your feet on the ground for a moment?* Like with most things she said, I never really understood them until she died. I wish I could hear her say it one last time.

Even here in Sorrowsong Valley, swimming brings me peace. Here, everything is going fine. Here, I don't feel quite so lonely.

For the first time today, the sigh that leaves my lips is contented and not exasperated. I'm weightless, floating in the calm that seems to surround this forgotten lake hiding below the castle walls. The last of the evening slips away like the water between my fingers, and I allow myself to feel a little pride that I made it to university despite all the obstacles before me.

When my muscles are spent and the sun is vanishing behind the dense tree line, I flip onto my back, stare at the sky, and tell my parents about my day. I tell them about Alex, about Sofia, about being in Nightshade. I tell them the little things—the things I'd probably tell a friend if I had one—like how the man beside me on the train ate a croissant in the messiest way imaginable, and how I finished a Sudoku book in a week. Only when I'm telling them about the god-awful weather up here does an uncomfortable sensation sweep over me, an awareness prickling my spine.

I feel like I am being watched.

Buoyed by the water, I sit up and scan the shoreline, every shadow between tree trunks looking more threatening than it did half an hour ago. Branches look like arms, leaves that catch the last of the daylight look like watchful eyes, but no one else is here. All is still, yet the feeling doesn't go away. The silence that had been

45

calming a moment ago now gnaws at my sanity, driving me faster as I swim to the water's edge. I haul myself onto dry land, scanning my surroundings once more.

Nothing.

I'm being paranoid, but I run the towel over my shivering skin and get dressed a little faster than usual.

I slip my tights over my feet and reach for my boots, but my hand freezes midair. The laces on my boots are gone. I spin around, eyes darting around the tarn twice as fast as they were before. For a second, I let myself believe it was an odd prank by the grounds-keeper, perhaps for ignoring his advice. Then I remember he left before I even got in the water.

My stomach sinks as my eyes catch on two black shoelaces tied in neat bows around a nearby branch. Someone was here. Someone is messing with me. My trembling fingers rip the laces from the branch and put them on my boots haphazardly, skipping half the eyelets in the black leather.

It's a harmless prank, but there's a loud voice at the back of my head that tells me this is all more sinister than it looks.

Legs wobbly, I break into a jog toward the castle, pretending I can't feel the unmistakable sensation of eyes on the back of my head, or the spiced scent of an unfamiliar cologne in the air.

Chapter 5

ALEX

How I've been roped into a two-mile trip to watch cold people splash around in a loch is beyond me.

My running shoes sink into the soft forest floor beside Vincenzo's, his shirt slung over his shoulder despite the bitter chill. Our night began in the Nightshade library, ended at the Snakeroot initiation party in the castle, and neither of us can remember what happened in the middle. All I know is we were awoken in the Snakeroot dormitories by Bella phoning Vincenzo to ask why he was late to help her run the swim trials.

I woke up alone, clothed, and on a couch, and Vincenzo woke up naked, in company, and in a bed, so we were both pleased with how the night turned out.

"*Che cazzo.*" Vin stops and puts his hands on his knees, cursing his sister in breathless Italian.

"*Ciò fa ben sperare ai provini per della squadra di rugby.*" *This bodes well for the rugby squad tryouts.*

47

He holds up a middle finger but doesn't straighten up. "Fuck you, rich boy. Your Italian sucks. And so does your hair."

I start running again, pulling my black hoodie off. It's sticky in this forest, the air thick with fog. "So do your manners. You're the one who dragged us here."

He catches up beside me, a bead of sweat running down the skull tattoo on his neck. "You've seen how scary Bella can be, she'll have my balls. She should be the next fucking capo, not me."

The forest thins, allowing us a distant view of the loch through the trees. It's nine in the morning and the sun looks like it's had enough for the day. Still, in my first seven days here, I think this is the first day it hasn't rained. "Perhaps she should be."

"Fuck no. There'd be a war in the first month. She's happy playing doctors and nurses."

I'm not sure Vin is any more calm-tempered than his sister, but I don't let that thought pass my lips. I met him in New York when he was nine and I was eleven, and somehow, I haven't managed to shake him off in the twelve years since. We sat and stared at each other in silence for three hours that day while my father made a shady deal to provide helicopters to the Morello Syndicate. When Vin's father, Rocco, asked my father how much it would cost to make one of his Russian enemies vanish in an accident, they asked me to stand outside.

The man in question died in a helicopter crash the next week. The official report was swept out of media coverage just as quickly, but the press said the Russian pilot was on Class A drugs at the time.

Every life has a price to my father.

As we trudge down the bank of the loch, I half wonder what mine is. Low, probably, but higher than my sisters'. And that annoys me.

Belladonna is yelling at Vin in rapid Italian before we're even in earshot, her hands darting around in front of her. I'm genuinely afraid for my balls.

My friend sheepishly rubs his chest as we approach, choosing not to respond to the string of curses that float our way. He's right; if Belladonna took over the Morello Syndicate, New York would be a war zone. "Sorry, Bella, we got buried in pre-reading for the financial module."

She shoves his head aside like she doesn't buy his bullshit. "Buried in a Snakeroot student, more like. You two can be lifeguards."

Vin rubs a hand over his brown, recently buzzed hair. "You said we'd be timing people. I'm not getting in that water."

"And then you were half an hour late." She kisses my cheek. "Alex, *amore*, you really must find a new best friend. Why won't you try out? We could use you."

"I was just thinking that," I mutter, dodging Vin's battered knuckles that swing at my jaw—wasn't he *just* talking about his sister's temper? "And I'm stretched thin enough already, I can't add swimming to my schedule." I pick a bottle of water from the ice bucket on the jetty and tug my hoodie back on.

Sorrowsong has a reputation for success in sports. It's not the reason I came here, but it helps. Rugby practice and the occasional rowing regatta have been shoehorned into the few gaps in my schedule. I'm sure I'll resent selling my sanity to impress Carmichael, but it's all part of my plan. It'll all pay off in the end.

I hope.

"Alex!"

I look up to see Sara Hamilton and Mura Sayari jogging over to me. *Supermodels*. They're *also* not the reason I came here, but they help, too, even if they are both wearing ridiculous heels on muddy terrain in the north of Scotland. I've met them both before at a social club in New York, but that seems a far cry from where we've all ended up now.

Truthfully, I don't really know why everyone comes here. Maybe we're all just trying to be as far away from home as possible.

"It's good to see you both. Terrific footwear choice," I say as Sara hugs me.

"Thank you!" she exclaims, looking down at her brown Manolo Blahniks that were probably peach-pink about an hour ago. "They're not even for sale yet; I just wore them for a shoot, and they let me keep them, and I said they really didn't have to do that, and then *they* said it's totally fine, and then *I* said—"

"He's being sarcastic, Sara," Mura interrupts, giving me a knowing smile.

Mura is one of my closest friends here, even if she did force me into a luxury fashion photoshoot with her last year. I did it for my mother, really, who proudly kept the magazine in a display cabinet.

Until she shattered it with a tennis racket, but that's a story for another day.

Mura has a sensible head on her shoulders, and she's always been kind to my sister, Fleur, supporting her through her first few modeling campaigns. "You look good, Alex. Family okay?"

There's an undercurrent to the question, a private look just for me. Mura and I, we understand each other. God knows how much of her soul she sold to be allowed to study here. I give her a tight smile, because it's easier than trying to articulate the black cloud that lives in my chest lately. "Yeah. Yours?"

Her smile doesn't touch her eyes, and I know she doesn't believe me. "Yeah. Anyway, you're here to swim?"

"To lifeguard."

"Oh, I *love Baywatch*," interjects Sara, beckoning over an attractive blonde who, judging by the towel robe she ties around her waist, is here to compete. "Have you met Colette DuPont?"

I cock my head at the newcomer. She looks vaguely familiar, like everyone else here. "I recognize you from somewhere."

She flashes me a shy smile, all platinum hair and tanned skin. "Well, I've been on the front page of every news blog for my very public estrangement from my family." A flush heats her face, like this is not information she wanted to discuss on her first time meeting someone.

I have seen her very public, very messy estrangement from the Luxembourgish royal family all over the French news, now that she mentions it. "I was in a Swedish yogurt commercial, too, but I doubt it's that."

I click my fingers as she says the second sentence. "That's it. I'm a *huge* Swedish yogurt guy. Watch all the commercials on the day they come out."

A grateful laugh leaves her lips, her hand landing over one of the ravens on my arm. "Maybe we can get a drink sometime?"

"Sure," I say, but it trails off as a flash of copper hair and dark clothing rushes behind her. Ophelia *fucking* Winters. She's everywhere. When I eat, she's sat in the dining hall. When I study, she's doing those stupid crosswords in the library. When

I go out running, she's floating in the tarn like an orange dish sponge.

She was intriguing in the car, out of line in the chapel, and downright infuriating in the library. I don't know what happened between those events that made her hate me, but I suppose it could be any number of things. My father angers a *lot* of people these days.

I nod a quick goodbye to Mura, Sara, and Colette, and join Vin where he sits on the end of the jetty. Ophelia glances in our vague direction. Was Vincenzo serious when he said my hair looked shit? I run both hands through it, tensing my jawline and my thighs beneath my rugby shorts.

What the hell am I doing? Why do I care? I can't stand the girl. "Look who it is."

My teeth clamp together as I watch her wave to Colette and drop her bag at her feet. "I've seen. If she starts drowning, I'm not going in."

"I will," he says through a bite of an apple. "She's hot, and girls love that shit."

I shove my hood back up over my hair. "What, drowning?"

"No, shirtless men carrying them out of bodies of water."

The heat from Vin's lighter brushes my nose as I light a cigarette. I quit last year, but something about that ginger girl makes me want one. She looks like she'll get scared off before the first semester is up, which is good for me and my blood pressure. The sooner the better. "Hell will freeze over before I take dating advice from you, Vincenzo."

"Come on, you really think she's up to something? She looks like her idea of *bad* is parking without a ticket."

"She clearly doesn't want to be here, and she looks like she gets her clothes from Goodwill. She's up to something."

Vincenzo takes off his shoes and dips his gross feet in the water. I offer a silent prayer for the aquatic population of Sorrowsong Loch. *Death by Mafia bonehead feet*. Gotta be in the worst five ways to go.

"First of all, Goodwill is expensive nowadays. That's what Zia Patrizia says. Second of all, they don't even have that store here. Third of all, you don't wanna be here either. *Third* of all—"

"You've already done a third." I love the guy, but I'd bet each of my cars that he'll fail all his exams this semester.

"Whatever. She's not gonna last the month, anyway. Looked terrified at dinner yesterday."

The only thing I thought she looked at dinner yesterday was hot, but I keep that confession quiet. With her nose buried in a clothbound classic, a packet of tissues up her sleeve, and a miserable expression on her face, she's almost charming, in a depressing sort of way.

We both stand as the first men's heat begins, but my attention struggles to pull away from Ophelia on the third jetty along. She steps out of her tired, black sweatpants and pulls her shapeless sweater over her head, left in just a black swimsuit. I'd drawn some conclusions from her rain-soaked shirt and miniskirt from last week, but this confirms what I already know.

She's a fucking smokeshow.

Shame it's all wasted on that nasty attitude. I turn back to watch the race, because Vin can't keep his eyes off Colette and one of us has to at least vaguely pay attention. "Don't even dream of it, man. She's asked me for a drink."

His face falls. "Are you gonna go?"

"No." I have my reasons for being here, and none of them include getting involved with disgraced royals.

"Good." He rubs his knuckles over the short beard on his jaw. "Just imagine. Let me live my fantasy in my head."

As long as it stays in his head. Vin has a habit of bumping into a woman in a coffee shop for the first time and then planning all their future children's names the same day. He once matched with a girl on Tinder on a Monday and gave her the code to his Amex on the Wednesday.

Pretty sure she used it to book a flight to go and visit her boyfriend.

The men's heats come and go, boring and uneventful. Belladonna scribbles down the names and houses of the few that qualify, ushering everyone around with her usual ruthless organization.

"Odds on the one that wanted to be in Hemlock drowning?" Shawn Miller appears behind me and Vin, blond hair still wet from his swim. Even in the mudslide that is the Scottish Highlands in autumn, he's wearing loafers and no socks.

Horrendous.

I tend to socialize with people for one of two reasons. Because I like them, or because it's smart business. Shawn falls *so* far into the latter category. I'd rather put pins in my eyes than chat with him, but his father owns an investment firm and sits on the board of my father's company, so I can't toss him in the loch.

Yet.

"High," I mutter, watching her take her place at the edge of the jetty. Beside her, Colette dips a toe in the water and lets out a quiet yelp. No one here is handling the transition from expensive, climate-controlled, indoor swimming pools to a late-autumn Scottish lake very well. Sorrowsong does have a pool inside the conservatory, but Belladonna likes to watch people suffer.

I watch another swimmer from Nightshade mutter something in Ophelia's ear, and judging by the way her jaw tenses, it's not an offer of good luck.

One day in, and she seems to have made a *lot* of enemies.

She doesn't grace the other girl with a response, focusing on her stretches as the final stragglers take their places. Belladonna fires an empty rifle into the air and they all dive in. They all surface immediately, stunned motionless by the cold.

Not Ophelia, though. I can't see her. Shawn steps forward between me and Vincenzo. "Where's Hemlock girl?"

"Her name is Ophelia," I mutter, scanning the black surface of the water. Shit, I didn't *actually* want her to drown. Not that badly, anyway. Just a little bit. Silent seconds tick by, Belladonna's pen freezing on her clipboard.

Vin is already tossing his shirt aside and grabbing the life buoy when she surfaces about twenty yards ahead of the others, gliding across the loch like she hasn't noticed that it's cold.

To my left, Vincenzo tucks the buoy under his arm and claps as though she can actually hear him. "Girl can *swim*."

And she can. She glides through the water as if propelled by some external force, some desperate need to win. Whatever her motive for impressing Carmichael is, I doubt it burns hotter than mine.

She wins her heat by a mile, Colette coming in second, and then she wins the final by a few inches, pushing her athletic frame out of the water and stepping into a towel—wait, is that Shawn holding the towel? He's vanished from between us, holding Ophelia's towel for her and gushing over her performance. A small smile appears on her lips as he holds out her clothes, and when he laces up her sneakers for her, she fucking giggles.

"Fuck Shawn Miller, man." *Two-faced imbecile.*

Vincenzo snorts and jingles his keys in his pockets. "Would be a shame if someone scratched his Bentley later."

"A tragedy for the ages."

My phone buzzes in my pocket and I tug it out. The screen lights up with an incoming call. *Cain Green.* My mood sours. I've been in the UK for weeks, and this is the first time my father has contacted me outside of forwarding me financial statements he thinks I'll be interested in.

I press the phone to my ear. "Cain."

The rhythmic thud of footsteps punctuates his smooth voice, and I imagine him pacing the halls of Green Aviation's head office in Manhattan, barking at his secretary. "Alexander. You didn't reply to my email."

I stroll off the jetty and away from Vincenzo. "I've been busy. What was it about?"

"Looks like TechEon has pulled their stake in the Intrepid Air narrowbody deal."

I pause for a minute, trying to summon a single fuck to give. Just when I think I've got one, it fizzles away into the frigid air. "Wow, that's crazy."

"Certainly poses an opportunity for us. Deacon is putting together the proposal already. I expect you to be more active on your work email in future."

I toe a rock in the mud with my running shoe, keeping my sigh contained. "I'm kind of busy here."

His tone deteriorates from polite to bitter in a moment. "You don't know what busy is, boy. If you want to break your poor mother's and sisters' hearts and go to Scotland, that's on you, but I won't have it interfere with your training. Do you know how many men your age would kill for a position as CEO in twenty years?"

Twenty years. I'd sooner die than let it be that long. His second sentence makes the darkness inside me expand in my chest to the point that it hurts. My fingers itch to text each of them the two words that bounce around my brain for every waking moment of my days here.

I'm sorry.

"Harris told me you got a seventy-six on your pre-course assessment," he says, and I hear a door shut in the background. He must be in his office.

Jesus Christ. "Why are you getting so cozy with the chancellor?"

"Seventy-six, Alex?"

I'm surprised the phone doesn't crack in my hand. "It's the pre-course assessment. I've not taken the course yet."

"You've been joining me in the office since you were ten. Have I taught you to give seventy-six percent effort at work?"

"Is there a point to this phone call?"

He's seething, talking through gritted teeth. "The point is not letting my deadbeat son waste another several years of his life. The media are watching you closely. God knows our publicity people are busy enough as it is."

Deadbeat. I don't say anything, unable to think of a reply that won't split our family into two and make my mother worse.

A ragged sigh crackles through the speaker. "I push you for your own benefit, Alex, to make you stronger. One day I won't be around anymore. A son should not need his father."

I needed him a long time ago. I needed him when I broke my first bone at seven. When I had my first breakup at fourteen. When I first dialed for help for my mother at sixteen. When I first checked all my sisters into a hotel at seventeen. When I left Yale at nineteen. My life is a complex web of moments that could've been made easier by a present father.

I needed him then.

I need him now.

My tone is as flat as my mood. "Sure. Got to go to rugby."

"Sports are a waste of time."

"Always great to catch up, Cain." I punch the red button at the bottom of the screen with far more force than necessary and gesture to Vin that I'm leaving.

Having seen enough, I say my goodbyes to Belladonna and the others, and jog toward the forest's edge. A low fog hugs the base of the trees, and somewhere a raven lets out a shrill cry into the bitter air. We're on the cusp of October, but it feels like a New York winter out here.

As I veer left into the thicket, a small hand shoots out from the shadows and grabs my hoodie.

Warm cinnamon. The same smell that lingers on the passenger seat of my car. Christ, I wish we could go back to that car journey some days. Where for five minutes, a glimmer of intrigue sparked in my chest. When the pretty, down-on-life redhead was still a mystery and not a thorn in my side. "Fucking hell, Twist, you're obsessed with me."

She drags me deeper into the trees, caramel-brown eyes burning up at me in the dark. "Were you at the tarn last night?"

My smile is venomous. "I don't remember a lot of last night, Ophelia. Want me to wear an ankle tag just for you?"

Her grip on the front of my sweater tightens. "I swear to God, Corbeau, if you were fucking with me at the tarn yesterday, I'll kill you. It wasn't funny."

"Not if I kill you first," I bite back as a droplet from her wet hair runs over the freckles beside her nose.

"Just answer the question." The water trickles over the soft, pink curve of her bottom lip. She's shivering. I don't know why I notice. I don't know why I care.

I take a step back, freeing my hoodie from her grip. Cold air replaces the warmth of her chest and I find myself frustrated that I'm losing my cool, unable to pinpoint why she stirs such an intense reaction from me. My usual comfort blanket of apathy doesn't feel like an option around her.

Somewhere between the car and the chapel, she made her mind up about me, and that's fine. It's happened a hundred times before.

So why am I so bothered?

"No, Ophelia, I wasn't at the tarn. Can I run back to the castle now, or do I need to submit a map of my expected route? Wanna meet up at a checkpoint halfway?"

"Go to hell, Alex."

I jog backward away from her, my gaze fixed on hers. "See you there."

Chapter 6

OPHELIA

The first night in the Nightshade halls, I fell asleep at midnight and woke up to Sofia standing over my bed, grinning at me, two hours later.

I didn't manage to fall back asleep. I went swimming instead.

In the week since, she's managed to make my existence hell most nights. A rat in my bed, a knife to the throat, and, worst of all, missing biscuits from my biscuit tin. And all because she thinks I'm joining Vincenzo's side. Like having an opinion on a New York–based Mafia conflict is something that normal people have.

I'd retaliate if it wouldn't be the last thing I'd ever do.

She's in Jaden's room this evening, but I've been lying awake staring at the ceiling for hours. My body is exhausted, but my mind and my heart are racing. Coming to Sorrowsong was a mistake. Kicked out of school for nonattendance, denied university places for lack of exam results; my dreams burned to ash in that helicopter wreckage.

With bills piling up on my doorstep and loneliness gnawing at my bones, I begged the universe for a reason to get up. Then a white envelope with a red wax seal landed on the growing pile of mail beside my door; an opportunity to have a career, an opportunity to understand more of my parents' death. It felt like a glimmer of hope.

Now, though, I don't think I can do it. The sound of the staff shuttle helicopter taking off earlier this evening sent me into a crippling panic attack so bad that I couldn't get down to dinner.

Every time I close my eyes, I wonder how scared my parents were at the end. I see a ball of fire crashing into a dark forest, and I swear I can feel smoke burning the back of my throat. I thought I was coping well, doing better, but there are too many reminders here, too many ghosts trapped inside the castle walls. Maybe I'm not ready to confront my parents' death, after all. Maybe I'm content with the oddly vague incident report citing "weather-related causes" as the reason I was orphaned a few weeks after turning seventeen.

The Nightshade mansion sighs and groans at night, battered by the howling wind. I don't bother turning the lights on because darkness is preferable to eerie flickering.

I'm beginning to wonder if Lord MacArtain wasn't so insane after all, because it does sound like a woman is wailing, condemned to an eternity in this bleak valley. In the rafters above me, creaking and other strange noises persist through the night.

I don't know whether being awake or asleep is worse. The unexplainable sense of dread that started the second I saw the Sorrowsong gates sits heavier in my gut each morning.

In the dark, I turn on my phone and wait five minutes for one search on the internet to load—Wi-Fi doesn't really stretch to the first-year rooms and I have patchy signal in the mansion.

One by one, paparazzi photos of Alex landing at a London airport earlier this month look back at me. He looks immaculate in black suit trousers and a tailored black shirt, that one fucking strand of his hair perfectly out of place over his eye. I swipe left over my greasy phone screen, faced with a snap of him in bed with a model as part of a cologne advert.

No one our age should be built like…that. Tattoos decorate his rippling forearms, biceps, and chest as he gazes lazily at the camera, one hand behind his head.

It's probably Photoshop. I imagine an underpaid intern working overtime to make Alex's biceps look bigger. It makes me feel better.

I'm losing my mind here.

I click on the link I'm looking for. His biography loads line by line at a painful pace. I've read his father's biography so many times it's burned into the fabric of my soul. I've even pinned his face to a dart board, but I've ignored Alex's until now. I doubt the apple falls far from the tree.

I learn he has recently turned twenty-three, and that he completed two years of an architecture degree at Yale before abruptly dropping out four years ago, refusing to disclose the reason to the press. There are reports of his potential appearance in the Olympic rowing team, of a career as a pilot, but it all came to a sudden end. *Strange.*

I learn that he grew up with an American father and an English-French mother, his childhood split between London, Paris, and New York. There's a photo of him on the red carpet with a younger girl who must be his sister. There's a photo of him running a marathon for charity, and one of him sweaty and grinning with a medal hanging over his navy Yale Rowing top. Another of him unveiling a new model of private jet for Green Aviation.

Like his father's, his image is squeaky clean. The devil works hard, but it appears that the Green publicist works harder.

I'm going to have my work cut out for me.

For the millionth time, I type the same four words into the search bar.

Sorrowsong University helicopter crash.

No matches found.

It's *this* feeling. This unfathomable rage I feel when those three words get spat out at me is what keeps my heart beating on my lowest days. I've dreamed, fantasized, *yearned* for the moment that my screen is flooded with photos of Alex's father being depicted as the killer that he is—the man who cuts corners, accepts bribes, kills innocent people, and pays the press to remove all traces.

One day, the Corbeau-Green name will only ever be muttered like a curse word. Only then can I start to live again.

My finger trembles a little as I tap on the Contacts app. The list has expanded by three names this week alone. Belladonna—who only asked for my number because she captains the university swim team—Divya, who is very friendly, but spends all her hours studying—and Colette—who seems to genuinely like me.

Some guy called Shawn Miller asked for my number, too. He's a little bit cliché: a blond, all-American rich boy whose father works in finance, but he did seem genuinely sweet earlier. I didn't give it to him, but it might be nice to have a male friend here. God knows I could use the experience.

I click on Divya's name, opening up a text she sent me earlier.

Divya

Not coming to dinner?

> **Ophelia**
>
> Hey. Sorry, I missed dinner earlier—wasn't
> feeling well. I have a question for you.

Divya

People are talking about your swimming
abilities. And what's up?

> **Ophelia**
>
> Are you good at computer stuff?
> Programming, hacking, disks...idk.

Divya

The fact you just said disks tells me
you aren't. I'm a medical student. What
makes you think I can hack computers?

I sit upright in bed, the glow of my phone illuminating the
arched stone ceiling of the room. I shift uncomfortably, holding
my breath as though someone might creep out from a dark corner.

> **Ophelia**
>
> You asked me what graphics card was in
> my laptop. I don't even know what that
> means.

Divya
That's a low standard, but yes, I'm good
at computers. What do you need? Trying
to find exam answers already?

> **Ophelia**
> Where is your room?

Divya
I'm in the library. I'm studying for a
cardiovascular lab we have next week.

> **Ophelia**
> Stay there. See you in ten.

DIVYA IS AT one of the desks in the middle of the library, surrounded by dusty textbooks and leather journals. I sink into the chair beside her, looking at the annotated diagram of cardiomyocytes on her screen.

"*Jesus.*"

"I know," she says, rubbing her forehead. "What's up?"

"Do you know the Corbeau-Greens?"

"Everyone *knows* them. Their name is plastered on the side of half the private jets in America. I'm not friendly with them, if that's what you're asking."

I unlock my phone while she finishes talking and Alex's face is still on the screen. *Whoops.* "That is *not* what it looks like."

She beams. "You want me to hack his photo album?"

65

"*No.*" My face warms with embarrassment. "Absolutely *not.*"

"Wouldn't blame you, that man is…" She reaches over and zooms into a photo of him in his trademark black shirt, top two buttons undone. "Slutty."

"What does that even mean? Don't answer that. I don't want to know. I'm asking about his father."

Divya wrinkles her nose. "My mother says he's sleazy. I don't know what he did to make her say that, but it's enough to make me dislike him."

I lower my voice, eyes darting around to the dark corners of the mostly empty library. "My parents died in a helicopter crash a few years ago."

"What? You said they're political aides," she hisses back, and I hold up two hands to beg her to quieten down.

"I lied. They died here in Sorrowsong Valley in a Green helicopter crash."

A familiar look flits across her face, a gleam to her eyes I've seen a hundred times before. "Ophelia, I'm so sorry. That must've—"

"I don't want sympathy, Divya, I want revenge."

"What were they doing in Sorrowsong anyway? Even the locals keep away from here."

"My father was a chef here, and my mother a gardener. They died in the staff helicopter shuttle. With a healthy pilot. In a new helicopter that had no issues reported."

Her eyes widen. "You think someone sabotaged it?"

"Something like that."

"Shit. Ophelia…sometimes these things just happen. Pockets of air, or sudden storms, an unexpected mechanical fault."

Frustration bubbles in my throat, dangerous and volatile. "There's more to this, Divya. I know it."

"So take it to the papers."

"None of them will discuss it. He must have something over them, an NDA or something. Look at this." I open my final messages with my father and put my phone on the desk in front of us, hoping I can trust her.

Dad

How was school, O? Burger Friday? Xxx

> **Ophelia**
>
> Good. Aced my chemistry mock. Burger
> Friday sounds amazing. How is work?

Dad

I'm proud of you. Celebratory movie night
when we get back later xxx
Stay away from Cain Green.

> **Ophelia**
>
> Random. I don't even know who that is.

Dad

Keep it that way.

> **Ophelia**
>
> Are you okay?
>
> Taking off soon? Mum didn't pick up my call x

Have you taken off? I'm home so I can start
dinner. I got burger buns from the shop. The
good ones this time.
Dad?
Where are you both?
Tell me you didn't get on the helicopter.
Dad.
I'm coming up to Sorrowsong in a taxi.
Please just call me back.

The letters wobble through my tears as I stare back at them. I
screamed when I saw the crash site. I yelled when they dragged me
away. But the grief didn't come until I stepped back into the still,
empty cottage the next day. When my eyes landed on the three
stale burger buns laid out on the chopping board, I sank to my
knees on the kitchen floor and didn't plan to ever get up.

Then the anger came. Not the unpredictable, fleeting kind that
I felt at the crash site. This one came on slowly. It seeped into
my blood like a disease, and every day I woke up sicker than the
last. Every hour in the silent house rotted the calm inside me
away. Every extra million on Cain Corbeau-Green's net worth
made the fire in my chest burn hotter. Every whistleblower paid
into silence made me more determined to lift the curtain on that
heinous man.

The pink flush drains from Divya's brown cheeks. "Holy
shit. Why would he tell you to stay away? Did he catch wind of
something?"

I shrug, locking my phone. "Something worried him the day he
died. It has to mean something. Cain must somehow be to blame.

Police aren't interested without concrete proof. He's too rich to be touched by the law."

"How are you not…god, I'd be furious."

"I am fury itself, Divya. It's like a curse I've had for years, stopping me from sleeping well, eating right. Help me, *please*."

"What do you need?"

"I just want to know the name of one engineer on shift that week who touched that helicopter. It'll be on a maintenance log. The school orders a check of the helicopter every twenty-five flying hours, as well as a preflight check on Monday and Friday. There *has* to be documentation of that somewhere."

Her brown eyes are sincere as she nods. "I'll see what I can do, see how good the security on the drives is. I'm so sorry, Ophelia. That's…I can't believe it. Not a word to anyone, I swear."

I leave Divya in her world of arteries and ventricles, but I don't turn left out of the library. I head right, out of the mansion and into the starless night.

A few students smoke in a huddle outside, but the path to the castle is quiet. The occasional runner jogs by, the hoot of an owl punctuating the crunch of my feet over the pebbles.

The castle looks magical at night. Moonlight kisses the slate rooftops with a silver shine. The six turrets seem to stand taller, prouder than they do in the day. The cracks and crumbles aren't so visible, overshadowed by pools of warm, orange light that spills from pointed arch windows. The silhouette of a girl drying her hair obscures one, a couple dance in another. Dying houseplants and half-empty vodka bottles sit on the ledges of others.

It makes the castle feel more normal.

It makes me feel less lonely.

Creeping through the darkness of the chapel and back to Achlys's Hall, I can't even bring myself to look at her. I step up to the painting, running my fingers over the varnished canvas until I spot the rectangular dip in the paint. Holding my breath, I push on the door. It rattles, but it doesn't open.

Damn it. Obviously it would be locked.

A bird coos in the rafters, making me jump out of my skin. I take a step away from the door, a sudden sense of unease washing over me.

"There's a keyhole just below her left foot."

A scream bursts out of my throat, my back against the painting as I whirl around. Carmichael steps out of the shadows of the hall and paces toward me.

Fuck. The man is a phantom.

"Sorry, sir. I was just exploring."

"Exploring my office?"

Well, obviously not, because it's locked. "Oh, is that what this is?"

He unlocks the door and pushes it open so that Achlys's leg bends at a sickening angle. I peer inside the warmly lit office, a slave to my own curiosity. There's a desk just in front of the door, which must belong to his assistant, and behind that, a set of wooden stairs lead up to a mezzanine. The stain on the wooden banister is turning orange, the steps bowing in the center. I can't see much of the mezzanine, but I can see the walls are covered in shelves of boxes and books that extend to the intricate cornice on the ceiling.

There has to be something useful in there.

The glint in Carmichael's eye makes me nervous. "Come in."

"Um…no. It's okay. I should really get to bed."

"Oh, but you were so keen to see inside?"

The bird coos again, as if telling me to leave. A gust of wind howls through the hall. Achlys lets out a mournful cry.

"I had better go. Thank you, sir."

I back away from him for the first few steps, before turning away and jogging all the way back to the Nightshade mansion. Trudging back up to the fourth floor, I fish my key out of the front pocket of my Sorrowsong Swimming hoodie. My clumsy fingers fumble around in the dark, eventually putting my room key into the lock and twisting it right.

It doesn't move.

The door is already unlocked. *Christ*. If all my belongings get stolen one day, it'll be my own fault for being forgetful.

I step inside the empty room, and the tiny grain of fear at the back of my mind is realized. A distinctive scent tickles my nostrils: aniseed or cloves mixed with something unfamiliar. It's the same odd combination that followed me as I ran from the tarn last week.

My fingers tremble at my sides as I scan my side of the room.

I may have forgotten to lock the door, but I sure as hell didn't make my bed.

Chapter 7

OPHELIA

A text from Divya pings through while my Childhood and Youth Psychology lecturer wraps up our session.

I'm not completely sure, but I *think* it might have just woken me up. My nights have been increasingly sleepless, punctuated by strange noises that have me convinced I'm going insane. Still, the idea of Chancellor Carmichael catching me asleep in a lecture is mortifying. Must do better. I sit up straighter and unlock my phone immediately.

Divya
Apparently Carmichael has boxes of old
files in his office. Student records, staff
records, supplier records. Things like that.

Ophelia

On paper?! We're not in the sixties. Old
documents make me sneeze.

Divya

You'd be first to go in the apocalypse, you
know, but you're probably fine with that.
I found a Sorrowsong-specific training
manual online. It says monthly
maintenance records go into red boxes
for the chancellor to review should he
need to. Might be worth getting into his
office. No one seems sure where it is.

Ophelia

I know where it is. I'll see if I can find
anything out.

I need to find those red boxes.

"The lecture is finished, Ms. Winters."

I look up to see the last few students trailing out of the doorway and Professor Bancroft staring up at me from the lectern below, putting his brick of a laptop into a weathered briefcase. He is a kind-looking man in his early sixties who looks like he might have been worn down by the rough tides of life. His knitted sweater doesn't fit right, there's a coffee stain on his tie, and he has a weird, old-man musk about him.

He shoves his glasses farther up his nose, and I jump to my feet, gathering my books under my arm. "I'm so sorry. I was listening, I swear."

His smile is warm, thin wrinkles crinkling the aging skin around his eyes. "I believe you. Struggling to make friends?"

Ouch. I didn't think it was that obvious. I tuck a stray wave of hair behind my ear, the crimson-carpeted steps groaning as I descend toward him. "Maybe a little."

"They'll warm up to you. Don't despair."

I can't help my laugh. Unless I can pull a trust fund and the will to give a shit about the FTSE 100 Index out of my ass, I doubt it. "I'm not so sure. It's nice to have a friendly face around here, anyway."

His smile fades slightly as I get closer, lost in some past memory. The words that slip past his lips are scarcely a whisper, but I hear them well enough. "You look *just* like your mother."

His words punch me in the gut, and the wave of grief that follows almost knocks me to my knees. I *am* the spitting image of my mother. It took months for me to be able to bear my own reflection after I lost her, and even now, I turn the mirror in the bathroom around.

I have my mother's face, painted in my father's style. "You knew her?"

A flush creeps onto his wrinkled face. He has the grace to look a little mortified, at least. "I'm so sorry. That was a terrible thing to say. I've never had much tact, I'm afraid. Please forget I brought her up, I'm sure that isn't pleasant for you."

"No…it's…it's nice to hear someone talk about her." Especially after a certain airline executive swept her entire existence under the rug. "Was she well-known?"

"Oh, she was very popular here. Such a bright, cheery face in this dark castle, lighting up the dreary days. I see you've got her hair."

His words are both the knife that carves a larger hole in my heart and the salve that dulls the sting of the wound. "I miss them," I whisper, more to myself than Dr. Bancroft. I've had such a lonely few years that I'm not sure if I've ever said that out loud before.

He flicks the gold light switch as we leave, plunging the gothic lecture hall into darkness. "I can imagine it's been a very difficult few years. If you ever need to talk to someone, I'm always here or in my office in the eastern spire."

Someone is being kind to me, willingly. Things are looking up for the attendance rate at my funeral. I picture Divya, Dr. Bancroft, and May, my parents' ancient neighbor, awkwardly eating tuna sandwiches and commenting on the mediocrity of my life. *She was good at crosswords, wasn't she? I liked that green T-shirt she had. She had decent handwriting.*

Nice.

MY SOCIAL PSYCHOLOGY class is in the oldest part of the castle: a slightly slanted tower that oozes gothic grandeur. Glass windows sit beneath pointed arches and crumbling flying buttresses, the lichen-covered walls almost black in the rain.

I follow the map on my phone, winding down forgotten hallways and through overgrown courtyards where a few students sit and study in silence. In a hallway that's almost pitch black, I reach a large set of warped wooden doors, the handles shaped like twisted vines. The rusting hinges grumble as I push them open and step into a huge teaching room that looks like it's been untouched since the day the castle was built.

Shadows cling to the arches on the high, vaulted ceilings, intricate carvings run down to the weathered wood paneling on the walls. The front and back walls are covered in floor-to-ceiling bookcases, the air thick with the smell of aging parchment and dust. I like it here.

Between a few glares and whispers in my direction, a whistle shoots toward me. "You look good, Hemlock girl!"

Shawn jogs over and grins at me, his teeth the brightest thing in this room. They might even be veneers, which would be a real turn-off. He's immaculately dressed in a pale blue shirt, loafers, and sand-colored chinos, like a poster boy for the American dream. Still, it's kind of nice to have a familiar face here. "Shawn? I thought you were studying business."

"Business with psychology. We do one psychology module a year. It's the most popular combination here. Always good to be able to read people in business." His eyes sweep down over my checkered miniskirt and knitted jumper, and they're full of approval when they come back up to mine. I'm not sure if I feel flattered or uncomfortable.

He seems harmless enough.

"Makes sense," I mumble, following him between rows of time-worn desks and brown leather seats. He drapes himself over a bench on the second row and unlocks his laptop. He's looking at the Stocks app on his iPhone; the one that sits comfortably beside GarageBand in my I've-got-no-fucking-idea-what-they-do folder. I'm careful to sit a few chairs along. I don't want to give anyone ideas.

"Ophelia!"

I'm strangely popular today. I look up to see Vincenzo coming in the doorway, waving manically like he genuinely *is* excited to see me. I can't help but laugh. His inked, muscular frame is hugged by black cargo trousers and a black turtleneck that stretches over his chest as he slaps Alex's arm and says, "Look, it's Ophelia."

Alex looks as serious as ever. He doesn't respond or glance in my direction, which is perfectly fine with me.

Everyone in this room is either rich, famous, or both, but there's a certain aura around Alex that has other people staring at him too. He moves like a shadow, dressed monochromatically and carrying nothing but a black notebook and pen.

There's no expression on his face as they head toward me, but his eyes tell another story. I wish I could pinpoint the look that he *always* has in his eye; like beneath the stony exterior, a fire is burning so hot, so intense, that it consumes him.

I wonder what fuels it.

He doesn't protest when Vincenzo bounds over to the row of seats behind me, reaching over to squeeze my shoulder. "We're classmates!"

"I can see that, Vincenzo," I mutter, facing the front.

"Where'd you learn to swim like that? Why don't you like Alex? He's a good guy, really, you know? Has your roommate stabbed you yet? Have *you* stabbed your roommate yet? Did you have the salad or the pie at dinner last night? We honestly thought you'd drowned at the swim trials. Alex was delighted. *Did* you nearly drown? Want some gum? Shit, I forgot my gum. Have you got any gum?"

He peppers me with questions, which bounce off my back onto the carpeted floor beneath our feet, ignored and unanswered. He's annoying, but I'm grinning at my laptop screen as I type. I don't know what's in the air around here, but it must be strong if I'm considering befriending a cold-blooded Mafia killer.

As I type up a sentence about social influence, a perfectly folded piece of paper lands on my fading keyboard. I unfold it and look up at Shawn, who winks at me and returns to his writing. It's his phone number, scrawled in neat writing. It's *so* cliché, but I smile and add it to my contacts. I dropped out of school just as boys were turning from gross, mysterious creatures to intriguing, marginally less gross crushes. This is all new to me.

Another note bounces off my laptop screen, this one screwed into a ball so tightly that it looks like a piece of chewing gum. I sigh and open it up. It takes me a minute to read the almost child-like handwriting, pressed so hard into the paper that there are tiny holes in it.

Shawn Miller probably still breastfeeds from his mama when he goes home for Christmas.

"Vincenzo!" I hiss, spinning around to face him. He just grins, the little script tattoo on his temple crumpling. Beside him, Alex's notebook is unopened on the table, a crease between his eyebrows as he types something on his phone. He puts it on the table but immediately, it lights up again with an incoming text. He yanks it from the surface again and a muscle in his jaw tics.

Vincenzo peers over Alex's shoulder. "All good, brother?"

I turn back to the front, straining to listen to anything that'll help me nail his father's coffin. "Fleur's boyfriend has cheated on her."

The pencil in Vincenzo's hand snaps. "The skinny guy?"

Alex hums in response. "I've dealt with it."

I shudder, wondering what that means in their world. I wonder if Vincenzo knows anything about the helicopter crash. Probably, but I doubt he'd ever tell me. He's too loyal to be of use to me.

Professor Andersson introduces our coursework task, a joint essay on conformity, obedience, and strategies of persuasion. She's an attractive woman in her early forties with thick, blonde hair and an even thicker Swedish accent. She matches everyone into twelve pairs. Shawn is with the preppy clone of himself to his left, Alex is with Vincenzo.

I'm the odd one out.

"Ah. Ophelia. You can join another pair, or—"

"I can do it on my own." My nonexistent social life will help with that.

"Not to be advised, but…fine, I suppose," she says, turning a page in her notebook. She starts to speak again, interrupted by the huge doors creaking open. Sofia strides in, ignoring the lecturer as she stomps her way to a seat.

Professor Andersson peers over her red glasses at her. "Ms. Ivanov. You can do the essay with Ophelia."

Marvelous.

Sofia casts her eyes up to the ceiling. "I'm not doing it with her."

"You two can iron out your differences, I'm sure."

"It'll be your fault when I kill her," snaps Sofia, staying firmly in her seat.

"I'll go with Ophelia. Pick me!" shouts Vincenzo, through a mouthful of raisins. I can't help but laugh. He's ridiculous, but he's in my corner.

Andersson huffs. "You're all adults, for heaven's sake. Sofia, you can go with Vincenzo."

The whole room lets out a whoosh of air through their teeth. "Rival families. Bad idea," warns a girl at the front. Andersson mutters something about not being paid enough for any of this and pairs Shawn with Vincenzo, Shawn 2.0 with Sofia, and…

No.

"Ophelia and Alex."

I open my mouth to protest, because I'd genuinely rather work with Sofia, but the glare Andersson gives me makes me close it again. The heavy sigh from behind me tells me Alex isn't keen either. This is not good.

I'm momentarily distracted by an incoming text.

Divya
The week before the crash, someone
called Nicholas Papadopoulos emailed
Carmichael's PA with a photo of a
signed preflight check.
That's all I can give you. I don't want to
get caught and expelled.

Genuine gratitude expands my chest.

Ophelia
I can't thank you enough. I'm so grateful.
I will take a look later. PS I've just been
partnered up with Alex for an essay.

Divya
This is good, kinda? You might be able
to get information out of him. He might
let something slip accidentally.

     Ophelia
     Doubt it. He hasn't smiled or said a word in
     ages. I'll try, though. Talk later.

Divya
Huge party in the Nightshade mansion
tonight. Wanna borrow an outfit?

     Ophelia
     What's wrong with my clothes? And I'll be in
     bed with a cup of tea, living my dream.

Divya
Fine.
And you dress a bit like Oliver Twist.

Oh my god. I look down at my brown skirt and sweater. Maybe it has a tiny hole, but it adds to my rustic charm. *Doesn't it?* I spin around to Vincenzo. "Would you say my style is girl-next-door?"

Dark eyelashes flutter, a wonky smile appearing on his face. "Whatever you say it is, angel, I agree," he says, at the same time that Alex mutters, "Dickensian-orphan-next-door, more like."

I glare at him for a beat until he drops his phone to the desk and stares right back at me with that striking pair of eyes. Christ, he's a work of art. A twisted, heinous, evil work of art. "Problem, Winters?"

You're my problem, Alex. You're all of my problems. I grit my teeth, narrowing my eyes at him slightly before turning back to face the front, distracting myself with the lecture.

Two hours fly by, and I find myself genuinely interested in the content. Learning about how people can be influenced into doing bad things by powerful people feels relevant to my mission.

The same can't be said for Vin, who is watching some viral dating show with his earbuds in. He pulls out an earbud and slaps Alex on the shoulder with far more force than is necessary. "No fucking *way*. Andrea chose Michael. Even after Michael went in the hot tub with Ekuwa."

Alex lets out a wearied sigh, eyes fixed on his notes as he writes. "They're all fucking stupid, Vincenzo."

As Andersson wraps up, Alex rips a page from his book and slaps it on the table in front of Vin. It's an extremely simplified summary of the lecture in big block capital letters. Vincenzo pauses his phone on a shot of two bikini-clad women trying to pop balloons with their crotches. *Each to their own.* "Thanks, man. Dunno where I'd be without you."

Alex doesn't reply, closing his leather notebook and gliding down the steps toward Andersson as everyone else leaves. I linger around awkwardly, shuffling from foot to foot by the doorway as I wait for Alex. He's engrossed in hushed conversation with Andersson, hand rubbing the five o'clock shadow over his jaw as she shakes her head. Reaching into the pocket of his black slacks, he produces a wad of banknotes, tossing them onto the lectern between them both.

Andersson shakes her head again. He sighs and rests his elbow on the wood, a fabricated smile tipping the corners of his mouth up. He rakes a hand through his unruly hair, letting it flop over his forehead in *that* way. Whatever it is he's asking for, Andersson looks like she's about to give him it as she flips her platinum hair over her shoulder and flushes.

For fuck's sake. She's twice our age, flirting with a student who has even less personality than *me*, and that's saying something. I'm dryer than Dr. Bancroft's scalp.

Both of their eyes turn to me, and something flits through Andersson's expression that makes me turn away in disgust at myself.

Pity.

I push through the double doors and into the cool air in the hall, letting the embarrassment drain from my face. *Whatever*. I'll talk to Alex later—or maybe I won't; I doubt he'll be much help with the project, anyway. I breeze past faded portraits that sneer down at me, beneath thick cobwebs, over the stone floor that has been smoothed by centuries of footsteps before me.

I run my finger along the wall as I walk, watching the dust gather on my pale skin, and wonder if my mother walked this same hallway. Did she count down the hours until the end of each day like I do? Did she *really* like it here?

Behind me, the stillness in the hallway is fractured by a dull scrape, like the shuffle of two feet on stone. Unease prickles my nape, silence hanging in the deserted hallway. "Alex?"

I creep toward the direction of the sound, hovering outside a closed door. Tentatively, I turn the handle, and I'm met with a dark, empty teaching room. It's deserted, but I can't fight the feeling that someone is in here. "Alex?"

"Doing a tremendous job of convincing me you're not obsessed with me, Twist. Do you shout my name in your dreams, too?"

I step back from the doorway, spotting Alex lazily strolling down the hallway, too far away to have been the noise I heard. Someone must've been here, watching me again.

His voice is as soft as silk, melting over the goose bumps on my arm as he flashes me that famous smile. It doesn't fool me, but I give him one right back; just as cheerful, just as false. "Only when it's a nightmare."

He palms his jaw, thumb tracing the sculpted curve of his lower lip. It takes a few seconds to drag my gaze away. "So I'm on your mind."

"What did you want with Andersson?"

"Tried paying her to make you go away."

I hate him. "Yeah? And how did that work out for you?"

"Turns out, someone on this planet thinks you have potential."

"Or maybe she knows you'd fail the essay without me."

"How old are you, Ophelia?"

I narrow my eyes at him. "Twenty-one."

One eyebrow raises like he's surprised by this snippet of information. "Quite old."

"All right, DiCaprio, calm down. What do you need next, the name of my first childhood pet?"

"Please. The street you grew up on, and the three digits on the back of your credit card too." The bitter smile on his face evaporates, his body leaning closer. Close enough for me to notice every shade of green in his irises. "What I want to know is why a girl like you would come to this university three years late with nothing but a shitty bag of cheap clothes and some made-up stories about your parents. No one with your surname works for the government here."

How he has found that information out, I do not know, but my heartbeat rises to a sickly rhythm in my throat. Hearing a Corbeau-Green talk about my parents is nauseating on so many levels. I need to get this conversation on safer ground. "What my parents do is none of your business. We need to choose a day to start the essay."

He stifles a yawn like he's bored of the conversation. Bored of me. Bored of it all. "I'll do the essay. No time in each other's vicinity required. I'll forward it to you when it's done."

Tempting, but no. Carmichael does not need any excuses to get rid of me. "Tonight at six?"

"Got rugby training. Four o'clock in the library?"

"I'll be swimming. Eight? After dinner?"

His tone is sarcastic as he turns to leave. "Great. I'll wear a tux."

"I'll wear my pajamas," I reply, watching his powerful form slip through the doorway.

The hallway is silent once more, colder and darker than the rest of the castle. The same sensation creeps up my neck, a prickling feeling that I'm not alone. I hurry out of the castle, wondering how I'm going to survive an hour alone in Alex's company tonight.

"GREAT JOB TODAY, Winters." Belladonna tosses me a sports drink in the swimming locker room with an approving nod.

It turns out, Sorrowsong has an indoor pool after all. In fact, it's probably the most modern amenity I've seen in my time here. Belladonna just decided to have the trials in the near-freezing river because she's…Belladonna.

Colette hums her agreement, swiping a rosy gloss over her lips in the mirror. "You're like…really fast."

"Thanks," I mutter, stuffing my towel into my bag. My mind is elsewhere, lost in a cloud of black smoke infecting a rain-washed forest. A phone number for a helicopter engineer is burning a hole in the pocket of my jogging bottoms.

Nicholas Papadopoulos is the first shard of hope that Divya has discovered while trawling through maintenance databases and old emails. He was a Green Aviation contractor conducting safety checks at Sorrowsong for ten years until the month of my parents' death.

Odd timing.

Damp strands of my hair lash against my face as I step into the storm outside, hunched over to see the screen as I punch the number into my phone and press it to my ear. A long, monotonous beep bleeds out of the speaker.

No signal.

Of course.

"Dinner?"

Colette jogs out into the storm toward me. Her pink umbrella is inside out, and the Barbie pink skirt of her dress is a similar shape, but I respect her commitment to fashion. "Sure."

Wet gravel crunches underfoot as we hurry to the imposing main structure of the castle and out of the rain. My phone buzzes with a text in my pocket, but I'm distracted by the smell of food wafting from the dining hall. My stomach grumbles. I'm a firm believer that there are not many wounds that a giant bowl of carbohydrates can't fix.

"Want one?" Colette picks up a salad pot, hand hovering over another.

"Salad makes me sad," I reply, plucking an immaculately presented carbonara from the counter. I grab a bowl of fruit for good measure and join Colette and her friendship group.

As they ease into conversation about a celebrity divorce, I tug my phone from my pocket and stare at the notification in disbelief.

Unknown
My room at 8pm, Twist. I have a desk
and two chairs. -A C G.

> **Ophelia**
> I didn't give you my number.

Unknown
Ten points to Detective Winters. Are you
always this observant, or is this a good
week?

I puff out a frustrated exhale and ask Colette if she gave Alex my number. She wouldn't have meant any harm, but the idea of him having it is sickening. It's another betrayal of my father's final request to me.

"No, but he's texting you?" replies Colette excitedly. "Oh my god."

I rub my sweaty palms over my thighs and tap out a reply.

Ophelia
Delete my number. Email my student
address if you need me.

Unknown
I almost forgot you're stuck in the
Dickensian era. See you tonight.

I reread his first message and frown.

Ophelia
We'll meet in the library.

Unknown
It'll be fun, I promise.

Ophelia
I'd rather shit in my hands and clap than set
foot inside your bedroom. We'll meet in the
library downstairs.

Unknown
But I was excited to see your pajamas :(

If I wasn't so annoyed, the irony of Alex Corbeau-Green using a frowny face would force a chuckle out of me. I click on the icon at the top of the screen and block his number.

The delicious smell of the pasta turns rancid in my nose, the dish congealing into a scrambled mass in front of me. My skin prickles with an uncomfortable dread, unwilling to spend an hour in his company.

I down the last of my wine and mumble an excuse to the table, gluing my eyes to the top right corner of my phone the whole walk back to my halls, hoping for one little bar of signal to appear. I'm so transfixed on the screen that I slam into someone, staggering backward in the busy foyer.

Amid flashing lights and music, my eyes adjust fast enough to see Sofia's palm swing toward my face. I duck it just in time, drawing "oohs" and "ahhs" from the crowd of already drunk partygoers around us.

"What the hell?"

In the purple lighting, she looks crazed. "You stole my iPad."

"Incorrect."

Her bony fingers jab toward my face. "You're so desperate for attention, you've agreed to spy for the Morellos."

"Twenty pounds says it's in your wardrobe where it usually is." Sofia's wardrobe is like an allegory of the inside of my mind; open it just an inch, and a lifetime's worth of dusty old shit falls out.

She grabs me by the neck and the room whoops with excitement, but I force my breath to be steady as her bony fingers dig into my throat. "I'll kill you in your sleep, Winters."

Calmly, I prize her hand off me. "You can try."

THE FIRST THING I did when I got back to my room was open Sofia's unlocked wardrobe and find her iPad beneath a pile of fishnet tights and mud-caked boots. Now, freshly showered and dressed in a brown pleated skirt, thick tights, and one of my dad's knitted jumpers, I redial the most recent number in my call log. With each ring, my hope dwindles, until a hoarse voice crackles down the line. "Papadopoulos."

I'm so shocked to hear his voice, my delicately planned script doesn't come out. Now the moment is here, I'm grappling to find the words I want to say.

A ragged sigh muffles the microphone. "*Gamó*. Fucking spam callers."

Desperation knocks me out of my speechlessness. "No, wait. Wait. Don't hang up. It's Nicholas, right?"

I hear a slow exhale, imagining a puff of cigarette smoke leaving his lips. There's a pause before his thick Greek accent returns. "That's what I *just* said, and I'm not interested in your insurance. Not for my dog, not for my car, not for my life."

"I'm calling from Sorrowsong. I wanted to know—"

Another puff of air. "Don't work there no more."

I cut to the chase. "I know. I'm calling about the helicopter accident a few years ago."

The silence stretches on long enough for me to pull my phone from my ear and check the call is still active. "Mr. Papadopoulos?"

"What the fuck do you want from me?" he barks, his tone switching instantly from bored disinterest to visceral rage. "You people tell me to shut up and I do. You tell me to forget it, but you're making it very hard."

I open my mouth, but I'm cut off by the flat sound of the line going dead. I hurl the phone at the bed and press the heels of my hands into my eyes, the beginning of a migraine setting in.

90

I don't know what I'm doing here, suspended in some sort of half-surviving state, fueled by a mission I'm not even sure will be worth it. I just can't let it go, because the second I do is the second I have nothing left to wake up for in the morning.

I'm not ashamed to admit my parents are—*were*—my closest friends. I'd skip house parties to stay at home and play Scrabble with them, and I'd wake up without regrets. Successes, failures, heartbreaks, dreams, they were all poured down the phone line during my quiet evenings at home while my mother tended to Sorrowsong's gardens.

I wasn't always close to them—geographically, that is, thanks to their jobs at Sorrowsong—but they were always on the other end of a string. If I tugged it hard enough, they'd be there. If I tied a paper cup to each end, they'd be listening on the other side. When it felt like the world was crumbling, they'd stick it back together again with homemade apple pies and weekend camping trips.

Everyone has their string people—the people they are tied to, whether it be through blood or trauma or friendship. It's a luxury I didn't realize I had. A comfort blanket that was so constantly *there*, I never even noticed how warm it kept me at night.

I never considered I might lose it. Now my summers are quiet, my Christmases are silent, and when I tug on my piece of string, the other end slithers along the ground at my feet.

That is what the Greens have done to me. That is why I cannot take Nicholas's no for an answer, why I can't befriend Alex—or even Vincenzo—why I have to last here, even if it'll cost me my sanity.

I won't replace the people on the other end of my string, but I can ruin the people who cut it in half.

Chapter 8

OPHELIA

I step into the hallway a few minutes past eight with an odd sense of light-headedness.

Shrugging off a wave of nausea, I fire Divya a text about the uselessness of my call with Nicholas. As I hit Send, an email pops up at the top of the screen.

From: Alex Corbeau-Green
Subject: Punctuality (noun) *the fact or quality of being on time*
Date: Tuesday 1st October 20:04 BST
To: Ophelia Winters

I'm in the library. Look for the charming gentleman in the black shirt.
-ACG

I consider blocking his email, too, but I need good feedback from my lecturers.

From: Ophelia Winters
Subject: Patience (noun) *the ability to wait, or to suffer without complaining or becoming annoyed*
Date: Tuesday 1st October 20:05 BST
To: Alex Corbeau-Green

I'm on my way down now. Are you sitting to the left or the right of the charming gentleman?
Signing your emails with your initials is obnoxious,
Ophelia

I slide my phone into my tote bag and wind my way down the staircase to the foyer of the Nightshade mansion, clutching the ornate banister a little tighter as my head swims. All I had was one glass of wine. Perhaps I'm becoming a lightweight.

It becomes clear as I hit the second floor why Alex thought it was a bad idea to study downstairs. The thick stone walls grumble with each beat of heavy bass, and the cheers of drunk people occupy every floor.

I pass Nightshade, Hemlock, Cortinar, and Snakeroot students on the stairs, and when I hit the final step, I'm faced with half of the rugby team chugging beer from funnels held up by half-naked celebrities, the room so loud I can't hear my own thoughts. *Never mind, the library will be quiet.* I shove my way through the crowd of sweaty people and through the old double doors.

The library is not quiet.

Colette DuPont is dancing on one of the oak desks with another woman I don't know. Louis, a law student from my hallway, is passing neon whisky shots off a metal tray and out to the heaving mass of people occupying every square inch of floor space. Alex and Vincenzo's friend Jack is making out with two women at once.

"Jesus Christ, Vincenzo, that's a first edition!" I shout, watching Alex's friend put his overflowing beer down on the world's most expensive coaster. I snatch the book from under the glass and cringe at the circular mark on the cover.

"Ophelia!" he exclaims, slamming me with all two hundred pounds of his weight. "You came!"

"No, I didn't. I'm here to work."

"Huh?" he shouts, turning his mangled ear to me over the music. I shake my head at him and shove my way to the back of the room, where Alex sits on a corner desk by the window, typing on his laptop in a pair of fucking *reading glasses.* He pulls out an earbud, green gaze connecting with mine before it drops down to my midsection. "You wish."

I follow his eyes to the book in my hands. *Far from the Madding Crowd.* That would be nice.

His eyes coast over me once more, distant and disinterested. "You look disheveled, as ever."

His black shirt looks like it was ironed by Giorgio Armani himself, molded to his athletic frame in a way he does not deserve. "And you're comically overdressed. What's new?"

94

His smile wanes as a raucous cheer erupts over by the library's bar. "We should've gone to my room."

I pull my tangled earphones from my pocket and open up the report that Alex started on my laptop. "I'd sooner insert this pencil into my eye socket than join you in your bedroom, Alex. Have you started the conformity write-up?"

"Yeah, figured you could write up the section on obedience," he mutters, as his thumb traces the line of his jaw. He looks over the screen of his laptop at me, eyes glittering with some sort of private joke.

I pause my irrationally enraging fight with my earphones. "Something to say?"

He leans back in his chair, interlacing his fingers behind his head. I fight to keep my eyes on his face, and I hate that I must. "Not at all."

For twenty minutes, we're productive despite my growing headache. Then Vincenzo presses the Power button on my laptop to get me to join the party. Unfortunately for him, I cannot be stopped when I'm on an academic roll, even if my laptop takes another twenty minutes to start up again. It sounds like a 747 trying to take off.

The crowd in the library thins slightly, thanks to a game of strip poker finishing upstairs. I decide I need to start fishing for information. "The section on strategies of persuasion is interesting, don't you think?"

He doesn't look up from his phone, thumbs furiously typing. My fingers tighten around my pencil. "Alex."

He looks up. "Yeah, I guess so."

"Yeah. Like…if someone at your dad's company saw something was wrong and was persuaded to keep quiet…that would be kind of…interesting?" *Christ, Ophelia.* Real smooth. I strike police detective off my potential career list.

Lazily, he takes his reading glasses off and hangs them over the *V* at the top of his shirt. It reveals another inch of tattooed muscle. The desk groans as he rests his elbows on the wood and leans toward me slightly, his voice slow and quiet like he's about to reveal something secret. He smells good. "Ophelia, is this your first attempt at holding a conversation with someone?"

I retain my steely expression, but I know my blushing face betrays me. "Yes, how am I doing?"

His focus returns to his phone, raising my blood temperature yet another degree. "Horribly."

I square my shoulders and return to the report, but the letters start jiggling at the edges, a ringing piercing in my ears as my light-headedness worsens. Maybe I ate something bad, or maybe it's just Alex's proximity. I look up and study the man sitting opposite me as he rubs the tension out of his left shoulder. He wouldn't have put something in my drink.

Right?

"I might…" The world tilts on its axis slightly. Something is wrong. "I might have to head upstairs in a minute. I'll catch up tomorrow."

Alex doesn't look up, sitting farther back in his chair with his hand glued to his phone. It's the final straw. I scrape my chair back, yank my overheating laptop from the table, and swipe the stupid phone from his hand. "A phone addiction is an extremely unattractive characteristic, Alex. Come back to me when you can be bothered."

He pushes his sleeves farther up his forearms and nods down at the device in my hand, expression neutral. "Please, sir. Can I have some more?"

"Fuck you," I seethe, shoving it into his chest and storming out.

The sweaty sea of students churns like the tarn as I push my way through the dark foyer. Through the fog that seems to be pervading my vision, I vaguely see Vincenzo, who sounds like he's in a fishbowl even though he's right in front of me.

A shadowy figure hovers over his shoulder, but I can't quite make out who it is in the haze. Wobbling on my feet, I stare down at my hands, watching them slowly shift back into focus. When I glance back up at Vincenzo, my arms seize at my sides, body rigid with terror.

It's Achlys. The woman from the painting and the stained-glass window.

She's real, and she's staring back at me.

Her eyes are raw from crying, her wet hair is stuck to her face, strewn with algae as though she has just been pulled from the darkest depths of the tarn.

And even though I can hear her strangled sobs over the boom of the music, what's left of her teeth form a chilling grin. Something about her is so awful, so *abominable*, that my legs start propelling me backward of their own accord. I stumble back through the crowd, but two lifeless eyes follow me the whole way, never blinking.

The banister is cold as my trembling hands find it. The skin over Achlys's cheek melts away, like her soul is rotting her body from the inside out. Her cackle turns to a mournful wail that makes my ears bleed.

No one else reacts. No one else is scared. It's hard to breathe. The foyer is spinning, my footsteps are faster. I run up the stairs as fast as my body will allow, stumbling into my bedroom before the yawning black hole engulfs me.

All I hear as the world fades to nothing is Achlys's bony fingers turning the door handle and following me inside.

Chapter 9

ALEX

Honestly, I hardly noticed that the ginger girl left the library until I got this odd feeling like something was missing. Then I realized it was her unrelenting complaining and her weird lines of interrogation.

And maybe the soft sound of her blowing a piece of unruly red hair out of her face only for it to land exactly where it started.

When I watched her tattered tote bag swing around the double doors, I did feel a little bad, but my sympathy dwindled by the time I took my next breath. Sure, she's a loner, but she brings it on herself. She's rude, and where's her sense of fun? I get the impression the highlight of her day every day is doing Wordle, or finding a misshapen cornflake in the box, or something.

In a way, I'm envious of her constant foul mood. There was a time once when I had the energy to care. When my mind was capable of any emotion that wasn't lukewarm apathy. Nothing matters to me these days. Rugby games, essay grades, girls, my career, they all sit in a dusty box in the attic of my mind with a peeling label that says *for when the world has color again.*

It's not that I'm sad, either. I'm just…blank. I can't remember the last time I had a label to slap onto my mood. Can't remember the last time something drummed up enough excitement in me to make me look forward to waking up in the morning. So though Ophelia's constant anger irks me, I think it'd be worse to see it go.

There's a gray cloud inside me, a shapeless, faceless monster created by my father. He rolled me in his palm, flattening all my edges and peculiarities; my creativity, my empathy, my passion, until I was a perfect sphere of his creation. Until the monster inside me matched the monster inside him.

But his monster, it walks outside his body, threaded through each of his actions and his words. It's in the way he tears down others, and the way he can spin anyone's enthusiasm into self-doubt.

But mine, mine is trapped between the boundaries of my flesh. It won't creep past my lips or bleed into my deeds, no matter how hard I try. It tears *me* down, churns *my* optimism into self-doubt.

Cain Green planted the seed of evil inside me, nurtured it, watered it, fed it every day, and then made my skin so thick it couldn't get out.

If it wasn't for my sisters, for my desperation that they don't get a gray cloud of their own, for my plan to win over Carmichael, I'd have succumbed to it already.

But I can't and I won't. Not until they're all safe.

Shutting the lid of my laptop in the darkest corner of the Nightshade library, I turn my attention back to my texts with my eldest sister.

NIGHTSHADE

Fleur
Mom is bad today.

> **Alex**
> Can't be any worse than Dad.

Fleur
Hahaha. Very, very true.

> **Alex**
> Need me to come home for the weekend?
> How bad is it?

Fleur
You can't fly from the UK to New York
just for the weekend. Mom will be fine.

Vincenzo appears behind me, two tequila shots in his bruised fist. He scans my phone screen, his expression sobering. He sets the shots down and watches the three dots on the bottom left of the screen until a message pops up.

Fleur
She threw all the wine glasses into
the pool in front of Josie, screaming
something about tulip glasses being out
of fashion. I rang her doctors and they
picked her up.

The new housekeeper made a great
spaghetti alle vongole though, so you
win some and you lose some.

"Jesus fucking Christ," I mutter. I imagine the scene in my parents' ostentatious home and try to gauge each of my sisters' reactions.

Fleur, at the ripe old age of sixteen, has more emotional maturity than any adult I know. At fourteen, Mia and Evie pretend they have no emotions, like watching their mother lose her sanity is a regular phase of adolescence for everyone. Éléanor isn't really interested in anything that isn't Taylor Swift, but it's Charlotte and Josie, not yet out of elementary school, who I worry about most.

Alex
Is Dad home?

Fleur
He's at a sustainability conference in
Boston. The irony, right? He's back
tomorrow. Tennis match now, byeeee.

My mood sinks faster than Vin sinks the tequila, and for what might be the hundredth time today, a wave of guilt slams into me and reinforces what I already know to be true.

I'm awful for leaving them. Noble quest or not, if anything happens to any of them, I'll never be able to forgive myself.

Somewhere along the line, our childhood morphed from idyllic to troubled, turning my relationship with my little sisters from brotherly to fatherly. Then, as we all ate cereal on the floor of our ridiculous pantry on a day when my mother's mind was particularly fractured and my father's fuse was particularly short, I promised them that no matter what happens in life, they'd always have me.

And they still do, but I'm three thousand miles away. Fleur understands why I'm here. She understands that my silence is not truly apathy. It's molten rage churning beneath the surface, and one day, that rage will melt the flesh off Cain Green's wretched body.

Fleur is the only one who *really* knows. I can't trust the others. They're young and loquacious. They'd spill all my secrets for a bag of Hershey's Kisses and a new lip balm if given the chance.

I gather my things and return to my room, flicking the gold switch on the wall. No power, *great*. Half my evenings here I've spent studying by candlelight in a dungeon—like Gondor, or Gandalf, whatever his name is.

In the eerie dark, I swap my black shirt out for a hoodie of the same color, tugging some sweatpants over my legs. Outside, the rain picks up, trickling over inky ivy and down the Tudor mansion windows. The dark silhouette of Sorrowsong looms through the fog, dotted with warm, orange lights from windows.

If spending three miserable years kissing ass in this shitty, dark castle is what I have to do for the seven women in my life, I'll do it. I just hope they don't hate me in the meantime.

And God, I hope I don't mess this up.

Tugging the hood of my rugby sweater over my head with the omnipresent weight of expectation on my shoulders, I run my hand along the back of my desk drawer until my fingers find what I'm after. A master key. I took it from a cleaner's trolley this morning in the business wing.

My phone buzzes with a text from my second youngest sister. It's a picture of her arm, decorated with a friendship bracelet with my name on it.

Charlotte
Is it nighttime where you are? Night
night, Ally.

I fire back a picture of the matching one hanging from my room key and wait a depressing amount of time for it to send.

Alex
It is. Get off your iPad and do your
homework.

Charlotte
Boooring.

A warm glow settles around my cold heart, and I make my way out into the rainy night.

Chapter 10

OPHELIA

I wake up with a racing heart and a sheen of sweat cooling my skin.

For once, my nightmares were not of a helicopter plunging into a thick forest, but of Achlys wailing at the end of my bed. Downstairs, the thundering bass has been replaced with low chatter, quiet enough to let me hear the howl of the wind through the rafters. The party must've wound down.

In the dark, I tug on the cord of my nightlight, but the power is out.

My heartbeat hasn't slowed. The sense of dread looming over me hasn't lessened, and all of a sudden, it hits me why that is.

There's a smell in the air. That *same* smell. The scent of licorice and nutmeg followed me in the tarn, it clung to my freshly made bed the other night, and now it lingers in the frigid air of the bedroom. I roll onto my side and make out Sofia's sleeping form in the other bed and realization sinks into me.

It's her.

She's my strange stalker. I don't know why I'm surprised. She is the only other person with a key to access this room, and God knows she's not my biggest fan. She must've spiked my drink last night too. I bolt upright in bed, trying to decide what to do with this new knowledge. I turn on my phone and squint at the time.

4:23 a.m.

Then a notification distracts me. An email to my personal account, sent an hour ago. I don't recognize the name, but I open it all the same.

From: Alan Sine
Subject: Ode to a Nightingale
Date: Wednesday 2nd October 03:04 BST
To: Ophelia Winters

My heart aches, and a drowsy numbness pains
My sense, as though of hemlock I had drunk.
—John Keats.

I frown down at the email. *Alan Sine.* It isn't remotely familiar. My gaze lingers on the word *hemlock* for an extra second, a sinking feeling in my stomach. It's too apt to be a coincidence.

Perhaps the name is an alias. My gaze lands once again on the other person in the room, and I stomp out of bed and yank her onto her back.

My voice is far louder than I intend, but I am *so* sick of her. "What the fuck is—"

Sofia is cold beneath my fingers. Colder than any human should be. Her skin doesn't dimple beneath my touch like it should do. She's missing the hum of life that I never realized people have until now.

No.

A scream is lodged in my throat, fighting my heart for space. A bead of sweat runs down my spine. My lungs beg me to breathe, but it's fruitless.

Time grinds to a halt, and for a few sickening seconds, I'm paralyzed with shock.

Then a flash of lightning illuminates every corner of the room, and the scream finally escapes. Sofia stares up at me, unblinking and emotionless, and placed ever so delicately in her mouth is a small bunch of white hemlock flowers, tied neatly with a ribbon.

My trembling hands cover my eyes for the next lightning flash, because I can't bear to see. I can't breathe. I need to get out of here. It takes five tries for my fingers to hit three consecutive nines on my phone screen, and one try for the woman in the speaker to tell me my call cannot be connected because I have no signal. I hit the Dial button again and again and again until a dense ball of dread is lodged in my throat and I finally find the strength in my legs to stumble out into the hallway.

A low voice pierces the quiet. "Twist?"

No. No, no, *no.* What is he doing here? Will he kill me next? Alex has a key in the door at the end of the hallway, his hair so wet beneath his hood that it drips onto his muddy shoes.

My back hits the wall with a thud, needing somewhere to hide. I'm trapped. Trapped in the hallway with the son of a killer. Trapped in the hallway with Sofia's killer. I don't feel anything as my back scrapes down the rough stone, sinking to the floor with my hand over my mouth.

He takes in my appearance, and in that moment, I'm everything I prayed I'd never be. Scared of a man. Scared of a Corbeau-Green. *Weak.* "What's the matter? Done a Sudoku wrong?"

I can't talk through my hyperventilating breaths, can't think, can't move, can't escape, can't do anything but sit and stare at the lifeless shadow in the bed beside mine. Alex's gaze follows my own, his brow creasing. He tugs his phone out of his joggers and turns on the flashlight as he stops beside Sofia's bed.

He's emotionless, silent for a moment. And then another. Eventually, he swipes up on his phone, switches off the flashlight, and slowly turns to face me. "Fucking hell, Ophelia. You didn't have to kill her."

I—*what?* "I didn't," I whisper, looking up at him as he fills the doorway. "You don't get to pin this on me. You did this."

"I heard her scream. You're the only one who's been in there."

I rise to my feet, knees trembling. "That was *my* scream, genius."

"Sure." His focus returns to his phone, opening his contacts. His finger hovers over the green Dial button.

"What the hell are you doing?" I whisper-shout, lunging for the device. I catch a glimpse of the name Carmichael on the screen and intensify my efforts.

He holds the phone above his head. "Getting you out of here before you kill the next person that annoys you."

"Yeah? And when I say *it wasn't me, but Alex came running in with his face hidden at four-thirty in the morning, maybe you should check the CCTV?* You look *just* as suspicious as me."

His nostrils flare, thumb shutting off his phone. "I have no reason to kill Sofia, you do."

"Such as?" I hiss, feeling woozy. I'm all too aware of the dead body just a few yards away.

His eyes are almost glowing in the dark, alight with frustration. "She was making your life hell."

I scrub my face in my hands, pacing into the hallway. I'm surfing a colossal wave of adrenaline, but I know I'll be broken when I fall off it. "I don't know what parallel universe you live in, but that's a reason for me to steal her body lotion, or something, not fucking murder her!"

He stands opposite me and remains silent, mouth set in a firm line. I think he's a killer. He thinks I'm a killer. I look suspicious. He looks suspicious. We're at an impasse, two suspects beside a dead body, unsure if we're on the same team or not.

One large hand tugs back the hood of his rugby sweatshirt, his damp hair tousled beneath. "So what are we now? Study buddies who bury bodies together?"

"*What?* The day I bury a body with you is the day I lose my mind. We are not covering this up. That's not fair on her family."

"Her father is a shithead."

I hate his complete lack of empathy. "A shithead who lost his daughter."

"You got a better idea, Twist?"

I open my mouth in the hope that something clever will fall out of it, but the silence is shattered by the sound of voices outside.

Distant shadows obscure the translucent stained glass in the hallway door, laughter creeping through the gap beneath. Panic slices through my stomach, the dwindling wave of adrenaline finding a second wind. "What now?" I whisper, frantic.

A figure moves on the other side of the door, snapping Alex into action. He points to the key in the lock of the room at the end of the hall. "My bedroom, Ophelia."

His bedroom? Alex shares my hallway? I said I'd never set foot in his room, but a manslaughter charge in my first month here feels worse. As Alex makes my bed with a speed I can only admire, my shaky fingers turn the key and I dive inside.

I hardly have time to notice that Alex's bedroom is actually a whole apartment, because as soon as the door closes behind him, he yanks his wet hoodie and T-shirt over his head. My heartbeat roaring in my ears, I stand awkwardly by the king-sized bed, wrapping my arms around myself.

I don't mean to look, but I do.

A birdcage curves around the side of his ribs, and out of the open door flies a raven that spreads its wings over his abs. Another raven soars over his left shoulder, and another over his broad chest. They dance down rippling arms, over his muscular back as he chucks his muddy running shoes into the bathroom and shuts the door.

Alex Corbeau-Green is an evil, depraved work of art.

"There is a universe outside of my arms, you know."

I feel my cheeks warm. "You're a gold-plated turd, Alex."

He rounds the bed in nothing but dark gray joggers. The sound of voices in the hallway gets louder, the thud of my heart in my ears deepens. "Get in the bed."

"*What?*"

He's so close I can feel the heat of his bare chest through my pajama shirt. "Get. Into. My. Bed."

My next breath is heavy, riddled with loathing and something unfamiliar. "And why would I do that?"

His hands find my shoulders and gently but firmly push me to the mattress, his face hovering above mine. I focus on the scar through his eyebrow. The five o'clock shadow that kisses his jaw. The way the rain clings to his lashes. Anywhere that isn't the pools of green beneath them. His voice comes out a hoarse whisper. "Because for some reason, I'm willing to be your alibi."

He steps back from between my legs, tossing the duvet over my shivering form before peering through the peephole in the door. His voice is muffled by the door, but I hear his gravely command. "Wear your hair down."

"Why?"

"The last letter is *Z*."

Am I in a different universe to everyone else at this school? I never know what is going on. "Huh?"

"Sounds like you're always stuck on the penultimate letter of the alphabet. It's all you ever say." He turns back to the bed. "Wear your hair down, Twist, because that's how I would've wanted it."

What? Butterflies do odd things in my stomach. Not for him, though. They'd do it for anyone.

I don't know why my fingers tug my red waves loose, but they do. Eyes still glued to the hole in the door, he holds up three fingers, then two fingers, then one. A visceral scream for help from the hallway makes my blood run cold, and Alex flicks off his phone torch, plunging us into darkness.

With my eyes unadjusted, I can't see a thing, but I feel the bed dip beside me under the heavy weight of him, sense his head on the pillow beside mine. I don't dare breathe, don't dare tell him this is my first time in bed with a man, don't dare tell him that this is all bringing back awful flashbacks of the worst day of my life.

Ancient grief has wriggled its way out of the cracks of my heart and tied my tongue in a knot.

I forget the man beside me is my worst enemy and anchor myself to the steady, calm rhythm of his breaths and the warmth that emanates from his skin. I ignore the shouting outside, ignore the yawning hole of panic trying to drag me under, ignore the tears that sting my eyes.

After a few minutes of waiting with bated breath, I feel Alex's body stiffen as a gruff voice grumbles outside. "It's Carmichael."

My heart skips a beat. "In the hallway?"

"Yeah," he whispers, holding his breath.

His leg brushes mine, the contact enough to make us both take a sharp inhale. I jolt back, reminding myself once more of why I hate him. "Are you giving me an alibi, Alex, or using me as one?"

He sits up beside me, lighting a candle on the side table with a Zippo. "Now is really not the time, Ophelia." He looks down at me in the dim light, and with careful, steady fingers, he undoes the top two buttons of my sleep shirt without ever grazing my skin. I'm paralyzed, forced to watch his hands as they drop the fabric and gently tousle the lengths of my hair.

Copper strands wind between his index finger and thumb, neither one of us willing to shatter the silence. I'm so starved of connection, so hungry for intimacy that I don't stop him. Even a fabricated moment with the wrong person feels better than loneliness.

His focused expression relaxes and he stills a moment, breaking eye contact to look at my mouth. The pad of his thumb skates along my lower lip ever so slightly. "If you weren't so unbearable, I'd make you look freshly kissed," he whispers.

His words snatch my retort away. If he was anyone else, anywhere else, perhaps I'd agree. I roll my head away from his hand in time for a sharp knock to rap on the door. The dread that was just beginning to dissolve from my body seeps back in at the edges.

What if he thinks it was me? What if it *was* me?

Alex rolls out of the now-messy bed and pads over to the door, his voice almost inaudible. "Look...flustered, okay? And cry."

Look flustered and cry? What kind of instruction is that? Fortunately, flustered and crying is my default mode.

Alex lazily swings open the door and rubs his chest sleepily. "Good morning, Harris."

Harris? Are they buddies? The chancellor looms in the doorway, and I swear the temperature drops ten degrees. *Could he be Alan Sine?* He doesn't seem to like me, and he does give me the creeps. He'd have a key to my room, surely. And what is he doing fully dressed in a waistcoat and blazer at this hour? Even his mustache is perfectly shaped into a handlebar.

"Alex. I don't suppose you saw Ms. Ivanov or Ms. Winters this evening?"

He muffles a yawn with a tattooed forearm. "I saw Sofia at the party at ten or eleven. Ophelia is in here."

Carmichael's eyes drop to me, filled with ill-hidden surprise. "Oh?"

I don't have to fabricate my embarrassment because I know what Carmichael must think of me. Seduced by the son of Cain Green, the reason behind all of my problems. "Hello, Chancellor Carmichael."

"Are you all right, sir?" asks Alex, turning his attention back to Carmichael. "Seems an odd hour for a chat?"

"Ms. Ivanov was found dead a short while ago."

I can't fake cry, but I can think about how far off track my life has gone.

It doesn't take long for the tears to fall, but I wish they didn't splinter my soul on the way down. I wish they were fake, and not tears of grief for the life Sofia won't live, for the goodnight text I didn't get from my dad, for all the hopes and dreams I had that now sit in a dusty bedroom back home.

I'm a mess.

Alex and Carmichael share a hushed conversation at the door, and it's obvious they know each other well already. The chancellor listens to what Alex says with a strange sort of respect, and when he swears neither of us killed Sofia, he accepts it without doubt.

Thank God.

Carmichael tears his attention from my new fake lover and stares at me. The longer he does, the colder I feel. He glances from me to Alex, back to me. I get the strange sensation that he sees inside my head.

Now that Alex is my alibi, I can't accuse him. *Smart.* And if it was Carmichael, I don't want to poke the bear. Not now I know that the bear has a creepy penchant for literature and access to a fucking poison cabinet.

I blurt out the obvious question, mostly to end the silence. "Can't the police investigate it? Like every other murder?"

Carmichael's eyes flash with something strange. "This is being handled...internally."

Of course it is. The police can be bought, it seems. He checks his pocket watch, which is unnecessary because there's a clock in each hallway. "Well, do come back to me if any information...," he almost snarls, "...resurfaces."

Carmichael leaves and I hop out of the bed like it's on fire while Alex tugs on a black, long-sleeved training top.

My legs threaten to give way beneath me, my whole body trembling with residual shock. "I don't believe you didn't do this."

His nostrils flare, fingers tightening around his phone. It's the first glimmer of anger, or of any emotion, really, I've seen from him since I got here. "No, Ophelia, I didn't do this, because any rational student here would know that this makes Vincenzo look guilty."

I feel blood start to pool back in my limbs, the ringing in my ears relenting. "Then maybe he did do this. Aren't they at war?"

Alex pinches his nose and exhales a slow breath. "Because Vincenzo would say—and has always said—"

"We keep the women out of it," finishes a gruff voice. Vincenzo's broad frame fills the doorway. "You think I'm a murderer, darlin'?"

I shake my head and lean it back against the cold wall behind me. I spent so long trying to escape the silence of my lonely life back home, and now it's all I want. I'm leaving tomorrow.

She didn't deserve this.

And though I didn't do it, I wished her gone on so many occasions. Now Kirill has lost his best friend and her parents have lost a child. The thought turns my anger into sadness, sitting like a lead weight on my left shoulder while guilt weighs down the other.

Alex and Vincenzo fall into serious conversation, and then the Italian rings one of his men to ask for protection for him and his sister. It's another world I never knew existed.

Tears still trickling over my cheeks, I fill my mind with menial thoughts about a small mark on the wood flooring, like how it got there and how long ago, because if I think about anything else, I'll crumble.

And if I think about how my stalker isn't Sofia but someone else entirely, I might not last the night.

A sock covers the mark, and beside it, a glass of water lands on the bedside table. I feel the weight of two striking green eyes on me.

"Is this a joke?" I whisper, looking up at him.

Alex looks down at me, and for the first time, I see the hatred I feel for him reflecting back at me with the same intensity. He thinks I've put his friend's life at risk. I think his father caused my parents' death. "I don't know, Ophelia. Are we laughing?"

"You spiked my drink and now you're giving me this?" The glass scrapes against the wood as I push it back toward him.

"I spiked your drink," he repeats, as though he didn't hear correctly. He breathes out a soft laugh and leans forward so we're eye to eye, and I'm cloaked in his shadow. "You vastly, *vastly*, overestimate my interest in you. You're just a sad girl with a made-up backstory. I don't know what your obsession with me is, *Winters*, but it is not reciprocated. I swear, if even a whisper of an accusation of Vincenzo leaves your lips, I'll make you disappear."

The second sentence is salt in my already broken heart, and the last sends my blood temperature plummeting.

He *is* his father. The apple hasn't even fallen from the tree. He's a rotting core behind a beautiful facade.

"Surely, Ophelia is the only one that could've done this," says Vincenzo, coming out of the bathroom. I don't understand how they're both fine. A girl is dead, and they're just...*fine*.

Vincenzo is supposed to like me. I feel the first strings of madness thread their way through my conscience. *Could it have been me?* I wasn't in my right mind last night. I don't know what happened after the world went black.

I shake my head. I know myself. Even at my lowest, I wouldn't take a life. "It wasn't me; it was Alex. He spiked my drink, he sent me the email, he killed Sofia."

Alex snaps his focus back to me. "What email?"

Something stops me from explaining. "Alan" is either Alex or Carmichael, and I don't think he'd take kindly to either accusation. "Nothing."

The two of them head toward the door, my eyes tracking Alex. He moves like a panther, gracefully threatening. "Don't go anywhere. We're just checking that Belladonna is fine."

The door clicks shut, and I'm alone in his bedroom.

I can't face the questions from other students, nor can I even think about going back to my bedroom, so I remain in place as instructed.

Alex's phone is on the small side table, his laptop on the desk, illuminated by two candles that bathe the room in a low light. It feels like a trap, all too convenient. I wipe my damp cheeks with the back of my wrist, pacing the perimeter of the room for any snippets of Alex I can find. The floorboards creak beneath my feet, punctuated by the occasional rumble of thunder and the trickle of rain through the gutters.

It's obvious he has two main hobbies outside of sports: sketching and reading. Intricate drawings of gothic and baroque buildings are pinned to a board above his desk, and if he wasn't so unpleasant, I'd say they were very good. Beside his MacBook is the leather sketchbook I saw in his car on the first day, open on a half-completed drawing of a female form sketched in orange pencil.

Almost all of the remaining wall space is occupied by bookshelves. I run my finger over delicate clothbound titles until it pauses on one particular set of books. *The Complete Works of John Keats*. My saliva turns to sawdust. In a day full of strange coincidences, it feels like one too many.

Even in the dark, I spot a scrap of paper sticking out the top of one of the books. Glancing over my shoulder to check I'm definitely alone, I tug it off the shelf and creak open the spine to the bookmarked page. For the second time tonight, a knot constricts in my throat.

Ode to a Nightingale.

The book lands on my toes, but I barely feel it. Dread has its hand wrapped firmly around my throat.

A shadow caresses my shoulder, and for some reason, even in a room full of people, I would know it was him. "That was expensive."

My whole body goes rigid. "Get away from me."

He does as I ask, and I hear the bed rustle as he flops down on it. "Not a fan of John Keats?"

"You sent me the email," I whisper, staring at the book on the floor as if it might reach up and smite me down. "You killed Sofia, you took my shoelaces." My rage builds up with each accusation that slips through my lips, until he's lying back on the bed and my

118

hands are around his neck. All I see is red, and all I feel is defeat. Like I've watched the last threads of my sanity unravel over the last few weeks and not been able to stop it.

Somewhere in the distance, somewhere far away, I hear him tell me he didn't do those things. I hear him tell me to stop. He doesn't fight me, though. Doesn't touch me.

But it doesn't matter. I'm too far gone. Too angry, too desperate to pin the blame on someone. It is him. It has to be him. For my own soundness of mind, I *need* it to be him. By the time I manage my next sentence, my voice is hoarse with unshed tears. "You spiked my drink, you made me think I was insane."

I'm yanked back by two firm hands, rapid Italian dragging me back to Earth. Vincenzo grasps me by the shoulders, eyes wide with alarm. "She's fucking crazy, man. I know you hate that word, but she is."

"He's torturing me," I choke out, tears scorching a path down my cheeks.

Alex sits up, the imprint of my palms on his neck as he sucks in a heavy breath. "She just woke up next to a body, Vincenzo, what do you think she's gonna do? Start making a cup of tea?"

"It's preferable to accentuation!"

Despite the tension of the moment, the faintest hint of a smile crosses Alex's expression. "You mean *asphyxiation*?"

Vincenzo breaks into a laugh. "Fuck you, man. I'm trying."

His giant hands come up to shield his face as Alex clubs him around the head with a thesaurus, but I just stand there. An outsider looking in.

Sofia is dead, and something deep in my gut tells me it's my fault. That she was killed for merely being my roommate.

On shaky legs, feeling like I'm living somewhere outside of my body, I stagger into Alex's oversized bathroom and stare at myself in the mirror.

Blotchy cheeks, puffy eyes, and a nose the color of my ugly pink pajamas. I look awful, and I'm suddenly desperate to be gone. Out of this bathroom, out of this mansion, out of this university.

And God above, I'm sick of feeling sad, sick of not knowing how *not* to feel sad. I'm worried my worst fears are coming true. That I'm so damaged that I'll end up incapable of loving or being loved. As I stare down at my trembling hands over the sink, I'm so weighed down by grief, so overwhelmingly *alone,* it's hard to imagine how I'll get through my next breath.

Alex appears behind me. "You know, you can stop crying now."

It's the final straw. A throwaway comment, not laced with any animosity, but at the end of such a vile night, it's the thing that tips the scales. An ugly sob strangles my throat, self-loathing burning me from the inside out. I barge past him, past his friend, and out of that awful mansion.

Chapter 11

OPHELIA

The spider in my bedroom has extended its web from the
ceiling to the window.

The rugby team won their first match of the season in
Edinburgh.

Cortinar won the monthly swim tournament this week.

Around me, the world moves on. Inhaling and exhaling a steady
beat of everyday happenings and extraordinary events, but for me,
time stopped a week ago.

When Sofia's father held a gun to my head and asked me what
happened, and I saw the rage in his eyes was just an ugly manifestation of the grief of a father.

Jaden Adeoye was reported missing shortly after Mr. Ivanov's
arrival, but I know he wasn't to blame.

Glued down by the feeling of blood on my hands and the sadness in my heart, I haven't managed to leave my bedroom this

week. On Saturday the sun came out, but it only illuminated the decaying corners of my mind.

I know I'll have to leave soon, mostly because by my calculations I'm due to run out of shortbread biscuits by this evening.

And also because I need to eat something, anything that isn't shortbread.

My phone chimes with a notification, a sound that, a couple of weeks ago, made me feel less alone, but now it just fills me with dread. I roll onto my belly to see the phone on the floor. There are two notifications from this morning, and Vincenzo's makes me smile. I'd like to live inside his head for a while.

Vincenzo
Unblock Alex's number, he wants to ask
you about the coursework. Also, I think
he feels bad about whatever he said to
you in the bathroom. PS Do you think
my white sneakers or black boots will
go better with my darker jeans? You
know the ones. Belladonna can't be
trusted with this advice.

Colette
Missed you in the pool today, honey.
Want to get dinner with me?

Dinner. Dinner means dining hall, and dining hall means hundreds of people. Hundreds of eyes and hundreds of questions. I shut the screen off and roll onto my back.

I've never felt as torn as I do now. I dreamed of a university space for a long time, watched my dad proudly tell supermarket cashiers and dentists alike that I'd be the first in my family to get one. Maybe I didn't envision it here, but I envisioned it somewhere.

But then I remember my dad cried when I broke my ankle at seven. Cried when I felt lonely at school at ten. Cried when I first looked in the mirror, pinched the skin below my belly button, and said I'd do anything to look like someone else. That man would cry if he saw me now, and I know in my heart he'd tell me that no victory is worth it if you lose yourself on the way.

Maybe a better way to honor my parents is to just live a beautiful, blissfully ordinary life.

I swing my legs over the side of the bed, my feet planting on the cold stone floor. Stretching my arms above my head, I take a failed attempt at a deep, calming breath. I swear, I've forgotten what it's like to have two unblocked nostrils, but if I ever get to experience such bliss again, I'll never take it for granted.

I pad into the bathroom and for the first time in a while, turn the mirror back around. Heavy violet circles sit under my eyes, my skin so pale it's almost translucent. Even now, I see my mother staring back at me. It's an odd thing, to look so much like her. It's a reminder of how lucky I was to have her and how bereft I am now that she's gone.

I turn the shower to freezing and step under the spray, letting the cold breathe life into my rotting limbs again. I allow myself to feel grateful my stalker has been silent since Sofia's death. Perhaps it was her after all.

By the time I've dried my hair and stepped into my joggers and giant jumper, I feel like a human again.

A human with a mission.

I crack open my bedroom door and creep down the stairs. Two Nightshade students in the foyer raise their eyebrows as I hit the bottom step.

"Almost forgot you existed, Winters."

The other one snorts. "Careful, mate. She'll kill you in your sleep."

I shove my headphones over my ears and keep walking through the mansion and out into the gray drizzle outside. If people talk to me, I don't notice. I breeze under the portcullis and into the castle courtyard, through the chapel and into Achlys's Hall. She sneers down at me like she knew I wouldn't last here.

"Fuck you," I mutter, rapping on the well-concealed door in the painting. The hall is silent for a few moments until the sound of heels clicking on tile draws nearer and the door swings open. Eva, Carmichael's PA, looks me up and down beneath her thick eyeliner. "Ms. Winters."

"Please can I see Chancellor Carmichael?"

She pushes her red glasses up her nose and spins on her heel like a soldier. "Follow me."

We traverse the wooden steps up to Carmichael's office in unfriendly silence, and she gestures to the red chesterfield sofa opposite his desk. "He will be free shortly."

I nod, running my eyes over the infinite books and boxes that cover every wall of the office. Even in this era of smartphones and unmanned drones, Carmichael's office is lit solely by candles and dull light from the windows. I wait for the sound of Eva's heels to fade away and stand, pacing the perimeter of the room. My mission to avenge my parents' death sits abandoned at the back of my mind, but as the minutes stretch on, the three red boxes on the second to top shelf look *so* tempting.

Too tempting.

I'm up on the sliding ladder before I know it, lifting the lid from one of the boxes. My fingers carve three lines through a thick layer of dust.

I flick through year after year of the staff shuttle helicopter maintenance sheets, moving to another box until I hit one from the month and year I lost my parents. A rush of adrenaline courses through me as I tug the file from the box and open the faded brown cover sheet.

There's a record of preflight checks for every time the helicopter is used on a Monday morning and Friday evening. I run my finger down the November dates, stopping on the final one. The helicopter had a full annual service the day before it went down.

Beneath, the words *aircraft scrapped and recycled due to age* are scrawled across the remaining empty boxes, and the paper crinkles in my fists. *Scrapped* is an interesting word for crashed. The initials in the final box are *M.S.*, and a desperate part of me wants to find out who that is and what they know.

"Has a book taken your fancy?"

I jump so hard I nearly topple off the ladder, hunching over the box to try to block Carmichael's view of the shelf as I shove the file back and close the lid. I must come back to get it. "Um…yeah. Sorry." I hold up a random book and wave it in his direction.

"*The Male Body, an Owner's Guide?*"

I glance down at the clothbound book in my hand and wish I'd fallen off the ladder. "Yeah…always good to be…informed, you know?" *Christ.*

He strokes his goatee and eyes me suspiciously. "Indeed."

I descend with very little grace and sink onto the sofa. "I came to tell you I need to leave."

"You are free to come and go from the campus as often as you please, so long as it does not impact your attendance."

I fiddle with the tassel on my joggers. "No, I want to leave. Quit. Unenroll, whatever you want to call it."

He takes his thin-framed glasses off and places them on the giant desk. "Your father would be most disappointed."

It's a punch to the stomach, but I square my shoulders. "Do you think you're doing a good job of running this university if students can just kill other students?"

"People will kill other people, Ophelia. It's a sad but inevitable fact of life. It happens in universities, schools, hospitals, prisons, homes. I can, however, try to create well-rounded individuals who know how to cope with hardship. As Shakespeare said, 'death, a necessary end, will come when it will come.'"

The quote triggers an alarm bell at the back of my head where it joins the growing pile of literature quotes I have been fed since I joined Sorrowsong. I narrow my eyes at Carmichael, trying to discern between meaningless coincidence and a well-hidden confession. "I'd like to leave."

"Leave if you wish. Your first term's fees will be due at the end of October."

My mouth drops open. "My fees? You said I was on a scholarship."

"Yes, should you complete your degree, you'll receive your scholarship."

"*What?*" I rake my hand through my hair. "I obviously don't have twenty-five thousand pounds lying around."

"Twenty-three."

"Oh," I throw both hands in the air, "twenty-three! Excellent. You should've said so before, I can pay that now."

"Can you?"

"No!" My head drops down into my hands. "Why are you doing this?"

"I am sorry that Mr. Ivanov interrogated you. That was an oversight on my part. It is not a reason to give up on your degree."

"It's not just that. It's the creepy anonymous texts. It's the students. It's the dead girl in my room. It's the weather." Tears sting my eyes, but I'm on a roll. "It's the sound of that fucking helicopter taking off on a Friday afternoon. It's the fact that I know my mother planted the geraniums outside the Nightshade mansion. I'm sick of it all."

He regards me with a serious expression, the gray mustache on his top lip moving as he presses his lips together. For a moment, I think he's considering my request. He checks his pocket watch. "Shouldn't you be in a social psychology lecture? Wouldn't want to lose your scholarship due to lack of attendance, would you?"

The sofa scrapes along the floor with the force with which I stand. The edges of my vision are clouded red, but I force myself to appear calm. "Have a *wonderful* day."

"And you, Ms. Winters."

I don't have my laptop, textbooks, or my notepad, but I wind my way into the pointed spire in the farthest corner of the castle for my social psychology lecture. I can't think a week, day, or even an hour into the future, so I just focus on the next step. *Left foot. Right foot. Don't cry. Open door. Close door. Don't cry.*

There are murmurs as I walk into the lecture hall, where everyone is sitting in their pairs for the project. Half of them believe a false rumor that I murdered my roommate for snoring, the other half believe I've seduced *the* Alex Corbeau-Green.

Unfortunately for me, Divya has fallen into the first category. I don't blame her. She knows I wouldn't sleep with Alex.

Even if both rumors are falser than Colette's eyelashes, I think I've impressed some people, and that can't hurt. Ascending the carpeted stairs, I sink into the seat beside Alex, sliding a little lower down the wood. My fingers itch with the urge to text someone, *anyone*, about my talk with Carmichael, but I'm not sure who'd care.

Beside me, a low, soft voice cuts through Professor Andersson's lecture. "You ignored my emails. I shouldn't have made that comment in the bathroom, I'm sorry."

I stare down at my hands, picking the brown nail polish off with my thumb. "I haven't checked them."

"Two weeks ago, you lectured me about not pulling my weight on the coursework."

"That was before I woke up beside a dead girl."

His fingers pause over his keyboard, and I sense his eyes turn to me. "Are you all right?"

The one question I've longed to hear, from the only person I don't want it from. "I'm doing fine."

"I think your T-shirt is backward."

I look down at the neckline of my jumper where the label of my top pokes out from beneath my sweater. I scowl at him. "Deliberate."

His voice drops to a husky whisper, his scent filling my nostrils as he leans toward me. "Given a rumor that we're together holds

128

up our dreams of being, oh, I don't know...*not in prison*, maybe you should act like you're not physically repulsed by me?"

"This is me trying."

I look up at him to see him pressing his lips together in an effort not to smile, flecks of gold glittering in his irises. "You didn't like our alibi?"

"I think it's sad you had to make up a whole story just to convince people you could last an hour in bed with me."

He tips his head back and laughs. It's genuine and throaty, and like the rest of the room, it makes it impossible for me to look away from him. He doesn't seem to notice. "You're funny, Twist, when you're not actively being insufferable." He resumes his typing. "I could show you the best ten seconds of your life."

Now *I'm* laughing, and I don't know if it's at his dumb joke or at the hysterical state of my life, but it does feel good. "I'm all right. Cheers, though."

He angles his laptop so I can share the screen, opening up our report. His sections are almost finished already, as well as half of mine. My chest sinks. I'm drowning here. I'm behind on my other modules too. "I'm sorry. I'll catch up."

"You can repay me by not strangling me again."

Whoops. I almost forgot I did that. That whole night is a tangled mess of memory and hallucination. "It was an accident."

He raises an eyebrow. "An accident?"

"Tripped and fell onto your neck. That's how I remember it anyway."

He grins, but I sober my expression, horrified at the small upturn in my mood. I cannot get friendly with Alex. He's probably only here to take on his father's wicked empire. He *is* his father.

Professor Andersson's heels click to a stop at our desk, her red lips forming a smile in Alex's direction. "How are you two getting on?"

"Fine," we both say, a little too tensely.

She hums in disapproval. "Maybe you'd benefit from a little icebreaker, you know? Get to know each other?"

"Oh, they know each other well enough all right," interjects a student somewhere behind us. I roll my eyes, ignoring the look Andersson is giving Alex that says *I wish you weren't my student.*

The girl in front of me swivels round to face us, eyes brimming with curiosity. "How was it?"

I give her a shy smile. "It was great. The big ones hurt, so…Alex is perfect."

He laughs in disbelief beside me, leaning forward to be closer to our curious neighbor. "Best two inches of her life."

She turns back around, face laden with disappointment. A warm breath tickles my ear, a hard thigh pressing against my own. "Ophelia, Ophelia, *Ophelia.* What am I going to do with you?"

Something hot and unfamiliar unfurls in my lower stomach. "Leave me alone, hopefully."

A gravelly hum sounds in his throat. "No longer an option."

His thumb presses against the spot where my pulse hammers below my ear. My breathing betrays me, but his does too. He shifts in his seat. I press my thighs together. The ping of his phone injects some common sense into me, shattering the strange atmosphere around us. I shuffle away from him on the bench, trying to lose everyone's attention.

When the mortified lecturer moves on in a swish of platinum hair and red lipstick, Alex rests his chin on his palm and stares over at me beneath long, dark lashes. He's playful, but something about him seems sinister, like he's luring me into a trap. "Maybe she's right, Twist. We *should* get to know each other."

"That would be pointless." The second I hit Submit on this project, I'll never see Alex again.

"Awh, come on. I want to know things."

"Such as?"

His eyes flicker with something that isn't his usual disinterest. Sinister curiosity. His fingers drum on his lower lip. "Such as, what's your real reason for being here?"

I fire back a question of my own. "Do you get on with your father?"

"Why'd you lie about who your parents are?"

"Why'd you drop out of Yale?"

I watch the shutter of indifference fall back over his eyes, the line of his shoulders tensing. He turns his gaze back to his laptop. "You're right. This is pointless."

I press my lips together, a flicker of regret slithering up my spine. I've hit a nerve, but I don't apologize. Hating him is easier when he hates me too.

We return to our notes in complete silence, neither one willing to open up to the other. I wish I wasn't so aware of him, of the aftershave that clings to his rugby hoodie, or the gold ring on his pinky finger. Of the low exhale that leaves his lips when he stretches his arms over his head, or the way the tattoos look when he brings them back down.

It's superficial attraction, but it's infuriating all the same.

My phone buzzes on the desk, and I grab it before Alex can see.

From: Alan Sine
Subject: Don't leave me
Date: Thursday 10th October 15:32 BST
To: Ophelia Winters

You wouldn't leave me to rot in this castle alone, would you?

The warm ball of hope in my chest punctures. My stalker is still alive, meaning my stalker is more than likely a killer.

Attached to the email is a photo of a page from Shakespeare's *Much Ado About Nothing*. One line is circled.

When you depart from me, sorrow abides and happiness takes his leave.

I can't drag my eyes away from the subject line.

There's only one person in Sorrowsong who knows I was intending to leave.

I've had a gut feeling about Carmichael since the first time I met him.

Somewhere in the last few hours, my dread has bubbled into fury. Once I have the culprit in my hands, perhaps the rumors about me won't be false after all.

I KNOCK ON the open door of Professor Bancroft's office just as he takes a bite of a sandwich, sending a splotch of mayonnaise onto his chartreuse shirt.

He makes a garbled noise through the bread in his mouth and sits up, gesturing to the spare chair beside him. I awkwardly sink into it, watching him swallow the comically large mouthful by unhinging his jaw like a snake. "Ophelia. I missed you at the lectures this week."

"Sorry, I…it's been a hard week."

He smiles over at me sympathetically, a breadcrumb clinging onto his bottom lip for dear life. "I was very sorry to hear about your roommate. If it's any consolation, I don't believe you'd kill her in a million years."

"Thank you," I reply, my voice hoarse with emotion. "I…haven't really slept since it happened. I'm completely trapped here. Some days I don't feel like I can do it."

"I lost my parents at a similar age to you," he says, his weathered hand picking up his cup of tea. "It took an awfully long time for me not to feel lonely again, even when I was out with my friends."

"I'm sorry that happened to you," I mumble. A question about Carmichael is on the tip of my tongue. *Do you think the chancellor would stalk a student?* It would be so easy to ask, but something stops me. If they're close friends and Carmichael finds out I'm suspicious of him, God knows what he might do.

I decide to wait for better proof.

Professor Bancroft's brown shoes shuffle over to a printer where he removes a couple of sheets of paper. "Here. These will catch you up on all you missed." He smiles warmly. "I've cut out my endless waffling."

I breathe out a grateful laugh, staring down at the notes on change and transitions in childhood. I open up my backpack and stuff them inside. "Thank you, sir."

"*The Great Gatsby*," he says, nodding at the book in my bag. "Your mother loved that book."

"She did."

A fond expression crosses his face. "She was reading in the libraries often. I'm not sure how much she liked it here."

I offer him a tight smile as I sling my bag over my shoulder, unsure what to say in return.

"And Ophelia," he says, stopping me as I reach the door. "You are never alone. Your parents are in your heart."

I stare down at my feet until the burning behind my eyes fades. I hate it when people say that. "I just wish they were outside of it too."

Chapter 12

OPHELIA

I kick the space behind me, my arms feeling heavier with each stroke. I vaguely hear Belladonna and the swim coach shouting as I break for air, but I dip back under. This morning marks my return to swimming, and I'm being well and truly punished.

At least Belladonna didn't make me swim in the loch again.

Lungs crying out for air, my fingertips finally hit the end of the pool. I place my forearms on the tiled edge and see that Abbie, a second year from Hemlock, has beaten me to it. Colette hits the tile next, and then the others. Belladonna shakes her head at me. "Six thirty, Winters. Six. Thirty. I think my nonna could swim faster than you right now."

I tug my hat off my head and try to catch my breath. "Harsh."

"We have Loughborough, Bath, and Glasgow here for a tournament next month, and you're supposed to be our best for the four hundred. If you fuck it up, you're off the team."

"Watch out, Bella, she'll strangle you," says the Nightshade student in the lane next to me.

Colette rolls her eyes, wringing out her blonde hair. "Shut up, Honor. You're just mad she can swim better than the rest of us." She leans over the lane divider rope and grins at me. "Do you want to watch a movie tonight?"

"Like…a movie? At the cinema?"

"Well, we can't be bothered to drive an hour to the theater, so we'll watch it here. But my driver picked up some clothes for me from Inverness and he came back with popcorn and everything."

Threads of color leach into my graying heart. "I would love that. I would really love that."

"Yay! Wear your pajamas. Vincenzo, Jack, Ariana, Alex, Hattie, Magda, and Jenna are all coming!"

The threads slither back out. "Oh. I…I'm not on great terms with Alex, I'd rather not."

She pouts as we both push ourselves out of the pool and dry off. "Oh, that's a shame. I've really missed you this week."

I'm grinning like a fool as I slip into my flip-flops. Her words mend a little part of my soul that tells me I matter. "I missed you too. It's complicated with Alex."

Her slight German accent intensifies as she clasps her hands together. "Oh, I know complicated. My last boyfriend had a wife."

"What? Oh my god." *My lover isn't actually my lover, I just said that to avoid a murder investigation, but his father had a hand in my parents' death.* It doesn't have such a good ring to it.

I grab my bag from the benches, watching the pool's surface ripple silently. Ironically, the swimming pool at Sorrowsong is my favorite pool I've ever been in. It's modern-day technology, elegantly wrapped in classical charm. A top-of-the-range, heated pool sits inside an ornate Victorian conservatory, sparkling glass panels held in place by black iron struts. If Belladonna didn't guard the keys like a dog, I'd be in here every night.

A RARE SHARD of sun pierces through the thin sheet of cloud over the valley, illuminating my path back to the castle after my final lecture of the day. After two days of heavy rain, it feels like the Highlands have nothing left to give. The trees sit in quiet stillness, and the mist is clear enough for me to see the sea in the far distance.

It's silly, but I needed that reminder. Needed to remember that there's a world outside Sorrowsong. All my favorite things; the hustle and bustle of Covent Garden, the quiet bookshops of Edinburgh, the lambs in the fields back home; they're all still rattling on in my absence. And if I miss them too much, I can always visit them.

There's something about Sorrowsong. A spell that seems to be cast over it that makes you believe that the only hallways in the world are eerie and cobwebbed, that libraries simply *must* be poorly lit, and that ghosts lurk in every shadow. But it isn't true.

I feel a little bit lighter and a little bit stronger.

I wander around the castle walls under the gaze of the crumbling gargoyles, waiting for a bar of signal to appear on my phone. I'm halfway down to the tarn when I finally get any, and I redial an old number.

The voice on the other end is gruff from a life of smoking. "Papadopoulos."

"Nicholas? I rang you the other week and—"

"And I said I don't want to talk to you people."

"Wait!" I beg. "I don't work for Green. I promise."

"Fucking journalist," he grumbles bitterly.

"No," I interrupt, before he can hang up. "I'm not, I swear. I have one question and that's it. The week before the crash—"

"It didn't crash, it was scrapped due to age." He sounds like an automated robot.

A six-year-old helicopter scrapped? Seems likely. "Okay, fine. In the days before it was *scrapped*, it was checked by someone with the initials *M.S.*"

"You don't get to bring Mike into this. He was the victim here, okay? He was a good guy. Stop fucking calling me."

"My parents were in the helicopter," I blurt out, desperate.

There's a long pause. A drag of a cigarette, and then another pause, until he finally breaks the silence. "You're Andy Winters's little girl?"

"Yes," I whisper, furiously wiping a hot tear from my cheek. "I just need some answers."

"I can't tell you what you want to know," he mumbles back. "I have a little girl too. I can't...I can't take any risks."

"I know. I get it. I just...I miss them."

"He...he was excited, that day. For the burgers."

A sob rips through my throat. A memory as mundane as burger buns on a chopping board, and it's enough to bring me to my knees on the damp earth beneath my feet. "So was I," I manage, my voice hoarse.

Seagulls squawk on the other end of the line, a child's laughter followed by a splash of water. I picture him somewhere sunny, maybe in Greece, and it warms my heart.

I hope he forgets about all of this one day; that all his children ever know is comfort and warmth. "Look...Mike...Mike is dead. I can give you his daughter's number, Laura. She lives in Inverness, but she might not want to speak with you."

"Thank you. Thank you, thank you, *thank you*," I repeat, scrawling the number as he recites it.

"Please don't call me again."

"I promise."

The line goes dead, the trees around me silent and still. I dust off the knees of my tights and stand, letting out a shaky exhale. I feel nauseous, my stomach flooded with adrenaline, hope, nerves, and dread.

Someone has a hold over Nicholas. Someone is desperate for him not to talk. I've always known it wasn't just a simple crash, but the confirmation that something is amiss is a weight off my shoulders.

Forget quitting. I'm not leaving Sorrowsong. Not until I've finished what I came here to do.

I trudge back up the muddy path, arriving back in the central courtyard just as the rugby team returns from training. Vincenzo beckons me over, shouting my name.

"Could your shorts get any shorter, Vincenzo?"

He grins and pulls them farther up his giant thighs. I swear he's chipped another tooth since last week. "Is that a request? Because I'll do it. You're coming to our movie night, right?"

My eyes flick to Alex, who is pacing on his phone a few meters away. His hair is damp, hanging over his forehead. Mud obscures the tattoo that sits above his left knee, but I think it might be

another bird. If I knew him better, I'd say he looks stressed. "Um…
I'd better not. I have loads of classes to catch up on."

"Come on, Pheels."

"We're not doing 'Pheels.' That is not a nickname. And no, you
know how it is between me and Alex."

"It doesn't have to be like that. He's a good guy beneath the
whole dark and broody thing."

Oh, if only you knew. I hold my tongue as Alex joins us. "I have
to go to New York."

Vincenzo's face falls. "What? When?"

"Now, tonight. Business emergency."

Business emergency. My jaw tenses. Alex will leave Sorrowsong
as a darker-haired, tattooed version of his father, and that enrages
me. Vincenzo clicks his fingers at me cheerily. "Looks like you can
come after all."

NEATLY SANDWICHED BETWEEN Vincenzo and
Colette in Alex's giant bed wasn't where I thought my evening
would end, but I'm not really upset about it. I wasn't delighted to be
using Alex's room, but after the fourth cider, Vincenzo started making sense. It does have the biggest TV, after all.

The Breakfast Club blares on the fifty-inch screen, mingling with
the sound of Colette's popcorn rustling and quiet chatter from her
friends watching from the floor.

It's all so wonderfully ordinary, I feel almost giddy.

As I finish what may or may not be my seventh drink, my phone
lights up with an email from Alex.

From: Alex Corbeau-Green
Subject: Rearrange (verb) *change (the position, time, or order of something)*
Date: Friday 11th October 21:19 BST
To: Ophelia Winters

I'm going to be on a flight back into the UK for our social psychology session on Monday. Can we catch up on a call tomorrow instead?
—ACG

The message is overly formal, as ever, but the subject line makes me smile. My alcohol-riddled brain doesn't see any issue with that. He's just a man. I'm just a woman. I'm allowed to think he's pretty and hate him all at once. I hit Reply, but my phone is snatched out of my hand by Colette before I can type anything.

"No," I screech, grappling for the phone as Colette hammers out a response and hits Send.

From: Ophelia Winters
Subject: RE: Rearrange (verb) *change (the position, time, or order of something)*
Date: Friday 11th October 21:20 BST
To: Alex Corbeau-Green

Omggg. Why so formal?!

141

We're not in a business meeting.
Ophelia xx
Sent from your bed.

"Oh my god, Colette, you are the worst," I grumble, as she gives it back.

Vincenzo peers over and grins. "Bet he's kicking his feet on the plane."

"Shut up." I only get halfway through my damage control email before his reply pops up.

From: Alex Corbeau-Green
Subject: Hypocrisy (noun) *the practice of claiming to have higher standards or more noble beliefs than is the case*
Date: Friday 11th October 21:21 BST
To: Ophelia Winters

"So formal" because you blocked my number. Block this email, too, and we'll resort to fax or telegram.
Enjoy the bed. There are Jelly Babies in the left bedside table.
—ACG
PS Catastrophically drunk before 10 p.m. is embarrassing.

I *love* Jelly Babies. Right now, I love Jelly Babies more than I love my pride. I pull open the bedside table and yank them out. Popping one in my mouth, I tip my head back and let out a contented sigh. Alex's bed is the best. Cocooned in a soft mattress and crisp cotton sheets, I burrow farther down into the duvet and bask in the unfamiliar bliss of companionship.

I let my heart be mended by the glorious lack of silence and the heat of other bodies around me.

For the first time in a while, I let my body drift into a restful sleep.

Chapter 13

OPHELIA

I'm dancing to a strange song.

Waltzing down Sorrowsong Castle's somber hallways to the sound of high-pitched bells and tinny chimes. The portraits tip their hats at me, the sconces burn brighter as I pass. Even the spiders seem to lift their webs as if to tell me to keep on going.

I reach junctions and crossroads in the tunnels, but I never stop to ponder the direction. My feet take me where they wish—I am merely a spectator. I spin down a hallway, the door at the end left slightly ajar. A soft, orange glow spills from the opening and onto the cold stone tile. In the dreary hallway, it looks so tempting. Like it would warm my cold toes and caress the most forgotten corners of my soul.

I dance faster toward it, whirling around with some invisible partner. The tapping of my heels echoes around me, the door becoming closer and closer. I want to run. I want to go through it, but my feet step together again, the line of my back arching like in some Viennese waltz.

After what feels like an age, I stop outside the door. The bells itch at my skin, screeching in my ears. I peer around the door, teetering on too-high stilettos into the orange room.

I get the sensation of coming home after a long, arduous journey.

"Dad?" I whisper as he stands. My mum appears behind him, too, then everyone I've ever lost. Oscar, my childhood dog, bounds up to me. Mr. Rogers, my elderly neighbor, is sipping a cup of tea opposite my grandparents. My aunt is doing a crossword on the floor.

It's a room full of everything I've longed for. Of every birthday wish I've made since seventeen.

My dad extends his hand. I've missed that hand. The safety and security of it. "Come here, love."

I'm trying. Trying to step over the threshold, but my feet are stuck to the floor. The bells change pitch, painfully out of tune. My skin crawls.

It looks warm in there, but I can't escape the cold. My father's face falls like I've betrayed him. "Come in. Don't let her get you."

"Who?" I glance over my shoulder and my heart hits the floor. Achlys is here again, staggering toward me. Her clothes and hair are wet, leaving a wet trail behind her on the stone. She cackles and sobs all at once. I scream at my feet to unstick, beg them to let me into the warmth. The song gets louder and louder. More familiar.

It's my alarm clock.

Achlys gets nearer, the stench of rotting flesh filling my lungs, but I can't bring myself to wake up. Not when my parents are in front of me. I'd take whatever cruel punishment she has for me if to remain in their presence for another moment.

But they fade away, and Achlys's wails at my back get quieter. I'm losing them all over again. It all pales to a hollow emptiness, until all I can hear is the sound of my alarm, and all I can feel is the giant ball of grief that sits beneath my ribs.

Each night is a new opportunity to lose them, each day is a chance to find new ways to notice their absence.

I swing my eyes open, trying to anchor myself to the little things. I watch the way the pale sunlight kisses the windowsill, stretches her fingers through the curtains, paints the flecks of dust gold. I listen to the sound of gravel crunching under shoes on the path outside, feel the way the cool morning air tickles my skin.

This feeling, this loneliness, is the price I pay for loving them so much and so deeply. Though it eats away at my happy moments and sinks my bad moments lower, I know I'd rather grieve them than feel nothing at all. It keeps our love alive.

I hit Snooze on the alarm and check my phone. The screen is too bright, the birds outside too loud. A text from Vincenzo pings through.

Vincenzo

Hungover? Pretty sure Colette and Magda
threw you into bed and then passed out
on the stairs. They really like you.
Wanna get a coffee and a sausage roll?

They really like me. I'm grinning as I type out my reply.

Ophelia

I have swimming and then social psych
coursework. Thank you for hanging with me
yesterday. I've been kind of lonely.

Vincenzo

Maybe if you didn't kill your roommates
and be mean to handsome airline heirs,
you'd be less lonely.

Ophelia

Whatever.

My first order of business for the day once I've washed the
melted Jelly Baby out of my hair is to call the number Nicholas
gave me. I sit at the end of the hallway to get better service, praying
someone will pick up.

The voice that comes is tense with suspicion. "Hello?"

"Hello, is that Laura?"

"Who is this?" she replies, an edge to her voice. She sounds
shaky, out of breath.

"My name is Ophelia…I'm sorry to call on you like this. I wondered if I could ask you something about your dad?"

"He passed away," she whispers, so quiet the microphone barely
picks it up.

"I'm sorry," I say, even though I hate it when people say the
same to me. Seven stupid letters that try to patch a hole far too
great for words to mend. "I lost mine too. That's kind of what I'm
calling about. I wanted to ask about the helicopter."

"You work for those…monsters? That company Mr. Green owns?"

"No! God no. I'm trying to prove their wrongdoing, and someone told me you might be willing to help."

There's another trembling breath, a heavy pause that even I can tell is filled with things she's desperate to say. An inhale filters down the choppy line, and I brace myself for whatever truth she's about to tell me.

The call drops.

I hit Redial, but it rings and rings without answer. I try it once more, but the automated voice tells me the number is unavailable.

She's blocked my number. Great.

I SIT DOWN at a desk in the Nightshade library at ten on the dot, the early morning sun having given way to sheets of rain that pelt the arched windows. The power is out in the mansion, so three candles burn on the desk beside me and one of the portable power packs sits at my feet.

As my laptop crashes for the third time this morning, I send Alex an email.

From: Ophelia Winters
Subject: Technical difficulties (plural noun) *technical problems, problems with equipment*
Date: Saturday 12th October 10:02 BST
To: Alex Corbeau-Green

I am joining the call; my laptop is just having a moment.
Ophelia

A reply comes back quickly.

From: Alex Corbeau-Green
Subject: User Error (noun) *technical problems caused by the human user*
Date: Saturday 12th October 10:03 BST
To: Ophelia Winters

No problem.
It always helps to lift the lid and turn the laptop on.
—ACG

"Fuck you," I mutter, finally logging on. I panic-clean my greasy webcam, dusting the shortbread crumbs from the keyboard. Alex appears on my screen, a steaming coffee mug between his hands as he stares off to the side. For once, he's dressed in something that isn't his rugby gear or a black button-up shirt. A gray workout top hugs the contours of his torso, his hair damp from a shower.

I don't think I've ever seen someone quite so striking.

Even through my blurry screen, I get the same odd feeling about him as I did that first day in the car. On the surface, he looks dangerously attractive. But he *seems* boring. A man without feelings, goals, direction, or passion.

But there's something sinister about him that extends beyond my hatred for his father. The way he does things, the way he carries himself; sometimes it feels like a mirror. Like he's searching for some kind of revenge just like I am.

149

He notices me on the screen and frowns. "You're so weird. Like a girl in a horror movie, just lurking, never speaking."

I flash him my middle finger, studying the floor-to-ceiling windows, stone arches, and modern light fixtures behind him. "You're not winning any conversational awards any time soon either. Sorry I was late. Is that seriously your house, or is that one of those green screen things?"

"My dad's house. Did you get caught up doing one of your crosswords?"

I feel my cheeks flame. I was late to the call because of my laptop, but I was late to the library because I was hunched over in the shower doing a crossword on my phone like an intellectual prawn. "I like my crosswords. What time is it for you?"

He puts the coffee down, the lines of his forearms rippling. I wish he didn't look like that. "Five in the morning, but I'm jet-lagged and can't sleep, so it's fine."

"Oh." I open up the report and see he's already there. We work in mostly polite conversation for an hour, finishing the introduction and the literature review. Alex seems tense, constantly rubbing the muscles of his shoulders.

I don't bother asking.

He leaves to refill his coffee, and I refill my tea at the bar in the library, sinking down into the chair and warming my fingers over the candles on the desk. He hasn't returned, giving me a chance to study the room he's in.

I hate that I notice the little things. I hate that they sting. My mind is desperate to make itself miserable, constantly in a state of comparison.

There are photos on the dresser. I can't make out the faces, but there's a family photo above them all. Four dirty cereal bowls sit beside a sink, one of them pink and covered in fairies. There are jars behind glass cabinets, each one brimming with food. A stuffed toy sits on the windowsill.

I have to look away.

He returns with another mug of coffee, rubbing his jaw. He picks up his phone, his index finger and thumb on his eyebrows. For once, just once, I let myself remember he's a human. "Are you okay? You seem kind of stressed."

"Fine," he replies, sitting up straight. He's not willing to let me make the conversation personal, and it feels like I just lost a competition between us. He glances down at his notes and slides his reading glasses on. I minimize the tab to stop myself looking.

We're fifteen minutes into our persuasion and blackmail write-up when a mop of curly, blonde hair appears behind him. "Whoa, are you chatting to a *girl*?"

He slaps a palm to his chest and turns around. "Oh my god, Josie. You scared the crap out of me."

Two beady, green eyes appear at the bottom of my screen. "Hello, Alex's girlfriend, I'm Josie."

Alex glares at the little girl. "She's not...we're not...what are you even doing up?"

"I was too excited for my birthday."

"Which isn't even today," he grumbles. He slides off his stool and swings the girl over his shoulder, bending over to look in the camera at me. My lower abdomen tenses beneath the desk. "I'll be back, Ophelia."

The girl shrieks as he swings her around and they both vanish from view. Laughter echoes through his camera, and then another girl's voice joins in.

Jealousy is *such* a pathetic emotion, but it's one I've never had any control over. It's an ugly manifestation of my own insecurities, a way to pinpoint blame onto people when it has nowhere else to go. I stare at the dirty bowls on the counter and hate myself for letting such trivial things get to me. Loneliness has been my only dependable friend for years, but I'd trade it all in for a sink full of dirty dishes and a round of laundry for more than one.

Alex sits back down, and I swallow the lump of emotion in my throat. "Sorry. She's back in bed now."

"Your sister?"

"Yeah. One of the six of them. She turns eight tomorrow."

"*Six.* Jeez. Also, we only have two weeks to finish this."

"Two weeks and we won't have to talk to each other anymore."

Good, because the more I see snippets of Alex's humanity, of his family life, the more at sea I feel. Will my plans to tear down his father impact Josie's life?

If I released the information today, would it ruin her birthday?

I don't think I want the answer.

The sound of bare feet on marble comes through my headphones, and a second girl appears, this one much older, with big, almond eyes and dark hair that falls to her hips. I've seen pictures of her and Alex on news sites before. She's already a model. Alex doesn't even look up. "Fleur, I'm working."

"Well, Josie came into my room and said you have a girlfriend, so obviously I had to come and see." She waves at me and grins. "Oh my god, she's pretty. I knew redheads were your type!"

152

He looks up at the camera like a character in a sitcom, eyes wide with exasperation. "Let's pick this up on Tuesday, Ophelia."

"Pretty name, Ophelia!" is all I hear before he hangs up.

I shake my head. I don't want to know about his family. I don't want to know about his perfect life. I don't want to hurt his sisters, only his father.

Blowing out the candles as the chandelier flickers overhead, I check my texts and frown at the top one.

Unknown
Can't talk on call. Too risky. 17
Macquarie Close, Inverness. L.

A glimmer of hope sparks in my chest. I plug the journey into my phone, and it dwindles slightly. Ninety-six-minute drive. There's no way I can pay a taxi that, even if they were willing to come here.

And hell will freeze over before I ask Carmichael to hitch a ride on the staff shuttle helicopter.

I've never dreamed of the extreme level of affluence that those at Sorrowsong have, but man, would it be nice to have my own driver.

"Going to Inverness? Eike will drive you! He loves the views on the route."

Colette perches on the edge of the desk in a cream miniskirt and blazer combo that is so inappropriate for the weather it's almost funny. It takes a minute for her offer to sink in. "Seriously? I can pay you."

She hooks one knee-high boot over the other. "In a polite way, I saw you put biscuits back on the shelf in the student shop. They're, like, one pound." She taps away on her phone, chewing her pink bottom lip before her face brightens into a smile. "He can take you in the morning!"

That was because I am now sick of shortbread, but I don't argue. My finances are in tatters.

I guess I'm off to Inverness tomorrow. Nerves wriggle their fingers through my mind. I'm scared of what I'll find out. "That…that would be so helpful. You genuinely have no idea."

She eyes the tissues on the desk. "Are you okay at the moment?"

"I've not been crying. I'm just ill all the fucking time. But…" It would feel so good to tell someone at least half of the truth. "I have a stalker."

She giggles. "Honestly, Vincenzo's just too friendly. Like a puppy. He does it with everyone."

"No, I'm serious," I reply, and her face falls, hardening into a frown as I show her the emails and explain what happened at the tarn. "At first I thought it was Alex, or maybe just a stranger. But now…now I think it's Carmichael."

She sits opposite me and pulls out a purple journal. "He does have a super strange vibe but…why would he do this?"

"I don't know." Maybe it's to do with my parents' death. Maybe he feels guilty.

She flips to a blank page and draws out an empty mind map, and I have to admit, it's nice to have a friend.

Chapter 14

OPHELIA

Eike, Colette's driver, sits in stony silence as we wind our way beside Loch Garve, the green curves of Ben Wyvis to our left. He's a *very* good-looking, dark-haired man in his thirties with a gruff voice and a short beard.

I half wonder why he agreed to such a strange job.

It stopped raining twenty minutes ago, and the rugged scenery of Scotland is that myriad of shades of green and orange that only come out after an autumn shower.

I may moan about Sorrowsong, but I *love* Scotland. I spent most of my childhood here, and despite the fog and the rain, it's all golden in my memories.

There's a pride in Scotland. It's in the heart of the people and the veins of the landscape. It's in the way people carry themselves, in the way people stop to chat on the hiking trails, in stories at the pub, in the deep gold of the whisky. My father was born and raised here, and it'll always be special to me.

I just wish it didn't have a giant black stain on it now.

Without the dense Sorrowsong air hanging on my shoulders, I feel ten times lighter.

Eike pulls into a petrol station in a small village not far from Inverness. "Can I get you anything, ma'am?"

"No, thank you. You've already done more than enough."

He nods once, taking his black blazer from the passenger seat and shrugging it over his broad shoulders. He refuels the Mercedes and heads inside to pay. I drum my fingers on the window, riddled with anxiety. I don't know what to say to Laura, don't know what she'll say to me. I'm nervous she won't say anything useful, but mostly I'm nervous that she will.

I'm scared she'll hand me the bullets for Cain Green, and I'll have to find the courage to pull the trigger.

Eike pulls his car door open again and I jump out of my skin. He deposits a bag of Jelly Babies onto my lap. "Colette said you would want them, miss."

To be loved is to be known, and this week, I feel both. "Oh... thank you. These are the best."

He glances in the rearview mirror and peels the car back onto the road. "I'll take your word for it."

It only feels like a few more minutes of silence before he stops the car outside a small terrace of run-down houses. "This is the address, ma'am."

I look out the window at the tiny, overgrown front garden. The white paint is peeling off the door, exposing the rotting wood beneath.

The door says number one, but there's a silver seven that's fallen onto the faded doormat beneath. The lights are off inside.

It looks like my house back home. "Thank you so much. I really appreciate it."

"It's what I'm paid for." He rolls down the window to get a better look. "You seem nervous. Is it safe?"

"It's safe," I reassure him, clambering out of the car with great care. I cannot afford to accidentally scratch the black paint.

Straightening my stiff limbs, I move the broken gate aside and knock on the door, shuffling from foot to foot.

I let a minute pass in silence before I knock again. I glance back at the car where Eike eyes me suspiciously. I push the rusty mail slot inward and call Laura's name, but my hopes are dwindling.

The house looks completely uninhabited.

Just as I turn back to the car, I hear the handle turn and the door creak open. A dark-haired woman peeks around, eyes wide with anxiety. She looks like she's only a few years older than me, but she's frail and thin, her cheeks hollow. "Ophelia?"

I give her what I hope is a reassuring smile. "Laura."

She opens the door just enough for me to step inside, slamming it shut the second that I do. "Tea?"

I walk into a tiny living room. There's only one dent in the sofa. One mug on the coffee table. The house is freezing cold in a way only those who visit lonely relatives would understand. *God, I'm dreading going home in December.* "Yes, please."

I sit down on the fraying sofa, listening to the kettle boil in the next room. There are old photos of Laura and a man who must be her father on the side table. She looks happier. Her cheeks fuller and pinker, her hair not so limp.

Is that what people would think about me?

A teapot rattles on a metal tray as she comes back in. "Milk? Sugar?"

"Milk would be lovely, thank you."

She cringes as her shaking hand pours the tea into two stained mugs, and I want to tell her it's okay, that I understand better than anyone. But the words are stuck. I'm too nervous. "My father never had any milk," she whispers eventually.

I smile as I pour some into my mug. "Mine had too much milk and too much sugar. I always told him it would affect his health. He…he died in the helicopter crash."

Her face pales to a ghostly shade of white. "That's why you're here. For revenge. You've got it all wrong, it wasn't him."

A knife appears out of nowhere, the tip against my throat. I shake my head as much as I am able. "I'm not, I swear."

Her fingers tighten on the handle. I feel a warm bead of blood pool on my skin. "It wasn't his fault."

I don't feel afraid. Now it's just me left in my world; my death would not happen to anyone but me.

But I do want to taste revenge before the end.

"I believe you," I whisper, holding her gaze as gently as I can.

Her eyes widen, the grip she has on the knife weakens. I watch her brain short-circuit, not knowing what to do. Like perhaps she's been fantasizing about hearing those three words for a long, long time.

"You do?"

"Yes, and I'll make everyone else believe you, too, if you'd just tell me all you know."

She sinks down onto the fading brown sofa, her hands shaking violently over her face. "It was my fault," she chokes out, her body wracked with a sob. "It was all my fault."

My heart hammers in my chest, torn between shaking her shoulders out of desperation for information and being patient with a woman who is clearly even more broken than I am. "Please explain."

She begins again, whispering even though we're alone. "My father was asked to…tamper with the helicopter."

The tea threatens to come back up. "And?"

"His supervisor at Green Aviation asked him to loosen some bolts on the rotor hub at the next full maintenance check. He refused, of course. He knew what would happen. He was a good engineer and an even better man. The most senior mechanic who visited Sorrowsong. But a week later, he had a visitor." Her bottom lip trembles.

"I was stupid. I skipped school to go shopping, and a man came and told me I'd make a good model. He said he'd take a headshot of me outside and…I was so stupid. I went with him. They sent Dad a video of me with my hands and mouth bound." Her shoulders shake with sobs. "I think about it every day. Every *minute*."

The sharp tang of iron coats my tongue, my teeth biting so hard on my cheek. "So he did it? He tampered with it?"

She buries her face in her hands and nods. "He was at gunpoint, believing his daughter was the same. They said it would kill one man. One criminal who deserved it. He didn't know. He didn't know."

"Who was the visitor?" I whisper, swallowing the bile in my throat. I don't want to ask. I don't *need* to ask. But I do it all the same.

"It was the CEO. Cain Green."

My heartbeat slows to a dull, syrupy thud in my ears. My mouth feels like it's full of cotton wool. I feel sick. Disgusted with myself from the past few weeks. How could I stray so far from my values that I got into Alex's bed, *twice*, whether he was there or not?

My palms are clammy. I rub them on my skirt, but it only makes them feel too hot.

Breathing becomes a labored effort. I want to grab her shoulders and shake her. Scream at her for not doing more the same way I've screamed at the mirror for not telling her parents she'd be fine if they just drove and were a little late to dinner. Here in this moment, I want to break her.

But she's already broken. She's on her knees asking for my forgiveness like her life will be on pause forever if I don't grant it. She is me, and I am her. A grieving young woman let down by far more powerful things.

So instead, I clasp her cold hand in mine and tug her into the tightest hug I've given someone in a very long time. I try to glue her shattered pieces together with the remaining ones of my own.

"Do you have any evidence?"

She nods into my shoulder. "He told me that same week it happened. He was crushed, but he left it on a tape before he…before the guilt killed him."

I squeeze my eyes shut and my arms tighter. She's suffered as much as I have. "Thank you for telling me. I just don't understand why."

She pulls away and wipes her red eyes with her sleeve. "I don't know. I don't think my father knew."

"Why haven't you done anything with this information before?"

"At first, I was scared of what they'd do to me. I had dreams, you know? But I've given up on them now. If Cain kills me, too, I'll be ready, as long as he comes down with me. I tried to approach two journalists, but they dismissed me." She hiccups another sob. "Everyone is wary of saying anything about that fucking university. The students there have too much power."

Tell me about it.

As I stand to leave, I find myself laden with more questions than when I arrived. What would the CEO of an American private airline want with a chef and a groundskeeper at a Scottish university?

And also, what the hell do I do now? I hover awkwardly in the doorway. She looks up at me questioningly.

"The tape?"

"I can't give you the tape."

My chest falls. I knew this had all gone too well. "Why not?"

"The tape was his…the tape was his suicide note. It's all I have left of him. I can't give it up to you. He wishes me goodnight each night."

"Let me use it to prove Cain's wrongdoing. You'll get it back. I'll clear your father's name."

"I can't. I'm sorry."

"Can I have a copy made?"

"What if…what if they damage it? You can't take it. It's all I have left." She shakes her head to reinforce her point, and I know she will not be convinced.

I press the heels of my hands into my eyes. For each step forward I take, I take another back. Crestfallen, I trudge back down her path, so overcome with such a spectrum of emotions that I don't know whether to scream or laugh or cry.

As I pull open the car door, Laura calls my name from the doorway, her thin frame casting a shadow on the doormat.

"Yes?" *Please just give me the tape.*

"Maybe after all of this…maybe we can be friends? Have coffee? Or text each other?"

I'm too angry to consider that right now, but I give her a smile. "Okay."

I slide into the back seat and let one small sob out as a treat. But it's not enough. More come, and then the tears start to fall, hot lines of frustration that carve a path through my cold skin.

I catch Eike's eye in the mirror and shake my head. "Don't try to help. Just ignore it. If we both ignore it, it'll go away."

He takes a packet of tissues from the center console and passes them back, pulling out of Laura's road and leaving my optimism behind.

I thought not knowing what happened was bad, but knowing and not being ready to do anything about it? *Agony.*

Chapter 15

OPHELIA

I've managed to avoid Alex since last week. I canceled our next study session without reason, working on the project alone instead.

And on my laptop and a USB stick, a long report into the series of events behind my parents' death is nearing completion. But I know if I even *found* a journalist willing to look at it, they'd ask me for concrete proof. My proof is stuck inside a tape player in Inverness.

I tug my Doc Martens over my fluffiest socks, slinging a brown scarf around my neck. I told Colette I'd join her in watching the second home rugby game of the season. She doesn't really understand the rules, but she loves to watch men in short shorts roll around in the mud.

Frosted leaves crunch under my boots as I join Colette, Magda, and Hattie where they wait for me outside the Nightshade mansion.

Magda is the daughter of an American property tycoon and a Polish fashion designer, and Hattie is the daughter of a racehorse trainer, very distantly related to the king. They all look runway-ready; Colette and Hattie with bouncy blowouts and Magda with fresh braids.

I did my hair nice yesterday, but then it rained. Now half of it is up in a feeble effort to make it look less frizzy.

We wind our way around the outer perimeter of the castle, past the swimming pool, and onto the row of sports fields. A seating stand is already filling up with the burgundy colors of Sorrowsong and the occasional Nottingham fan in green. Rubbing my chilly hands together, I settle onto the metal bench of the stand with a warm sense of nostalgia softening my heart.

I used to sit and watch football games with my dad in the winter. He'd yell at the referee over a steaming cup of Bovril, and I'd nod my agreement with a mouthful of chocolate buttons and a stomachache.

The rows of freezing spectators clap as the players jog onto the mud bath that we're calling the pitch. "Oh my god, Ophelia. Your man looks hot."

"He's not my man," I mutter, refusing to look at him.

Magda leans over, removing the lollipop from her mouth with a wet pop. Her brown eyes twinkle with curiosity. "But how was it?"

Colette huffs. "She's being super coy about it all. Won't tell us *anything*."

I blush, even though I haven't so much as touched Alex. "That's just…private information."

Hattie, a second-year veterinary medicine student, peers over the line of players as they finish taping up their legs. "Which one's Vincenzo?"

I blow on my flask of tea. "Number four. Second row."

"That means he's really fast and *really* strong, right?" asks Colette, and I laugh into my drink. I don't think she can decide whether she's in love with Vincenzo or her driver.

I recognize Alex and Vincenzo's friend Jack, a second-year medical student, as he warms up. He's the fly-half, giving orders to the rest of the team. Clearly, his quiet personality, oversized knitted jumpers, and perfectly pressed slacks have been hiding how athletic his frame is.

As the match gets underway, I bury my chin farther into my scarf and allow myself to watch Alex play on the back line. He's the outside center, and the number thirteen on the back of his shirt seems fitting enough.

White tape wraps over the patchwork tattoos on his biceps, black strapping over his left knee. His shorts sit high on his muscular thighs, already streaked with mud. My stomach tightens as he dips low, tackling his Nottingham counterpart at the hips and sending him flying back.

Magda fans her face, all hot and bothered. "*Wow*. Look at them all fighting. You know, they'd cover a lot more ground if they just threw the ball forward and not backward."

I hide my smile in the scratchy wool of my scarf. "It's a wonder they've not thought of that."

At the sound of the referee's whistle, I wrestle my phone out from my ninety-five layers of clothing and open my latest email. It's another Shakespeare quote.

From: Alan Sine
Subject: Could it all have been different?
Date: Sunday 20th October 9:10 BST
To: Ophelia Winters

Suspicion always haunts the guilty mind.

I read it once more. After last week's visit to Laura, the quote rings true. But the email doesn't make me afraid anymore. Only annoyed.

I picture Carmichael having a creepy little chuckle to himself as he sends them, trying to burden me with the responsibility of my parents' death. I will not take it. As the players gather around for halftime, I send "Alan" my first reply.

From: Ophelia Winters
Subject: Get a hobby, Alan.
Date: Sunday 20th October 9:29 BST
To: Alan Sine

I am no bird; and no net ensnares me.
—Jane Eyre

Watching the first scrum of the second half, I do start to believe what Vincenzo says about rugby making him forgetful. He skirts the line between legal and illegal aggression, blood trickling down from his ears as he locks the players into place.

The bench dips slightly as a large frame sits beside me. "Hey, Hemlock."

I cringe internally. That name started losing its appeal the second Carmichael put me into Nightshade, but the night Sofia died really put the nail in the coffin. "Hey, Shawn."

He pulls his Burberry jacket tighter around himself and smiles down at me. I wish he conjured the same visceral attraction as Alex does in me, but maybe it'll grow. "Still good for dinner tonight?"

"Can't wait." I *can* wait, actually. I'm kind of dreading it. I accepted in a moment of loneliness, when the idea of being a sad, Wall Street trophy wife sounded quite good.

This is my first real date as a…as a woman, I guess, even if I still feel like a sixteen-year-old girl sometimes. He's taking me to a fancy restaurant with a tasting menu half an hour away from Sorrowsong.

A gust of wind breezes by, but not a single blond hair moves on his perfectly gelled head. "Wear a dress for me."

As with most things Shawn says, there's nothing wrong with it, but there's nothing right with it, either. But I want to give him a chance. Plus, the more I think about him, the less I'll think about Alex and his little sisters.

I'm not sure I even have a nice dress here with me.

Colette all but falls off her seat as one of the Sorrowsong players lifts Vincenzo by the hem of his shorts high enough for him to snatch the ball during the opposition's lineout and toss it to the fly-half. Alex darts through two green shirts, running with Jack past the twenty-two meter line.

Nottingham's flanker slams into Jack with a force I'm sure would break my ribs, but not before he tosses the ball to Alex. He catches it with one arm, squeezing it to his chest as he breaks into a run. Before I know it, I'm on my feet beside the others, watching him weave between players, fake left to avoid a tackle, and dive over the try line for another five points to the home team.

I keep my emotions contained amid the roar around me, but Shawn pumps his fist into the air. "Fuck yeah! Touchdown!"

I don't even bother correcting him.

Eighty minutes ends with a raucous cheer as Jack sails a drop goal between the posts for a 23–19 win to Sorrowsong.

The players bundle into a rowdy circle at the base of the stands, but as my eyes skim over Alex, his land straight on me. They don't leave mine as he pulls his black and white mouth guard out, or as the back of his hand slowly wipes the mud from his lower lip.

Something about the action makes my scarf feel like one layer too many.

Pulse drumming in my throat, I break eye contact first, gathering my things and following the lines of people off the rattling stands.

I slip and slide my way through the mud at the back of the stand, past the fabric that hangs from the top row.

A tanned hand pulls me through the black mesh and onto the browning grass beneath the rows of seats. Footsteps hammer on the metal above my head, a titanium-white smile reflecting back at me.

Shawn might as well lick his lips with the way he stares at me. I peer over my shoulder and through the mesh, at my friends wondering where I went. "What are you doing?"

"I just can't wait."

"To what?"

"To kiss you."

Anxiety scratches at my throat, a battle forming between my desire to say I'm not ready and the ugly fear that I'll become boring and undesirable once I've said that. "Later."

He pulls me closer by the ends of my scarf, one hand drifting to the outside of my thigh, just beneath the hem of my skirt. "I love this outfit on you—holy fuck, are these stockings?"

I shut my eyes and whisper a silent wish that the ground would swallow me up. I am comically behind on my washing, hence the stockings. They were a mistaken purchase last month.

When a sinkhole fails to open below me, I swing my eyes back open.

They're met with emerald green.

Alex freezes in his tracks as the black mesh falls into place behind him, staring straight at me. "Hold on. I gotta go," he says, into the phone pressed to his muddy ear.

Shawn turns around and holds out his fist. "Hey, bro. Amazing game."

Alex graces Shawn with a brief glance but returns his gaze to me while he quickly sends a text on his phone and chucks it into the gym bag on his shoulder. Shawn returns his fist to his side. "Far be it for me to criticize your game, *bro*, but you couldn't have picked a shitter spot for it."

Shawn laughs, but Alex seems unable to summon a smile. "You're totally right, man. But we have nicer plans tonight, don't we, Ophelia?"

"Yeah," I mumble, staring at the grass at my feet. Why is it always the woman left feeling ashamed? Why do I feel dirty, when Shawn looks so goddamn proud.

Shawn frowns down at his buzzing phone. "*Huh*. Vincenzo just texted. Says it looks like my bedroom door is open. I better go. See you at seven."

"What the fuck, Ophelia?" snaps Alex the second he's out of earshot.

"What?" I fire back, even though I know exactly *what*. I wrap my arms around myself, the October chill seeming colder all of a sudden.

A muscle in his jaw twitches. "Here's a crossword clue for you. Two words. Five and six. First letter *S*. A massive wanker who pays for a tanning bed in the Scottish Highlands."

"Shawn Miller." *Man, I love crosswords.* I couldn't hold the answer in even if I wanted to. "He's nice to me. He asks me about my day."

"Jesus fucking Christ, you're worse than my sister," he mutters under his breath. His exasperated sigh contracts the broad chest muscles beneath his wet rugby shirt.

Not that I notice.

"Meaning?"

"Meaning your standards are on the floor. If he asked you to split the bill fifty-fifty you'd thank him for paying his half."

"No, I wouldn't." I frown at him, eyes flicking up to the bleeding gash above his eyebrow.

He sticks out his bottom lip, tone dripping in dry humor. I hate that it's endearing. "It hurts."

"Not more than the silver spoon stuck up your ass, surely?"

"Maybe even a little bit more."

I shake my head, at the end of my tether. Why am I talking to Alex, anyway? I turn around and head through the tear in the mesh and onto the field outside. I stride toward the silhouette of the castle through the late morning fog, grateful not to hear him follow after me.

Shawn is slimy but harmless. Alex, however…Alex has an unexplainable darkness to him that seems so deeply rooted that it forms the makeup of his entire being. Every smile is a sinister threat, every casual comment is garnished with a vengeful look in his eye.

If I didn't know about his sisters, I'd say he seems like a man with nothing left to lose.

"HONESTLY, I WOULDN'T even be that trusting of those articles. I think now is a *great* time to invest in cryptocurrency. I mean, just think about it."

Shawn's voice trails off as I stir my elderflower cocktail with the glass rod. I'm so bored, I've counted the peas that surround my salmon and velouté three times. As a woman without a *return-on-investment* kink, this first date is not going well.

I've said *Wow, that's crazy* three times and he's *still* going.

The restaurant is exceptionally beautiful, set in a small cottage looking out over the choppy waters of the Northern Minch. The atmosphere is warm, mostly filled with couples and small families, but I recognize a few groups of Sorrowsong students, too. The menu is a proud display of all the treasures that Northern Scotland has to offer.

Shawn and I *should* get along. We're both the best first years on the swim team, we share some modules, we both like food.

Although I've never met someone who proudly claims to hate food, so I strike that off the list.

But still, we have things in common.

So why am I thinking about pulling a wooden stick from the olives and inserting it into my retina?

On the plus side, I've got the best phone signal I've had in weeks. The first two movies of *The Lord of the Rings* trilogy are already downloaded, and *The Return of the King* is at sixty percent. My weekend is sorted.

"I'll help you get started if you want."

I smile around a bite of food, which I have to admit is delicious. "That'd be great." *If they accept Monopoly money as currency.*

"You seem quiet."

I shift in my seat. In all honesty, I'm self-conscious. I'm in a borrowed green dress with makeup that's not mine, either. I never dress up, and Shawn hasn't said anything at all about my outfit. I'm worried I look ridiculous. Coupled with the fact that he's only managed to not talk for a cumulative total of forty-eight seconds since we got here, his observation doesn't come as a surprise.

"You're just...very chatty, and this food is really good."

He has the grace to look embarrassed. "Sorry. I've just had such an interesting life, you know? I'm really blessed. What about you? Got any secret hobbies?"

I blush. "Well, I like puzzles. Crosswords, Sudokus, cryptic crosswords. They calm me down, you know?"

"Okay, I can see why you were quiet now," he replies, a condescending expression on his face. I chew the inside of my cheek and stab some food onto my fork. There's few feelings worse than someone making you feel stupid for your interests.

My mind wanders back to my conversation with Alex. *A massive wanker who pays for a tanning bed in the Scottish Highlands.* The thought makes me laugh, and Shawn looks pretty proud of himself.

His lecture on inheritance tax makes me consider ending it all, but the deconstructed sticky toffee pudding is a welcome hand that pulls me back from the metaphorical edge.

As we both order an espresso to finish, Shawn excuses himself to go to the bathroom and I allow myself to check my phone.

No one's here to judge my sins or my pathetically confused emotions, so I let the only notifications make me smile.

Vincenzo

I'm so drunk I. Just sat. In the fireplace
and set fire to a chair. But if Sleazy
Shawn tries
Sorry sent early
If Sleazy tries anything Shawn, text me
and Alex will come pick you up. He's not
drinking.
He's sober.
He likes you. I know it.
Did Colette mention me earlier?

> **Ophelia**
> She was watching the game with me.
> Maybe have a glass of water?

Vincenzo

Alex here. He's passed out. I'll make
sure he's fine. Enjoy your evening.

Shawn reappears, sinking into the chair opposite. "I think the soap in the bathroom is cheap soap in expensive bottles."

Christ. "Maybe people kept stealing it?"

"Who steals something as boring as soap?" He sniffs his hands and wrinkles his nose. "Anyway, I heard a rumor about you and Alex."

I wave my hand in the air like some sort of flailing seal. "It's nothing, I swear. We're not together."

"Okay, good." He leans in a little. "Between you and me, you really don't wanna go there."

My interest piques. If Shawn knows anything about Cain's shady business practices, it would make my whole year. I bet his and Alex's parents know each other. "Really?"

"Bad genes. His mom is batshit crazy."

I don't know how, but I instantly know it's an insensitive choice of words. "What makes you say that?"

"You haven't seen?" He tugs his phone from his pocket and loads an internet search. I recognize his mother immediately. Most people would. She was one of the most famous models on Earth in the early 2000s. In the thumbnail, she's in a chic white shift dress and boots, her waist-length hair a little messy.

I take his phone in my hands, my heart beating a little too fast. I feel like I shouldn't be looking, but this is on a trashy but public news site. *Anyone* could see. I could've just stumbled upon it myself.

Pressing on the white Play button, a shaky, hand-filmed video of his mother appears, taken the Friday before last. Right before he flew back to New York.

The video loads at a slow pace, until the thin frame of Elise Corbeau starts to move. She sweeps her arm over the jewelry counter of a luxury department store in Manhattan, screaming something about none of the gems being the perfect color. Diamonds worth more than my existence bounce across the marble floor like cheap beads from a shitty bracelet. My stomach sinks to the bottom of the Minch as I watch a security guard pin her to the floor.

"She's been like this for years now. That family is so high maintenance."

It doesn't take a genius to see that this isn't high maintenance. It's an illness.

The phone drops from my clammy fingers onto the linen tablecloth, and I wish I didn't watch to the end. I wish I didn't hear as she cries out for someone to get her eldest son and not her husband.

I wish a steady patter of rain didn't quash the anger-fueled fire that has kept me alive these last few years.

I wish that for the first time in four years, I didn't feel completely lost about what I want to do.

ALEX CAN EAT his words about Shawn. He paid the eyewatering bill very happily. I managed to get a whopping *three* sentences in on the drive home, and he walked me to the mansion doors. *And he didn't seem too mad when I said I didn't want to do anything physical at all.*

God, maybe my standards are on the floor.

Phone flashlight guiding my way, I climb the winding stairs of the Nightshade mansion feeling too many emotions to count.

I can do normal things. I can date. Maybe I'm not emotionally stunted, after all. Maybe I can be capable of love.

I text Colette with a summary and Shawn with a thank-you as I hit the third floor.

I don't want to go out with Shawn again. Whether I dislike Alex or not, I don't like the way he talked about his mother. The video played on repeat in my head the whole way home.

I think about his last-minute trip back to New York. To the little blonde girl on his webcam.

What was her birthday like? Did her mother get to be there? Or her father?

Did the responsibility of making her feel cherished land on Alex's shoulders? Is he the steady parental figure in their lives?

An odd combination of confusion and melancholy stings the corners of my heart.

Candles flicker on the walls of the hallway as I fish my key out of Colette's clutch bag. A small storm pooling in the base of the valley is making the power choppy. The sound of a woman wailing carries over the hills and through the rafters of the mansion.

"How was the date, Twist? Did he wear Velcro shoes?"

I slap a hand to my chest as Alex comes out of his bedroom and locks the door. He slowly takes in my skintight dress and rubs a palm over his mouth like he's desperately trying not to say something. "And you say *I* lurk."

His expression remains stony. "How was the date?"

I can't even meet his eyes. I know things he wouldn't want me to, and I feel guilty for that.

And most of all I feel guilty for something I haven't done yet.

I realize I haven't even answered the question. "It was…nice."

"Nice?"

I unlock my door, but don't open it. The silence weighs heavy between us. "Yeah, nice."

If he was sober when Vincenzo was texting me, I don't think he is now. He's standing behind me, close enough that his chest kisses my back each time he inhales. "He didn't deserve it."

My shoulders tense. "The date?"

"That dress."

I hate that his words hold the power to light little candles of confidence in the back of my mind. "Don't say things like that."

"You look beautiful." He says it so simply, like it's not an opinion but a fact; not up for debate.

"The dress is Colette's," I whisper. I can't hear my own words over my sticky pulse. I don't dare tell him that I spent half the date imagining *him* pulling it off me, not Shawn.

"It was made for you," he says, voice thick with desire. I press my thighs together. "Did he pay?"

The heat building between us fizzles out. It's information he doesn't need to know, information he has no right to know. I'm frustrated, panicked about the way his gaze alone makes me feel completely naked in the hallway.

A depressing fact sinks its claws into my brain.

Something in the way Alex looks at me, something beneath the anger, makes me feel pretty.

"Did he?"

"Why do you care?" I snap, finding the sense to push the wooden door open.

His next words are throaty, feeling like warm honey on my exposed back. "Ophelia, I'd start a Crowdfunder for the pigeon that shat on my car last week if I found out it had gone on a date with Shawn Miller."

I don't know if it's the video, the cocktails, or the fact that I don't feel so insecure in his company, but my lips press into a reluctant smile as I look back over my shoulder. We're almost nose to nose. "What about the pigeon that would pee in your cup holder?"

The devastating curves of his lips form a smile of their own, but beneath his black lashes his eyes are clouded with that omnipresent darkness that seems to follow him around.

"I'd leave that stupid, ginger pigeon on the rainy path outside the university gates."

Chapter 16

OPHELIA

*S*tupid, ginger pigeon.

It's the worst way a man has ever described me, and yet I've never felt so seen.

I bury my head under yet another blanket as a flash of lightning illuminates the room. No matter how many layers I hide under, I can always see it.

My phone tells me it's five in the morning, and I'm *still* waiting for sleep to drag me under.

I'm scared.

Forty minutes until the Monday morning staff helicopter comes in. My shitty headphones don't drown it out. My fingers can't block it out. My pillow somehow makes it louder.

Each time, the panic attack seems worse.

I can't lie here and wait anymore. It's torture. Instead, I roll out of bed, tug on some warmer clothes, and make my way outside.

I want the folder from Carmichael's office.

I don't know yet what I'll do with my case against Cain Green, but I want it to be as strong as it can be.

My parents never got a proper funeral. Never got any justice. The official records haven't even been updated from *missing*. They were simply erased from this planet without a trace.

My feelings for Alex and his mother may be increasingly murky, but my feelings for his father are very simple.

I pull my hood over the wavy mess that is my hair as I jog along the deserted path to the castle. Sorrowsong is cloaked in quiet darkness, the last remnants of the storm fading away.

The sound of Alex's mother crying out his name echoes through my mind.

What burden must that have on a child?

Perhaps Alex is not his father at all.

The hallways of the castle's central structure are dark enough to make me walk faster, as if something is lurking in the black abyss behind me. I don't pass anyone as I walk past the Cortinar halls and down into Achlys's Hall.

She's illuminated in the moonlight, looking over me with that blood-curdling smile. "Piss off," I mutter, looking up at her.

I swear her smile grows.

An early riser as always, I hear the *click clack* of Eva's heels on the inside of the door. I rap on the painting, waiting for the door to swing open.

Eva is in a suit so intensely purple that it burns my corneas. My eyes flick to the photo of the car pinned to the wall behind her desk. "Ms. Winters. The chancellor has not arrived for the day yet."

"I'm here to see you, actually. I was just on a run and…is the red Mazda yours?"

"Yes." She pales. "Is she okay?"

"The alarm was going off is all. Not sure if the storm rocked it, or…"

"Oh no." She pulls on her raincoat. "I better check."

She leaves in such a hurry, she forgets to lock the door.

Shame.

I take the steps to Carmichael's mezzanine office two at a time, rolling the sliding ladder to the right. I'm on limited time. I cringe at the mud my shoes leave on the ladder as I throw myself up it, pulling the third red box forward.

I flick through the months of the year my parents died. August, September, October.

November is missing.

No. I flick through every folder again.

And again.

I rip the lids off the other two boxes going over every file twice.

November that year is gone without a trace.

When I opened that box a few weeks ago, the cardboard cracked open, stiffened with age. My fingers left paths in the dust. No one had touched it for years.

And now it's gone.

My fingers tremble as I haphazardly stuff the maintenance records back into the boxes. Who'd have taken it?

No one saw me in here except…

My phone chimes with an email.

From: Alan Sine
Subject: Trespassing
Date: Monday 21st October 05:24 BST
To: Ophelia Winters

Anne Brontë said it best.
I love the silent hour of the night.

I don't care if I'm poking the bear. Carmichael can wither to dust. I reply with a favorite quote of mine.

From: Ophelia Winters
Subject: RE: Trespassing
Date: Monday 21st October 05:25 BST
To: Alan Sine
Galileo said it better.
I've loved the stars too fondly to be fearful of the night.

I replace the lids on each box, clambering down the ladder so fast I almost fall. I freeze at the sound of voices below.

Eva isn't back, but Carmichael is. *Why is everyone up so early?*

I lunge for the door in Carmichael's office, the one that leads onto the mezzanine of the chapel, but it's locked.

Fuck.

The bottom stairs creak with slow footsteps, and I'm standing in the middle of his office at five in the morning like a thief caught red-handed.

His emails may be harmless, but murdering my roommate was not. My breaths come quick and ragged as I look for somewhere, *anywhere*, to hide.

I come up short.

As the first gray hairs of Carmichael's head appear over the top stair, I frantically throw myself onto the Persian rug at my feet and wedge myself under the sofa. There's only just enough room for me to inhale, but I'm holding my breath as he steps into the office.

Two Bottega horsebit loafers shuffle to a stop at the edge of the sofa, inches from my head. I don't smell that nutmeg-licorice scent that lingered at the tarn and on Sofia's body, but I know it's been him this whole time.

I clasp my hand over my nose and mouth in a bid to remain undiscovered. Each of my breaths sounds like it's through a megaphone. I watch the maroon leather shoes move a few paces away, over to the ladder.

My eyes widen like I've just taken a kick to the stomach. My sharp inhale slips through the gaps in my fingers.

I left the ladder out of place.

You idiot, Ophelia. Carmichael rolls it back into the corner of the room where it belongs, the scrape of the wood too loud, too jarring, against the fragile skin of my ear on the floor. He paces a slow circle around the room. I squeeze my eyes shut, my head swimming with a desperate urge to breathe properly.

"Don't just wait there. Come and sit."

Oh fuck. I let out the exhale I've been holding, trying to come up with any excuse for why I'm lying under the sofa. Nothing comes. Just as I start to roll out, a second voice joins us.

"Morning, Harris."

I freeze again as two familiar black boots come into view. What is Alex doing in Carmichael's office at this hour? The boots pace toward me, and I brace myself.

Please don't choose the sofa. Please don't choose the sofa. Please *don't choose the sofa.*

He flops down on the sofa lazily, the red leather pressing down onto my already constricted stomach. My face is pressed between the sofa and the floorboard, lungs desperate for air.

Alex sets his notebook, phone, and keys on the floor beside his feet, so close I could touch them. I feel the base of the sofa shift as he leans forward toward Carmichael's desk. "Brontë fan?"

Oh my god. My gasp is so loud that I'm sure I've been caught.

It's him. It's Carmichael.

"Not particularly."

"Did you read my proposition?"

"I read it."

"And?"

"And I think you're twenty-three years old."

Even through my muffled version of the conversation, I can sense Alex's anger. "So you're out?"

"Alex, abusing my position as the chairman of the board of your father's company is unwise."

Carmichael is on the board of Green Aviation? My whole body pulls taut.

Does he know what I'm doing here? Is that why he's trying to break me? So the truth never comes out?

Somewhere in my head, a puzzle piece clicks into position.

Alex's voice rises. "Did you read section four?"

"I did."

A fist lands on the sofa, and I swear it bursts my eardrum. "Then do your fucking job, Carmichael!"

I don't have time to ponder Alex's uncharacteristic outburst, because the whir of the helicopter flying in over the valley rumbles the wood beneath my head. I clench my sweaty fists tighter. Unable to breathe and unable to move, I feel like I'm about to be hardened into steel like the suit of armor in the corner of the office.

I can't guide myself through the panic.

I don't have my crossword book, or my headphones.

There's no shower for me to crawl into.

Only the sticky leather that feels like bugs crawling across my clammy skin.

I can't breathe.

I'm going to die under this sofa, a mouse trapped in the lion's den.

Not in a ball of fire like my mother and father, but in silent stillness. My lungs will turn to stone.

I'll die alone. Broken and bitter like the painting outside.

I *am* Achlys.

I don't care if Alex feels me move beneath him. I use all my power to push the sofa up enough to press the heels of my hands over my ears. I keep focus on all the things that I can see. The delicately crafted foot of the sofa. The black leather of Alex's boots. The piece of lint by my face.

I count the keys on the clip beside his phone. A gold one for his room. The small, black fob for the Nightshade mansion, a smaller one that might be for a window, and the cleaner's master key with the green tag.

I almost hear my mind screech to a halt. The cleaner's *what*? I reread the tiny, fading writing on the green plastic.

What the hell does he have a stolen master key for?

The helicopter touches down, the whir of the rotor blades getting slower and slower until it stops altogether.

As it always does, my heartbeat mirrors the rhythm of the blades.

The gold rings glint on Alex's hand as he picks up his phone. I try, *really* try, to listen to their conversation for useful information, but when Alex mentions the words *fiscal year*, my brain powers down.

I see my screen light up beside my head, and dread lances into my chest like a knife. I don't switch it onto silent fast enough, and the chime of an email pings loud and clear in the quiet office.

Alex clears his throat. "Sorry. That was my Green work phone."

From: Alex Corbeau-Green
Subject: Claustrophobic (adjective) *having an extreme or irrational fear of confined places*
Date: Monday 21st October 05:43 BST
To: Ophelia Winters

I'm just *dying* to know the reason you are lying beneath me right now.

I read the email in utter disbelief. How does he know? Does that mean Carmichael knows? I'm just going to throw myself in the tarn and never get out.

I type a shaky reply with one finger and switch the phone to silent.

From: Ophelia Winters
Subject: Asphyxia (noun) *a condition in which the body is deprived of oxygen*
Date: Monday 21st October 05:44 BST
To: Alex Corbeau-Green

Can you shift to the right a bit? You're right on my fucking lungs.

I hear Alex breathe out a laugh as Carmichael drones on about whatever it is he likes to drone on about.

From: Alex Corbeau-Green
Subject: Oneirology (noun) *the scientific study of dreams*
Date: Monday 21st October 05:44 BST
To: Ophelia Winters

In the nineteen times it's happened in my head, my first time on top of you didn't look like this.

He thinks about me.

My breath catches in my throat. My thighs press together. Somewhere between yesterday morning and now, there's another element to our conversations.

One that makes me feel unfamiliar things. One that feels so wrong and yet so sinfully right. I think of the Alex who put his little sister to bed. The one who crossed a continent when his mother called his name.

Here in this moment, I let myself believe Alex is not his father.

I picture him sitting opposite Carmichael, and maybe the residual adrenaline of a fading panic attack makes me braver, because my reply sends a thrill through me.

From: Ophelia Winters
Subject: 1 Across
Date: Monday 21st October 05:46 BST
To: Alex Corbeau-Green

Nine letters. First letter *U*.
I'm not wearing any.

Each beat of silence takes another bite out of my confidence, until Carmichael clears his throat with a tone laced with annoyance. "Have you got something more interesting going on?"

I feel Alex shift in his seat, and when his voice comes, it's hoarse with desire. "Honestly, sir, you have *no* idea."

From: Alex Corbeau-Green
Subject: 2 Down
Date: Monday 21st October 05:47 BST
To: Ophelia Winters

Two words. Five and six. First letters *H* and *A*.
I'm about to have one.

I smother my laugh in my elbow. I like the idea that I could give him a heart attack.

From: Ophelia Winters
Subject: Fiscal Year (who the fuck knows?) *who the fuck cares?*
Date: Monday 21st October 05:47 BST
To: Alex Corbeau-Green

Please wrap this meeting up. I'm ten minutes away from the stomach rumbles.
Bonus points if you can bring the old fart with you when you leave.

His laugh makes me feel ten feet tall. I hear the click of his phone shutting off and watch it clatter back down to the floor. "Sorry, Harris. You know how funny Vincenzo can be. Can we talk outside? I'm always more focused in nature."

"Very well," the chancellor grumbles. If I had a millimeter of space to tip my head back with sheer relief, I would. Two pairs of shoes creak across the floorboards. I hear Carmichael rap his knuckles on the banister twice to get his secretary's attention. "Eva, please email Ms. Winters and tell her she is welcome in my office anytime. There's no need to sneak in."

Fuck.

"She's a strange one, that one," mutters Alex as they descend the stairs. Carmichael mumbles his agreement.

I shut my eyes and let my stomach sink with a slow exhale.

I don't know what I'm doing. I couldn't even pull off secret missions in *Club Penguin*, I don't know what inflated my ego enough to make me think I can take down a Fortune 500 CEO.

With about as much grace as a fish out of water, I start to shuffle out from beneath the sofa and sink myself into the wingback armchair opposite the desk and let my eyelids drift shut. All my hopes in secrecy lie in ruins, so I pick the cobwebs from my hair, get comfortable, and wait for Carmichael's return.

CARMICHAEL TOOK LONGER than I thought. By the time he comes back up the stairs, I've eaten half of the humbugs in the bowl on his desk and obliterated BieberLover6969 in an online game of Scrabble.

I sit up straighter. "Morning, sir."

"Ophelia. Do help yourself to the mints."

Whoops. "I haven't had breakfast yet. I can replace them."

"Did you find what you were looking for in my office?"

"Were you, at any point, intending to tell me that my parents didn't die in an accident?"

It's infinitesimal, but I notice the way his body freezes on the way down into his chair. The leather creaks as he leans back and looks up at me through those strange, pale eyes. "I considered it."

My next exhale comes out shaky. "So this is not a surprise to you."

"It is not."

I'm out of my chair before my next breath, clenched fists leaning on the wooden surface in front of him. "And you didn't think it was the sort of information I deserved to know?"

"I fail to see what use that information is to you now. There are few things more painful in life than the things we cannot change."

I'm three seconds away from throttling him. "It matters because my life has been on pause for four years."

He has the audacity to look bored. "*You* paused your life. You could've done any number of things after that helicopter went down, but you chose stagnation."

My knuckles crack against the cherrywood. Wrath bubbles up to my throat, sour and bitter. There it is; the disappointment, the expectation that trauma has to turn into an inspirational story. That a life changing injury should end in a Paralympic gold and an awful childhood should fuel your meteoric rise to success.

Just surviving is achievement enough.

"You owe me the truth. You owe me the reason that a helicopter full of ordinary people was sabotaged." My voice rises to a shout, because I'm worried that if I don't shout then I'll cry. "You owe me the reason it was allowed to happen under *your* nose, *your* roof, *your* authority."

His palms slam down on the desk twice as hard as mine, his slender frame rising to his feet. I watch him snap in front of me.

The pensive, antiquated gentleman melts away to leave nothing but acrid vitriol behind.

It's a new side to Carmichael, and as he looks at me with nothing but fury in his eyes, I'd say it's the first time he's looked truly alive. His shout comes even louder than mine, crackling through the air like an electric current. "Your mother was *not* the angel you remember her to be."

"What is that supposed to mean?"

"I know what you're doing here, and you would do well to cease your investigations. Your scholarship was a kind offer of a second chance at life, not a chance to dig around in matters you ought to stay out of."

"Scared of what I'll find out? Scared I'll damage your fortune in Green Aviation stock?"

If I don't kill him, he looks like he may kill me first. He snaps his fingers twice. "Eva, escort Ms. Winters out, please."

Eva's heels click against the stairs to the mezzanine. "Does the name Alan Sine mean anything to you?"

"Eva, escort her out."

"Is there a reason you're trapping me here?" I shout, as I'm all but dragged out by Carmichael's bright purple guard dog, eyes fixed on the dull gray sheen to his as the door slams in my face.

Fuck him.

Fuck him, and fuck this university. I repeat it like a mantra as I storm through the castle and back toward the Nightshade mansion.

A twig snaps, fracturing the wintry air around me.

Alex stands at the end of the forested path to the mansion, green eyes piercing through the haze of smoke from the cigarette dangling from his lips. Beneath the dull light of the struggling sun, he looks huge.

I stop walking.

He takes a slow, lazy drag, nostrils flaring slightly with frustration. "I don't like it when people encroach on private conversations."

"I don't like it when people encroach on private burglaries."

Everything about him makes my heart run faster. Pacing toward me, he rolls up the sleeves of his shirt, like he's burning up even in the autumn chill. "What did you want in his office?"

I'd never tell you. "It doesn't matter."

"Matters to me."

"Shame."

He takes a step forward. "Don't make me chase you."

I take a step back. "I have stamina."

"I'd rather find that out a different way."

My next step falters, heel catching in the mud behind me. I fall, but I don't hit the ground. One tattooed arm wraps around my waist, strong and warm.

Alex gazes down at me, the cherry of the cigarette glowing as he takes another drag.

"Smoking raises your blood pressure," I whisper, my voice more hoarse than it should be. It's a stupid comment, a feeble attempt at dissolving the tension between us, at getting back into the familiar hatred and out of whatever *this* is.

His grip on my waist doesn't loosen, the heat of his large hand scorching through my hoodie. "*You* raise my blood pressure."

"How?"

His eyes drop to my lips for the smallest of moments. "That backless dress from last night, for a start."

The chatter and pounding feet of a small group of runners travel up the path, and Alex drags us into the bushes.

My back hits the trunk of a small ash tree, chest rising and falling faster.

The cigarette hisses as he puts it out against the bark just a hair's breadth away from my ear. The light is lower, casting soft shadows over the contours of his face. His palms land on either side of my head, and then his thick forearms.

"Don't." *Don't touch me. Don't kiss me. Just don't.*

"Bold of you to assume I want to."

But he does want to. I see it in his body language because I see it in my own.

I never wanted to meet Alex. Never wanted to see him, touch him, want him. None of this is right.

I'm adrift at sea; so far off course, I don't know what I'm doing anymore.

The cold metal of the ring on his index finger grazes my skin as he lifts my chin. "Do you want to know how I knew you were under the sofa?"

I look away, focusing on a knot on the next tree along. "No."

He grasps my face in his left hand, firm but gentle, forcing me to look at him. It's too hot, too humid, too dense beneath the trees. "Because *everything* smells like you." He leans in closer. Close enough for me to see the cut and bruise on his face from his rugby match. Close enough for me to see the usual storm in his eyes has been replaced by something else entirely. "The passenger seat of my car, the couch in Carmichael's office, my fucking bedsheets. You're *everywhere*."

He's so close I can almost taste him. Taste my own weakness, my confusion.

I feel like I can hear the drumming of his heart, feel it against my chest in time with my own.

But I must be wrong, because I've never believed he has one.

The atmosphere is so heavy, so thick with desire that it feels like sticky syrup around us, dripping down the neck of my hoodie. His eyes are on my mouth when he finally speaks. "Whatever secret reason you're here for, tell me Shawn Miller is all part of it."

My hand wraps around his forearm, and I don't know if it's to touch him or to stop him getting any closer. "It wouldn't matter if he wasn't."

"You're too good a woman for a man like him."

"And you'd be better?"

A dark chuckle vibrates in his throat. "Ophelia, love, I'd be significantly *worse*. But I can't watch you with him."

Somehow, we've ended up closer, my hands against his chest to keep a precious gap between us. "Then look away."

He looks at me like I've asked him to pluck the moon from the sky and bottle it for me. "Can't."

"You don't know me at all." You don't know what I came here to do. What I still might do.

You don't know what I might do to your family.

To your mother.

I'm a monster. Just like Cain Green. An eye for an eye. A tooth for a tooth. A family for a family. He burnt away my kindness, my compassion. The ash he left behind is bitter and calamitous.

I look up at him, desperately trying to convey the words I can't bring myself to say. *Stay away from me. You don't know what I'll do to you.*

His lips hover over mine, forehead to forehead. And beneath the panic, the horror, the knowledge that this is wrong, a tiny part of me is just grateful to be close to someone, grateful to be wanted. "Did he kiss you?"

"You have no right to know that."

His voice is strained, like he knows that but asked it anyway. For a second, I think he's going to do it. The quiet voice at the back of my head is on its knees, pleading for more. My lower abdomen clenches. "Put me out of my goddamn misery, Ophelia."

"Yes," I whisper. It's a lie, but the gap between us cools as he pulls away a fraction.

The frosty curtain closes over his eyes again. "So you really like him, huh?"

"Yes."

I don't know if he believes me, but he does respect it. He pulls away to let me step back onto the path. I suck in a deep breath, the air cool and crisp once more.

My environment may be clearer, but my mind is just as foggy as it was in the trees. "Our relationship doesn't extend beyond studying, Alex."

He straightens his collar, running a hand through his hair. "Of course."

We walk back to the Nightshade mansion in tense silence, but for some reason I'm biting my lip to hold in a laugh.

This is all ridiculous.

Alex pierces the quiet first. "I bet Shawn jumps up and down in the club."

The laugh escapes like water from a burst pipe. It's cathartic, hysterical, and quite possibly manic, but I don't care. I'm stuck here in this place I hate so much it's almost funny. "With his finger in the air, too?"

Now Alex is laughing. "And talks about the perks of cryptocurrency between songs."

"Hey, the Federal Reserve has literally *just* cut the interest rate. The market capitalization of cryptocurrency has had a great boost. Risk appetite is high right now."

Alex smothers his laugh in both hands. It's beautiful. "He did *not*."

"The *whole* fucking date."

"Oh my god."

"He's sweet."

Alex scans his card at the impressive double door of the mansion. "He probably still sends out his Snapchat streaks in the morning."

I blurt out the question burning at the back of my mind. "Why do you have a stolen master key?"

He doesn't miss a beat. "It lets me into the Grand Library past opening hours."

"I don't believe you."

He opens the door to let me in, looking down at me in a way that makes my traitorous cheeks blush. "It doesn't matter whether or not you believe me. Just like it doesn't matter that I think you can't stand Shawn any more than I can."

Can't argue with that.

We ascend the first two floors in silence, but we're almost at the top when he breaks it. "Why all the crosswords?"

I shrug as his footsteps echo behind mine. "Just to occupy my mind."

"So you're like me."

"In what way?"

"Worried about where your mind will go if left unoccupied."

Ten words. Ten words that I've been trying to articulate for years. Ten words that make me think I've had it all wrong about Alex Corbeau-Green.

Ten words that make me feel less alone.

"Yeah," I whisper. "They're a cage for my thoughts."

We stop on the top step, staring at each other like two astronauts that have bumped into each other on a faraway planet. "I understand," he says, his voice buttery soft.

I'm too close to doing something I'll regret. Something I cannot do. "I need to go to the gym. I need to train my shoulders," I blurt out.

"Okay, are you asking my permission, or…?"

"I have to go." I scan my student card at the door to our hallway about fifty thousand times and barge through it, bolting into my bedroom like my life depends on it.

I sink to the floor on the other side of the door like I've just run a half marathon, head in my hands.

None of this is happening.

I'm not really here.

I'm not really trapped.

I'm not really growing fonder of *him*.

Chapter 17

OPHELIA

Ninety-one percent. Best in the class.

Vincenzo jumps into the air to celebrate his forty-eight—a pass—like he's just won the lottery.

Alex shuts off his phone screen, closing the results email as we all grab our bags to leave Andersson's lecture hall. "I guess we make a good team, Twist."

"Stop calling me that."

"You don't like the nickname?"

It's kind of ironic. I *was* orphaned, but he doesn't know that. "It's marginally better than fish food. But a Dickensian orphan, it doesn't really make me feel...like a woman."

"So what should I call you?"

"Oh, I don't know, how about Ophelia Winters?"

"What should Shawn call you?"

I blush. Shawn is pretty relentless, but I've managed to use swimming as an excuse not to see him so far. "I don't know…What do men call their girlfriends? Sugar?"

I regret it the second I say it, but Alex raises an eyebrow before I can retract my statement. "Sugar. You want to be called sugar."

"No, not sugar. Something else, like…" I scratch my head. I have no idea.

He presses his lips together. "Sugar."

I shove him out of the way, feeling my cheeks flame. "*Not* sugar. Honey? No. Not honey. Muffin? *No*."

He looks exasperated with me. "Jesus Christ. What's next? *Eggs? Preheat oven to two fifty? Baking soda*, I'm home!"

I smother my laugh in my mittens. He's right. I have no idea how a relationship works. "Shut up."

"I guess we have no reason to see each other anymore," he says as pulls his phone back out of his pocket and frowns. I wonder if everything is okay at home.

Then I wonder why I care.

"I guess we don't."

"At last."

"At last," I repeat firmly. I've been counting down to this date for weeks.

So why am I not ecstatic?

Alex's phone lights up with an incoming call, and I catch the name Evie before he looks back up to me. "See you around, *sugar*."

I hate the nickname, but my pulse flutters. The way he says it, it sounds sinful and not sweet. Dark and twisted.

He says it like a promise. Like he'll be looking for me.

I turn away, grinning into my scarf as his phone's ringing stops and starts back up again. "Later, *muffin*."

I trudge out of the psychology wing and into the mid-November air. An early winter chill rolled in over the valley last week, and it doesn't seem to be keen to leave. Autumn seemed to give up on her mission.

Like me.

Last week, paparazzi photographed Alex's mother running in Central Park in her dressing gown.

He left his rugby match halfway through and flew to New York the same day.

His father didn't leave the climate conference in Washington.

Alex is quieter and quieter. The storm in his eyes is more and more violent each day. Usually so cold and calculated, I watched him in an extremely heated fight with Carmichael in the car park while on a run this week.

I said when I met him that he seemed like an elastic band waiting to snap. Somehow, it feels like he's been stretched even further.

My lack of evidence and my nightly internet searches about his mother and his oldest sister, Fleur, do nothing to stoke the fire of revenge in me.

All the times I've considered just ending it all, the need to see Cain Green in shackles has been the hand that stops me.

It was easier when the Greens were just words on an internet article. When I hadn't seen photos of them on Alex's Instagram, or watched a stupid video of him twirling his eight-year-old sister around the kitchen on Fleur's Instagram story.

I always knew I'd be ruining a family.

This was always part of the deal.

Carmichael hasn't sent me any more strange emails since our altercation in his office a few weeks ago. Maybe I've panicked him. Maybe he knows I already know too much, that his gargantuan retirement fund is at risk. Either way, it's been twenty-three days of swimming competitions, drinking with Colette, walks back to the mansion with Alex, and hiding from the sound of the helicopter.

Life feels almost normal.

An email pings through as I amble down a busy corridor in the castle's central structure. It doesn't worry me anymore. I open up the message from the mailing room and frown. I have a parcel waiting for me. Odd. I haven't had so much as a letter, postcard, or parcel since my elderly neighbor got dementia three years ago.

I excuse myself from the group of chattering psychology students and follow the chaotic map on my phone down endless winding tunnels and into the shortest turret on the outer perimeter of the castle. Given the trajectory my life is on, I know the package is almost definitely a severed hand.

But I never get mail, so whether it's a severed hand or a threat in a box, I *will* get my fun unboxing. Maybe I'll even film it and post it to my private Instagram account with zero followers.

Maybe it'll go viral.

I'm getting ahead of myself. I clear my throat as I round the doorway. "Hello?"

The woman at the desk simultaneously sighs and chews her gum. "Name."

"Ophelia Winters."

She yanks a battered box off the rows of shelving and shoves it toward me. I don't know what's stronger, the coffee on her breath or her Glaswegian accent. "Sign for it."

I pick up the pen and write my name. "Do you know who sent it? Was there any indication?"

She cracks the chewing gum in her mouth. "I'm paid by the parcel, love. Not by the hour."

"Right." I tuck the small box beneath my arm and hurry my way back to the Nightshade mansion.

I toss the package onto my bed and examine the writing on it. It was shipped to my parents' cottage an hour and a half from here, and then redirected to the university.

Intriguing.

I split what's left of the duct tape with my room key, tearing open the box. A messily scrawled note sits on top, written on the back of half an envelope.

It's what he would've wanted. —L.

Underneath it is an object wrapped in a dirty T-shirt and a tea towel. Wondering if I need a hazmat suit, I pinch the T-shirt between my fingers and pull it out of the box.

A tape clatters to the floor of my room.

I pick it up shakily, the writing on the label fading away. *Laura, my darling, I'm sorry.*

I drop it again like it gave me an electric shock, lowering myself to the floor beside it.

The final bullet in the barrel.

The grenade in Cain Green's home.

Only, he's not home alone.

I stare at the tape, wracked with indecision.

The two girls inside me—the *girl before*, and the *girl after*—want different things. One wants war, to make others suffer the same as she has, to not be alone in her misery. The other one just wants a quiet life of crosswords and peace.

One wants to mail the tape back to where it came from.

One wants to pull the trigger.

I opt to do what my father would. Sleep on it, decide tomorrow. But I do order myself a tape to MP3 converter.

Just in case.

THERE'S ONLY BEEN one foolproof way to clear my mind since I got to Sorrowsong, so I put my swimsuit on beneath my joggers and knitted cardigan, pack my towel and swimming float into a tote bag, and head down to the tarn.

The world feels silent as I take the winding path down to the lake. The temperature has dipped well into the single digits, too cold for groups of students to sit around and smoke on the trail.

A bitter wind chases me down to the water's edge, biting at my heels. My trainers don't even attempt to hide the cold around my feet as I dump my bag on the soft bank.

A rustle sounds in the hedgerow behind me. My eyes scan the length of it, suddenly aware of how alone I am here. All is silent and still, so I slip off my shoes and socks, letting my feet sink into the mud.

I'm just clipping my small orange float around my waist when leaves crunch louder behind me. I reach for the penknife in my bag, gripping it in my fist as the branches in the hedge bounce.

My attempt at steadying my breath fails. I'm as useless as the horror movie heroines I've spent my evenings yelling at.

Oh god. I'm going to die. Why did I provoke Carmichael? The man probably has hit men working for him.

I'm going to die, and I haven't even done today's Wordle.

A fox darts out from the bushes, scampering away into the inky green mass of the Solemn Woods.

I breathe out a shaky laugh. This university is making me overly paranoid.

I do Wordle at the water's edge, though, just to be sure.

The water is cold enough to freeze my mind. Freeze my worries—freeze the racing thoughts that treat my body like a racetrack. By the time my shoulders sink below the waterline, I can't feel my legs.

I tread water for a split second, trying to work the stupid fitness watch Belladonna gave me to track my swim speed.

My mother would know. She'd always fix the TV right before Dad was at the stage of punching it. She was clever.

She'd have caught my stalker by now.

My body falls still in the water.

Alan Sine.

It's an anagram of my mother's name.

All of those puzzles. All of those crosswords, and it's taken me almost two months to realize that Alan Sine is an anagram of Annalise.

It doesn't change anything; not really. It doesn't change what they've said or done. But it makes it all feel twice as sinister. Twice as personal.

A twig snaps in the trees to my right, and somehow it feels different. Different to the fox, different to the peace I've known for the last few weeks.

Something deep inside me tells me to return to the castle. Something is wrong.

My limbs too cold to be of much use, I make my way to the bank and stumble out of the water. Another twig crunches in the trees.

"Just a fox," I repeat, over and over, even though the snap is too loud to be a fox. Frantically, I rummage around in my bag for my knife. My legs are shaky, fingers devoid of feeling.

The wind howls over the valley. Achlys screams for help. My breaths are hyperventilating.

I don't know why I'm so scared, don't know why I reach for my phone to unblock Alex's number. It takes me too long to find his texts to me, too long to click on them. I don't hit Unblock in time.

I'm too slow to react when a heavy footstep lands behind me.

Two hands slam down on the back of my neck, sending me flying onto the bank in front of me. My face lands in the shallows of the water.

I try to roll over, try to fight, but a large hand pins my face into the water, the other pressing on the back of my neck. I scream, but it's a garbled cry that tastes like dirt and earth and *dread*.

I fight. God, I fight. I fight like I never thought I would. I fight like a girl who has something to come home to at Christmas.

I slam my head back. It collides with something, someone. I hear a furious grunt through the water that blocks my ears.

But it's not enough. The hands don't move. Before my head is slammed back onto the bank, the sickening stench of cloves and anise fills my lungs.

My legs kick in the mud. My lungs burn for air. My hands grapple behind me. They brush a forearm—a male forearm—and they claw at a ringed finger at the back of my neck.

I need to inhale.

I feel the *girl before* die inside me. I watch her hopes and dreams of noisy Christmases and sinks full of dishes slither into the water.

The *girl after* fights for longer. She screams again, bubbles spilling into the dark brown water. She kicks and thrashes even after the energy has left her limbs, fueled by hatred.

But like everything she's ever done, it's just not enough.

Water invades places only delicate enough for air.

My hatred and my malice join my compassion and my kindness at the bottom of the tarn.

The world fades to black around me.

Just black. No orange room. No music. No crosswords. No Mum, no Dad.

Just black.

I'm sorry.

Chapter 18

ALEX

Even through the phone, I can sense Dr. Harwood's exasperation with me.

I'd been doing better for a while.

He stands at the window of his office, staring out at the New York skyline beyond. "You're frustrated that Harris isn't interested in your proposal."

I recline back at the desk in my room, watching with mild interest as Ophelia walks across the gravel path to the mansion with a box tucked under her arm.

Christ, she's beautiful. Her hair whips around her face like threads of burning copper, spun into soft waves by the wind. Her brown miniskirt sits high on her muscular thighs, covered by thick, black tights. She's swamped her athletic frame in a brown trench coat that would probably fit Vincenzo and a scarf that has seen better days.

I don't even bother trying to look away. I drink in every minute detail like I'm dying and she's the cure. Somewhere in the last few days, I've ventured so far into denial that I'm out the other side.

I shift in my seat and bring my body back under control. *I want her.*

She's impossible to get close to, though. She's like that dumb Jenga game. You think you're getting somewhere, and then the tiniest move in the wrong direction and every little bit of progress I had made with her is gone again.

I guess she shuts people out because it's easier than getting hurt. I get it, but it still irritates me. I think we would be good together, but she doesn't agree.

And that sucks.

My jaw tenses watching a second year's gaze follow her a little too closely. She doesn't notice anyone admiring her; in her own world all the time, stuck in a mindless loop of her own thoughts. I know, because I'm in a similar torture of my own.

Dr. Harwood would say I have an addictive personality and an immature streak. He thinks I had to step up and raise my sisters too young, that I didn't have time to explore my emotions before I shoved them into a box. I cope with the stress of life by clinging to one thing all the time. It was drinking, then it was smoking, then it was running, drawing, working. Now, I think it might be her.

Watching her with Shawn Miller was easier before I realized her tights were stockings.

Life was easier before I realized her tights were stockings.

"I'm frustrated at everything."

"Everything?"

The outside world blurs as I home in on my reflection in the window above my desk. At the fading cut on my forehead left there by Loughborough's flanker last week, sitting beneath the bruise left by my own father. "Everything."

"Carmichael's reaction can't have come as a surprise, surely? He chairs the board of a billion-dollar company. It's his job to do what's best for the business."

"But it's not the right thing, ethically."

"It's a rare occasion that ethics and smart business align."

"I don't pay you to depress me more."

He sits back down in his red desk chair, examining me through the webcam. His hand rubs the dark brown skin of his bald head, dark eyes narrowing. "How is your mother?"

"I called her doctor this morning and asked him to keep her for another night." I drum my pencil on the desk. "He wants to increase her Clozapine again, but I don't think it's a good idea. They say it's my call."

"This is a very heavy weight on your shoulders to manage from afar."

I almost crush my coffee mug in my fist. I opt for a cigarette instead. "I know, *Robert*. Don't you think I don't know it was wrong of me to come here? But what else would you have me do? I need Carmichael to convince the board that my father has to go. I can't spend another week in that house, watching him play them all like puppets. I stay and I lose, I leave and I lose."

"That's not what I meant. I meant you need to get more help back in New York."

The laugh that escapes my lips is bitter. "From who? My father? My fourteen-year-old sisters? It'd be easier if they could move to

London or Paris, but Cain won't allow it." His family man, father-of-seven image is perfect for the press. "As soon as he's gone, everything will be easier."

"Tell me about the other things in your life. Not your mother and not your sisters."

"There is nothing else."

He sips his tea, and I can almost smell the Earl Grey from here. "Your studies?"

"Are just a means to impress Carmichael, which is a means to help my mother and sisters."

"Your rugby?"

"The same."

"Rowing?"

"Gave it up. No time. I've been sketching when I can't sleep."

"And the girl?"

I told him about Ophelia a few weeks ago in a moment of weakness, right after I'd found her sitting under the sofa listening to my conversation with Carmichael, right after our moment in the trees. I wasn't in my right mind, riding whatever euphoric high it is that I get whenever I've just seen her. Dr. Harwood knew something was different, anyway.

I've never been so perplexed by someone. She's fucking *miserable*, yet she makes me feel alive. She stains the corners of my gray cloud orange, but I have a feeling I make her bright colors gray. She never really smiles around me. I've always been like that to people. "She's interested in someone else. And I'm not interested, anyway."

"Why not?"

I sigh, drawing endless circles in my sketchbook. "What's the point? What's the end goal?"

"Love?"

I snort. Love is so far at the back of my priorities at the moment. "She's not that sort of girl. She wouldn't want me to love her. We don't speak anymore. Why are we even discussing her?"

"We're discussing her because you need a break from your home life. You need to *give yourself* a break from your home life."

In the trees with Ophelia a few weeks ago. That was a break. A moment when my mind was in Sorrowsong and Sorrowsong alone. I thought of little else that day. She felt perfect against me; soft and strong all at once

I should've kissed her.

"Two and a half more years," I say flatly.

"Stick with it. It'll get better. You'll be glad you stayed by the end."

"Yeah." I agree because it's easier than not. A text pings through from Fleur. It's a picture that Josie has drawn of me. I have seven fingers on each hand. It makes me smile. It reminds me why I'm here. *I'll be glad I stayed by the end.*

If my plan works.

My limbs ache with inactivity. "I gotta go work out, Rob. See you next week?"

"Yes. Virtually again?"

I scribble inside a circle. "Depends on my mother."

"Don't let it depend on your mother. She's in good, capable hands. I'll visit her myself if I need to."

I nod and hit the red button to end the call, staring out at the mountains beyond the tarn.

I'm losing a battle with the gray cloud inside me.

• • •

212

"I'M PRETTY SURE it has, like…chia seeds in it? Or maybe they're poppy seeds? I dunno. The small ones. They look like bugs. But I put Greek yogurt in it this time instead of oat milk, and it makes a big difference. It's way thicker. You could probably eat it with a spoon, honestly."

Mia, my fourteen-year-old sister, bleeds on in my AirPods, describing her smoothie in a level of detail I never imagined smoothies could be described in. On the plus side, Jack has invited Shawn and his Cortinar buddies to work out in the Nightshade gym, so she's doing a terrific job of drowning them out.

I drop my final deadlift with a low grunt, undoing the belt at my waist. The gym is as dimly lit as the rest of the mansion, the lighting warm and flickering slightly. Oak paneling rises up to high, corniced ceilings. It looks like something from the Elizabethan era, save for the state-of-the-art equipment everywhere. "I'll have to try it."

"Yeah, I'll make it for you. Are you coming home this weekend?"

Three two-day trips back to New York in four weeks, alongside my studies and my calls with select board members of Green Aviation, have burnt me out. "Not if I don't have to. I'll see you when I'm home for Christmas in a few weeks."

I'm excited for Christmas, for once. I've missed all my sisters more than I thought I would, and my father will hopefully be busy working.

Mia's voice is pensive on the other end of the line. "Do you think we'll still go to Paris? If *Maman* is ill?"

"Hopefully. Was the smoothie the only reason for the call?"

"Yeah."

"Okay, well, I better go. I'm at the gym. Who's at home with you all?"

"Ingrid and Russel, but Dad gets home early tonight. He's taking us to watch Evie's ballet." *The housekeeper and the driver.* I'm sure they don't get paid enough to essentially parent my sisters. "Also, I got a new phone case. It holds my lip gloss."

"I'm sure that's a solution to a nonexistent issue."

Her giggle makes unloading the barbell easier. "It's pretty!"

"I bet. I'll call you again next week, M."

"I love you."

"I love you, too. Take a video of the ballet and send it to me, okay?"

"I will. Bye!"

I hang up, sliding the weights onto the squat rack.

Shawn comes over right as I find my footing beneath the bar. I grit my teeth together. He's working out in a golf shirt, for fuck's sake. "Hey, bro. Amazing touchdown at the game last week."

Idiot. I try to be as civil as I can. "Just trying to work out, man."

"Looks like Ophelia kind of swapped you out for me, huh?"

What's that supposed to mean? Are they sleeping together now? My knuckles crack around the steel across my shoulders. "I'm trying to work out."

"Was she uptight with you?"

I can almost see my reflection in his overly gelled hair. I'd club him around the head if the sheer amount of product wouldn't shatter the club.

Seconds pass, and he's still in front of me. Breathe in. Breathe out. In. Out. "Would she want you to be asking that?"

He must be completely devoid of hearing, because he carries on. "She's frigid to a new degree, man. Was she like that with you?"

I'm going to kill him.

214

I can't kill him. His father is on the board.

I'm going to kill him.

His father is on the motherfucking board.

"Well?"

I turn the volume of my earphones up, trying to muffle his incessant whining. "If you were talking about one of my sisters like that, I'd crack your skull, Miller."

"Good job it's not your sister then." He flashes his overly white veneers in a salacious grin, and I drop the weight back onto the rack and duck underneath it to get closer to him. Jack pauses his workout to watch us in the mirror warily. "I tell you what, next time I take her out on a date, it'll be a fucking great job she isn't your sister. Reckon Ophelia is as quiet in bed as she is outside of it?"

My blood smolders in my veins. I shove him back. "She's not even quiet, you dick, you just don't shut up."

"Whoa, there. Better keep a check on those emotions, Green. Wouldn't want to turn into your psycho mother, would you?"

A red mist sinks in around me, swirling around the rows of dumbbells behind us. I don't even remember pushing him, taken over by a violent fury. The glass mirror makes an audible crack behind Shawn's head. My fists clench his ugly top by the collar, as I glare down at him. "My *what*?"

He looks terrified. Scared and small, as he should be. His pulse drums beneath my fingers, fast and heavy. A sickening satisfaction runs through me. It would be *so* easy to become my father. So easy to snuff out a life. "I didn't mean anything by it, man."

I slam my fist into his nose. And again and again and again, until Jack pulls me off him and Vincenzo appears out of nowhere to drag me out of the gym. "Don't."

I stare down at my bloodied fists. "I need to finish him off. I'm doing all of us a favor."

Vincenzo pulls me into the library, away from the gathering crowd in the foyer. "Over Ophelia? She's just a girl. Let it go."

"He called her a psycho."

Vin pales slightly. "Your mama?"

"Yeah."

He looks like he might go in there and finish Shawn off, but he shakes his head and stays in place. For once. "You need his father on your side, man."

"I've fucked that plan already."

"Just go. Clear your head. I'll deal with Shawn. I'm sure my dad will have some dirt on him or his father I can use. Just go."

I stagger out onto the path outside, hands on my knees as I suck in a desperate lungful of air.

I can't do this anymore.

It's Yale all over again. It's all too much. Too much for me, too much for my mother, too much for my sisters.

I have to go back.

I break out into a jog through the forest, punching a number into my phone. It only rings once before my father's PR agent picks up. "Andrew speaking."

"Hi, Andrew," I say as my feet pound the forest floor. My tone is sickly sweet. Andrew is the human equivalent of wet cardboard; fucking useless and smells weird.

"Mr. Corbeau. Good morning."

"There are videos of her online again."

"Ah yes. I've seen."

"So what the fuck do we pay you for? Get them taken down."

"I'm working on it, sir."

"Well work faster. I can fire your team just as easily as Cain can."

"I'll have them down today, sir."

I hang up, winding my way through the Solemn Woods that sprawl out at the castle's feet. My demons chase me between centuries-old pines and mangled oaks. They follow me through shallow streams and over jagged rocks. I run and I run, but nothing tires me. Nothing quiets the darkness. I can't outrun my problems anymore. There are so many things on my mind; I'm tempted to keep going and never come back.

One mile melts into two, which melts into five and then ten. By the time I calm down enough to loop back toward the castle, the afternoon is slipping away between gaps in the gray cloud.

I take the muddy track that runs along the far end of the tarn and up the left side back toward the castle. The tarn is still, undisturbed by the soft breeze.

I'm about to veer back into the trees when something catches my eye. A neon orange balloon, or a float of some kind, drifting across the black water. I follow its path to the bank, where a small figure lies passed out in the shallows.

I swear my heart stops beating.

Dread shoots up my spine like a bullet, my feet breaking out into a sprint beneath me. She's far enough away for me to jump to a hundred conclusions as I run.

She's dead.

She drowned.

No. She's the best swimmer I know.

She can't have just drowned.

I dial Belladonna on the way but she doesn't pick up. I try again, and again once more, skidding to a halt when I reach her.

My pulse hammers in my throat. This isn't apathy, this isn't gray. This isn't *nothing*, this is pure and utter dread.

She's lying on her back in nothing but a black swimsuit when I fall to my knees in the soft mire beside us. The icy water laps around her head, licking at the skin on my legs. A bitter chill sinks deep into my bones.

She looks like her Shakespearean namesake.

With my heart in the firm grip of terror, I drag her out of the water, feeling a weak pulse beneath my fingers. She's devoid of all warmth. Her lips are blue, limbs white. Dirt and blood are smeared down the side of her face. She's breathing, just.

This was no accident.

"Ophelia, can you hear me? Jesus fucking Christ, Ophelia."

I don't have time to panic. Don't have time to think, feel, or pause. I pinch her nose, sealing my mouth against her frozen lips, breathing a steady breath into her lungs.

I have to be calm. I have to hold it together for her.

Belladonna's name lights up on my phone as I breathe a third breath into Ophelia's limp body. "Bella, I need you on the bank of the tarn. Emergency." I seal my lips over Ophelia's again.

Don't die.

Don't leave me.

You occupy my mind.

Those stupid crosswords. You're those for me. You're the cage for my thoughts.

The busy sounds of a ward filter through the loudspeaker. "I'm on rotation at Raigmore. Is Vin okay?"

"Then I need a goddamn air ambulance."

"Is Vincenzo okay? Hold on." The phone goes quiet. She picks it up a moment later. "It's out on another call. I'll send another fifth year down now."

I cover Ophelia with her towel and my hoodie, but not before I spot the finger-shaped bruises on her neck.

I swear, I've never felt a fire like it.

"No, don't." I can't trust anyone. "Ophelia's been drowned."

"She's drowned, or *been* drowned?"

"Just fucking talk me through it. She's hardly breathing."

"Open her mouth and breathe for her."

She's so cold beneath my fingers. Her lips are so still beneath mine. I should've kissed her in the trees. Should've made her see how much she mattered. "It's not working. Fuck, it's not working."

"Alex, the calmer you are, the easier this'll be. You know chest compressions, yeah?"

I've done them for my mother once before. I shrug the memory away before it drags me into the cloud. "Yes."

"Start them. Harder than you think you need to."

I layer my hands over her chest and press. Blood trickles across her cheek and down her neck, onto the mud below. There are claw marks from her fingers beneath her.

The anger threatens to incinerate me.

Belladonna is calm on the other end of the line. "More breaths."

"God, Ophelia. Wake up," I whisper between them. I start the compressions again. "Please wake up."

Wake up, Maman. It's me.

I shake my head, focusing on the body beneath me. If I can't save her, I'll be everything my father always said I'd be.

"Breaths again. Does she have a pulse?"

I grit my teeth. My heart beats too fast between my ribs. Hers doesn't beat fast enough. "Yes."

"That's good."

It goes on forever. Until my arms are burning and I'm losing hope. She's cold and still and silent. The fire beneath her skin is missing. Does she know I'm fighting for her? Does she believe she's worth fighting for?

Her chest contracts with a cough beneath me, wet and ragged and weak. "She's choking."

I hear a car door slam on the other end of the line. She barks rapid Italian at her driver. "That's good. That's *great*, Alex. Roll her onto her side. I'm on my way."

Belladonna must've texted Vincenzo, because he's running toward me with blankets in his arms. I roll Ophelia onto her side, watching her cough up more water than anyone should.

Her breaths steady out. Her pulse builds to a steady drum beneath my fingertips. Gratitude gently prizes the claws of dread from my chest, allowing me to take a full inhale. If I could cry, now would be the time.

I pull her frozen body onto my lap, wrapping her in blankets. "I have you," I whisper against the dirt on her forehead. "You're okay."

A quiet sob escapes her lips, her whisper barely audible. Her head leans into me the smallest amount. "I'm cold."

I tighten my arms around her limp frame and don't intend to ever release them. I feel like I could vomit. "I know. I know, baby. I'm so sorry."

Vincenzo presses her freezing finger against the button of her phone and opens up her meager list of contacts while I dry her skin. He rings her dad, but it goes straight to voice mail.

He hits Dial on her mom's contact. It rings three times. Then four. I'm frustrated with them. Angry with them for not picking up.

Don't they care?

I brush strands of Ophelia's beautiful hair from her face, wrapping her hands in blankets. I run my finger over each of her eyebrows. *Does she know she matters?* "Try them again later."

I can't look away from the bruises on her neck, blinded with rage. "Ophelia, who did this to you?"

I don't get my answer. She's fast asleep in my arms. The rhythm of her chest is slow and steady in time with the briny water lapping the bank. I focus on each breath. It's the final remaining chain on the cage that hides the monster inside me.

She's alive. *You did enough, Alex.* Dr. Harwood would be proud.

Like she's made of rice paper, I carry her back to the mansion, hiding her face from curious watchers. I put her in my bed until Belladonna arrives, because I don't know what else to do. Vincenzo tucks a Glock into his waistband and leaves on a manhunt.

Ophelia's damp hair spills over the white sheets, the muscles of her legs covered in bruises and scrapes. She looks like that stupid painting in the hall outside Carmichael's office.

I want to put my fist through the wall.

I sit with her head in my lap, a bowl of warm water beside me as I wipe the cuts and scratches across her face clean. I can't bear not knowing who it was. I need her to wake up.

I brush my lips against her hair and tell her she's okay, and that she's doing fine. That I have her where no one can get her. I hope my voice permeates the fog.

"*Cazzo*. What the fuck happened?" asks Belladonna, finally arriving with a green duffel bag of medical supplies.

I run my fingers over Ophelia's scalp like my mother used to do for me, like I do for Josie when she can't sleep. I hope it brings her comfort. "Someone attacked her."

Belladonna pegs a fucking IV treatment bag to my headboard and gets a sharps disposal kit out of the duffel. "Who?"

I clench my fist so hard my nails leave moon-shaped cuts in my palms. "If I knew, I wouldn't be sat here. Vincenzo is out looking."

"Did he take someone with him? Kirill and his men are looking for any chance they can get to kill him."

"He took two men with him."

She nods, but the line of worry between her brows doesn't smooth. I get it. I spend my whole life worrying about my siblings.

Bella works for two hours. By the time she's removed the IV therapy bag and walked a half-awake Ophelia into my bathroom, every bruise, cut, and scrape on her body has been carefully disinfected.

The sound of the bath tap running filters beneath the door. I sink to the chair at my desk and rest my head against my palms. It's been a long time since I've felt so deeply. Hell, it's been a long time since I've *felt*.

I've known it since I almost ran her over in the car. Since I first watched her swim, since I found out she must be the only person under the age of fifty to wear mittens, since I found out she does puzzles to escape the gray cloud of her own, since I watched her close and reopen the lid of her laptop to try to fix every IT issue

222

under the sun. Since I heard her in her room, laughing and sobbing at a movie in the same thirty-minute period.

I could go on forever.

I'm obsessed with her. Desperate for her. But I could never be good for her, and for reasons she doesn't make clear, she doesn't want me to love her.

Belladonna steps out of my bathroom. Ophelia is crying quietly inside. "She'll be fine. Physically, at least. I'll ask Carmichael to see if CCTV picked anything up."

I nod, not sure what to say. I'm tired.

I knock on the bathroom door. I hate crying. I hate it when my mother cries, when my sisters cry. I hate it when Ophelia cries, too. "Can I come in?"

"If you want to."

She's sitting in the lukewarm water of the bath, a wet towel around her shoulders. Her face is badly bruised. Two of her fingers are in a bandage. I fight to keep the anger under wraps, because anger is not what she needs from me. I kneel at the edge of the bath. She doesn't look at me. The circles under her eyes are so dark, a tinge of blue beneath her almost translucent skin.

"Can I help you?" I offer, stroking her hair but careful not to touch her.

She shakes her head, her voice broken and hoarse. "I'm trying to stay away from you."

It sounds like a lie, no conviction behind her words, but pointing that out won't do either of us any favors. "I know. Just let me help." I glance at my watch. It's almost seven. "Let me help you until midnight. Tomorrow is a new day. We can go back to how we were."

She nods weakly, and I open the cabinet to take out a spare toothbrush, picking up her left hand to start cleaning the mud caked beneath her nails. This is as selfish as it is selfless. Helping her keeps the gray cloud at bay. "We tried calling your parents, but we couldn't get hold of them."

She shrugs, bottom lip trembling. Her gaze is glassy and unfocused, blinking like the bathroom is too bright. She looks like her spirit is broken. "They're bad at phones. They don't understand them."

"I'd never have guessed, looking at your technological prowess."

A small smile graces her pinkening lips, and my god, it's a smile that's going to ruin my life. It's a smile I'll replay in my head each night as I lie in that blissful space between awake and asleep.

A tear runs down her cheek. I brush it away with my thumb. "I'll call them later. Don't worry them."

"Okay," I whisper, lowering her clean hand back into the warm water.

"I don't like you," she repeats. "This isn't...this doesn't mean anything."

I sense her panic, though I don't understand it. I ache to kiss the freckles on her shoulder where the towel has slipped off. "Ophelia, this doesn't have to be anything more than one heartbeat helping another."

She nods, falling silent for a while as I clean her hands and feet.

"Belladonna says you saved my life."

"Not without her help."

I move behind her, running a brush through the copper waves that run down to the small of her back. A small sob splinters the silence. And then another. "I'll thank you one day, when I'm grateful."

I can't help it. I rest my forehead against her shoulder blades, taking comfort in the rhythm of her heart beneath her skin. "You don't owe me anything."

Ophelia feels like finding another human after months in the desert. A light permeating the thick black cloud. When my wayward mind wanders, it staggers back home to her.

She's everything I've been asking the universe for, and she fucking *hates* me.

I brush her hair at the pace of a snail just to drag out the time I can be this close to her, rinsing it with warm water. Only the gentle dripping of the tap and the sound of her sniffling fill the room. "I need to know who did this to you. For my own sanity, I need to know."

"I need my phone."

I grab it from her bag, carefully drying the tips of her fingers so she can use it.

She opens a long thread of emails, crying like showing me was the last thing she wanted to do. Like she hates herself for it. Her pale skin turns even whiter. "There's a new one. From thirty minutes ago."

"A new what?"

"A new email."

I peer over at her screen. There's an email from a name I don't recognize. It's a Hamlet quote, so sickeningly perfect for this afternoon that my breath catches in my throat.

Too much of water hast thou, poor Ophelia, and therefore I forbid my tears.

She places the device on the edge of the bath and buries her face into her hands. "I fucking *hate* this place, but Carmichael won't let me leave."

I scroll through the emails. They range from creepy, to strange, to downright terrifying for her. Sofia, the emails, *this*; she's had too much on her plate. I put the phone down before I snap it into two. The burning need for blood that I'd quashed after my fight with Shawn comes back twice as strong. "Who is Alan?"

I'll kill him.

"I don't know. He comes into my bedroom when I'm not there. He watched me swim at the tarn before, back in September." She wipes her tears away. "He killed Sofia. He drugged me. I thought it was you at first."

I try hard not to be offended that she thinks I'd do those things. Maybe she's right. I might rot into my father as I age.

Her next statement is quiet, like she's not sure if she can trust me. "I'm ninety-nine percent sure it's Carmichael."

Carmichael? It feels unlikely, but I'm wary of not believing her. "Why?"

"You said he had Brontë out on his desk when I was under the sofa in his office." She scrolls to an email from that morning. "I got this a few moments before. And a few weeks ago, Carmichael shouted at me. He said my mother was no angel, but he said it like he hated—*hates*—her."

I reread each email one by one and frown. Carmichael does love classical literature, but I've known him since I was seven, and he couldn't hurt a fly. And he so rarely sends emails. He still uses a typewriter to send letters. "Anyone else you can think of? Could it be Shawn?"

Maybe he was so mad that I almost killed him, he took it out on her at the lake. I should've killed the bastard.

The muscles in her shoulders tense, her head rolling on her knees so she's staring at the dark green tiles on the bathroom wall. "You don't believe me."

I run a cloth down her arm, trying to satisfy the deep-rooted need in me to look after her. It's one of the few good things I've got as a result of my father's shitty behavior. "I believe you have a stalker, Twist. I'm just trying to work out who it is so I can help you."

When she doesn't reply, I change the subject and stand, tugging a warm towel off the rail. "Do you want to come out?"

She nods. The wide, innocent look in her eyes almost knocks me back to my knees. "You won't look down?"

I fix my eyes on hers. On the color of caramel and Scotch whisky. On the brown lashes that fan out above them, clumped together with tears. "I won't look down."

I don't break eye contact as I help her up on shaky legs. As I steady her shoulders while she runs the towel over her naked skin. I don't break it as I lay out my sweatpants for her to step into, or as I tie them at the waist.

I don't break eye contact, and I don't want to.

I want her trust.

I deposit her back onto my bed, swamped in my clothes. She doesn't complain, or maybe she's just too tired to. Until I have *Alan* buried underground, I want her here. I drop a text to Rocco, Vincenzo's father, asking him to get his men to keep an eye on Ophelia whenever I'm out of the country.

"This doesn't mean anything," she repeats.

Not to you.

I know I'm only making life harder for myself, but I lie down beside her. I've split myself into so many pieces for so many people, I haven't got the fight left in me to be selfless anymore.

She rolls onto her side with a wince that makes me want to burn the world down; she's gazing over at me. The soft expression over her delicate features is enough to slow my racing heart. "Why'd you drop out of Yale, Alex?"

I'm in uncharted territory, unsure whether to trust her when she clearly doesn't trust me. "Why'd you lie about your parents?"

Fresh tears pool on her lashes. I swipe them away with my thumb. "If I told you, you'd judge me for not telling you sooner. I can't get close to you. Can't trust you with my heart. We just won't work together, Alex. I have to stay away from you, I just can't find the strength to."

Welcome to my world. I trace the subtle curve of her jawline with my fingers, gaze stuck on the bruising that stains her neck. Her lashes flutter shut. "Until midnight you can."

"And then we won't speak again?"

"If that's what you want." It might finish me off, though.

She sighs. "My life is boring. I don't have a big family, or an eight-bedroom mansion. I don't have big, exciting holidays or lavish Christmas plans. Or *any* Christmas plans, really. My parents aren't fancy government officials."

There's something in her eye that makes me feel it's not the whole truth, but I don't push her. Every inch with Ophelia feels like a mile. "You're not boring. Not to me. You've lost yourself, but I can see you. I agree that you're complicated. What's the alternative? That you're simple?"

Now doesn't feel like the best time for the *ogres have layers* spiel I give to my sisters.

My thumb skirts onto dangerous territory, over her chapped bottom lip, freeing it from her teeth. "I left Yale because my mother was—*is*—unwell. I stayed at home for two years to try to…fix her. She didn't cope well with me moving out, and my father didn't make her treatment a priority, so I left. Someone had to be at home to help, and I was happy for it to be me."

"You switched from architecture to business when you came here."

"I switched from pipe dream to practicality."

Her tears run over her endless freckles. I fight the urge to kiss them away. "Will she get better?"

"I don't know." I roll onto my back and stare at the vaulted ceiling. I don't know what makes me open up. I don't know why I spill my secrets to a girl who hates me. I've run out of self-discipline for the week. "I know what I need to do. I just can't do it."

She's holding her breath. "Which is?"

The cloud fills every corner of my chest, constricting my veins, shrinking my lungs. "Find her a live-in facility." Away from my father. "But my youngest sisters are eight and ten. They'd go from breakfast in her bed to weekend visiting hours."

Her hand wraps around mine. "Your father?"

My father. The monster bangs on its cage inside me, desperate to get out. "The only comment my father has made on the matter for months is that she's bad publicity. He used to love her. Not so much now."

She buries her head farther into my chest, like she's as desperate for my warmth as I am to warm her. I wrap both arms around her.

Four hours until midnight. I want each and every one. "How did it all start?"

My fingers tangle in Ophelia's hair. "It was gradual. The fame ate at her. It still eats at her. She spent so long in the spotlight. Every mole, freckle, hair, outfit, gram of fat on her body blown up on the front covers of magazines for years on end. After Josie was born, she had seven children. Her body had changed. I watched the lines on her body be picked apart in a way that lines on my father's were not; in a way that men's bodies are not. She started to believe what they said. That she'd lost her value, that she had *expired*. She started getting more erratic. Chopping her hair off, burning clothes that were out of season. The media call it 'high maintenance.'"

She holds me like she thinks I'll snap, but I won't. While they need me, I'll be unbreakable. "And what do the doctors call it?"

"Depression. Bipolar. Severe schizophrenia."

"I'm so sorry," she says on a broken sob.

I don't cry. Can't cry. Emotionally stunted, just like my father says he and I are. Even with the thought of my mother slipping away from me like sand between my fingers, I can't. If I pricked my finger now, I think I'd bleed gray.

It's the smallest of touches, but her lips press against the fabric over my chest. It spreads through my skin like a false promise.

I loathe her at that moment.

That she could do these things to me but tell me she hates me. That she could fill my chest with poisonous hope, knowing I can't stay away. Knowing that she wouldn't accept my love if I tried to give it to her.

Ophelia is my deadly nightshade. She's bad for me. I know what she'll do to me, but she's too beautiful. Too enticing. She's too deep in my bloodstream already, painful and ecstatic all at once.

She falls asleep with her head buried in my chest and her legs tangled around mine. I'm not strong enough to untangle them. I'm not strong enough to leave her when the clock hits midnight.

For once, I take what *I* need, do what *I* want. For the first time in a long time, I fall asleep with all the pieces of myself united here in Sorrowsong Valley.

Chapter 19

OPHELIA

D ivya sits at the foot of Alex's bed, painting my toenails a
deep purple. Maybe matching your nails to your bruises is
a trend I'll start.

"I'm so sorry I believed you killed your roommate."

"No, I get it. The alternative was believing I got into bed with
the son of Cain Green."

"Yeah, I couldn't imagine you doing that, but…"

But I'm in his bed now. I understand her confusion, because I
don't really know what I'm doing here, either. I sleep well here.
Alex put an extra lock on the door for me. I have a toothbrush here.
And he has a bath in his bathroom.

"It's complicated with him, I…I don't know."

Her eyebrows wiggle. "But how is it?"

"We haven't." I feel my cheeks flame. "I've never been with
anyone."

"Neither have I," says Divya on a sigh. "My father will never forgive me for being asexual."

"Maybe he'll come around." I fiddle with the bandage on my hand, oddly nervous. "I've put normal things on pause for a long time. I haven't worried about boys or panicked over my appearance or gone clothes shopping in forever."

"You do kind of need a new wardrobe. Or maybe just *one* item of clothing that isn't brown."

My bruised fingers pick at lint on the blanket. "You sound like Alex."

"Maybe he's not that bad. His life is kind of thrust into the spotlight against his will. He doesn't seem like his father. And he can draw, and he plays rugby. And he's in *great* shape, and he has a big dick."

I choke on my own inhale. "You've seen it?" I don't know why I'm praying she says no. I have no right to be this possessive over someone I keep saying I don't want.

"There was this whole thing last year. He went running in Central Park in gray shorts. Google 'Alex Corbeau-Green Viral Gray Shorts.'"

"Uhh…no, thank you."

"Your loss."

"Is he paying you an hourly wage to say this?"

She laughs, sending a smudge of purple over my toe. "Yeah. How'd you think I paid for my new car? He's got a lot on his plate, and he seems like he treats his family well, is all I'm saying."

I breathe out a long sigh and drop my head against his giant pillows. "I know, but it won't work with him. I'll either have to swallow the fact that his father let that helicopter go down and get over it, or I'll have to make his family the subject of a huge media storm. He wouldn't forgive me for that."

"He might."

"And I've not been honest with him; I've not told him about my parents, or that I only came here to ruin his home life."

"I'm not sure he has much of a home life left to be ruined."

"He does. He has his sisters."

"Maybe it's just not meant to be. You'll find someone else." She hides her smile. "Anyone but Shawn Miller."

I rub my palms down my reddening cheeks as she switches over to my other foot. "I have bad taste. I'll need to strike the balance between the poster boy for investment banking and the spawn of Satan."

Even if the spawn of Satan has a voice that gives me goose bumps and eyes that could burn me to ashes.

Between Divya, Vincenzo, and Colette, no one has left my side since I woke up the day after Alex found me on the bank of the tarn. Even Belladonna has been by to check on me. I keep pinching myself to check if this is real. In some twisted, strange way, it feels like having a family.

Three days, a mild chest infection, and two broken fingers later, I don't feel much stronger than I did when I lay in the shallows of the water.

All I can remember is *him*.

The warmth of him. The desperation in his voice as he begged me to wake up, and the desperation *I* felt when I couldn't open my eyes for him. The feel of his lips against mine. Not erotic, but primal. One body breathing life into another.

And then the way he ran the hairbrush through my hair in the bathtub. The way it filled an aching hole in my chest, a desperate need to be cherished.

And the way he spoke about his mother. I've cried about it since. It made my compassion for her swell, but it has made my hatred for his father burn so much hotter.

Nothing scorches like the self-loathing, though. The crushing guilt that under the soft moonlight, lying between his sheets, Alex opened up to me in a way that no one ever has, and that I fed him a string of half-truths in return.

I don't know what he sees in me, but I can't accept his love.

I feel *so* deeply. I always have. Every emotion that runs through me goes through an amplifier on the way in. The tiny inconveniences feel like mountains, the annoyances become insurmountable wrath. I cry at charity adverts, laugh at dogs in the park. I can't watch someone feel blue and not let it stain me too.

My mind is a chaotic blend of too many colors, too bright, too busy, too loud. The color red threads its way around all the others.

Mike's dying confession is on an MP3 file on my laptop. It only took three hours of angry crying over the instruction manual to manage it. It sits at the base of four years of evidence, of deleted articles and whispers of corruption at Green Aviation. Rumors of decay that start at the very top and drip their way through board-rooms and into the shop floor below. Four years of sleepless nights, and Laura's tape is the bow that ties it all together.

I wish I had that folder from the red box, but more than that, I wish I knew what to do.

Alex left during that first night, after his sister rang him to say no one had come to her ballet. He's been radio silent since. Perhaps he's honoring my request for space. I'm grateful, but I wish it didn't ache.

I watch him shave slivers of himself off each time that phone rings. It's a miracle there's anything left.

The mattress dips as Divya sits back on her heels. "All done!"

I wiggle my toes and smile. They're pretty. "Thank you."

"Hey." She grasps my hand. "We're going to catch him. And when we do, Colette will jam a stiletto in his eye."

"I hope so." I squeeze her hand tighter. I'm so grateful for them all. So grateful to have friendships, contacts in my phone, borrowed clothes in my drawers. "Thank you for staying with me, I mean it. And I'm really sorry about…everything. I've been a mess. My career dreams are abandoned, I'm scared to go swimming, and I'm not even sure what to do with my report on Cain."

"There is no shame in changing your priorities. You can forget the report for now, see where things go with Alex, or find someone else entirely." She stands, armed with a marker and sticky notes, and returns to the evidence wall we started earlier. Every possible stalker is mapped out, complete with drawings that made us laugh so hard we nearly died. If Carmichael saw my attempt at drawing him, he'd expel me.

Under Carmichael's likeness, *keeping Ophelia trapped here* is scribbled out. I got a signed letter from the chancellor, waiving all tuition fees should I choose to quit. It's a relief, but it also triggers an alarm bell somewhere in the back of my mind. If he is my stalker, would he be so willing to let me go?

Every time I think I'm sure, I start to doubt myself. Part of me wants to ask Alex for help, and the other half would rather drown. Again.

I can't stop thinking about him.

What are his visits back home like?

Divya attempts to draw Shawn Miller, the distance between his eyes approximately the length of a football field. "What is that?" I screech, pointing to what looks like a dick hanging off his top lip. My bruised ribs ache with every sob of laughter.

She folds over, snorting so violently that both her hands land on the floor. I think we're both past the point of sanity. "His nose! I'm a medic, okay? I can't draw or write."

A door sounds at the end of the hallway. Footsteps approach, heavy and slow. *Shit.* Isn't he in New York?

Alex's broad frame fills the doorway, eyes scanning the wall of nightmare-inducing caricatures. If I look tired, he looks *exhausted*. His black shirt is undone at the top, tucked into black slacks, and a belt at his tapered waist. His hair is longer, messier than when I first met him, damp from the rain outside. His sculpted lips are parted, slightly breathless. He drops his heavy bag at his feet, both hands grabbing the frame above the door.

He's a masterpiece. A culmination of the universe's finest work.

"What the fuck is going on?"

"Uh…brainstorm," I blurt out, like someone who has never interacted with another human before.

"I was just leaving," says Divya, sticking a dick-nosed Shawn Miller on my forehead.

Alex looks like he's too spent to ask questions, stepping inside and tossing his car keys onto the desk.

I lock the door behind Divya, gathering my books from the bed. "Sorry, I'll go back to my room. I just…I thought you were still in the States."

He pulls the yellow sticky note from my forehead and peers down at it. "Shawn Miller."

"*What?*"

"It really captures how much of a wanker he is."

I bite my lip to contain my smile. I heard a rumor that Alex beat the shit out of Miller in the Nightshade gym. He sticks the note on the wall and cracks the arch-shaped window beside his desk. The cherry of the cigarette tucked between his lips smolders as he lights it. His eyes glow yellow above the flame. "Why haven't your parents visited?"

My hands pause where they pack up my things to leave. "What?"

"You were five minutes from death, and they've not come to see you."

"It's complicated. They're…not around to visit me."

He smokes in silence, free hand in his pocket as he stares out the window. I'm not sure if he's waiting for me to elaborate, but I don't. Telling Alex about the reason I came here feels like my final resignation; confirmation I've given up.

As always with him, I wonder what runs through his mind. He keeps his emotions so buried; I'd kill to know just one of them. I get the impression the inside of his mind is not a good place to be.

The strong cords of his forearms flex as he stubs the cigarette out on an ashtray. The air is thick with words neither of us want to say and actions we both know we shouldn't take. I press my thighs together and force myself to look away.

He paces over to where I sit at the edge of the bed, each of his legs landing either side of mine. I shudder, wondering how he can make me feel so naked without ever touching my clothes. I hold my breath and shake my head. "Don't."

238

"Don't what?"

"Don't kiss me."

He cocks an eyebrow, walking his hands over the bed until I'm lying on my back and he's hovering over me. "No? And why not?"

He smells of smoke and bourbon and something that's just so Alex. The solid curve of his chest brushes mine on his next inhale. *Bloody hell.* What is a girl meant to do? His scent clings to the sheets, his heat caresses my skin. I need out before I do something stupid. "It'd probably be a letdown, anyway. Too much anticipation."

A soft pair of lips brush my cheek. "Oh, but I think the anticipation would make it even sweeter." They trace the lobe of my ear. "Even more *satiating*." They find the sensitive skin of my neck. His voice is a husky grumble. "Did you miss me?"

Yes.

I ignore the question, but I only feel his wicked grin widen against my throat. "Did you miss me, Ophelia?"

I shuffle my body against his, regretting it instantly. We both let in a sharp exhale as the hard muscles of his thigh brush the soft inside of my own.

I'm being suffocated by my own treacherous desire.

He pulls away, verdant eyes gazing down at me with a tender expression that scares me and nurtures me all at once. "One down. Seven letters. First letter *O. I've had a long day, and I want her for dinner.*"

Holy *fuck.*

He says the last sentence so hungrily that it makes me drag my knees up to try to put distance between us.

It doesn't work.

The two people stuck inside me can't decide what they want anymore. *Make sweet, gentle love!* screams one. *Let him break your bed!* shouts the other.

Traitors.

I let my lashes drift shut and pretend the hand that carefully skirts around the bruises on my neck belongs to anyone but him. "Two across. Eight letters. First letter *A*. *The quality of being unpleasantly proud.*"

"You think I'm arrogant?"

I think he's one of the most incredible people I've ever met. "Yeah."

"Tell me you missed me."

I look back up at him, at the hunger in his gaze. "I'd rather choke you."

His eyes smolder, lips part. "You could've told me that was an option."

I run my fingers down his back over the crisp fabric of his shirt, feeling the ridges and dips beneath. It's a new world to me. *He's* a new world to me. I breathe out a curse and let my limbs flop down to the bed, coming to my senses.

"You got selective hearing, sugar?"

I laugh at the nickname, stroking my chin as if deep in thought. "Yeah, and…oh man. It looks like you've not been selected. Good luck next time, though."

"You're a fucking nightmare, Winters." He lowers from his hands to his forearms, his body flush against mine. I grasp the bedsheets tighter, breaths coming shorter.

God, I want this.

"What's stopping you?" he asks, eyes suddenly sincere. His fingers interlace at the top of my head, his elbows by my ears, caging me in. I'm hyperaware of the weight of him, the heat of him on top of me.

I've never felt like this before. It's not just desire. It's *more*.

"It's complicated."

He drops his head down to my neck in a way that's so endearing, so un-Alex, that an embarrassing whimper escapes me. "Doesn't matter. I'll find it and I'll fix it for you."

"Can you fix the fact that I don't like you?"

He doesn't call me out on my lie, instead tapping my phone screen beside us to see the time: 4:32 p.m. "Like me until five. Then we can go back to before."

I want to believe that there's some alternate universe where he and I could be together. Where it wouldn't matter that his father killed my parents and that I made it public. Where his sisters could forgive me, and I could look at him and not see his father, or helicopters, or endless NDAs.

I wrap my hands around his arms to push him away, but they linger there, momentarily mesmerized by the feel of another life beneath my fingers. For so long they've known inanimate things. It's been an age since they've felt the buzz of a pulse, the soft way that skin dips under pressure, the way that a current of warmth seems to flow through the points of contact between us, thawing my insides.

To feed the starving loneliness inside me, I selfishly let myself touch him. I undo another button of his shirt and run my fingers over his chest, feeling the heart that beats for everyone except himself. He lifts his head, tracking every small movement of my fingers like he can hardly believe they're real.

I press his forehead against mine and close my eyes. I want to lose myself in him. Just once. One last time. I almost give in. But no—it's kinder this way, for him and for me.

"No," I whisper. "I just *can't*."

He rolls off me immediately and shuts his eyes as if in pain. "*Why?*"

"It's complicated."

A ragged growl fills the air between us. "I hate that fucking word."

"It's the only word for it."

"I don't see how it's complicated." He scrubs his face in his hands. "Do you want me or do you hate me? You can't do both. You can't have both. It's not possible. In a world full of complicated, Ophelia, my feelings for you are extremely simple."

"Things aren't black and white. Not for me."

He looks defeated, like somehow it's his fault that I'm not happy here. I long to wrap my arms around him and tell him that he's doing fine and that he's doing enough. But it's not my place.

He'll find someone right for him. Someone who can love him without complication. Someone capable of emotions that aren't tainted by anger. Someone else will know the feeling of his body against theirs. The thought makes me feel unwell. And then the fact that the thought makes me unwell makes me feel even sicker.

I have to get out of here before I'm in too deep. "We can be friends?" I offer, to assuage my guilt. I cringe as soon as I say it. It sounds dumb, and neither of us wants to be friends.

"Friends who fuck each other's brains out?" he offers, like it's a business negotiation.

"Friends who say hi in the hallway."

His smile lightens the mood, tone unserious. "Friends who fuck in the hallway?"

I decline his compromise, but it does make me laugh. He looks around the room as if searching for a distraction. "Can I borrow your laptop?"

"What for?"

"I want to track the emails you've had. See if I can find anything out."

I take my laptop from my bag and log in, closing the open document before he gets a chance to see. Guilt pangs in my stomach.

He takes the laptop and plugs it into his own on the desk, opening the bottom drawer. He tugs out a few more cables.

My eyes land on the brown folder at the bottom of the drawer.

The folder from the red box.

The folder I've been looking for.

"What's that?"

He shuts the drawer and locks it. "Just a folder."

My voice is strained, but he doesn't notice. "You strike me as an electronic sort of guy."

He snorts, logging into his laptop. Some sort of code appears on the screen. "I am. It's just work stuff for my father."

Work stuff. Is that what the crash was? Work stuff? Did Alex know it was going to happen?

He hits Enter on his keyboard. "Give it a couple of minutes."

"You're not stealing all my files, are you?" I ask, half joking.

Maybe a little less than half.

243

He steps into the small kitchenette and pours hot water into a cafetière and a mug, chucking a teabag in the mug for me. He sets it on the desk in front of my fidgeting hands. I whisper an inaudible thank-you. This all feels too familiar, too homely. "Yeah, I'm really desperate to read your Lord of the Rings fan fiction."

"Shut up. You don't even know who Gandalf is." And that was *one* time when I was eleven, and technically Thranduil is in *The Hobbit*.

Why is that folder in his drawer?

He puffs his chest, fiddling with the spaghetti of wires in front of us. How do people just know how to do these things? "Yes, I do. It's the kingdom with the men."

"That's Gondor. I swear you do this stuff to annoy me."

He leans over my shoulder and types something on my laptop. His voice is low and gruff in my ear. "I thought that was the hot guy?"

Now it's my turn to sigh. "That's Aragorn."

"What? Isn't that the spider in Harry Potter?"

I shake my head and give up. He stifles a yawn, sitting back down at the desk that now looks like something out of a sci-fi movie. "Let's take a look at the IP address and device info."

"You can see an IP address from an email?"

"Surprised you even know what one is."

"Well, that's rude."

"Ophelia, you don't even know what a page break is. You just hit Enter fifteen times. I spent the whole coursework deleting them all. If a caveman were here, he'd say you were even shittier at technology than him."

"If a caveman were here, he'd probably say *oog* or *ugg*."

His laugh stokes a fire in my chest. The skin beneath my tights sizzles where it brushes against his thigh. I nibble my thumbnail, trying to ignore the way he's gazing down at me.

Why has he got the folder?

He turns his focus back to his screen. "They were sent here at Sorrowsong, from a laptop and not a phone."

"How'd you know?"

"I'll teach you." His large hand wraps around the leg of my chair, pulling me closer to his side. The move leaves me weak at the knees. "From this top line here. Does the name mean anything to you? Alan Sine?"

I shake my head. I could tell him the truth, but then he'd know my mother's name. He'd probably be able to figure out she worked here. He'd probably be able to figure out she died here, too.

I'm an awful person.

Whatever this stalker has planned for me, I deserve it.

I cannot have Alex and not tell him my past. I can't be with him and tear his family into two like I always dreamed I would. The two can't exist together.

If I want him, I have to come clean.

Chapter 20

OPHELIA

My return to the real world and to Sorrowsong is gradual.
I've not seen Alex in days. It's harder than I expected;
I have no good reason for missing him, but I do. I miss
the way he laughs at my bad moods and runny nose.

I miss his quiet belief in everything I do.

I'm trying to keep my mind busy with swimming and studying.
Colette has been kindly letting me into the Cortinar gym so I can
avoid the Nightshade one, and I even spent an evening in her halls.
While the Nightshade mansion looks right out of a Regency horror movie, the Cortinar halls are plucked from between the pages
of an F. Scott Fitzgerald novel.

Rich velvet drapes sit beside geometric artwork, sleek grand
pianos, and glitzy cocktail bars serving dry martinis. You can't hear
the wind howling, only the soft sound of jazz filtering through the
jukebox. I'm a little bit bitter that I wasn't in a different house.

And all the while, Carmichael's letter burns a hole in my pocket. Now that my revenge plan is wavering slightly, my long-abandoned childhood dreams are creeping in to fill the void. There was a second reason I accepted my place here, though I have lost track of it over the last few weeks. A chance to swim at nationals, a career in child psychology; Sorrowsong is my free ticket to them all.

Now that I have the chance, I can't quite bring myself to leave.

My effort to get good grades begins with a study session with Dr. Bancroft. I'm behind on all my modules, but he's patient with me. He explains each lecture between mouthfuls of wasabi peas. His clothes are crumpled as ever, the gray hair of his eyebrows so long it almost droops over his eyes.

"I promise I'll be better next year," I say, sticking a Post-it note in my textbook.

"Don't worry, you're doing fine. Although, I might not teach here next year."

"Oh." That's a little disappointing. "Why?"

He paces the length of his office, dusting the green wasabi dust onto his black trousers. "Sorrowsong is losing its charm for me. Just look at what happened to you. I think I'd like to go to a normal university, where my biggest worry is whether the student shop has a good bakery."

"That makes two of us. Carmichael is looking into what happened to me. The CCTV in and around the mansion was erased that day."

"That's terribly convenient."

247

"Maybe he'll find something out." I'm determined to be optimistic. I pick up my phone and swallow down my smile at an email from Alex.

From: Alex Corbeau-Green
Subject: Begging (noun) *ask someone earnestly or humbly for something*
Date: Friday 21st November 16:48 BST
To: Ophelia Winters

Unblock my number. This is getting old.

I type out a quick reply, instantly regretting it. He's like an addiction I'm trying to drop.

From: Ophelia Winters
Subject: RE: Begging (noun) *ask someone earnestly or humbly for something*
Date: Friday 21st November 16:49 BST
To: Alex Corbeau-Green

There's nothing humble or earnest about you.

His reply comes immediately.

From: Alex Corbeau-Green
Subject: Not focusing on my workout anymore
Date: Friday 21st November 16:49 BST
To: Ophelia Winters

Meet me under the rugby stands. I'll get on my knees and show you just how humble I can be.

Fucking hell. I sit up straighter and stare at my notes even though I cannot at this moment remember where I am or what I'm studying.

Bancroft stops pacing. "I'm surprised you'd trust Harris with that."

I shut off my phone and my wayward thoughts. "Why? What do you know?"

"I shouldn't say. Carmichael is a…he's a man with great power. Not just here in Sorrowsong, but all over the world. He's on the board of multiple companies. He has millions, *billions*, even."

"Please," I whisper, my hands together. I'm tired of half-truths and throwaway comments.

"Carmichael was not fond of your mother. Not at all."

My leg starts drumming nervously beneath the table. So he did hate her. Did he hate her enough to bribe Cain to kill her? "Why?"

Bancroft seems unwilling to answer my questions. Maybe Carmichael is holding something over him. "I'd be very careful of upsetting him, or you'll…"

My whisper is almost inaudible. "Or I'll what?"

He doesn't reply, but the words linger between us all the same. *Or I'll end up like my mother.*

I feel nauseous. I throw my textbooks into my bag, dizzy on my feet. "Thank you as always, sir."

"Ms. Winters," he calls, stopping me as I hurtle out the door. I glance over my shoulder at him. He looks genuinely worried. "Don't let Carmichael know I said anything."

"I swear."

I check the time as I speed down the steps of the tallest turret. I've stayed too long.

The Friday afternoon helicopter is going to come in any minute. I'm not going to make it to my room.

I run down the hallway and out into the courtyard, begging it to be a few minutes late. I can't face the noise. Not the week of the fourth anniversary of their death. I'm waiting for the bang. Waiting for the distant sound of it hitting the hillside. Waiting for the stench of death and smoke.

I'm going to die. I can't untangle my fucking earbuds.

A pair of heavy footsteps lands beside mine. "Why are we running?"

Oh *great*. I swear he must be having me watched. "Leave me alone."

"How's that going?" asks Alex, nodding down at my earphones.

A low rumble reverberates through the air around us, my fingers desperately trying to undo the knots in the wires. "It's not funny," I snap, hands shaking too hard.

He takes the earphones from my hands, making quick work of the wires and handing them back to me. "Your audiobook addiction is getting out of hand."

I don't retaliate, shoving the buds in my ears and turning my music to full volume.

Even with the music, I know when the helicopter is landing. I press my palms over the earphones as I hurry in the direction of the mansion. The floor vibrates beneath me, rattling me down to the marrow in my bones and knocking the breath from my lungs. Alex must notice, because his hands settle over my shoulders to stop me in my tracks.

His eyes hold mine, silently asking me, *telling* me, not to let go. Gently, softly, a pair of warm hands settle over mine, dulling the last of the noise.

I'm so stunned by his gesture, I barely notice the touchdown. He presses my forehead to his chest, letting the outside world bleed into empty nothingness until all that's left is him and me. The rotors whirl to a stop in the far distance. My heart slows. The sickening feeling of dread ebbs away.

Embarrassment trickles in to replace it.

I force out an awkward laugh as he removes his hands from my ears and delicately hooks his pinky finger around the left wire of my earbud to remove it. "Sorry. Just wanted to listen to Sinatra. Love the guy."

He doesn't mirror my amusement. "What happened?"

I chuckle again, like an antisocial clown on his first day of the job. *What the fuck is wrong with me?* "Just a funny moment."

"A funny moment." He watches me wipe my trembling hands on my skirt. "Are you afraid of helicopters?"

"Yes."

"Is that why you don't like me?"

He probably said it as a joke, but it's the closest he's ever been to hitting the nail on the head. "Pretty much."

We step out of the castle courtyard and onto the forested track that leads to the Nightshade halls. His hand sits on my lower back, warm and reassuring. He feels so unfortunately right, but my mind is full of unknowns. Why is the folder in his bottom drawer? What did my mother do to earn Carmichael's hatred? What does Professor Bancroft know? What do I do with the report on my laptop?

And the one that burns the back of my head all day every day: Does Alex know about what his father does behind the shiny businessman facade?

If so, can I ever forgive him?

An iridescent sheen of frost decorates the browning grass outside the castle, littered with tracks from foxes and deer. It looks like a festive greeting card out here. It's almost December; almost Christmas. The thought makes my chest tight. My summers are difficult, my Easters are lonely, but Christmas…Christmas is horrendous.

It used to be chaos. My mother would set the lights on that awful flashing setting that everyone else ignores. My father would burn the turkey to within an inch of its life. My neighbors would bicker over the orange cream biscuits in the selection box.

I used to think my Christmases were kind of sad. I never realized how wrong I was until it was too late.

Sorrowsong breaks up early. I'll have at least a month at home. My limbs feel heavier with each step I take, and Alex must notice the downward shift in my mood because he gives me a comforting squeeze on the shoulder.

I wish it didn't soothe my soul.

My desire for revenge is the reason my heart keeps beating, and with every kindness, every gentle gesture, he strips my purpose away. I'm scared he'll leave me with nothing; no one to fall asleep with and no reason to get up when the sun rises. "I'm too complicated, Alex. I'll only ever hurt you in the end."

"I hate it when you say that. It makes me want to punch whoever put that idea in your head."

"You want to punch everyone, all of the time."

His laugh comes out as a white puff of air. His rugby shorts ride up the thick muscles of his thigh, sitting just above the black raven inked above his knee. I forget about the cold entirely. "That is true."

We walk beside the lichen-covered walls around the perimeter of the castle grounds. I sneak a peek over at him. Dappled sunlight spills through the trees, painting his face in shades of silver and gold. It kisses the strong line of his nose, the sharp angle of his jaw, the remarkable shade of his eyes. Whichever artist sketched him, I doubt they've ever produced another piece like it.

He catches me staring and I blush like a schoolgirl, frozen mud crunching beneath my boots as I almost stumble over. He blushes too; barely noticeable, but so endearing. He clears his throat. "I have to ask you a question I've been dying to know. Just so I can finally sleep at night again."

Worry slithers up my spine. "Go on."

"Under the stands after the Nottingham game."

I cringe. "Shawn dragged me under there."

"Did I hear the word *stockings*? It's research, for...science."

My laugh bounces between the trees around us, relieved as much as it is amused. "I'd run out of washing, okay? It had been a rough few weeks."

"If there are forks wedged in all the laundry machine filters tomorrow, it wasn't me."

I muffle my giggle in my scarf as we walk toward the Night-shade mansion's impressive facade. My next sentence sneaks out without my permission. "Same goes if you find all your shorts have been turned up another inch tomorrow."

He grins like this has made his day. "You like my thighs?"

"Nope. You misheard me."

"I'd pay good money to watch you grind on one of them."

I halt in my tracks, all my blood rushing south. I frantically bat away the erotic visions that fly toward me. "*What?*"

"Nope. You misheard me," he echoes. He glances back over at me, expression sobering. "You could've called me today, when you were scared."

I don't know what to say back. I long for someone to call, he's just the last person I ever wanted or expected to fall for. "I struggle with asking for help."

He presses his palms together like he's praising the universe. "Oh my god. She's becoming self-aware."

I can't squash my grin. "It feels like I've been alone in my corner for a long time, okay?" I sober my expression. "I've built my walls too high."

"They're worth the climb."

"They aren't."

We stop on the mansion steps, his tone soft. "They are. For me, they are."

He scans the door and lets me in, standing in the doorway so my body brushes his on the way in. His touch feels electric against my skin. We reach our hallway and I open my mouth to say goodbye, to tell him I'll see him around, that I hope he'll have a good Christmas if I don't see him before. But the words are snatched out of my mouth as we both stop in the hallway.

My door is ajar.

Alex's arm shoots out to stop me from moving farther, like someone in a spy movie. I almost roll my eyes, but a sinister feeling hangs in the air around us. "Did you lock the door?"

"Yes."

He pulls me into his room and leaves me standing in the middle of the rug. I watch in horror as he tugs a gun from beneath his desk. A real-life gun. Like, an actual one that shoots bullets.

"Alex, what the *fuck*?"

"Don't move."

He stalks back out to my room, hand hovering over the handle. My heart is in my mouth. Does everyone have guns here? Does Carmichael? Does *Alan*? Oh God.

I can't watch him get hurt for me.

Alex steps inside the room and I wait, suspended in time in the silent bedroom.

My fingers tremble at my sides, bracing for a gunshot. "Alex?"

There's no sign of a struggle, so I creep into the hallway and bite my bottom lip so hard it bleeds, calling his name again. Something slides beneath my snowy boot, making me jump. I stoop to pick up the Polaroid photograph, feeling the blood drain from my face.

The green T-shirt in the photo is the same one buried at the bottom of my wardrobe here, the ginger hair is the same shade as the one I try not to look at in the mirror. Her face has been scratched away, but I know immediately that it's my mother.

255

Alex's voice sounds far away, like it's underwater. I feel faint. "Go back into my room, Ophelia."

I swallow the bile rising in my throat, trying to make sense of the photo. I'm scared it means I'm wrong. Carmichael is happy to let me go. Carmichael has washed his hands of me. This person hasn't.

I look around the doorway, frozen in place by a sickening feeling of disgust. The room has become a collage of photos of my mother. Every single one has her face scratched out. Alex tries to pull me away, back into the hallway. I can hear him talking, but the words don't register. There are unfamiliar pictures of her here.

Photos of her in underwear. Photos of her in bed. Photos of her sleeping. Photos of her in a bedroom that isn't one of the ones at home. Photos of hands on her body that aren't my father's.

Alex quickly takes down each one of her undressed while I stand in the center of the room like my world is ending around me. Achlys's cry over the mountains sounds too much like my mother. Calling for help. Calling for forgiveness. Calling out for a lover that isn't my father.

A Shakespeare quote is sprawled over the wall in red paint.
Villain, I have done thy mother.

A small laugh bubbles out of my throat while the world tilts on its axis. "That is a terrific choice of quote, Alan."

Alex lowers me to the bed with two gentle hands on my shoulders, watching me warily like he thinks I might disintegrate. I might. All I have left of them are memories. Carefully preserved and dangerously fragile, constructed into delicate houses of cards that start to tumble down around me. Every happy memory morphs into a question mark. Every family dinner decays at the edges.

Did my father know?

I pluck a letter from the headboard, trying to steady my hands enough to read it. It's my mother's curly handwriting.

> **My darling,**
>
> **I won't see you next week. It's O's birthday. We can't leave before her birthday.**
>
> **I dream of you every night. Dream of the life we can build in Spain or Portugal. If Andy suspects something, he hasn't said. He's always been like that. Spineless.**
>
> **Not like you.**
>
> **She'll be lucky to have you as her new father. She'll come around.**
>
> **Your Anna. X**

My tears drip onto the paper. I'm broken for my father. I hope he didn't know. I hope he didn't die with sadness in his heart. I hope he didn't die feeling unwanted.

A horrible feeling seeps beneath my skin as I fold the letter in half. During sleepless nights, with nothing but eerie darkness and my own conspiracies to keep me company, I had wondered if my stalker and my parents' killer were the same person. This feels like proof.

A violent shudder wracks my spine, the anger I feel toward Alan bubbling over into full-blown fury. "I'll end him."

Could it be Alex's father? Would he have been having an affair with my mother? It just seems so far-fetched. My stalker must've ordered the hit on my parents, and Cain was more than happy to comply. The paper crumples in my shaking fist.

Alex's rugby boot lands beside my feet. I wrap my arms around myself. I feel too exposed. My skirt is too short, tights too thin. I don't want him to look at me. I don't want him to see me cry.

Two strong arms lift me off the bed and carry me away from the mess in my room. He drops me on his bed but I sit up, shaking my head. "I don't want this," I say, ignoring the tears that run down my cheeks and praying that he ignores them, too.

His forehead lands against mine, thumbs tracing my cheek-bones. "I know."

"I don't want to be with you." I sound like a broken record, stuck on repeat for so long that neither of us is really listening anymore.

"So why haven't you put me out of my misery and left me alone."

"I'm trying," I choke out. "God, I'm trying. I've been trying since September. You're bad for me, Alex, but I'm drawn to you by some invisible force. Why can't you help me out?"

He shakes his head like I'm expecting too much of him. "I can't stay away from you, Ophelia. I've never pretended I can."

My trembling fingers run over his knuckles. "You make it *so* hard for me."

He pulls away and rakes both hands through his messy hair. He's exasperated with me. "So what is it, Ophelia? What have I done that could possibly be *so* bad?"

"What's your dream, Alex? Why are you here?"

There's nothing but sincerity in his words when he speaks. "To take over my father's company."

It's the answer I knew was coming. It stings my heart all the same. "I'm going to leave this room, and I need you to leave me alone."

"Right after you tell me why that's an issue."

He tosses the gun into a desk drawer, stands at the end of the bed, and looks down at me with that unreadable expression. He looks imposing, intimidating. He looks like the man who almost ran me over. He looks like the man who runs Green Aviation.

"I *hate* your father, Alex. I hate what he does. I hate who he is. I hate that you'll end up like him."

He looks like I've slapped him across the face. "You think I'm like him?"

"Do you know what he does? What he can be bribed to do?"

"Of course I know what he does."

Nausea churns the seven Jaffa Cakes in my stomach. Or maybe the seven Jaffa Cakes are what churns my stomach. I choose to believe it's a physical reaction to him; a warning sign from my body. "And you're fine with it?"

His chest falls, voice softens. "It's complicated. Business is complicated."

I now know how he feels when I say those words. I understand his bewilderment, because how could it possibly be complicated? A staff shuttle goes down with five innocent people in it; pawns caught up in some chess game being played by the rich and powerful.

It's black and white. Right versus wrong. It's anything *but* complicated. In the back of my mind, three burger buns sit untouched on a board. A bottle of petrol station wine remains unopened. My chest hurts. "I hate you."

His laugh makes my blood white-hot. "For the love of God, Ophelia, Make. It. *Believable*."

"I hate you, Alex. I hate that you're studying business and not architecture. I hate that you flew home three weeks ago to unveil a new jet with your father. I hate that your boundary between right and wrong is complicated. They're real people, Alex; the people who end up as collateral. The whistleblowers who go missing. The people who die in accidents. Hell, even the Mafia bosses with blood on their hands, they have families too. They're not *business*; they're mothers and fathers, daughters and sons."

"I know!" he shouts, interrupting my tirade. "I know they're real people. I am *not* my father, Ophelia. I'd rather die than watch myself decay into him."

I sink deeper into the bed, my mind stuck in my bedroom, surrounded by Polaroids that serve as reminders of the fact that no one is ever who they say they are. "I don't believe you."

"I don't want to be anything like him."

"You just said you want to take over the business."

He paces over to the window and stares out at the trees and the castle beyond. It's started to rain, fat droplets snaking down the thin glass. "It's complicated, Ophelia. I have a plan."

"We just won't work."

"I know you have trust issues. You don't tell me about your home life, but I know it's messy. And I get that this," he turns back toward me and sweeps his hand in the vague direction of my bedroom, "has probably made it messier. Your mom has let you down, and maybe some other people have too. But *I* won't."

"I'll let *you* down, Alex. You have enough on your plate without adding me to it too."

I hate that he fights for me so hard. Hate that he's so blatant about the fact he thinks we'll work. I don't deserve it. "Give yourself a chance, Twist." He closes the gap between us and gently pops open the tiny locket at my neck, staring at a photo of my father and me when I was six. "Give *her* a chance. Why don't you give her any patience?"

I wipe the tears from my nose and snatch the necklace from his fingertips. "You don't know anything about her."

"Why is it so hard for you to admit to yourself that you want this?"

I almost hear my patience snap, my final shred of self-control landing on the rug between our feet. "Fine, I want this. I want *you*. I can't escape you, Alex. You're like the sun. I turn away, I look down, but I can still see you reflected in everything at my feet. If I draw the curtains, you slip through the cracks. I can't fall for the moon instead because it's you that illuminates it. None of that changes the fact that we just won't work. You're not the problem here. It's me, and things out of my control."

Like your shitbag of a father.

His knees straddle my legs on the bed, large hands flipping me onto my front. He sinks his full weight onto me, pinning my body to the mattress. "It's you who's the sun, Ophelia. I am the moon. You keep me in this tortuous cycle, lighting me up for the shortest time before you disappear again and make me invisible. Don't give me that *it's not you, it's me* crap; I hate it."

That's how he feels about me? My natural instinct to push people away rears its ugly head, but Alex's fingers on my shoulders dissolve it away before it engulfs me. A soft exhale escapes my lips. I'm as turned on as I am confused. "It's the truth."

"You can't go back to your room like this. The lock is broken on your door."

"Bet you say that to all the girls."

My attempt at lightening the mood fails. "Whatever it is that makes you think you can't be loved, we'll work through it."

"*Alex*," I sigh, leaning my neck back into his touch.

He feels so good. He feels like home. He feels like I don't *have* to use the file on my laptop. Like just for tonight, none of it matters.

"Let me talk, Ophelia, please. Promise me you'll listen. Not just hear me but listen, too."

I feel my resolve bleed into the mattress beneath me. It's not an unreasonable request. "Okay."

His fingers sink into my scalp, teasing, pulling, massaging. I moan into the mattress, prompting a tortured curse from Alex. His thighs are thick and solid against my back, heavy enough that I couldn't escape even if I wanted to.

"My father is the worst of society. The shiny CEO is just one side to him. He has this darkness within him, a desperate need to do bad; he'd kill people even if he didn't get any money for it. Everything he touches rots at the heart. Most people at the top of the chain are like that. They have sadistic tendencies, violent cravings. Money does that to people."

"It doesn't make it right."

"No, it doesn't, but it's the way it is. It's the way Vincenzo will have to be, because if he isn't, he'll be killed. I know Vin seems like a joker, but he gets a sick thrill from death like the rest of them. It's the way my father has raised me; that we matter and those below us don't. He reached into my chest and set his darkness free, but I don't want bloodshed. I don't dream about someone dying beneath my hands—not beyond your stalker, at least. My darkness isn't like his."

I roll over beneath where his arms cage me in, his shoulders so broad that he eclipses my view of the ceiling. His eyes are genuine and so full of patience with me. "What does your darkness tell you to do?" I whisper.

He doesn't need to answer. His eyes say it all. It hits me what that unnamed look is. It's a battle between his inner demons. The panic that sweeps through me, the sheer horror that he'd hurt himself, takes me by surprise.

He finds so much strength for everyone else that there's none left for himself. "Don't. Please don't."

His lips brush my tears. He smells like rugby, the forest, and complete and total acceptance. "I won't. Not all the while they need me. I'm here to convince Carmichael on a vote of no confidence in my father, to show him I know what I'm doing. He wants to watch me closely. The rugby, the grades, the endless meetings in his office, the four years I spent working beside my father instead of being at Yale. It's all a careful plan. I have no intention of spending my life as CEO of Green, but the board is divided, jealous of one another."

"You want to replace your father?"

"Temporarily, until I find a better replacement. The ones who still have a moral compass think I'm nothing like my father, the rest of them think my father's raised me as evil as he is."

I clock on. "You're the best shot at a majority vote."

Pride flits through his expression. My desperate need for praise hums happily, swinging her legs with glee. "*Atta girl*. My mother, my sisters, and I, we're all in his prison. They'll never be free until he's behind bars. Ophelia, I'm only *here* to ruin my father."

My laugh of disbelief is hoarse. He's here for the same reason as me.

His features soften at the sight of me. "Anyway, my shrink says I have to do something for me. Something completely selfish. Something that revolves around what *I* want." Gently, he tugs my cardigan aside and plants a kiss on my collarbone. "You're that for me. You're not charity, you're not a sympathy project. You're not in my room right now because I feel sorry for you, or because I think you couldn't take down your stalker alone. You're what *I* want, my ultimate selfish act, my darkest desire. So let me work for you. It's therapeutic for me."

"But when I let you down in two months, or when we fight in a year, or in three years you're just tired of me, we'll both be more broken than we were before." His grin widens with each word past my lips. "Stop laughing at me."

He looks down at me like he sees me. Like he *knows* me. Like if I handed him my fragile heart, he'd treat it with tender kindness. "Can't help it. You're the most miserable person I've ever met. Have you ever been optimistic about anything, ever?"

"No," I grumble.

"Let me give you an alternate scenario." My hands snake around the back of his neck, hanging onto him for dear life. "Right after we've lived out our secret fantasy involving you on my thigh, we'll hatch a plan for catching this wet sponge who calls himself Alan. Then we eat dinner here tonight. I've got instant ramen in the cupboard and Jelly Babies in the bedside table for dessert. We can do a crossword, or watch a movie. We spend the night in my bed, if that's what you'd like." He taps his phone. "It's almost six o'clock now. Give me until midnight. For my own sanity, let yourself be loved until midnight."

There's only so much willpower a woman can have. Soft lips land on my neck, and for the first time, I let myself relax in his company. I surrender myself to his stupid plan. "Midnight."

"Midnight, a hundred years from now."

I laugh and shove him off me. "That wasn't in the deal!"

"You should always read the fine print, Ophelia," he says, his voice husky. Butterflies unfurl in my lower stomach, but my own guilt sticks their wings together like an oil spill.

"I've not told you the whole truth about me," I whisper.

"Have you lied about the way you cry at movies that aren't even sad?"

He can hear that? I hope he didn't hear me sobbing at *Ratatouille* last week. Linguini really shouldn't have put that little rat in the jar. I feel myself blush. "No."

"Have you lied about your passion for swimming?"

I shake my head.

"Have you lied about the way you keep going, despite everything that's happened to you here?"

I shake my head, biting down a smile.

"Did you lie about the way your reaction to any kind of hardship in life is to pull out a crossword book?" His fist curls into the hair at my nape, voice roughening. "Have you lied about this hair? These legs? That laugh? Those *freckles*? Your stupid brown outfits?"

My hands land on my cheeks, mortified and flattered all at once. "No."

The atmosphere switches, no longer playful but thick with tension. His body is hard and heavy on mine, cocooned in warmth by the copper sun sinking low over the tarn outside. He plants a scorching kiss against my neck. I feel it down to my toes. "Then I think I'll manage just fine."

Slowly, like we have all the time in the world, he trails kisses over each of my collarbones. I wish I could explain the way each one makes me a little bit stronger, a little bit more receptive to the fact that I could be happy again.

"Can I kiss you?" he asks, looking at me through those incandescent eyes. The storm in them is quiet, still, like his mind is here and here alone. His lips hover over mine, so close, so *achingly* close. And when his next word tickles my lips, I know I'm done for. "*Please?*"

"Please," I repeat, heart pounding in my chest.

His hand snakes between my shoulder and the mattress, finding a firm grip on the underside of my neck. Something glitters in his eyes; something feral. "Gotta make sure you don't run away again."

Impatient and nervous, I squirm beneath him, but he's solid and unmoving, his heartbeat slow and heavy against my fast and erratic. His hand tightens behind my head, tugging gently on the sensitive strands of hair there. Tiny pinpricks of electricity skate along my skin.

I'm glad I can't speak French, because whatever he's saying under his breath sounds like it would make me delete the file on my laptop and become a hermit that never leaves his bedroom. My mouth pops open slightly in a quiet plea, and like that was exactly what he was waiting for, he puts me out of my misery and touches his soft lips on mine.

My soft gasp is buried in his mouth, hot and possessive as it melts over mine. The hand beneath my neck traces the curve of my throat, skates along my waist, caresses the line of my hip. He feels so right. Everything I dreaded he'd feel like and more. He takes a slow inhale through his nose, the tiny shift of his hips enough to make me feel like a sinner.

I swear, something dormant awakens deep inside me. It drowns out the voices, the constant bickering in my head. The self-doubt, the feeling that this is too good to be true, the idea that I'll be a disappointment, my mother's betrayal; they all stand in stunned silence, watching as the kaleidoscope of too many clashing colors bleeds out of me and into him.

"I knew you'd feel like this," he whispers, against my lips, hunger threaded between each syllable. The hand returns to my neck to pull deeper into him, and the low hum in his throat is fuel for me to thread my fingers through his hair, desperate for something to hang onto.

It doesn't matter that I'm not sure what to do, because Alex is. He kisses me like he's been planning how he'd do it for months, the monster inside him possessed by some primal need reserved just for me. Planting a strong hand on my waist, he snakes a leg between mine and rolls us both so I'm on top.

A ragged rendition of the word *mine* leaves his mouth, his teeth gently tugging on my lower lip. I'm on a cloud, floating far above Sorrowsong, too far to think about all my problems. The last of the day's sun feels like honey melting over my skin, warmed by his touch.

I don't break the kiss, holding his face between my hands as if I'm worried it'll vanish if I don't. My sharp breaths mingle with his irregular ones, chests heaving in perfect time as he sits up to get closer to me. My tights are so thin, offering no protection from the feel of his thigh between mine. It's new.

All of this is new.

He pulls away first, sending disappointment lancing through me. Gazing up through long, dark lashes, he steadies me on top of him with two large hands resting atop my thighs. The cool metal of his rings burns through the fabric of my tights. His fingers flex and unflex against me, like he's desperately trying to keep himself on a leash. "You still think the anticipation ruined it?"

My cardigan slips off my shoulder as I shrug. His eyes home in on the sliver of pale skin like a starved animal desperate to take a bite. "I don't know. A sample size of one is too small to draw conclusions."

He tugs his muddy hoodie over his head, exposing a strip of golden, tattooed skin across his abs. The garment joins my pride and my patience on the floor. "If you end up being the death of me, Winters, I couldn't ask for a better end."

His fingers settle on the first button of my cardigan, eyes laden with an unspoken question. Nerves creep back in, my fingers landing on top of his to still them. I can't remember when I last shaved my legs, but I'm pretty sure my roommate was alive when it happened. I keep readjusting my tights so the hairs don't poke through. And what if he takes my cardigan off? What am I supposed to do with my boobs? I guess I can't really do anything *with* them; they sort of just sit there. That's kind of their appeal.

I'm overthinking this, I am sure. "I'm not…I've not…"

"This doesn't mean we'll go any further than your sweater coming off," he says, quieting my internal panic.

His fingers undo each green button, eyes locked on mine the same way they were in the bathroom after I was attacked. Slowly, gently, he slides it off my shoulders, over the goose bumps that rise on my arms. He hooks a finger beneath the thin strap of my camisole, tugging it aside to see the three tiny fine line circles inked over my heart.

"What does it mean?"

My mother's betrayal is a knife in my spine. Were we ever really three perfect circles? Had the helicopter landed safely, would three burgers have been eaten that day, or two? I offer a small smile. "It's complicated."

He puts the stretchy fabric back into place over the symbol, covering it with his hand. It's such an intimate gesture, I'm momentarily spellbound. "I get it."

I hook my pinky beneath his training top, lifting it slightly to see a black raven's wing stretching over the golden skin of his waist. The muscles across his stomach contract where my skin grazes his. "Are they your sisters?"

He pulls the shirt over his head and lies back down, watching me closely as I examine the ravens over his sculpted chest and the ones on his thighs. "One for my mother and six for my sisters." He twists at the waist slightly, letting me see the broken birdcage on his ribs from which all of the ravens have escaped. "And one for my father, of course."

The document on my laptop burns at the back of my mind. It might help rid him of his father, but at what cost to his mother? For the first time, I consider telling him about it.

It's nothing he doesn't know already.

"Bloody hell," I whisper, prodding his firm stomach. "I have got to stop having two dinners."

He laughs, dragging me down to kiss him. "Don't you dare. Watching you polish off two bowls of spaghetti over a crossword in the dining hall is the highlight of my week, every week."

"It's not my fault it's all the fine-dining-tiny-portion food over here. What if I don't want tomato *foam*? I just want a tomato, made of tomato. What happened to a roast dinner so heavy you can't move until Monday? This country is crumbling."

He grins underneath me. It makes me want to lock this door and never leave. All the while, his hands encircle my waist, run up and down my rib cage, trace the crease between my thighs and my hips as though he'll keel over and die if he stops touching me. "I actually agree. Every time I fly back to New York I eat *so* much shit. I miss pizza."

"Same. And sausage rolls." My hands clasp my cheeks in despair. "Or *chips*." Jesus Christ, when was the last time I ate chips? At least I'll have access to chips at Christmas.

I'm smiling like an idiot. So is he, and I know why. This feels uncomplicated. This feels like raspberries in June and hot drinks on cold days. So wonderfully ordinary that it's euphoric for the soul.

It's like stumbling home after four years of being completely and utterly lost, and by the wordless awe in his eyes when he looks up at me, I can tell he feels it too.

He tugs me back down to kiss him, my body melting against his. His hands fly to my hips, grinding me against the muscles of his thigh in a slow, scandalous circle. A delicious warmth unfurls low in my belly, my mouth dropping open on a quiet moan.

I feel his grin against my throat as his teeth graze the delicate skin there. A violent shudder wracks my body. "*Fuck.*"

He kisses me harder, hotter, *deeper*, shifting his thigh to brush against the sensitive space between my thighs. I arch forward on a desperate shudder, hands gripping his shoulders as his fingers sink deeper into the flesh of my hips. "Trust me?" he asks, pulling back a little.

I nod, because for some reason, I do.

I watch, mesmerized as he guides me onto my knees and sinks his thumbs into the fabric of my tights, tearing them at the seam without ever touching my skin. This cannot become a regular thing; shredding tights in this economy.

Cool air licks the delicate skin where the fabric used to be. His eyes return to mine, pupils dilated and lips parted. "It'll feel better this way."

He lowers me back down onto the hard ridges of his thigh, placing my hands over his chest. "Take what you want, Ophelia." He keeps his eyes on mine and plants the softest of kisses on the inside of my wrist. "Use me."

I shift my hips, gasping at the jolts of pleasure that spark through my core. It's tentative at first, but when I see what it does to him, see the fire it ignites in his eyes, see the evidence of how I make him feel, I can't help but move faster. Riding his thigh, it feels obscene; so wrong that it's right, but with every moan that leaves my lips, another whispered string of praise comes to meet it.

Minutes blend into each other, Alex's groans of approval meld into mine, each one winding me higher into the apricot sunset outside. "You look so beautiful, Ophelia. So powerful."

A desperate plea escapes my lips, inhaling the heady scent of his skin as I bury my head in his neck. His hands take over, setting a pace that my hips cannot, every drag of my thong along his skin like a hot wire to my nervous system.

Hoarse exhales rip from his throat too, like this is as good for him as it is for me. My breaths come shorter, whimpers higher, muscles tighter until he sinks his teeth into the skin of my shoulder and sends me tumbling over the edge. He buries my cry in his mouth, wrapping two arms around me while I ride out the wave of ecstasy.

The sun finally kisses the tarn, red light bleeding into orange cotton clouds and setting the water alight. The shudders that wrack my body subside, the skin between my thighs so sensitive I can't bear to move. I'm overwhelmed with emotion, completely lost in him.

He doesn't talk, and for that I am grateful. He just holds me, a hand between my shoulder blades and another on the back of my head, tangling in my hair.

When a knock on the door drags us out of our trancelike state, the sky is black and my heart is content. Alex pulls away, brushing strands of hair from my face in the low light of his room. His voice is low and quiet, filled with reverence. "I wish I could pause time here."

I trace my finger over his bottom lip, slightly swollen from me. From *us*. A shy smile creeps across my face, a realization of what we just did sinking in. I've kissed a few people, but not like *that*. A kiss has never given me a desire to sit in a confession booth before. "Me too." My eyes skirt to the door, to the shadow beneath it. A frisson of worry prickles my skin. "Was I too loud?"

"*God, no.*" He pulls his hoodie down over my camisole, basking me in warmth and his addictive scent. He grasps the drawstrings and tugs me forward, planting the softest of kisses on my forehead. "You were perfect."

I'm done for. Whatever revenge plan I had has been fractured into two.

The tattoos over his back flex as he tugs open the door. A broad, bald man in sunglasses and a sharp suit stands outside, like Pitbull on steroids. His shades are so dark I can't tell where he's looking.

I wrap a blanket around my shoulders, self-conscious. They exchange a very brief conversation in Italian before Alex turns back to me. "What time did you last leave your room before it was broken into?"

"Before swimming at seven."

Pitbull drops a set of keys into Alex's outstretched palm and a cardboard box at his feet.

Alex shuts the door and tosses the keys to me. "Your room has been cleared and the lock has been changed. The photos of your mom are in the box."

The lock has been changed. It's the smallest thing that feels like such a relief. A ball of emotion chokes my throat. He cares. He really cares. "Thank you. Who was that?"

"One of Vincenzo's men. He's got a fingerprint from one of the door handles. He'll run it and get back to me."

"You were wrong when you said I could take this guy down alone. I don't know what I'm doing. Thank you for…" *Being patient with me. Meeting each of my insecurities with equal kindness. Kissing me. Letting me believe I might be worthy of love. Giving my lonely heart a safe place to rest.* "Everything," is all I can manage.

"I like looking after you. It makes me feel better." He swipes up his T-shirt from the floor and catches sight of my bottom lip creeping out. He laughs, letting the T-shirt hit the rug once more. "I feel like a stripper."

I watch the *V* of his abdomen clench and press my knuckles to my grin. "You *look* like a stripper." I shuffle on the bed. "You didn't…"

He strolls into the kitchenette and fills the kettle, pulling two cups of instant ramen from the cupboard. The power is temperamental tonight, so I busy myself lighting candles. "I didn't what?"

My cheeks flame. I wish I had a bit more experience to come into this with, or at least *some* knowledge. He leans on the kitchen doorway to gaze at me and his expression softens. "Ophelia, if a genie appeared in front of me now, kissing you while you dry hump my thigh for an hour would be all three of my wishes. Don't worry about me, I've got shower material for the next thirty years."

I'm sure my smile is cracking my face in two. I bash my desperation to watch one of these showers down like a mole in that Whac-A-Mole game. *Not now.*

His words settle into my chest, warm and welcome, while I light the candle on his desk. There are sketches pinned to the wall behind it, and a child's drawing has pride of place.

Six girls and one boy stand under some trees, the words *good luck at uni (again)* scrawled along the top in crayon. A pink friendship bracelet sits on his desk, a letter from Mia beside it. It's obvious that he lives for his sisters. It chips the armor around my heart that little bit more.

I want him. God, I want him. "Still, I…I want to, I just don't know what I'm doing."

His voice mingles with the sound of water being poured into plastic ramen pots. "Then we'll go as slow as you like."

Easy as that. Everything is simple with him. Whatever the opposite of my overthinking mind is, it's Alex.

"We need to talk about your mom. Are you going to call your dad?"

I pick at the skin around my nails, shoulders slumping. I need to crawl back to reality at some point. I need to sit down and think about the implications of today's discovery. I need to face the fact that my mother wasn't who she said she was. I just don't have the strength to do it tonight. "I'm not ready to talk about my family with you."

I hear his sigh, but he doesn't argue. We pad into a third room, a small sitting room with another wall full of books and a comfy sofa, warmly lit by flickering sconces, a log burner, and a banker's lamp on the side table. Other than the giant TV hanging from a bracket on the wall, it looks like a cozy library in a Georgian mansion.

He sprawls out on the cushions, dragging me to be closer to him. He smiles down at me, hand splaying over the soft flesh of my stomach. I let my body relax, let his finger trace the curve of my waist, let my soul mold to his with each synchronized breath we take.

He clears his throat like I'm not the only one struck with a jarring sense of completeness. This is too much feeling, too soon.

He queues up *The Fellowship of the Ring* on the giant flat-screen, pausing a moment to send seven goodnight texts from his phone. An unfamiliar feeling fills my chest, so sweet and *so* dangerous. "You love this film, right?"

A laugh bubbles out of my throat, tears in my eyes. All I ever do is cry. "Yeah. Yeah, I really do."

We eat the ramen in contented silence under the light of the candles. It tastes better than anything else I've eaten this week, and the steady beat of Alex's heart against my back makes it sit warm and comforting in my stomach.

TURNS OUT, ALEX'S gentlemanly demeanor doesn't extend to food. There was an odd number of Jelly Babies in the bag, and even though I'm *still* crying over Boromir dying, he's got out a set of vernier fucking calipers to measure each half of the last one.

"It's bigger!" I shriek, looking at his half.

"As if." He peers at the number on the caliper. "Yours is bigger by half a millimeter."

"Then let me have yours if it's bigger."

He clutches his chest with laughter. "No way."

"Because you know yours is bigger," I snap.

He picks it up, gathering powdered sugar on the tip of his tongue. "I licked it so it's mine."

"Are you four years old?" I lunge toward him, sending us both toppling backward. He reaches for his half, accidentally batting it under the sofa. We both look at each other, and then to the orange pair of legs, unscathed on the empty packet. "Don't even think about it, Corbeau. That's my half."

His gaze makes my thighs clench, his voice so thick with desire that I'm not sure if we're even talking about the sweets anymore. "Oh, I'm thinking about it."

I slam the Jelly Baby into my mouth before he can, his expression melting into utter outrage. He lurches forward, hand grasping my neck and lips landing on mine. I'm not sure if he's trying to taste the Jelly Baby or just kiss the life out of me, but it works.

He kisses me with so much force, so much intensity that all I can do is hold onto his arms and hope I don't get swept away.

When he pulls away, he looks happy. Not the silly, fleeting kind, about new purchases or shallow compliments. His eyes are glittering, like the happiness has grown new, delicate roots inside him.

I have to delete that file before I damage them.

Someone making *you* happy is one thing, but seeing the demons in someone's eyes go quiet when they look at you? It's something else entirely. "Stop looking at me like that, Alex."

His hips grind into mine. "Like what?"

"Like I'm the only woman on the planet."

His eyebrows shoot up in very convincing surprise. "There are other women on this planet?"

I grin up at him. I'm embarrassingly elated, torn between not letting my hopes get high and just wanting to enjoy the moment. But I've suffered enough for one decade, and he's looking at me like I'm something worth looking at, so I let myself feel each emotion without insecurity.

He slaps the discarded packet on the floor as if he is in denial that it's empty. "I can't believe you, Winters."

I flip his wrist to read his watch. "Forgive me until midnight."

"And if I've forgotten all about it by midnight, that'd be okay too."

I plant a hot, wet kiss in the center of his bare chest, delighted at what it does to him. He makes me feel so pretty. I sit back on my heels between his legs, the hazy glow from the fireplace warming my toes.

He looks down at me through heavy eyelids, picking up my hand and sucking the icing sugar from my fingertips. Something deep inside my stomach clenches. His smile is nothing but wicked. "Oh man. Corrupting you is going to be great."

Chapter 21

OPHELIA

I wake up with a warm body wrapped around my own.

The air outside is crisp and cool, chilling the tip of my nose, but beneath the duvet it's heaven. Alex's watch on the side table tells me it's not yet six in the morning.

Three more days until Christmas break.

Five mornings in a row I've woken up in this bed. Five nights of movies and ramen and soul-wrenching kisses. Five nights of watching all that Alex does for his sisters, from nightly phone calls to emails to their teachers and physicians.

Not only does he have a black heart, but Cain Green is also fucking useless. He kills people, blackmails people, treats his workers like shit, but nothing enrages me like what he does to his children. He teaches them that they're not worth coming home for.

He's let Alex believe he's not good enough to be loved.

His son, however, is all my favorite feelings tangled up in a six-foot-one masterpiece. At some point in the last two months, he's become the closest sensation I have to a home. He calls me beautiful as if it were my name, touches me as if it keeps him alive, kisses me like he wants to brand himself on me forever.

Ophelia from two months ago would slap me.

In the peaceful dark, I trace my index finger down the space between his brows, gently so I don't crack him more than he's already been cracked. He makes it all look easy, but I know it isn't. I wake up in the night to find him scrolling through trial drugs for his mother, or catch him reading a story to Josie over the phone, all the while keeping his grades in the nineties and body fat below fifteen percent.

I'd be lying if he didn't make me feel a bit guilty about my weekends in bed, eating crisps and crying over fictional rats.

My finger dances over one of the ravens on his chest, watching its wing flutter with each inhale. I like it when he sleeps, because it's the only time he's not living for anyone else.

We were up late last night. Delicious flashbacks of Alex's head between my thighs flit back to me, and then ones of him teaching me to return the favor. Of him looking down at me like I hung the moon in the sky, my name a breathless curse from his lips.

Now I know he whimpers—fucking *whimpers*—I'm truly screwed.

My body hums with a calm sense of exhaustion, but I can't sleep. How cold will the house be when I get back there? How quiet will it feel on Christmas Day, when no one is there in the morning and no one kisses me goodnight? When no one will tell me to stop eating chocolate or to not shower for so long?

279

That thing I used to call freedom, it's festered into isolation.

A macabre sunrise slips through the burgundy curtains, an inky mess of brown and purple and yellow. Alex's phone lights up on his side table, buzzing with an incoming call from his mother.

Those lashes flutter open, and for a second I get the calm; the tranquil pool of green that I got for all of last night, free of stress and trauma. He smiles drowsily at me. "You're beautiful this morning."

I trace a finger over each of his brows. "You said that yesterday morning, too."

His voice is low, roughened by sleep. "You just keep on getting better."

I want to indulge, but instead I tuck a messy lock of hair behind his ear and nod my head toward the table behind him. "It's your mother."

"Shit."

He sits up against the headboard, a sliver of light running over his naked abdomen. I quash the urge to run my tongue along it. He hits Accept and presses the phone to his ear. "*Maman. Qu'est-ce qui se passe?*...Oh. Is she okay?" He stands up and paces to the window, giving me a chance to admire him in full. Muscular shoulders taper down to a slim waist, the broad lines of his thighs flexing. "Did she? Was Dad home?"

I bite my fingernails and watch him talk, watch him lazily chuck a few clothes into a bag as he does. Pocketing his passport, he swipes two pairs of my underwear from his desk and stuffs them into his jacket pocket, mouthing the word *souvenir* at me.

He's going home early, probably for the rest of the year. My stomach sinks. I slip into his bathroom and turn on the shower, trying to catch a hold of my emotions before they spiral.

I have some real abandonment issues for a girl who's never really been abandoned by anyone in her life.

By the time Alex steps behind me in the thick, eucalyptus-scented steam, I've pulled myself together. He takes over from my hands where I massage shampoo into my head, meeting my gaze in the mirror above the sink. He snakes his hand between my legs, tracing the delicate skin while his other hand scratches my scalp. "I licked it so it's mine."

He's ridiculous. I bite down my smile, tipping my head back to meet his shoulder. "How is she?"

His hands return to my sides. "Having a bad day. She gets these voices that tell her she looks wrong. That her nose shape is outdated and she's too fat to walk the runway and her clothes are out of season. I know it sounds superficial, but it's torture for her. She'll be fine; I just hate my sisters being around that sort of ideology."

I reach my hand up and behind me, scratching my fingers through his hair. "I'm so sorry."

His next sentence sounds like an apology. "I'm going to fly back for Christmas."

"Today?"

His fingers work deeper into my scalp, his hard chest against my back. "This morning. It just makes sense for me to. I'm going to go to Charlotte's parent-teacher conference. I don't have to, but the alternative is that no one goes, and that's not fair. She wants to be a doctor one day."

I stare at the water running down the tiles and swallow. I hate that he's leaving, but mostly I hate that a twenty-three-year-old is having to go to parents' evenings for his sisters. "Okay."

"Vincenzo's man will keep a watch over you while you're still here." He sighs, his chin coming down to rest on my shoulder. His frustration about my stalker is palpable. Every time we think we're onto something, we aren't. From vague IP addresses to disabled CCTV, they're covering every track they leave. "They couldn't find a match on the prints in any database, UK or US. This guy has no criminal record."

His strong fingers move down to my neck, kneading and rubbing the tension away. I'm sure it should be me doing this to him. "It's possible I don't even know the stalker. It could just be someone who knows my mum, but not me."

"We'll find them."

I turn around and wash his hair how he likes. "The police lose interest the second I say the word 'Sorrowsong.'"

"Doesn't surprise me. When will you go back?"

"I'm not sure. I don't think I actually *have* to be off campus until Christmas Eve."

He frowns, catching my wrists to stop me from rinsing his hair. "Don't tell me you're staying here that long."

"I might stay a couple of weeks more."

"Please don't."

"*Alex.*"

"I get things are shitty with what's happened with your mom, but don't stay here. Not with Alan here. I'd be so much more relaxed if you left."

My hands run down his chest and over his abs. He sucks in a lungful of steam, pupils dilating. The look in his eye hasn't darkened, his shoulders haven't slumped under the new weight on them since the phone call. I have this desperate urge to make this man the happiest man alive.

"I'll think about it, I promise." My knees land on the warm tile at his feet, and I blink up at him with my most innocent look. "Have you got time?"

He leans his head back against the wall and casts his eyes to the ceiling like he's thanking a god he doesn't believe in for my existence. His hands lift my wet hair into a ponytail, wrapping it around one fist and pulling it, hard. It's in contrast to the softness in his eyes. I love that; how rough he is with me all while staring at me like he'd bend the tides or steal the moon to see me happy.

I want him to be my first. I want him so much it's probably unhealthy, but I don't care. I want the faces he makes and the noises that leave his mouth and the way he takes control.

I want it all, but we're on two vastly different levels of experience.

He tips my chin up as I brace my hands on his thighs. "You make me finally understand what people mean when they say life isn't long enough."

I READ A new notification on my phone, overstimulated by trying to pack my bag. One day I'll learn how to fold a T-shirt correctly, but for now, I'll stick to swearing at them and squishing them into the corners of the bag.

From: Alex Corbeau-Green
Subject: Ophelia (verb) *my favorite morning activity*
Date: Thursday 27th November 00:12 BST
To: Ophelia Winters

Landed safely and on the way into the city.
Started replaying this morning's shower in my head when I sat
in my seat, and when we touched down at JFK I'd only just got
to the part where you sat backward on my shoulders.

Oh my god. I hope they don't monitor our emails. The IT guy is
probably having the time of his life.

I lie back on Alex's bed between his room key hanging on my
key chain and piles of my unfolded clothes. I've booked a taxi and
a train home for a few days' time. My mind has been so stuck on
last night and this morning that I don't think it would be safe for
me to drive even if I could.

From: Ophelia Winters
Subject: Obedience (noun) *compliance with an order, request,
or law*
Date: Thursday 27th November 00:39 BST
To: Alex Corbeau-Green

We can re-create the shower again after Christmas.

I'm packing up my bag, ready to leave in a couple of days.
I hope your mum is doing better.

He doesn't reply, and I try to imagine what he's doing in New York, sitting in the back of a driver's car, pulling up outside the Corbeau-Greens' famous brownstone near Central Park. Is there a man standing at the door to open it, or does he just put a key in like a regular person? It's not a world I've ever lived in or even experienced from afar.

Do they have family dinners? Who do the girls eat with when Alex is away, Elise is with her doctors, and Cain is in the office?

Alex has made it clear that the media is the wedge that splinters his mother's health. That for her, *all* press is bad press.

I can't bring myself to publish that document online, not now I know the family it would ruin. I need to find another way to bring Cain down, and I need to decide whether to do it alone or with Alex.

Chapter 22

OPHELIA

My front door catches on a pile of spam letters and overdue bills gathering on the peeling doormat as I push it open.

A family portrait of the three of us stares back at me from the entryway. I can't bear to look at my mother. How long was she sleeping with someone else for? How could I have been so stupid as to miss the signs?

Like someone returning to their hometown after an apocalypse, I pace around the tiny property in complete silence.

The house is just as I left it, only colder and dustier. The chill is deep in the foundations of the house; the furniture, walls, carpets, and curtains all icy to the touch.

The houseplant I left in the kitchen is dead. At some point, the freezer has broken. Whatever was in there fills my nostrils with a putrid scent. The boiler by the front door coughs and splutters as I turn it on, struggling to wake up.

I hate myself for crying. I don't remember when I became so weak, but I don't know how I'm going to cope.

Cup of tea. All good plans start with a cup of tea. Leaving my mittens on, I turn on the dusty kettle and pull a mug from the cupboard. The words *dad joke fuel* are fading against the white ceramic.

I miss him.

The white puff of my breath joins the steam from the rusty spout as I pour boiling water over the bag.

A text pings through. My phone is too loud, too shrill in the silence of the house.

Alex
Did you make it home okay?

Ophelia
All good, thank you for paying for my taxi.

Alex
I'll come visit you over the Christmas break. I'll take you out for dinner, christen your bed at home.

I try to think of an excuse, a valid reason I wouldn't want a boyfriend to come and visit. I'm not embarrassed about my childhood, my financial status, or the size of my home, but I don't really want him to see my life here. Despite the mess he has at home, he's rich in ways far more valuable than money. His cupboards are full and his breakfasts are loud and busy. There is love between the walls of their mansion.

Ophelia
Don't worry about it

My screen flashes with an incoming call. I hit the green button and smile. "Hey."

"Hey, beautiful."

"Are you driving?"

"You're on Bluetooth. Cars have that now."

"Shut up. Where are you going?"

I hear the rhythmic tick of an indicator. "Just going to pick Mia, Éléanor, and Evie up from dance. I gave the driver a day off. You seemed sad over text."

"I'm okay. I'm great. Excited for Christmas." I cringe as I say it. It doesn't sound remotely convincing.

He picks up on my tone, of course. "Does your dad know? About the photos of your mom?"

I cup my mug to try to warm my shaking fingers. "Alex, I don't want to talk about that."

"I'm here for you, though. You know that?"

He can't see my smile, but he can have it anyway. "I do. It's more than I deserve."

His voice is sure and comforting. I let it soothe my soul. "We deserve each other."

"Until midnight."

I can hear his grin. "Until midnight, a hundred years from now."

I stare at the black mold that rots the windowsill. I have a to-do list longer than one of Bancroft's lectures. "I gotta go."

"Bye, baby."

288

I hang up and drag my bags upstairs, dumping them on the single bed in my bedroom. A cloud of dust puffs into the air when I throw them on the mattress.

I don't think I'll ever bring myself to take the main bedroom.

I strip my bed and carry the sheets down the stairs, stuffing them into the washing machine and turning the dial.

It doesn't start.

"Give me a break," I mutter, unplugging it and plugging it back in. No luck.

I decide it's an issue for another day. Who needs bedsheets, anyway? I'll lie on a towel.

I sit on the fold-out dining table in the kitchen and dial the number for the nursing home down the road.

"Benmara Care Home."

"Hey, Sarah. It's me, Ophelia."

"Ophelia! You're home already?"

"Yeah. Sorrowsong has short terms, like Oxford. Do you need extra hands over Christmas? I could really do with the company."

"We're *always* in need. May will be very excited to see you, and I will, too, of course. I can't wait to hear all about university."

"If she remembers who I am. I'm free every day."

"Can you come in tomorrow for dinner service? Is that too short notice?"

"I'll be there."

"It's great you're back, Ophelia. Your mother would be very proud of you."

Would she? I'm wondering how well I knew her at all.

◆ ◆ ◆

THE FIRST THREE weeks of Christmas break go by quicker than I had dreaded they would. I go to the nursing home every day and visit my old neighbor, May. She and her late husband, Mr. Rogers, were a big part of my childhood. In the absence of biological grandparents, they were it for me. They'd come at Christmas and take me out on walks, and if my parents got stuck late at Sorrowsong, I'd eat dinner with them.

Mr. Rogers passed peacefully in his sleep six years ago, and a few years after that, May was diagnosed with dementia. Still, she's the closest I have to family, and I live for the moments when a glimmer of recognition sparks in those hollow eyes.

And I've become a professional at reading bingo.

Sarah pays me to help, too, even though I'd do it if she didn't. My first two weeks of wages paid off the water bill and a washing machine repair, my third week paid for a freezer repair. I hope I have earned enough during the break to pay the electricity bill and to fix the heating.

The time between shifts is *hard*. It's so cold in the house that it stops me sleeping. The dreams are bad, too, alternating between helicopters crashing and a stalker breaking into this house.

It's too quiet. Too still. Too lonely. I fall asleep crying and wake up with puffy eyes. I never thought I'd be counting down the seconds until I have to go back to Sorrowsong.

Alex tries to call me every day, but he's busy. I know how full-on it is with his mother and his talks with Green board members. He spent the first week in New York, then he took his sisters skiing in Aspen, and now his whole family is in Paris for the week.

I roll over in bed with a groan, the delighted squeals of children outside reminding me that it's Christmas morning. I just have to get through today. Then I'll be over the worst of it.

I open a text from Vincenzo. It's a photo of Belladonna drinking from a bottle of champagne. The surroundings make it look like they're in some kind of Italian villa, and in the background, there must be fifty other family members. *Merry Christmas, Pheelz.*

I shut off my phone, envious and lonely. Something makes me pick it up again. It's this self-isolation, this misery, that keeps me lonely, stops me from making friends. I need to make an effort to change. Instead, I text him a cheery reply. Another text pings through at the top.

Alex
You up?

Ophelia
I'm awake.

My face appears in front of me like some kind of horrendous jump scare. Christ, is that what I look like? I mutter a curse into the freezing bedroom air. *FaceTime.* The bane of my life. I can't roll out of bed and look good like Alex does. I sit up and smooth a hand over my hair in the darkness, squinting at myself. I swear one eye is bigger than the other.

His face appears on the screen, that fond warm smile on his face that I've come to know so well. It sounds like utter chaos in the background. "Hey. Merry Christmas, sugar."

I smile, burying my blushing cheeks into my blanket. He's blushing too, expression warm. "Merry Christmas."

"You look beautiful."

"That's factually incorrect. My lips are crusty."

"I haven't mentioned my crusty lip kink?"

Despite the heaviness in my heart, he drags a laugh out of me. "It hasn't come up yet, no."

He presses the phone to his chest as someone shouts something at him in French. I wish I *was* the phone. He shouts something back, but I can't translate it. His face appears again. "That was my mom. She wants to say hi. She's really good today."

"To me?" I squeak, hand blindly fumbling around for my hairbrush in my side table. "You told her about me?"

"Yeah, like, six weeks ago."

"*What?* Was I that much of a done deal?"

His grin is boyish and so unlike him. "I have a way of getting what I want, and I really, really, *really* want you."

Christ, I think I love him.

"*Viens ici, Maman,*" he says, beckoning someone over. I panic, sitting up in the dark and running the brush through my hair. This feels serious. This feels like *more*. I flick the dim, orange bedside lamp on.

Elise Corbeau sits down beside Alex, and I'm momentarily stunned. She's as beautiful as she was when she was twenty, just in a different way. I occasionally forget his mother is one of the most famous models of all time. Her dark hair is loose and glossy, down to her hips, and the same dark shade as Alex's. Her green eyes peer down at the phone, pink lips turning up into a smile. A gentle flush caresses her olive skin.

Alex is the spitting image of his mother.

Elise plants her hand on her son's arm and looks up at him, back to me, and back up at him with a delighted expression on her face.

"Oh, Alex, *elle est vraiment belle*." She takes the phone from his hand and angles it away as if to keep me to herself. "You are *very* pretty, Ophelia."

"Hello, ma'am."

Ma'am? What the hell is wrong with me? I sit up straighter and remind myself that Alex's mother is not a drill sergeant.

"He *always* had a thing for redheads. He used to have a crush on that tigress in *Kung Fu Panda*."

I file that knowledge for later. "Oh, so did I, to be fair."

I see Alex's hand slap over the camera, trying to grab the phone back. Elise bats him off. "Alex, love, go and make yourself useful in the kitchen before Mia burns the place down."

One familiar green eye appears in the corner of the screen, making me laugh. "Blink twice if you need help, Ophelia."

"Oh, he is so dramatic," says Elise. A frail hand brushes her hair from her face. She's painfully thin. "He seems so much happier this week. I've hated watching him struggle to stay alive for so long, mostly because of me and the stress I put him under."

My heart constricts. I loathe the thought of Alex losing a fight with the monster inside him. He's very transparent with me about his depression. Some days he wakes up and fires me a text to let me know he'll be quieter today because it's one of the bad ones. "He's more than I deserve."

"You deserve each other."

I feel warmer, like I'm in the chaos of their giant living room in Paris and not the dark gloom of my bedroom in a miserable town in Scotland. "He says that too."

Her expression is warm. Happy. Contented. *She's really good today.*

I look at her smiling down at me like I saved her son's life, and a realization seeps into my veins, bitter and welcome all at once. I can't post my report online, can't send it to a journalist anonymously.

I can't do anything with it at all.

I can't bring more bad press on to this woman, no matter how much I hate her husband.

The last four years have been for nothing.

"Are you with your family for the day?" asks Elise, replacing my depressing thoughts with even more depressing ones.

Her question knocks me sideways, derailing my plan to be cheerful. I stall for a few moments, trying to think what to say. "Um…well, it's complicated. My parents aren't around. You know how families can be sometimes."

Her face softens with understanding. "I'm sorry, sweetheart. You're not alone, are you? We can fly you out here in no time."

And be in a house with Cain Green? I think I'd rather die. Somewhere in the background, six girls shriek with laughter. My eyes sting with jealous tears, and I beg them to go away. "I'm working at the nursing home later, so I'll have company there."

"I can see why he likes you so much."

Alex appears over her shoulder again, placing a glass of orange juice in his mother's hand and a gentle squeeze on her shoulder. He sets a small cup of pills down on the arm of the sofa. He's dressed casually, for once. A black, relaxed-fit T-shirt drapes over the muscles of his chest in a way that shouldn't be legal, the tattoos on his arm stretching as he rubs his neck.

I say a happy goodbye to Elise as Alex walks me into a quieter room.

"You're giving me a look," he says, chugging a glass of water.

"It's lust," I reply simply. "I wish you were here."

He chokes on the water. "This is how I've felt since you got into my car in September. It's like being a teenager again. The things I would do to you if I had you here."

Fuck. I desperately search for a new line of conversation before I get naked on FaceTime, *again*. "Your mother is so beautiful."

"She doesn't believe me when I tell her. Like you." He frowns at the camera. "Are you outside?"

"I'm in my bedroom."

"I can see your breath, Ophelia."

Shit. "Uh…the window is open. Fresh air and all that."

His expression remains serious, a *V* forming between his brows. "I thought you got the heating working?"

"Please just don't." My voice wobbles. I hover my finger over the End Call button, because it's easier than letting him see me cry.

"Don't hang up, Ophelia. Stop running from everything. Turn your camera off if you want to, but don't hang up."

I put the phone down on the bed, brushing my tears away with my sleeves. "I hate Christmas Day."

"How is your dad? Does he know yet?"

He's dead, I want to scream. But I don't want to do it over the phone. Can't admit I lied or admit I only came to Sorrowsong to tear his family apart on a FaceTime call. The second I see him at Sorrowsong again, it'll be the first thing that leaves my lips. "He's not here."

"Is your mom there?"

"No," I whisper, resting my head against my knees. "Alex, I…I have to tell you about them, I just don't want to do it over the phone." I'm terrified he'll leave me when I tell him, terrified that if I do it over the phone, I won't see him again.

"Hold up. You're alone?"

An ugly sob makes my chest ache. "I'm alone."

I hear him breathe out a curse, watch him run a hand through his hair. "I'll head to the airport now. Wait for me, okay?"

Alex leaving their thirteen-million-euro mansion to find me surrounded by snotty tissues in a rotting council house is something of my worst nightmares. "Please don't. This is why I didn't want to say."

"Please let me."

"I'm working in a few hours, anyway. I'll be busy. Let yourself have this day, Alex. Enjoy time with your mother while she's doing so good."

He looks so torn, his face wrought in an anguished expression. "She wouldn't want you to be alone."

"I'll be at work, I won't be alone. These good days with Elise are special."

He can't argue with me. They are special. "But what about after work? What about dinner?"

I furiously brush the tears away, but they keep coming. "I'll stay late and eat there."

"Jesus Christ, Ophelia. Why didn't you tell me? I'd have come and got you days ago. Were you alone when I called last night?"

"Yeah." *And the twenty nights before that.*

"Holy fuck, am I that obtuse I didn't notice? I feel terrible. Why didn't you say so?"

I cover my face with my hands. Shame weighs me farther into the mattress. He doesn't even know the half of it. "I'm sorry. I'm caught up in my own dishonesty."

"No, *I'm* sorry. I wish I was there."

"I wish you were, too."

"Is your heating broken?"

"It finally gave up last night. It needs a new seal. I'll get one when the shops reopen."

"Fucking hell."

"I'll be okay. I can cope."

He gazes down at the phone. "That's never been in doubt, Twist. Not for me."

"I had better go. I'll call you after work, okay?"

"I'll be waiting, beautiful."

I can feel the warmth of his body through the phone screen. It seeps through the frozen air between us and into my own, settling around my heart. He always says the right things, finds the perfect balm for my wounds.

"Alex! Come and open presents!" shouts a girl.

"Yeah, come on!" says another voice.

I try to muffle my sob in my knees. It's such an ugly thing, to be envious of other people's joy. I know Alex's home life is even more difficult than mine, but I'd do anything to have my parents back. I'd ignore the tense remarks, pretend I didn't know about the affair. I'd slap a happy face on if it meant there'd be a sink full of dirty dishes and a bin full of wrapping paper at the end of the day.

"Ophelia, I can have a jet at Inverness in less than two hours. You'd be here by lunch."

"*No.*" It comes out louder and harsher than I expected, my tone bitter. The idea of going in any aircraft, but a Green aircraft especially, makes panic wrap its hand around my throat. And then after

I landed, sitting across the table from Cain Green? I swallow the bile in my throat and soften my tone. "No, thank you. I'd better go. Go open presents."

"Call me after work."

"I will," I whisper, hanging up. I lie back on the bed and bite the inside of my cheek so hard it bleeds. No more crying. Not today.

I drag myself out of bed, checking the thermostat. Twelve degrees Celsius. The heat is on high, but it's not doing anything. Still, a shower helps warm me up, and the four layers of clothing I tug on afterward.

Wiping the steam from the mirror, I turn away from my reflection in disgust. Alex might be the one person who can understand the depth of my hatred for his father, and I've shut him out. All morning I've been rehearsing a way to tell him.

Did you sleep well? Yeah, cool, your father killed my parents, or at the very least, he accepted a bribe to kill them. Yes, that's correct, I did lie to you. And wait until you find out I've been trying to put your family in a huge public scandal for years.

I'll keep rehearsing.

THE NURSING HOME is quiet. Those with children—or rather, children that can still be bothered—have been collected and taken to their family's houses for the day. Only those with nowhere else to go remain. But that's okay with me. It's less stressful this way. I have more time to divide between fewer people. Having just finished reading an Enid Blyton book to everyone, I sit opposite May's armchair, painting her nails a bright red. It would be easier if she didn't keep wiggling them and saying *Oh, aren't they pretty*, but I can't resent her.

I haven't heard much from Alex, but I did log onto Instagram and look at his sister's story to see them out for lunch at one of the most expensive restaurants in France. I've paused the screen a hundred times on the moment where Fleur pans the camera around to Alex, sitting with his arm around Josie as he helps her build a new Lego model at the table.

His usual black shirt and slacks have been swapped out for a Henley and black cargos and *holy fuck*, I'm not coping. He's *huge*. I'll never forgive Instagram for not letting me zoom in on a story. Can Fleur see that I've rewatched this a hundred times? *Shit*. I hope not.

Even Alex posted a rare story, a mirror selfie of all his family bundled into an elevator with the caption *a Corbeau Christmas*. I wonder if it's an intentional dig at his father.

A few weeks ago, I'd never used Instagram in my life, and now I'm a stalker.

I paint a shiny topcoat over May's nails, rubbing some hand cream over the fragile, mottled skin around them. Janet in the chair beside her leans forward and hums in approval. "Would you do mine too?"

I grin and shuffle my chair over. "Of course I can."

I need some more friends my age, because I've only got to Janet's index finger by the time I've told her and May about Alex. Maybe May's been faking her frailness, because the second I mentioned I'd met someone, she sat bolt upright in the chair like Charlie Bucket's grandfather.

Even Sarah abandons dishing out pills into cups to see as I scroll my camera roll to find the only picture of Alex that I have. I don't want a generic one, one that anyone could find on the internet. His head lolls lazily against the pillow, half-lidded gaze looking just above the camera, right at me. I took it right after he showed me how to give him head for the first time. He looks sleepy and sated, no darkness in his eyes at all.

I'm beginning to love the need for control that lives inside him. Maybe there's a darkness in me, too, because I don't want him to hold back for me. I don't think I want gentle.

May squeals like a woman a quarter of her age, pressing her thin fingers to her lips. "Oh *my*. He is just splendid."

"Isn't that Alex Corbeau-Green?" shrieks Sarah, snatching the phone.

"Yes, you know him?"

"I follow his Instagram. Those viral pictures of him running in those shorts last year were my entire life. Oh my god, Ophelia."

Oh, right. I forget he's famous. She knows *of* him. She doesn't know him, but I do. I feel a little giddy. "Find another picture," demands May, slapping my arm.

I type Alex's name into a search engine. There's a fresh set of photographs from an aviation conference this week. I open one up, drinking in his sharp tuxedo and undone top button. His pocket square looks familiar.

"Wow," whispers Janet, leaning closer.

"Oh my god," I whisper, zooming in on the small piece of red fabric that peeks out of his breast pocket. "That's my underwear."

May shrieks. Janet squeals. Sarah drops her cup of eggnog. I clasp my hands over my cheeks.

He had better have washed them.

I end up painting all the ladies' nails, and even one man too. All the while, I'm grilled to within an inch of my life about Alex.

I think the whole town knows. So much for not getting my hopes up. If this thing with him goes south, it'll be crushing.

If this thing with him goes south, it'll be all your fault, the voice in my head says. I shove it down.

I eat dinner in a paper Christmas hat surrounded by people four times my age, reminding them all of my name between each mouthful. We watch a children's show that apparently is good for people with dementia and I end up having to help May spoon her food into her mouth, but oddly, it's been a good Christmas. My parents won't be around for me to care for them when they're elderly, so the least I can do is help the people here.

By the time Sarah and I have washed up twelve plates and bowls, cleaned the kitchen, and handed over to the night-shift carers and nurses, it's almost 9 p.m. I'm grateful it's so late. It's easier than passing the time at home.

Checking my phone when I leave, I have a festive email from my stalker; a quote from *A Christmas Carol.*

Sorry, Alan, I'm only interested in Dickens quotes from one man nowadays. Somehow, even now that I know how dangerous Alan Sine is, I feel strong enough to deal with him. I reread the quote with mild annoyance.

Happy, Happy Christmas, that can win us back to the delusions of our childish days.

I pull off my mittens to type a very short response.

Bah humbug.

I dial Alex twice as I walk down my parents' road. The bitter chill lessens when his deep voice filters down the line. "Sorry I missed the first call. I was putting Josie to bed."

My heart flutters. Both the people in my head want to have his babies. "Did she have a good day?"

"A great day. She got a Lego model of a train. She loves trains and buses."

I freeze in my tracks as I battle the weeds in front of my door. "Oh God. There's a giant parcel on my doorstep. It must be from Alan. Oh *no*. He has my address."

"Fuck, baby, I'm sorry. The parcel is from me. I should've texted. It's a new boiler for your heating. Someone is coming on the twenty-seventh to fit it."

"What?" I whisper, peeling back the cardboard.

"Do you want me to call someone to sweep your house for you just in case?"

"No…" I stare at the parcel, dumbfounded. I've always had an issue receiving presents, even before I lost my parents. "Alex, I…I've been saving for this. I can pay for half now and half later."

"Please don't."

"But I…" I run a hand through my hair. God knows how much he paid to have someone deliver that today. "*Alex*."

His tone is so warm, so soft and sure and full of affection. "Ophelia, my love."

"I'll take it inside, but I'll transfer you money for it."

"Okay. Pay me by midnight," he says, and I'm grinning at the unspoken sentence at the end. *A hundred years from now.*

"By midnight," I promise. "How is your mum? How are the other girls?"

"All very good. *Maman* ended up going to bed super early. Took her sleeping pills and ended the day while it was on a high, you know? Now it's just the housekeeper and me against a tsunami of pink glitter and lip gloss."

I huff out a laugh as I haul the boxes inside. They're ridiculously heavy. "You do so much for them."

"I can't let him break their spirit. How was work?"

"Good. You may have a small army of ninety-something-year-olds lusting after you."

He hums down the line. It's deep and sexy. "I guess I could be into it."

"Great. I'll get the hoist ready."

"Is the hoist for me?"

I clutch my ribs with laughter. Now that is a vision. "Do you want it to be?"

His words warm my freezing skin. "As long as you're there, I don't care."

"Nice pocket square, by the way."

"It's very versatile. Wore it as a bracelet in bed last night. Wrapped it around something else this morning."

And he didn't send me a picture? Rude. "I miss you," I whisper. It comes out dirtier than I intended.

"Fuck, I miss you too. You wanna have phone sex again?"

I bite my knuckles as I toss my keys and bag onto the peeling kitchen worktop and kick off my snowy boots. Alex's husky voice spewing all manner of filth into my ear at night, making promises I couldn't even utter aloud in the light of day, has only fueled my need to see him.

For three weeks I've heard him desperately choke out my name as he comes while I do the same, but it's not enough. I want the real thing. *If he forgives me for how dishonest I've been.* Guilt eats at my insides. "I really do, but I think I'm too cold to get naked."

"I'm *so* glad I bought that heating system."

Thank you. The words sit on the tip of my tongue, making me feel ungrateful. But a thank-you would mean acceptance, and I can't accept another kindness from Alex until I've told him the truth.

Chapter 23

ALEX

I do exceptionally well at not abusing my father's fleet of planes.

But Ophelia sounded so cold last night while I talked her to sleep that I'd had enough. My sisters understood; they're about as desperate for me to make it work with Ophelia as I am.

The wheels of the Gulfstream touch down at Inverness late on Boxing Day morning. A bitter chill sinks under my jacket as I descend the steps onto the tarmac. I bring up the details of the hire car as I walk into the airport, checking they match. Can't be too careful, not if Ophelia is going to be in it.

The one good thing about Inverness is there's no paparazzi as I walk through the empty arrivals lounge to the Land Rover waiting outside. I tracked Ophelia's phone to get her address. Stalkerish? Probably. But romantic? *Maybe?*

I've had girlfriends before, but I'm clueless with Ophelia. I don't want to ruin what we have.

I put her house into the GPS of the dark green Defender, peeling out onto the roads outside. They're surprisingly busy, full of Boxing Day shoppers looking for a bargain. I dial Fleur on speaker as I leave the city and head into the green and white countryside beyond.

"*Lovesick Fool's Hotline.*"

"Ha ha," I say, dryly. "Landed safe. All okay at home?"

"Yeah. Charlotte has made a key ring for Ophelia."

A wolfish grin spreads across my face as I turn left. "You know, I could still mess this up with her."

"Get her a Birkin. Can she drive? Get her an Audi."

"She can't drive, and she won't know what a Birkin is." I'm out of my league with Ophelia. She keeps herself so guarded that I don't know what she likes. Rich as we may be, I'm very wary of throwing money at her. It's the way all my father's rich friends are with women, but I'm not sure it's particularly flattering or romantic. "Better ideas?"

"Umm…food? Fluffy socks?"

Fluffy socks might work. "That'd probably be more effective. Ingrid and Emily are with you guys, yeah?" The new nanny seems really good with the little ones, granting me a bit more freedom.

"Yeah, yeah. And *Maman* is baking with Élé and Mia. Dad is home, too, working upstairs. Jeez, do you *ever* relax?"

I relax just fine when my head is being crushed between Ophelia's muscular thighs, but that's not a sister conversation. Maybe it's a therapy conversation. *Hey, Dr. Harwood, I have Daddy issues and I want legs as earmuffs, help.*

Jesus Christ, Ophelia's body. Thick, strong thighs and arms just as toned. Red hair that spills down to the small of her back. And freckles everywhere over her pale skin. Her addictive, charmingly miserable personality aside, no one's made my body react like hers does.

"Maybe I'll get her some lingerie."

Fleur squeals. Shit. I'd forgotten she was on the line. "Oh my god, *yes*."

"*No*. Okay, I better go. Call me if anything happens at all."

"Things are happening all the time. I just ate a cracker. That *just* happened. Oh, and I've just taken a step forward and picked up the empty box. The box is in the recycling, so that just happened."

God, give me the patience to cope with the eight women in my life. "If you actually put the box in the recycling, it'd be a first. Call me if there's any trouble."

"Will do, big bro. Love you."

"And you." I hit End and sigh. Christmas break has been exhausting. I have no idea how my mother coped with the six of them before she was sick and we got help. Dad being at home today doesn't relax me at all. I'm the only one he's turned physical on, but it's only a matter of time. I undo the top button of my shirt and grit my teeth.

Maybe I shouldn't have left them all.

The sad fact is, no matter how much I love Ophelia, I have to put my sisters first. It's not what Ophelia deserves, but it's the truth. I'm the closest they have to a parent at the moment, while mom is so bad and dad is so absent.

Once he's out of the picture, I can stabilize our home life, stabilize Green; give my whole self to Ophelia.

The drive to her small town isn't far, but the icy roads slow me down a little. I'm kind of nervous that she'll be mad. She doesn't seem excited about the prospect of me seeing her life outside of university. I wonder if her parents are not very involved, or not involved at all. Whatever it is, I've seen messy, I *know* messy; I'd never judge.

When I park the car where the GPS tells me to, I'm not sure I've got the right address. A man hobbles by, a thin plastic bag with a bottle of whisky hanging from his frail hand. He narrows his eyes at me like this part of town doesn't get a lot of visitors.

I check the door of the house to confirm that yes, it is number eighty-eight. It's a small house on a crumbling terrace, white paint chipping off the facade. The lights are off, the garden is so overgrown that weeds cover the bottom window. A small path has been trampled through the brush leading up to the front door, but otherwise it looks completely deserted.

I dial her number, watching for any sign of her in the windows. Her voice is quiet and croaky when it comes. "Hey."

"Hey. Eighty-eight Summerlea Terrace, right?"

I hear her breath hitch.

"Ophelia?"

Her voice has an unnerving edge to it. *Fuck.* Maybe this was a mistake. "Why are you asking?"

"I'm outside."

Even her breathing on the other end of the line stops. I've fucked this up. "Ophelia, I—"

"Drive away, Alex. I'll see you in a week and a half at university, anyway."

"Just let me—"

I know her voice well enough now to know that she's fighting tears. "Drive. Away."

308

"Are you home alone?"

"What part of *drive away* can't you understand?"

"Whatever it is, Ophelia, I won't judge."

"You will."

I hate that I've given that impression. "I promise, baby."

The call drops, and I sit in the car and wait for what feels like forever, until I'm wondering if I really should just drive back to the airport. Finally, I see a shadow behind the frosted glass of the rotting front door. She tugs it open, peering around with wide eyes.

She's beautiful.

I step outside the car, but she doesn't let me come to her, instead rushing out onto the icy road in bare feet and my joggers that mysteriously went missing. "Please go home."

Her eyes are *so* wide, so full of agony. I hate that the world has put it there, hate that she doesn't feel like she can show me her world. My sadness, I can manage, but hers? Hers makes me want to let the world burn. "Ophelia, I just want to see you. I'll sit in the car and book us a hotel somewhere while you pack a bag, if that's what will make you happy."

"I should've told you about them," she whispers, the words bursting out like they've been sitting on her tongue for weeks. Every muscle in her body pulled tight like she's terrified of what I'll do. The guilt in her eyes almost brings me to my knees.

"Let's go inside, baby. Then we can talk, if that's what you'd like to do." I lock the car behind me, following her over the weeds and between two wheelie bins that almost block the door. She doesn't say a word, looks like she can't say a word, as she leads me into an entryway so small that we both barely fit in it. The cheap vinyl floor bubbles under my feet, the unmistakable smell of damp filling my nostrils.

There's a family photo on the wall. Ophelia looks like she's fifteen or so, sandwiched between a grinning bald man in his forties and a red-haired woman who looks exactly like her. Her face is a little pinker, a little more happy than it is nowadays.

So she's an only child. I'd gathered as much.

Does she think I'll judge her because her house is small?

She shuts the door behind us and I'm struck by how cold it is in here. It sinks deep beneath my skin, raising the hairs on my arms. The thought of her shivering here every day is so depressing. I should've come sooner. Should've come when she first gave me an evasive answer about who was with her. The guilt makes it hard to inhale.

We walk past a completely empty bookshelf, which seems odd, and into a small kitchen. The windows are decaying in their frames, mold creeping up the wall. It's even colder in here than it was in the entryway. Her head is hung in embarrassment, and it makes me want to hunt down everyone who ever made her feel that her life was something to be ashamed about.

I'd stop at nothing to see her happy.

She still doesn't say a word, eyes on the ground like she can't bear to see my reaction to her house. I shrug my black jacket off my shoulders, opening a small door. It's a shoe and coat cupboard.

My coat hits the floor at my feet.

There are three pairs of shoes in the cupboard and three jackets. I recognize each of them as hers. I turn back around to the kitchen. No books, no food in the open cupboard. I open the final door downstairs to see a small living room. Empty shelves, a sofa covered in a thick film of dust. A TV stand with no TV. It's as devoid of possessions as the rest of the house.

Realization sinks into me like a knife. "Ophelia—"

She fits so much emotion in four tiny letters. "Don't."

"How long ago?"

I can't see her face through her hair. "Four years."

Four years. She was sixteen or seventeen. A giant lump of emotion clogs my throat. "Fuck, Ophelia."

She turns away, filling a plastic kettle and putting it on to boil. "Please just don't."

"Have you been alone here for twenty-four days?"

"I've been alone here for four years," she whispers, putting two tea bags in two mugs. "Sorrowsong was the first time I'd left this town since…since it happened."

My hands shake slightly at my sides. I place one on her shoulder, but the muscle bunches beneath my fingers as soon as I make contact. "Please don't."

There's another question on my lips but now isn't the time. Not while I can see she's reached breaking point and gone beyond it. Why did she lie? What was the point? Maybe to make her life seem less messy, but I can't believe that's it. She's not like that.

Her chest shudders with a sob, and I'm aching to touch her, but she won't let me. I run my hands through my hair to keep them busy. "Just don't," she whispers. "Don't touch me, don't say anything. Just leave me alone."

"I get you're independent. And now more than ever, I see why. But there's nothing you could say that would put me off you. I'm serious about this, Ophelia. Serious about *us*."

"Well, I don't know if I am," she says, hand shaking as she pours the tea.

I don't know why she's saying this, not when she's told me otherwise multiple times this week alone. It feels like she's preparing me

311

for something. Holding me from a distance so it'll be easier when I leave.

I'm not going to leave.

It's painful how much her own mind refuses to let her be happy. How she lets the bully inside her head tell her she doesn't deserve good things.

"How did they die?"

She shudders, boiling water spilling onto her hand. She doesn't react, doesn't even flinch. When she puts the kettle down and turns to face me, there's a haunting look in her eyes that sends my blood running cold. She looks half dead, half alive. "They died in a helicopter crash."

Somewhere, puzzle pieces start to clip together. Her fear of helicopters, her refusal to fly anywhere, her avoidance of all questions related to her family.

Her hatred of me from day one.

Oh my god.

I don't know how I know, but I just do. I feel like I could vomit into the sink. "It was a Green helicopter, wasn't it? The one that crashed into the valley?"

"I hate you," she whispers, tears running over her lips. The tinge of color that was in her face fades to white. "You know about it already. You knew people died and you let *him* cover it up. I hate you and I love you, but I hate you more."

"Ophelia. Fuck." Oh my *god*. Every cold interaction, every time she's tried and failed to let herself get close to me, gets shifted into a new light. This sensation I've had, like pulling Ophelia close to me is being made harder by a giant weight attached to her, suddenly checks out.

How hard it must've been for her to grow to like me despite what she knew. All the while I thought she was less interested in me; how hard she must've been working to put her past aside and give me a chance.

And my father let her parents die.

I keep my tone careful, like I'm trying to talk down a wolf. "Ophelia, I am *so* sorry."

"You're sorry," she echoes, turning away. The skin on her hand is raised and red from the burn, but she doesn't seem to have noticed. Her voice is shaking, brimming with untethered rage. I deserve every ounce. I'll take each ounce and hold it in my heart.

Finally, a quiet, disbelieving laugh cracks the silence. "You're *sorry*? I was supposed to be there for them, Alex. I was supposed to hold their wrinkled hands and remind them what day it is and watch them succumb to age. I was supposed to come here for Christmas and watch them fight over the vegetables and fall asleep on the sofa, and your father took that from me. And you *knew*. And your mother knew. And all the people around him knew what he was doing, and you all looked away."

"That's not—I didn't know about it until after it had happened." I don't know why I bother defending myself. She's right. I know what my father does and continues to do, working with Vincenzo's father and others like them to erase whoever they want to from the planet for the right price.

I place my elbows on the countertop and interlace my fingers at the back of my neck. There's nothing I can say to fix this. Nothing that will bring them back for her. The only thing I can do for her is get my father out of his seat as CEO and behind bars, because the latter will not happen until the former does. He's too powerful to be arrested for anything right now.

I could kill Carmichael. He must have known about this, and he didn't think I'd care to know that the woman I was seeing was tangled up in my father's mess.

"There's nothing I can say to make this right," I say, straightening out. "And if you want me to fly home, I'll do it now. No questions asked. But I promise I hate him as much as you do. I'm working around the clock with the members of the board I can trust. I'll have him out within the year, I swear to you."

I pull open the freezer to get some peas for her burnt hand, but it's empty save for a few frozen fries and a bag of ice. The fridge is empty, too, hollow like the space between my ribs. Instead, I cover the hand towel in cold water and drape it over the reddened skin as she sinks down at the small dining table.

There's a faraway look in her eye, like she's not really here.

I can see why she said we can't be together now. I can see why she struggles to look at me sometimes, why she said we would never work. Why she shuts down whenever I talk about Green. Why the helicopter sends her running for her headphones. I'm flooded with a new appreciation for her I never had before.

I can't lose her. I can't *not* be with her, and I know how much I'm asking of her by saying that.

More than anything, I can't leave her in this house again.

"Ophelia," I whisper, sinking down opposite her. "Do you want me to leave now?"

She shakes her head, taking me by surprise. Thank *fuck*.

"Do you want me to run you a bath? Or book us a room somewhere?"

"A bath would be good," she croaks. She can't even look at me.

The monster inside me is laughing in delight. *This is what happens to people like you and Cain*, it says, pounding on its cage to be let out. I desperately keep it locked up, because the day it escapes is the day I'll lose the battle against myself.

I have so much to fight for.

It strikes me that Ophelia doesn't. She's a stronger person than I am. It's my family that makes me put the gun back in the drawer on my darkest days.

Every breath she takes is an achievement.

My only way of dealing with anything is looking after people, so the bath is a lifeline I grab onto with both hands. I retrieve my bags from the car and carry them up the narrow stairs, into the small room I recognize from our FaceTime calls. The bed is tiny, but I'm not banking on getting close to her anytime soon. I'll be lucky if she lets me stay the night.

The bathroom is small but clean. A short, narrow, white bathtub sits below a showerhead at the far end. The tap stutters as I turn it on, waiting for the water to run hot.

It's fucking freezing in here.

With Ophelia downstairs, it gives me a chance to sink to the floor, letting my legs outstretch before me with my back to the wall. I bury my head in my hands.

I've never felt as gray as I do now. Hollow and empty, devoid of anything. Even now, I can't summon red anger or blue grief. Only gray. I'm messed up.

In the absence of my father here in this house, all of Ophelia's anger and all of my hatred are going to the next best person: me.

I could've done better. If I'd started my plan earlier, never gone to Yale, maybe her parents would still be here.

My chest splinters into two, agonizing and numb all at once.

Two gentle hands lift my chin, a pair of small feet stepping either side of my knees. She looks like an angel. *My* angel. "I didn't mean to blame you," she whispers. "I know the blame lies with one person and one person alone."

That she would find the space in her heart to comfort me in this situation makes the hole inside me even bigger. "I could've done more. I'll ruin him for you, Ophelia. I swear, I'll break him. When his blood runs into the earth beneath my feet, it'll be your name on my lips."

A soft smile ghosts across her tear-stained face. "That would be a good Christmas present."

I stand up and gently tug her joggers down, removing the coat, knitted jumper, and thermal base layer beneath. Gently, I lower her into the hot water, keeping her burnt hand above the surface. She looks a little thinner than she did a few weeks ago, her muscles more defined as she turns to face away from me.

"My life stopped four years ago," she says, breaking the fragile silence. "I used to read. I used to bake cakes and make pottery. I used to have a friendship group. I gave up on it all the day they died. I only swam because the lake was so cold, I couldn't think about anything else. Your father buried their deaths. Erased all trace of them, sent out a hundred NDAs to a hundred of the right people."

Her next breath is a shudder. "I didn't get support from anyone. Didn't get financial support, or council support, because there was no record they'd died. The house was bought out by your father's company and gifted to me, but I was completely alone. No newspaper wanted to hear about it, no journalist would risk crossing your father. I couldn't bring myself to go to school, didn't sit my exams. I wanted to be a psychologist, but no universities had a place for a girl who didn't finish school."

"I'm so fucking sorry. I'll do everything to make it right." She's the strongest person I've ever met. I've given up trying to rationalize the strength of my feelings for her. Dr. Harwood says I get too emotionally committed to things, too fast, and maybe that's true. But I have this feeling about Ophelia. Like she's all my future Christmases and everything in between.

"You have enough on your mind already," she says, resting her head on her knees. Her free hand draws small circles in the bubbles, like I do in my sketchbook. "Everything about my life is just silent. Stagnant."

I run the bristles of a hairbrush down the wet skin of her back, just how she likes. "You won't know silence like this again. I'll fill each second until our last."

"You are my *worst* enemy," she whispers. It sounds like a lie. It tastes like a lie, smells like a lie. But if it's what she needs right now, I'll accept it.

I brush the tangles from her waist-length hair. Steam rises from her pale skin in the poorly lit bathroom. "Then I'll love you with the same intensity that you hate me. I'll hold on to you just as hard as you push me away. I'll fix you like you're fixing me. I'll always be here, Ophelia, I'll sit at the bottom of valleys and stand on the top of mountains with you. We're too good not to work."

She turns to face me, droplets of water running over her collarbones and between her naked breasts. Her whisky-brown eyes are red-rimmed and glossy. She looks like a Renaissance painting, achingly beautiful. "I don't know myself anymore. I don't know what I like, I don't know what makes me happy. I don't know how to be a girlfriend."

I squirt some of the nice shampoo I brought her from Paris into my hand and set it on the side of her bath. "I know you, love. I see you and I know you." I lather the impossibly long, ginger strands with the soap. "I know you get *so* mad when you can't get one across in your crosswords. I know your favorite book is *The Great Gatsby*. I know you're quiet because it's easier than putting yourself out on the line. I know that time spent with Colette and the other girls makes you happy in a way I could never fulfill. I now know you turn your mirrors around because you remind yourself of your mother. I know you, Ophelia, and it's a privilege."

"It's scary to be known," she mumbles. I get that. I feel it too. Ophelia has me in her hands, and that's terrifying. "Don't break my heart. It's fragile."

"I promise not to," I vow. "All this shit I do, all this effort I put in to make sure my sisters know they're loved and supported and capable, I do it all in the desperate hope that they'll grow up to be someone like you."

"Really?" she asks, meeting my gaze. Fresh tears pool in her eyes, but she looks more alive than she did before.

I can't quash my grin. "And I know you have an obsessive need for validation."

She threads her fingers through mine. I wonder if she knows that every time she does that, the darkness inside me shrinks slightly. "I really do."

I condition her hair only at the ends how she likes, rinsing it off and draining the bath. Pulling a towel off the rack, I wrap her up in it. She's the perfect gift.

"Do you and your psychiatrist talk about *your* obsessive need to look after people?"

I laugh as I usher her into her bedroom. "It's probably most of what we talk about." I pull my clean sweatpants from my duffel and help her into them. "He says I had to grow up too fast and now I'm emotionally underdeveloped."

Her eyebrows raise, perhaps at my honesty. "He said that?"

"Yup. Says I need to not get so frustrated when you don't want to accept my love."

Her face falls. "You think I don't want your love?" She presses her cheek to the center of my chest. "I do. I just…it's complicated."

"I see that now. Complicated was probably an understatement."

She pulls away and kisses me, and I'm almost embarrassed about how quickly she turns me on. A man's right hand can only do so much, and Ophelia's phone camera and Wi-Fi fucking suck. I had to make it work to a frozen screen of her eyebrows last week.

I'm feral for her. A strangled moan leaves her sweet, sweet mouth as I hitch her legs around my waist and bite the exposed skin of her breast. Her back hits the wall, fingernails raking over my back as I lavish my attention on her nipples.

"Please," she moans, head tipped back. "*Please.*"

A satisfied rumble sounds in my throat. I may only be a distraction, but I'll take it. "Good girl, begging for me."

Her hips jolt slightly, my grin hot against her skin. Ophelia comes alive when I praise her. I toss her onto the tiny bed, delighting in her squeak as she bounces over the mattress. I let the starving monster inside me creep out a little, let him take control.

I grip Ophelia's neck as I kiss her, so in tune with every moan that leaves her mouth. What she lacks the confidence to say aloud, I've learned to read from her body. The subtle cues: the heavier breaths, the fluttering lashes, the tensing in her stomach. I'm fluent in *her*. Her hands grip my face as she kisses me with equal ferocity, hot and wet and feverish.

Her cheeks are flushed, hips bucking of their own accord. I'm unraveling at the edges. Only when my hand reaches the hem of my joggers does she sit up, breaking the spell around us. "No. Not here. Not in this house."

I pull away completely, not trusting the animal that lives in my soul. Her chest heaves up and down, lips swollen.

Forget dying for her. I'd *live* for her. I feel like I could overcome all the darkness inside if only it meant I'd get a life in her company in return.

"I was worried you'd leave me," she whispers. "When you realized I'd hidden it from you all this time."

Fuck it. Maybe it's too soon, maybe I am emotionally underdeveloped, but I don't care. "I'm not going to leave you, Ophelia. *I love you*. And I know you're not ready to say it back, and I understand why. But I love you in ways I've never loved anyone before. My mind has been this shitty shade of gray for so long, and now there's this little thread of auburn copper." I wrap a lock of hair around my finger. "This little orange strand runs through the gray like a ray of hope. I love every piece of you, *especially* the parts that you've convinced yourself aren't worthy of my love."

Her bottom lip wobbles, the back of her wrist furiously brushes the tears away. "Thank you." She pulls me down to her and wraps her body around me so tight. "Thank you, thank you. For loving me."

"It's a pleasure." I pull away, meaning business. "Okay, I'm giving you a proper Christmas. I just need to get some food."

She checks my watch. "The food shop will be closed. They close early on Boxing Day."

"Shit. Is there a restaurant around?"

"Not really. Not one that'll be open."

I hum, bringing up a search engine on my phone. "Have you got Christmas lights?"

"Um…maybe?" She pulls my hoodie on and pads out onto the upstairs landing. I fight my smile. She's not *that* much shorter than me, but she looks ridiculous in my clothes. We head into the other bedroom, a larger, empty room with a double bed. I don't need to ask why she doesn't use it.

She squats down beside a pile of neatly packed boxes. Each one has a small note in her neat handwriting. *Mum's clothes. Dad's clothes. Board games.*

I have a new respect for Ophelia. In fact, it goes beyond respect and into reverence. I imagine a seventeen-year-old girl boxing up all of her parents' possessions alone. It's a miracle she's still here and breathing.

She pulls out a string of battery-operated lights from one box, flicking the switch. Her face lights up in childlike joy. "They still work!"

I'm *so* far gone for her.

"Okay, stay right here and wait for further instructions."

"You're obsessed with control."

I pull her to me with a rough grip on her jaw, planting a kiss on that smart mouth. "You have no idea. But this is about wholesome, nice things. Stop making me horny."

Chapter 24

OPHELIA

Alex is up to something. I'm not sure what, but his eyes are alight with a joy that makes my heart sing.

I have that sort of headache that you only get when you've cried way too much for one day. My burnt hand stings beneath the wet towel, my body aches, but I feel lighter. I thought Alex would leave me, but instead he met my confession with the same patience he usually gives me.

I'm going to delete the file from my laptop.

I sit on the bed, bundled in his clothes with a bowl of Pringles, a Sudoku, and a cup of tea, instructed not to move a muscle. I end up with three nines on my final row; my brain was fried at some point during our kiss, but I don't get angry like usual. I'm excited for Christmas. This *real* Christmas. Honestly, I'd rather it wasn't in this house, but Alex is making it feel better.

"Okay, come down," shouts Alex from downstairs. I juggle my book, Alex's present, my snacks, and my drink as I creak down the steps. He's by the front door, dressed in washed charcoal jeans, black Converse, and a hoodie. My mouth waters at the sight of him.

"We're going out?"

"I figured it's not easy for you to relax in this house."

He sees me and he knows me. I put on some slippers and practically bounce out the door with glee. I feel like a kid on Christmas morning. "Where are we going?"

"Well, first of all, we'll find food. It may be instant ramen."

"I love instant ramen."

The car outside looks *expensive*, and very equipped for snowy Scottish roads. The headlights illuminate the pothole-ridden street outside, a warm glow emanating from the windows. "Is this yours, too? And the Rolls and the other one in London? Why'd you need three cars in a country you don't even live in for half the year?"

"Calm down, Twist. This one is a rental. I do like it, though. I might get one to keep at university. Would be nice to have somewhere to rail you that has working lightbulbs." He cocks his head at me. "Did I say that last bit out loud?"

"Can't tell, I was busy staring at your ass."

He laughs and helps me into the passenger seat. I spin to look behind and clap my hands together in sheer excitement. *Presents.* I haven't unwrapped a present in a long time. The back rows are folded all the way down, creating a flat, spacious area behind the front seats. It's definitely big enough for us to lie down in. Not that I'm thinking about it.

The fairy lights are dotted around the perimeter of the car, bathing it in a tangerine warmth. A blanket covers the whole space, two more folded in the far corner. A crossword book and *two* bags of Jelly Babies sit neatly on top.

I've forgotten how good it feels to be loved. And to think I've been resisting this for so long.

Alex slides into the driver's seat, handing me his phone to put some music on. I do just that, and take an ugly close-up selfie on it too. He grins and sets it as his lock screen, pulling the car away into the night.

"Shit," he mutters, as the fish and chip bar comes into view. John, the owner, is just locking up. Alex pulls the car over and rolls down my window.

John nods at me. "Ophelia. Merry Christmas for yesterday."

"Hello, John."

Alex leans over a little. "John, I have a very hungry, *very* grumpy woman here."

"I don't envy you, lad."

"One portion of fries for her, I'm begging you."

My mouth waters. I would love some chips right now. "I've already locked up, mate. Sorry."

Alex pulls a giant wad of cash from the glove box. I'm practically hugging myself with elation. He loves me. "Name your price. Any price."

John slaps his red hand on the car by way of goodbye. "Can't put a price on the missus being angry that I'm home late. Also, they're not fries, they're chips. Put a bit of respect on my food."

Alex watches him leave in the rearview mirror. "Fuck."

"The locals don't love people who aren't Scottish."

"I gathered." He pulls away again. We do a loop of every take-away, restaurant, café, and shop in the town, which isn't many.

Finally, we reach an off-license on the corner of the street my old pottery studio was on. The owner is locking up when Alex gets out of the car and runs over.

I watch him hand cash to the man at the door and hurry inside. I don't know how much he gave him, but it looked like a *stack*. Alex emerges five minutes later with a steaming cup of ramen in each hand and four beers tucked under his arm. He slides into the seat beside me and sets the noodles in the cup holders. I can't drag my eyes off his profile. The way he puffs a breath through parted lips, the way his jawline flexes as he chews his lip, but mostly the way his eyes glitter when he looks up at me and smiles. "Bastard charged me twenty quid to borrow his kettle."

"Because you sound American."

"Well, my American friends tell me I sound French, my French friends tell me I sound English, and my British friends tell me I sound American."

I settle back into the leather as he turns the heater for my seat on and puts the beers behind us. "You do kind of sound all three."

His grin is so wide that it sucks his dimples in. I'm *doomed*. "And you sound Scottish when you're angry. It's like having Billy Connolly tell me not to steal his cookies."

That *is* true. My father was Scottish, my mother born and raised in London. For some reason, I do go Scottish when I shout. "They're biscuits."

He pulls away, away from the tiny town center. "Whatever."

This is one of the first times in a long time I've been neither at Sorrowsong nor at my house, and I feel lighter than air.

Our conversation is easy as he drives us through the night, and all the while I watch every detail of him. The passion while he talks about the architecture back in Paris. The pride in his voice when he relays how good Charlotte's parent-teacher conference was. The emotion in his tone when he explains how in love his parents were before it all soured, and the tiniest whispered confession that he still believes true love exists.

It's like he experiences the same breath of life when we're together that I do.

The cords of his forearms flex as he steers with his right hand, left hand sitting on my thigh. I'm glad it stays there, because if he ventured upward, he'd find out just how much I've been thinking about being in the back of the car with him. "What about you? You got a long-abandoned dream?"

"Child psychologist," I say, as he pulls the car up in a hiker's car park. It's where all the doggers hang out, but he probably knows that. Who am I kidding? That's probably why we're here. "It's not been a lifelong dream, but when my parents died, that was what I was doing in the fictional happy ending I built for myself. Helping kids with grief, trauma, that kind of thing."

He squeezes my thigh. "You'd be amazing at that."

"Oh, yeah. Everyone wants an emotionally unstable therapist."

His eyes drop to my chest. "I want *this* emotionally unstable therapist."

He leaves the engine running so that the heaters can stay on, gesturing for me to go into the back. Nerves race around my body. Does he know *how* inexperienced I am?

I can't face the cold outside, so I crawl between the front seats. I can only imagine Alex's view right now. I hear him clear his throat and shift in his seat before I feel a firm bite through the fabric of his joggers.

327

He follows me into the back of the car, a den of soft lighting and luxurious blankets. He settles beside me, draping a blanket over my lap and queuing up the second *Lord of the Rings* on his MacBook. I accept the lukewarm noodles he hands me, twizzling them around the plastic fork and willing myself not to cry.

This is one of the best Christmases ever.

"Thank you," I whisper. "For this. For coming. For not being angry I lied. Just for everything."

A soft kiss lands in my hair. "No, thank *you*."

I slurp my noodles up my chin in a way that *cannot* be flattering. "What for?"

I don't understand his response, not really, but he says it with so much conviction that I know it means something to him. "For yellow and green, for red and purple and orange."

"And brown?"

He laughs, making my heart stutter. "And brown too. It's my favorite color, lately."

As the level of my ramen goes down, the speed of my heartbeat goes up. I'm overthinking again. Will he ask me why, at twenty-one, I've never had a partner? Will he care? Should I just say I've had loads? No, definitely not. He definitely knows I've never slept with anyone. But when is the time to formally tell him? Now? Later? Is that presumptuous of me to assume he even wants to sleep with me today?

"I'm a virgin," I blurt out abruptly.

Thanks, *brain*.

He nods, swallowing his mouthful with a fond smile. "Cool. I'm not."

I nod right back, like one of those dashboard figurines with the wobbly heads. "Cool. Cool, cool. Nice. Good for you, I mean. Get in there, man."

Get in there? Did I just say that? Oh my god. I reach for the door handle, preferably to toss myself into the nearest ravine, but Alex grabs my hand, chest shaking with laughter. "Thanks, bro."

"Shut up." I hope he can't see how red I am. "And I haven't shaved my legs yet."

"I should bloody well hope not. You need all the help you can get in that fucking house." He eats the last mouthful of his noodles. "I haven't shaved mine either."

My next breath comes out a whimper. "You have *really* nice legs. Really...big."

"Ophelia, I sense you're spiraling."

"I'm spiraling."

He reaches over for the giant bag of presents, planting it on my lap and swiveling to face me. I postpone my sex-based meltdown for later. "I already know you're going to not accept these."

"So why bother?"

He rests his chin on his hand and blinks up at me with big, green eyes. It's *very* cute. "Because I'm desperate."

"I got you something, too, but..." I itch my neck, trying to think of a way to say it. "Money's not been great this year, somehow. Even though I literally have no presents to buy for anyone else. The washing machine broke and then the freezer. The nursing home pay is awful."

"You didn't have to get me anything. I don't want you to worry about money. I could pay off your bills."

Absolutely *not*. "Well, that's a conversation for another day. Jesus Christ, there's, like…seven things in here!" I'm flattered he got me a present, but mostly I'm flattered he knows me well enough to think of seven things I'd like.

"Five from me." He pulls out one in *Frozen* wrapping paper and one in the most expensive-looking wrapping I've ever seen. I look at each of the tags.

You're a brave woman going near Alex. From Fleur, Mia, Evie, Éléanor, Charlotte, and Josie.

"Fleur wrote that tag. Her whole life is dedicated to keeping me humble."

"They got me a present?" I whisper, voice hoarse with unshed tears.

"Yeah. I know you're only *just* coming to terms with us, but… I've been telling them about you for two months. Sorry."

I peel open the Disney paper and rapidly try to blink away the tears. I fail miserably. It's a friendship bracelet. Small and purple and messily homemade. It's everything I've ever wanted. Alex brushes my tears away with his thumbs. "Mia is desperate to Face-Time you. Actually, they all are."

Then there's the world's most expensive candle from Alex's mother, the kind you pick up and smell and put back once you see the price tag. It smells amazing. Not floral, just homely and warm. It smells like a busy house with cakes in the oven and a full kitchen sink. The note says *to warm you up if you're home alone.*

Then there's a pile from Alex, and a homemade Christmas card, too. It's a crossword, the word Ophelia running down the middle with the word Alex coming sideways from the end. He's such a romantic. It makes up for my emotional constipation tenfold.

He got me a giant crossword book, and the most delicious-smelling shampoo ever. And the best drying robe for wild swimming that has been sitting on my wish list on the website for two years. "Okay, before you tell me off for the last two, they're selfish gifts."

"I'm scared now," I mumble, unwrapping the final two. A Mac-Book and a pair of noise-canceling AirPods land on my lap. "*No*."

"Hear me out."

"No, no. Absolutely not."

He clasps his hands together, his voice a desperate plea. "Ophelia, you're too beautiful a woman for that blurry webcam. It's not fair on me. It doesn't do you justice."

I'd be lying if I said I wasn't swooning. The two women inside me have abandoned their constant fighting. They're on the same team now, bent over with their joggers down. "And the headphones?"

"You try untangling those stupid earbuds and you're in a bad mood for the next four hours. For the sake of my balls, use these."

Another no is on the tip of my tongue, but I know that accepting these gifts will nurture Alex the same way he's nurtured me today. I let out a deep exhale and press my lips to his. "Thank you *so* much. They'll help me with the helicopter sound, too. Will you help me set them up?"

He looks so content. "I would love to."

He holds my present. It looks tiny in his large, veiny hands. "It's not…it's in a different league to these." I motion at my pile of gifts.

"Well, I'm excited." He unwraps it neatly, turning over the small, orange sketchbook. There are fifty pages of premium drawing paper inside, and I've written a prompt on each one. Every page is different. *Draw something you love. Draw a Georgian window. Design a banquet hall. Design a church spire. Draw something at Sorrowsong.*

He flicks through each one with an expression that's so unlike him, it almost makes me cry again. He looks like a child at Christmas, a child that's realizing he really *is* loved.

"This is the best present *ever*," he declares, once he hits the final page. "And I'm saying that as a man who got the Sandy from *Grease* limited edition Barbie for his fifth birthday."

I crack open a bag of Jelly Babies and steal an orange one, chewing it through my amusement. "Oh, wow. I'm in esteemed company."

"Thank you, angel." He crawls over me where I sit so we're lying in the back of the car. "I mean it."

I let my thighs fall apart, letting him settle between them. The rough fabric of his jeans is hard against the cotton sweatpants. I don't have any underwear on, and I feel every shift of his body as his lips carve a hot path across my jaw.

"There's no one else around, love," he whispers between kisses. *So we can be as loud as we want* lingers in the sliver of space between us. His kiss is all-consuming, teeth tugging at my lower lip briefly before he goes back in for more.

There's a fire deep inside me and he's throwing fuel onto it with reckless abandon. "Please," I whisper, tugging at his hair. He groans into my mouth, tearing his top off and tossing it into the front of the car.

I sit up and do the same, the air in here warm enough that I don't feel too cold. He curses in French, fingers running over the pale skin of my stomach. The soft flesh dips beneath his touch;

something I'd tease my own reflection for that seems to be sending him feral. "My very own Aphrodite." His fingers slip beneath the sweatpants, pupils dilating. "Is this all for me?"

"I've been thinking about this all evening."

He looks *pained*. Like he wants me so much it physically hurts. I understand how he feels. Gently, his fingers move in a lazy circle, my soft moans filling the car. A carnal warmth spreads throughout my body, igniting when he thrusts two fingers inside, the heel of his hand pressing against the most sensitive part of me. My vision blurs from how good he feels. "Are you nervous?"

"Yes."

"Me too," he whispers, like he's letting me in on a secret. "I've never been so desperate not to fuck anything up."

I blush, unbuttoning his jeans. "You're…big." Understatement. "What happened to the best two inches of my life?"

He laughs. "Finally replied to those penis extension emails in my spam inbox." He tucks an unruly orange curl behind my ear. "You can take it, baby. I'll help you."

Fuck. Me. I'm panting like a dog, the windows of the car fogged up already. He arches the two fingers inside me in a kind of beckoning motion. My cry is so loud it takes me by surprise. I grasp the blanket beneath me, toes curling into the floor, spine bending as he drags me closer and closer to the edge, pulling away when I'm on the precipice. He frees himself and I swallow thickly, running my eyes down his tattooed abdomen. He *really* wants me. "I'm not on the pill."

He holds up a condom between his fingers, putting me at ease. I watch with mild fascination as he tears it open with his teeth and rolls it over himself, abs contracting with each heavy breath. He falls back down, palms landing on either side of my head. "We'll start like this, but I'm desperate to finish with you on top."

Oh God. That sounds advanced. I'm level one at this. The two idiots in my head are already pulling on their riding boots. He interlaces his fingers with mine, kissing me softer than before. "Will it hurt?" I whisper, eyes wide.

He kisses my forehead, my nose, each of my cheeks, gently sucking on my lower lip. My lower belly clenches. He releases it with a wet pop. "Maybe a little."

He tightens his grip on my hand, both of us silent. His heart beats against mine, just as fast. His forehead lands against my own, eyes burning as he shifts his hips forward an inch. My breath hitches in my throat, a delicious burning unfurling between my legs. It hurts and feels criminally good all at once.

His voice is rough and husky in my ear, gaze half lidded and lazy, like after a lifetime of wandering, he's finally home. "You're doing *so* well."

I plead for more, taken by a hunger unlike one I've ever experienced. He hooks my ankle over one of his shoulders. "Ready? Sure?"

"Yeah, and yeah," I reply, and he slams his hips against mine. The sound that leaves my throat is ragged and primal, my hand dropping his in favor of clawing at his back.

My name on his lips is a desperate plea, every muscle in his torso contracting. He gives me a moment to breathe, gives me a second to accommodate him, peppers me with worship.

And then he makes good on all the things he's whispered down the phone this week.

• • •

NIGHTSHADE

ALEX HAS BEEN at mine for *four* nights. Four nights crammed into the smallest single bed known to man.

We're official. Well, he says we've been official for a month and a half, but I'm coming to terms with it. He posted a faceless picture of me passed out on his bare chest in the Land Rover the other day on his Instagram, which according to Colette means he's *serious*.

He even tagged my account. @user802078 is kind of an internet sensation right now. Thankfully, I'm private, so only Alex, Sarah, Vin, Colette, and Divya can see my zero posts.

I do have about nine thousand follow requests, though. Horrifying.

I wiggle my toes in bed, unable to move any more. I woke up to find Alex sketching me from the end of the bed, so I have to stay still. It's a small price to pay for the *draw something you love* page in his sketchbook.

I'm sore in places I never imagined I could be sore. We've christened every surface in the kitchen. I think I've awoken some kind of animal in Alex. He's insatiable. He woke me up for sex at three in the morning.

I went along with it as a one-time treat but told him if it happened again he'd lose a ball. Three a.m. is an unsociable hour for me.

I deleted the file from my laptop. It's bittersweet; I cried after I did it, but Alex is my future. I'm sure of that. He is the definition of above and beyond.

"Breakfast?" he says, closing his sketchbook.

"After your therapy call?"

"You're sure you don't mind?"

"Alex, the world won't end if I go downstairs for an hour and you stay up here."

He buries his head between my breasts, his voice muffled. "Are you sure?"

"I'm super sure."

"Fine. I'll shower too." He kisses me once. Twice. Three times, dragging me with him into the bathroom.

He takes meticulous care in washing my hair, running soapy hands over every inch of my body. By the time we've brushed our teeth and strolled out of the bathroom, I'm struggling to look anywhere but the tanned muscle above the towel around his hips. He's a work of art, a mass of smooth skin and broad muscles.

I want to jump on top of him, all the time. Maybe *I* should take control for once. My eyes flick to the discarded robe tie in the bathroom across the hall. My internal temperature rises another degree. Alex tied up and whimpering, begging. Bloody hell.

"I was about to ring my dad, in case you wanted to listen or leave."

Well, that short-circuited my lust. "About my parents' death?"

"Yeah. He's in Japan at the moment, so I haven't caught him back home yet."

"I'll listen, but it might be too much."

He kisses the top of my head, bringing up his dad's contact. A familiar sense of panic starts to build in my chest as it rings.

"Nice to know you haven't forgotten about your old man."

Cain Green's voice makes my world tilt on its axis. I feel wobbly. Alex lowers me down to the bed, face creased with worry. "Afternoon, Cain."

"What could you possibly be calling me about? You're not so keen on friendly chats these days."

Alex's nostrils flare. It's clear his animosity toward his father isn't one sided. "I'm calling about a hit."

The line beeps and crackles, and Alex holds out my phone on the Notes app. *He's switching to an encrypted line,* he types. Cain chuckles. It's bone-chilling. "Who has dared to wrong my little boy?"

"I don't want to take someone out; I want to know about one that happened here in Sorrowsong."

His father yawns down the line. "That one was a shame."

I'm so sorry, Alex mouths at me. I'm glued to the bed by my own morbid curiosity, my apparent need to see myself suffer. "Who ordered the hit?"

"Me."

"Why?"

"Ah, it was complicated. I did feel a *little* bad."

Alex's hand tightens around the edge of the mattress. "Who was the intended target?"

"A woman, I think. Her and her husband. I can't recall their names. Annabel…Anna? Something like that. Wasn't anyone of importance; no one noticed they'd gone in the end, anyway. Probably one of the easiest cleanup jobs I've ever done."

Alex slips my new earphones into my ears, eyes filled with apology. I pull them out. I need to hear this. "Why'd you kill a random woman in Sorrowsong? Were you sleeping with her?"

My eyes turn to saucers. Does Alex think Cain was my mother's lover? Cain cackles. "God, no. Not my type. Someone had gotten

337

hold of some videos of me I'd rather not go public, and the hit was payment for their deletion."

I bolt upright. *Who?* I mouth at him, heart racing.

"Who was it?"

"Why the sudden interest?"

Alex picks up the box from the bedside table and lights his first cigarette of the week, taking a drag like he's struggling to get through the conversation. "Call it curiosity."

"Another nobody. But I'd rather your mother didn't see videos of me with Harris's PA—you know how *dramatic* she can be when she's upset. It would be bad press."

Alex looks livid. So angry he might burn the world down. Carmichael's PA? Was Cain sleeping with her? "Who was it that wanted the husband and wife dead?"

"I can't remember—no one of any significance. Never heard from him since. He worked at the university, too. Show your face at the company once in a while, will you? Don't make me change my mind about giving you my job in a couple of decades' time."

"Will do, Dad. Lovely as always."

"Who's the girl, Alex?"

I freeze in place as I pace the room. "No one you'd have heard of."

"Lose her."

"I'll think about it," he says, shaking his head at me. "See you around."

I sit back down, light-headed. My stalker and my parents' killer works—or worked—at Sorrowsong, was sleeping with my mother, loves classic literature. It's so much information, and yet I just don't know. I can't think who it could be.

"Surely Carmichael knows who it was," I say, head in my hands.

"I think he does, but he won't say. I've tried everything short of killing him. I'd waterboard him if I wasn't trying to win him over."

"Why? Why would he do that to me?"

"Blackmail, probably, or he's trying to protect his millions in Green investments."

"I hate him."

"So do I lately."

I lie back on the mattress, feeling it dip as he lies beside me. The file is in the Trash folder on my laptop. Gone, but not truly. I have thirty days to recover it. Thirty days to change my mind.

Alex wraps his arms around me, spooning my smaller frame. I have this awful sensation like everything is too good to be true, going too well. Alan has been too quiet, too silent. He's up to something, I'm sure.

I hate my mind sometimes.

Chapter 25

OPHELIA

We've been back at Sorrowsong for a week, and Alex has spent half of it in Paris with his mother's doctors. But the other half? Bliss. Drinks in the Hemlock halls with Alex, Vin, Bella, Jack, and Colette. Poker games in the Nightshade library. Unthinkable nights in Alex's bed. Shared desserts in the dining hall.

I could grow to like Sorrowsong if this is what it's like.

We both have a free period after lunch today. I thought a walk might be nice, but Alex, not so much. He's only really interested in one extracurricular activity at the moment. He is really good at it, though. *We* are really good at it.

"We need business cards. We fuck like professionals," he says breathlessly, making me laugh. Completely undressed, he sits up in bed with a lazy sigh, kissing the purple bruises on my naked breasts and reaching for the sharing bag of crisps on the side table. His phone lights up with a call.

"Mind if I get it?"

"Go for it."

He puts the phone on speaker, folding a hand behind his head. "Hello?"

"Hi, Alex. It's Ms. Dunn, Fleur's senior year mentor. Is now a bad time?"

"No, hit me."

"She says she's not sending any college applications at all? She's very bright."

Alex sighs. "I know she is. She's…we have a lot going on at home. She's struggling with it all."

"Should I urge her to reconsider?"

"She's a teenage girl. Asking her to do something will make her not want to do it. If she's going, she'll do it of her own volition."

"Her attendance is slipping this month."

He sits up. I wish I could fix things for him. I'm glad the report won't see the light of day. "I had no idea. I've not been in the country."

"I'll see you at her parent-teacher conference in February?"

"I'll be there, hopefully with my mother, too." He hits End Call and flops his head back on the pillow. The second he does, his phone rings again. I'm sure he doesn't have a favorite sibling, but when Mia FaceTimes him, his eyes light up.

"MiMi."

"Ally. How's you?"

"Good. Guess who's here."

Her face brightens. "Ophelia! Alex, get your ugly face off the camera and show me your girlfriend."

I laugh, waving to the girl on the camera. She has her father's blonde hair. "Hey, Mia. How was the party the other day?"

She lowers her voice. "I had a beer."

"*What?*" interjects Alex. "You're fifteen."

"Whatever, it was gross, anyway. I called to show you guys this."

She pans the camera round onto a loaf of sourdough. "You made that?" I ask.

"Yep. Wish you could smell it. I had to feed the starter every day to keep it alive."

"Christ. I have a hard time keeping myself alive."

Alex laughs, nuzzling my neck from behind. "That's why I'm here."

She turns the camera back onto her proud grin. "You guys are cute."

Alex rests his chin on my shoulder. "Very clever, Mia. You better re-create it next time I visit."

"Will Ophelia come too?"

Alex squeezes my hand gently. He knows as well as I do, I have a lot of personal development to go through before I can step into their house. He pulls me back down to the mattress, swamping us in the duvet. "It's far for her to travel. Next time we're staying in London, she might."

"You guys are so lazy."

He's anything *but* lazy, but that conversation is not appropriate for a fifteen-year-old.

IT'S LATE BY the time I reach the eastern spire of the castle for a study session. My phone pings as I climb the steps.

Alex

Sure you don't want to drink with us all?

NIGHTSHADE

Alex is in the Nightshade library playing poker with Vin, Bella, and Jack, the surfer dude turned trainee neurosurgeon turned nineties porn star from their rugby team. It's tempting.

> ### Ophelia
> I'm sure. I need to up my grades if I'm going to become a psychology master.

Alex
Can you use your degree to fix me?

> ### Ophelia
> Way above my pay grade.

Alex
Can't wait for later.

> ### Ophelia
> What's later?

Alex
Me, you, the shower, a blindfold.
One across. Two words, eight and five.
O and P. I'm gonna eat the fuck out of it
later.

> ### Ophelia
> Can I blindfold you?

Alex

Carte blanche, Ophelia. You can do
whatever you want to me.

Oh my god. I nearly fall up the stairs. I'm feral for him, even if
Ophelia's pussy is the worst crossword answer known to man.

> **Ophelia**
>
> Two across. Two words, five and four. A and
> D. I'm going to choke on it.

Alex

You're going to make me lose all our
money at poker. None of my blood is in
my brain right now.

Our money. The man is insane. There's no *too soon* when it comes
to Alex. But I think about what his therapist says, about his need
to fully commit because he wants to protect people, and my heart
softens. I can give him that, if that is what he needs. Plus, his protection doesn't make me feel pathetic. He makes me bolder, braver.

> **Ophelia**
>
> Better not. Bad boys get punished.

Alex

Oh my god. Where are you? I'll come to
you. There'll be a broom cupboard or
something we can use.

I laugh into the empty stairwell and chuck my phone in my pocket. There's no way he's focusing on the cards right now. Another text pings through.

Vincenzo
Thanks, amore. He's a mess. I'll give
you a cut of my winnings.

"Ophelia," says Dr. Bancroft as I sit down in his office. "Good Christmas?"

"It was nice, thank you. Yours?"

He smiles warmly, but it doesn't touch his eyes. "Quiet. Did you get a chance to do the essay questions?"

"Yes." I hand him three pages of my writing. "The third one was really hard; I didn't know what to say."

He paces the floor as usual, reading my answers. He nods his approval. "You're coming along very well. You've really caught up on the lectures you missed."

"Thank you, sir. Can I ask you…when you mentioned Carmichael before Christmas. Do you think there was ever anything going on between them? Him and my mother?"

He stops pacing. "It crossed my mind a few times, but she did seem to like your father."

My chest deflates. "I thought that, but apparently not."

"Ophelia, maybe all of this digging is bad for you. You look tired."

"I *am* tired."

He sits down beside me for once and picks up a red pen, scrawling on my top answer. As he sits, a whiff of his aftershave wafts

345

toward me. The reaction from my body is so visceral, so disgusted that I almost gag.

My pen falls from my hand.

Clove, anise, and cinnamon burn the inside of my nostrils. *Old Spice*. An awful flashback of being drowned slams into me, choking on the brown clay beneath my lips. I can't inhale.

A panic attack rears its head at the back of my mind.

It's him. It's Bancroft.

Ophelia, you fool.

I can't breathe. Can't focus. Terror clogs my throat, threatening to suffocate me. My hand violently shakes as I rifle around in my bag, pretending to search. "Damn it. Left my laptop charger outside. I'll just go and grab it."

"Isn't that it?" he says, pointing at the cable on the desk in front of me. Oh God. I'm going to die.

It's him. I don't even have time to process that it's him. I just need to get out of here alive. "Oh, yeah. I'll just use the bathroom while you mark my answers."

I'm up and out of the chair in a flash, typing a frantic text to Alex. I'm hitting all the wrong letters with my fingers, but I don't care. My breaths come faster, more panicked as I reach the door. I turn the door handle, but it doesn't move.

I'm locked in here. I try it again, frantically twisting the brass knob until a knife caresses the back of my nape, forcing me against the door. A hot, sticky breath brushes my ear, making the hairs on my neck stand on end. I hit Dial on Alex's number, but Bancroft slaps the phone to the ground and stomps on it until it shatters.

I screw my eyes shut as his body presses against mine, the knife at my throat now. His voice is different, no longer soft but gnarly and harsh. "You're just like your whore of a mother."

"You killed her," I whisper as he crushes my head against the wood.

"She was supposed to be mine!" he shouts, slamming my head against the door on the final word. Stars explode behind my eyelids. "She was supposed to leave with me, but she turned her back on me for *you*."

My penknife is in my bag across the room. I'm helpless as he runs the knife down my side and back up again. "One little video of Cain Green fucking Eva over her desk and he'd have done anything I asked. Anything to protect that shiny reputation. Killing a couple of nobodies was an easy decision to uphold his image."

I'm trapped into stillness by the blade at my spine. "I let you live, almost forgot about you, and then one day, there you are in my lecture hall." The knife draws blood at my neck, and I muffle a scream. "Like the universe is just *begging* me to end your bloodline. I gave you a chance to run. Spiked your drink, killed your roommate, but you were too obsessed with *him*. The tarn was my mistake, I'll admit. I thought I'd left you dead."

I feel sick, my skin crawling as he presses my body harder to the door. I scream Alex's name, rewarded with a knee to the lower back. "And there I was, thinking you'd hate Cain Green. Didn't take you long to fuck his son, did it?" The knife runs between my collarbones and all I can do is stand there and do nothing. If I step back, I'm dead. Every fiber of my body shakes. "Do you like it rough like your mother did?"

I wretch against the door. I don't struggle against the weapon, not now I have something to live for.

I want it all with Alex. I want the busy Christmases and the messy kitchens and a basket full of our laundry and I want to wash his hair until the end of time. I scream his name again, in the hope someone, anyone, will hear me.

I love him, and I haven't told him.

"What do you want from me?" I choke out.

His cackle makes my eyes screw shut. "Oh, darling. We're *so* far beyond bargaining. I just want to have fun with you."

I drop to my knees, sending him forward where he no longer has me to lean on. The knife lands in the door. I dart out from beneath his legs, kicking him where it hurts.

"You bitch!" he shouts, falling to his hands and knees. I can't find a key for the door. My only hope is killing him. I tear open the pocket of my rucksack, tucking my new earphones into my tights and reaching for the knife.

Earphones have trackers, right?

I'm too slow. A searing pain radiates down my arm as Bancroft slices over my hand. It hurts so bad I can't grip my blade. It clatters to the carpet, the sting from my hand making my vision blur.

Panic crushes my chest. What if Alex thinks I didn't want him enough to fight? Will he know I tried?

I kick Bancroft in the knee, his howl of pain reverberating in the repugnant atmosphere around us. He kicks me back just as hard, but I barely register the pain. I grapple for the giant knife in his hand, the blade nicking at my skin. His blood joins my blood, dripping down my arm like paint on a canvas.

"Fucking bitch," he seethes, crushing his palm onto my face. He kneels on me with all his weight crushing my lungs.

I'm light-headed from the bang to my head, short of breath from his weight. I'm all out of fight. His eyes are so dead, so empty as he covers my nose and mouth with his palm and presses until a hazy mist clouds my vision.

"Alex," I whisper, like there's some miracle by which he'd hear me.

My body feels broken. My mind proves to be the traitor it always has been. I hate myself for being so pathetic. Hate myself for losing to Bancroft again.

Only this time, it's Alex's soft smile that keeps me company as the room fades away. It's the kisses beneath my ear that wake me up each morning. It's the unwavering belief he's always had in me. It's the feeling of being *his*, so warm and so welcome.

If these are to be my last moments, I'm filled with nothing but gratitude for him.

For the second time, my world fades to black beneath Bancroft's hands.

Chapter 26

ALEX

I don't think Vincenzo has ever beaten me at poker in the almost twelve years I've known him, and he's obliterating me. That's what Ophelia has done to me. I'm a husk of my former self. I'd lose it all if it meant I could keep her, though. Half the time I can't believe she's mine.

She's beautiful in a way that makes me grateful nothing before her has ever worked out. In a way that makes me want to almost run her over on that rainy track outside the castle gates one more time, because I just know I didn't appreciate her enough the first time.

I can't remember the last time the world felt so colorful.

I make another sloppy mistake; another five hundred dollars down the drain. I'm *tired*. I spent half of last night buried inside Ophelia and the other half counting her freckles.

"Fold," huffs Jack, stroking his chin. A mustache has joined his messy mullet at some point over Christmas. A deep tan kisses his muscles from a December in the Maldives with his rich neurosurgeon parents. He's the perfect pornstar.

Vincenzo and Bella are fighting over the card game, as usual. And I'm just rereading my texts to my girlfriend like an idiot.

She left me on Read a while ago. I *hate* being left on Read. I'm not ashamed to admit I can be a little overbearing sometimes, and unfortunately Ophelia texts like your average sixty-year-old man. I passed my exam? Thumbs-up emoji. I wanna rail her into next week? Thumbs-up emoji. I narrowly avoided death at rugby? Thumbs-up emoji.

But she's new to it all, so I'll forgive her.

As Vincenzo deals out another hand, she finally replies.

Alex

Oh my god. Where are you? I'll come to you. There'll be a broom cupboard or something we can use.

Hot girl from uni
Banned Orifice

Banned orifice? The fuck does that mean? *Anal?* Jesus, my blood pressure is fighting for its life this evening. *Give a man a chance, Ophelia.*

Vincenzo catches me staring at my phone and smiles. He got a face tattoo over Christmas. Some Roman numerals extend from the bottom of his shaved sideburn to the corner of his jaw. He's going to run out of space soon, at the ripe old age of twenty-one. "How come she isn't here?"

"In some study session. She wouldn't let me go with her. Says I'm a control freak."

"You are. Who is she with?"

"One of the psych lecturers. Bancroft, or something."

Belladonna makes a face. "He's creepy."

I tense, dropping my cards onto the table. "Why?"

"Just weird. He took one of our third-year modules. He's just odd. He talks for hours on end and doesn't even hit the content he's supposed to." She sips her wine, tossing her dark ponytail over her shoulder. "He *hates* me."

"How come?"

"Caught him fucking one of the gardeners in my first year. I wasn't even gonna tell anyone anyway, but he threatened me. Said he'd hurt me if I told someone. I told him if he even dared, he'd have a hundred hot-blooded Italian men after him."

"Fuck yeah, he would," mutters Vincenzo. "What did you say his name was? Might pop over for a friendly chat."

Their conversation gets drowned out by ringing in my ears. I'm already out of my seat. "What did the gardener look like?"

"Female. Ginger. I can't remember much more than that."

A sickening dread sinks into my blood. "Fuck."

They all stand in unison. "What?"

"He's her stalker." I bolt out of the library and through the front door of the mansion, flying toward the castle. I call her number with the others on my heels. "Pick up, Ophelia, come on."

"Should we split?" asks Jack.

"Go to the car park. Don't let any cars leave."

"Got it."

My feet pound the castle courtyard, taking the stairs into the eastern quadrant three at a time. I dial her again with no success. Vincenzo and Bella are trying to reassure me, but it's not going in.

She's not fine. I have a feeling she's *not* fine.

Banned orifice. *Bancroft's office.* I've never felt a panic like it. Never felt so hopeless or so full of hatred.

"Up the turret," breathes Bella as we run into a stairwell. Vincenzo spears off to search the eastern halls.

The door to Bancroft's office is wide open when we reach it. The scene in front of me makes me want to vomit. There's blood on the carpet, a lot of blood. Her phone is shattered on the floor, her bag abandoned by the desk.

Belladonna curses in Italian. "It might not be her blood."

I tap her phone screen for a clue, but it's broken. "What was I thinking, letting her go anywhere alone?"

"This isn't your fault."

"It's all my fucking fault." I pull open every door on the top of the turret. It's deserted. My sense of despair is all-consuming. "Stay up here, they might come back. Call me if you see anything."

She nods, pulling a Glock from her waistband and holding it out for me. I almost take it, but I can't bring myself to. I'm not leaving Belladonna unarmed alone. "Keep it."

"*Alex.*"

I'm already descending the stairs. "Keep it!"

I knew better and I let her down. I should've been following her everywhere until Alan was caught. I let myself get complacent in his silence. I pull out my phone, bringing up the Find My app.

A wave of gratitude slams into me. Ophelia's AirPods are moving on the map. *Clever girl.* They jump around due to poor signal, converging on the forested edge of the tarn. Fuck. A strangling voice in my ear says he's dumped her body there. I push it out and grit my teeth.

She's not allowed to die until I say so.

I sprint out of the castle, traversing the path down to the water's edge, heart pulsing in my mouth. The place is deserted, covered with a foot of snow. There's no sign of footprints at the edge of the tarn when I skid onto it. "Ophelia, baby, where are you?" I whisper as I head into the woods.

The forest is silent and eerie as I jog through it, a low fog hugging the trees. I don't use a flashlight. I don't know how dangerous this guy is, or if he has people working with him. I can't attract attention to myself.

There's no sign of them. No footprints, no rustles in the bushes.

He could've abandoned her body, but I *know* Ophelia. I have some otherworldly connection to her that transcends what makes sense. In my heart I know she's alive, because if she wasn't, it would be aching.

I try to keep the anger aside, to focus on Ophelia's safety, but the monster inside me has crawled out of its cage. The colors bleed out of my brain, nothing left but malice.

I follow the blue dot until I'm so close it looks like I could reach out and touch her.

I stop, scanning the inky black abyss around me. My breaths are the loudest thing in the valley, each one a white cloud in the moonlight. There's no sign of Ophelia, no sign of Bancroft. A disconcerting silence falls around me. It's too quiet.

The dot moves to my left, and I head through a dense thicket of trees.

I slam into something—*someone*—as I round a thin tree trunk. Or rather, someone slams into me. Ophelia was sprinting through the trees toward the forest's edge. The large knife in her hand glistens with blood.

A terrified scream rips through her throat and I clamp a hand over her mouth to silence her, catching her wrist an inch before the knife sinks into my chest. "It's me," I whisper. "It's me, baby. I've got you."

She sobs into my hand, deep breaths heaving through her nose. Moonlight catches in the flecks of gold in her irises, wide and glassy. She looks terrified. I rake a desperate gaze up and down the soft contours of her body, searching for any sign that she's badly hurt. "I'm going to need you to be quieter, love."

When her ragged cries die down, I remove the hand from her mouth. "I love you," she breathes, like it's been on the tip of her tongue for hours.

I shake my head, clutching her to me. "No. You're saying that because you think we're going to die. Say it when you know we won't."

"He has a gun," she whispers, teeth chattering violently.

"Where is he?"

"I stabbed him."

That's my girl. "Take me there and then I'll get Vin to come and take you back."

"No. I'm not leaving you. Not now, not ever." She leads me through the night, my hand sticky with blood. *Her* blood. The monster rears its ugly head inside me.

"Are you hurt?"

She nods but keeps walking, dragging me through the trees. A rope dangles from her right wrist like her hands were bound before. A nauseating thirst for death, a lust for blood, courses through me.

Is this how my father feels all the time?

She hands me the knife in the dark, eyes wide with worry. It's such an act of trust, such a display of her belief that I'd protect her. Any other situation and I'd probably get down on one knee right here.

She freezes in a small gap in the trees, moonlight spilling like liquid silver over the forest floor. Her legs tremble beneath her ripped tights, eyes frantically darting between the shadows around us. A shovel glints in the cold lighting, discarded against a rock. He was going to bury her.

I have a feeling this'll take a long time for her to overcome.

Wet, sticky blood glistens on the leaves at our feet. A crow calls out in warning somewhere far away. Her breaths pick up, chest rising and falling faster. Unease prickles my spine. "I left him here. He was bleeding out right here."

I have to get her back to the castle. Revenge can go on hold as long as I know she's safe. We spin around to leave, but a twig snaps somewhere in the bushes. I wrap myself around her, hoping and praying that the muscle and bone of my body would be enough to save her if it came to it.

"Come out, man. Don't be boring."

Bancroft stumbles out into the trees, a gun aimed at me. He's vaguely familiar; a tall, gray-haired man whose existence is as miserable as his sweater. Ophelia has done a real number on him. A giant bloodstain sits over his abdomen, one of his eyes swollen shut. From the muddy footprints over his crotch, I'd say he's been through it.

I love her.

Even in the dark, it takes me all of ten seconds to see the gun is fake. Convincing, but faker than a three-dollar bill. It took Vincenzo a hell of a lot of effort to get his guns into the UK. There's no way this buffoon has got one. I tell Ophelia so, so quietly that I'm not sure she heard me. But her shoulders relax slightly in my arms, breaths steadying a little.

"Ophelia, love, would you go and stand over there?" I ask softly, slipping the rope from her wrist. "Might get messy."

"I love your mess, Alex."

I wonder what my shrink would make of the fact that, despite the situation, all I can think about is bending her over right here on the forest floor. My fingers sink into the curve of her ass, having to bite down my amusement as Bancroft points the gun at us with renewed determination.

A tiny, almost inaudible moan hangs in the dense air around us.

Oh, Ophelia.

I knew she had a fucked-up little monster of her own. I knew a tiny thread of depravity stained her gentle heart. Cute.

I calmly walk to Bancroft. He must clock that I know the gun is fake, because he drops it and turns to run. But he's slow, and I'm fast. He's old, I'm young. He's got nothing to run for, but I have *everything*.

It takes me all of three seconds to catch him by the back of the neck, dragging him into the middle of the glade and pushing his limp form onto its knees in front of Ophelia. She stares down at him, eyes alight with fury.

I twirl the knife between my fingers and let it land beneath his ear. "You and I are going to have a quick chat about Sofia Ivanov, and then we'll talk about what you've done to my girlfriend."

His squeal is nectar for the darkness inside me. For a man who likes to torture others, it doesn't take much force from the knife to get him to talk. By the time I've recorded his confession to Sofia's murder and the helicopter crash, he's clinging onto his life by the fingernails, begging for mercy.

I slide my phone into my back pocket, staring down at the withering mess on the floor. Evidence that I killed Sofia's murderer will be useful if I'm ever to cool my father's volatile relationship with the Ivanovs.

I move to finish the miserable bastard off, but Ophelia steps out of the shadows and shakes her head. "Let him die slowly."

She stands between his legs where he lies, sprawled out on the bloodied earth beneath us. Her body may be shaking, but her voice is not. She looks down at him as he lives his final minutes, reciting lines from *Ode to a Nightingale,* the John Keats poem that started this whole mess. She looks like a priest reading the last rites, and I don't intervene, *can't* intervene, too awestruck by her.

"'*That I might drink, and leave the world unseen, and with thee fade away into the forest dim.*'"

Angry tears roll down her cheeks, joining his rotting blood on the black earth.

Bancroft's chest heaves with a final breath, blood gurgling from his lips. The moonlight bathes Ophelia like a goddess, a silver statue painted in blood.

"'*Where palsy shakes a few, sad, last gray hairs, where youth grows pale, and specter-thin, and dies.*'"

She leans over and spits on his corpse, turning away in disgust. It's a forensic analyst's wet dream, but I decide to keep my mouth shut.

She sinks to her knees on the wet earth. Her next exhale is a desperate, shuddering apology to her father. The one after that is a bitter insult to her mother.

I kneel opposite her and she buries her head in my chest. "This doesn't feel like a win at all."

"It doesn't have to. You don't owe anyone gratitude."

"I love you."

I grin against her damp hair. "I love you, too."

Footsteps sound to our left, Vincenzo emerging between two trees with one of his men. They look ready for a cleanup job. Vincenzo chucks me a shovel, silently taking in the scene around us, gaze landing on Bancroft. "Ten points to Ophelia. You were a wreck the last time someone died."

I nod my agreement. "Character development."

Chapter 27

OPHELIA

Alex pushes the tip of the shovel into the mossy earth, stacking both gloved hands on top. In the navy forest around us, his eyes are supernatural. He brings his chin to rest on his knuckles, peering up at me with a boyish grin that has no business being so endearing at a time like this.

"So what does this make us? Study buddies that bury bodies together?"

I can't fight my smile. That feels like a lifetime ago. "The day I bury a body with you, Alex, is the day I've lost my mind."

He flutters long, black lashes at me. "You lost your mind, angel?"

"I lost it the day I got into your car."

His grin pulls in his dimples. "Really? I think I found mine that day."

Butterflies flutter somewhere behind my navel. Over his shoulder, a masked-up Vincenzo waves Bancroft's hand at me. Just his hand. The rest of him is still on the floor, being doused in some chemical by his bodyguard. Another of Vincenzo's scary Mafia men is scrubbing my blood out of Bancroft's office. Another is penning a false, cryptic suicide note. Vincenzo drops the severed limb onto the freezing ground.

I do have limits, and detached hands are well outside of them. I turn away and gag, trying to unsee the spectacle that lies in the center of the glade.

What a fucking mess.

Vincenzo is right. Something in me has changed. I'm stronger, more resilient than I was before. Covered in Bancroft's blood marbled with my own, shivering in a forest I never thought I'd venture into, I feel like I can do anything.

That's not to say I'm not planning on sobbing into a tube of soggy Pringles in the shower for two hours when I get back, because I am. There are things Bancroft said to me in the forest that I'll never unhear, old wounds that have been torn wide open.

Alex keeps me turned around, gentle kisses landing on the top of my head while they finish turning Bancroft into some sick and twisted salad. I don't look. I don't need a reminder that I have become everything I hate.

I pull his jacket tighter around me. I killed a man. I could go to prison. I *should* go to prison.

But more than that, what horrifies me most is the fact that when I finally slid the knife into his abdomen, a sharp thrill overpowered the dull wave of disgust. I'd be lying if I said ridding the world of another evil didn't feel good.

Manslaughter? Six out of ten. Enjoyed it—might not do it again, though.

361

Bancroft half dissolved and buried in varying locations around us, Alex steps behind me. The scorching heat beneath his shirt penetrates through his jacket, melting onto my skin. He makes me feel like everything might work out fine in the end. "I'm not going to bother asking you if you're okay, I'm just asking you not to shut me out when you spiral."

"I won't."

"Let's go home," he whispers.

"Home?"

Each gentle kiss on my hair mends another crack in my heart. "Wherever you want, love. It's home if we're there."

Chapter 28

ALEX

An orange sky drags the sun out of hiding, early morning light slipping through the curtains. Ophelia snores quietly beside me, fast asleep on her little throne of dribble. I don't blame her. It was two in the morning by the time we and Vincenzo's cleanup team went to bed, and three by the time we got to sleep.

I've dragged her too far into my world. I shouldn't have let her see Bancroft die. When she got back to my room last night, she cried in the shower for an hour. I don't know what he told her, but she's rattled.

And still, she surprises me. Stronger than I ever expected, and stronger than she herself believes she is. It's comforting, in a twisted way. Like if I were ever to lose this never-ending battle against myself, she'd be okay.

But I'll keep fighting for her, for my sisters, for my mother.

My fingers trace her freckles like a dot to dot that forms the prettiest picture. Bancroft's death is a victory, but it pales in comparison to what is still left to do. I have to get my father out. Have to put an end to what he does, have to get him away from the rest of my family.

I hoped to have him out by the time I was twenty-six and had completed my business degree, but that's not soon enough anymore. I took a folder from Carmichael's office to build a case against him, but I didn't need one. There isn't a single board member who doesn't know the full extent of his depravity already. There's nothing more I can tell them to convince them he's wrong, it's about convincing them that *I'm* right.

I have a solid relationship with most of them now, except Shawn's greasy father. Most of them have promised me their vote. I can't stall for much longer.

But God, if I fail, if my father catches wind of something, I don't think he'd be above killing his own son. Worse than that, he knows the girls are my weakness. He'd hurt them to hurt me, and I can't let that happen.

Speaking of my sisters, they've been suspiciously quiet. Not one request for help choosing a nail color from Fleur, not one raccoon meme from Mia, or a demand for details on Ophelia from Evie. Éléanor and Charlotte haven't told me how their dance show went, and Josie usually sends me a random emoji from her iPad once in a while.

Shit. I put my phone on Do Not Disturb last night to make out with Ophelia in peace. A nausea-inducing dread washes over me. I pick up the discarded clothes strewn about the rug, finally finding my phone beneath my jacket. I swipe up, my stomach swinging up to my throat.

One hundred and thirty missed calls. *What the fuck?*

I don't even know where to start. Thirty of them are Fleur, and seven of them are my mother's psychiatrist, who has never double-called me in five years.

Twelve—*twelve*—of them are my father.

Bile rising in my throat, I start to read the texts that have come through over the last few hours. From my sisters, from my lawyers, from the Green board members, from my old Yale friends.

Fleur
Maman is completely losing it
Pick up!!!
Dad just hit her. What the fuck do I do?
I know I said I'd never ask this of you,
but please come home

Élé
Some crazy article has gone live about
Dad killing people in Scotland.
Dad's scaring mo.
Fleur is trying to defend Maman
from him.

Charlotte
Fleur is hurt, I can't find Mom.
Someone said Ophelia did this, is it
true???
Is it true Dad did bad things?

As the words swim in front of me, a text pings through from Kenzo, my closest ally on the board. It's an article on a trashy blog. My mother's face loads onto the screen. She looks like a ghost, pushing her way through a swarm of paparazzi that swirl outside our Parisian villa.

"I'm sorry," she wails as the camera is thrust in front of her face. She sways on her feet, a black eye staining her skin. "I knew he had turned bad, and I didn't do enough. I wasn't brave enough. Are you going to cover my bruises with editing? I haven't done my hair."

Fuck. Fuck, fuck, *fuck*. I don't even bother packing a bag, pressing my phone to my ear as I grab my laptop from the sitting room. Mike, the director of technology at Green, picks up on the first ring.

"Where the fuck have you been, man?"

"I need a jet from Inverness."

"All Green jets have been grounded. Get your ass to New York before your father kills you."

New York. My chance at bringing my father down before he can blackmail his way out of this mess lies in Manhattan. But my terrified sisters? My unraveling mother? They're all in Paris.

I don't know what to do.

"Unless you want your plan to go down the drain, don't even think about Paris. Miller is rubbing his hands together. He wants CEO, and it doesn't look like Carmichael has your back. I have a jet landing at Inverness to take you to New York in an hour. Your dad is MIA."

Fuck Carmichael.

My finger hovers over the flight to Paris. *Fleur is hurt, I can't find Mom.* Where the fuck has Cain run off to? "I need security for my sisters."

"I'll get on it."

"Have you traced the leak?"

"Yeah, and I'd bet my ball sack she's in your bed."

"What?"

"I'd bury a bullet in her while you have the chance."

My voice is a hoarse whisper. "Ophelia?"

"Ophelia Winters."

The thought makes me feel sick. "It wasn't her. There's no way it was her."

"I'll send you the metadata if you want. It was sent from her email."

I'm in fight or flight, all emotions on pause while I grab my car keys and passport. "Send it over, but that has to be bullshit."

"Are you coming to us?"

Guilt makes my throat so tight I can barely choke the words out. Freedom for my sisters can only begin with Cain losing his power. "Yeah. Needs to be done."

I stare down at Ophelia, fast asleep in my room. The soft rise and fall of her breaths couldn't be further from mine.

I'm desperate not to believe Mike.

On my desk, I unlock her laptop and search her files, opening up her student email. Nothing.

I pull out her old laptop, the one that hardly works, waiting for her personal email to load.

I imagine the shitstorm at home. The CEO position I never wanted to have.

I don't expect I'll ever come back here.

A text pings through from Vincenzo as her emails load.

Vincenzo

I just woke up. I know more people
texting you is not what you need, but
fuck, brother. I'm so sorry. Whatever you
choose to do from here, I'm with you.

I type out a reply.

Alex

Can you go to Paris to be with them?
Belladonna too?

Vincenzo

We'll leave now.
They'll understand.

I doubt it.

Sitting in Ophelia's Sent inbox is an email to twenty journalists.
No caption, no subject line, just a report on my father and all that
he does behind closed doors.

"I gotta go, Mike." My voice sounds hoarse, broken.

I open up her drives, flicking through her university files. Like
her phone, her laptop has almost nothing on it, so it doesn't take
me long to find what I was desperately hoping I wouldn't. I recover
it from the Trash, almost amused that the file is named *Untitled
Document 2*. I flick through forty pages of screenshots, emails, texts,

and musings. There's a transcript of someone's dying confession, and a tape recording of the same thing. There's an accusation that my mother was complicit in it all.

My final shred of disbelief makes me open the file data, confirming it was her that created the document almost four years ago.

Betrayal fragments my chest into a hundred pieces. It physically *hurts*.

I should wake her. Beg her for any kind of explanation or excuse. I want to fight each other until all of this makes sense.

But that's another hour on my plan. Another hour away from the little ones. And I'm just *so* exhausted. Not the short-term kind, but down to the bone. I've got nothing left to give.

The gun in my bedside table gleams at me.

Wouldn't it be easier to just disappear?

If she tells me all of *this*—me and her—was some revenge mission, I don't think my sick brain could survive it.

My phone buzzes constantly on the desk.

I can't bring myself to look at her. Can't say goodbye. I can't face the fighting, the denial, the apologies, the excuses. I can't delay my plan to take over Green any longer. I can't put our relationship ahead of my sisters right now.

Mia

I'm scared, Ally. If something happens, I
love you.

          Alex

          Hold tight for me. I'll be there
          as soon as I can.

I can't imagine how I'm going to get to midnight without ending my life. I can't attempt to articulate how I'm feeling, so I slip out of that room and leave without a word.

I call Fleur as I yank my car door open. Vincenzo's matte black Maserati roars out of the car park at breakneck pace, and beneath the panic and the nausea, gratitude for him seeps in.

When my sister picks up, she's sobbing. I can hear Josie crying in the background. "Why didn't you pick up?"

I start the engine, putting my seat belt on while I pull away and hit the gas. "I'm so sorry. I fucked up. Where's Mom?"

"Hospital. The housekeeper left; Dad pulled a gun on her." I can picture her glassy eyes, wobbling lower lip. It crushes me. "When does your flight land?"

For the first time since I was a young child, I feel hot tears scorching a path down my cheeks, running over my lips. The road blurs in front of me. "Fleur, I'm…I'm not coming. Not today."

"What?"

I clasp a hand over my mouth so she can't hear me cry. "I have to go to New York."

Her sob makes me want to die. "I need you here."

"I'm so sorry. I need to get rid of Dad."

Josie howls somewhere behind her. The gray cloud strips the strength from my limbs. "Please. You're our dad, Alex. Not him. It's never been him. We can all run away, he won't find us. He'll go to prison. We can just run away."

She's seven years behind me. I've had seven more years of believing in the good in the world and being let down. It won't work out that way. "I'll be there as soon as I can."

"You're just like him. Green over family, always," she spits out, tone acidic.

She hangs up on me, and I don't blame her.

My fingers itch for someone to call. My mom. I need her. I need the version of her I had six years ago. The one that always knew what to say.

I'll never get that woman back.

On cue, Harwood's name appears on the screen in the car. I hit Accept, the sob finally bursting free. "I want to die."

He's calm on the other end of the line. "I know. Are you driving? You shouldn't be driving."

"Mike said it was Ophelia."

"It might not have been."

"It doesn't matter now. I have to move back to the States. I won't see her again. I didn't even wake her."

"That's good. I think a fight with her would've been one thing too many. Let's worry about Ophelia tomorrow, okay?"

My fingers shake over my lips. "I missed all of their calls. They needed me and I wasn't there. I put winning Carmichael's vote ahead of my sisters."

"You did it *for* them. None of this is your fault. Slow down if you're driving."

"I want to die," I repeat, hitting the accelerator harder.

"Are you going to New York or Paris?"

I can't bear to say it out loud, so disgusted with myself. He must know what that means, because he doesn't ask again.

"I think it's the right thing."

"Thank you," I repeat, over and over. "I can't be a CEO, Robert. I can't raise six girls. I can't manage her care. I can't do any of it." My voice cracks, a hoarse whisper. "I'm twenty-three."

"Slow down, Alex."

"I'm twenty-three," I whisper.

"I've watched you do most of those things before just fine. You're the most capable man I know."

"I've never been fine." Not until *her*.

I knew she'd poison me in the end. She warned me a hundred times, but I didn't listen. My lungs are so full of her, there's no more room to inhale.

My ray of sun has blistered my skin, my orange thread of hope is a noose around my neck.

Chapter 29

OPHELIA

I sit up in bed. I think I slept *too* well. My eyelids are heavy, limbs aching. The cut on my hand looks better. Alex isn't here, but all his clothes are. His laptop is still on the desk. Maybe he's out for a run.

I roll and grab my phone to text him, faced with seventy unread messages.

Bitter ribbons of hate fill the screen. I scroll through insults, threats, and the odd person calling me brave.

What the fuck is going on?

I google Alex's name and clasp a hand over my mouth. Article upon article upon article about his father's long history of crimes kept under wraps greet me. I click on one, unable to watch the video of his mother. She looks nothing like the woman I spoke to at Christmas.

It's the moment I dreamed of. The moment I lay awake and begged the universe for every night for years.

It feels fucking awful.

My eyes halt on the bottom line. *Source credit: Ophelia Winters.*

No, no, *no*. I swallow down the bile in my throat. This wasn't me. Does Alex believe it was me? I run to my old laptop, open on the desk, and type in my password.

An unfamiliar email pops up, sent from my account. I stare at it in horrified silence, calling Alex. The line is busy, but I call again. And again. He doesn't pick up. I dial Vincenzo, too, but he declines.

Ophelia
Alex, it wasn't me. I swear.
Please call me back when you can.
Where are you?

I run out into the hallway, traversing the quiet path to the castle at a pace I've never achieved. The Cortinar halls are quiet as I run into them, begging a student to let me in. I hammer on Colette's door, waiting a tenth of a millisecond before doing it again. She opens it in her pajamas. "Was it really you?"

"No. Of course not."

Her eyes are full of sympathy. "I didn't think so."

"How quickly can Eike get me to the airport?"

"Faster than most," comes a gruff voice. Eike pulls on a black bomber jacket and sunglasses, swiping his keys from her desk.

Colette blushes. "I swear it's not what it looks like."

I feel like it's exactly what it looks like, but now is not the time. "I'll pay you back."

She shakes her head, eyes full of worry for me. "Go, go. You two are too good not to work."

• • •

EIKE DRIVES THE whole way to the airport like a bat out of hell, both my hands holding onto the handle on the roof as the engine roars beneath us. He's run three red lights and gone the wrong way down a one-way street, stoic expression completely unreadable beneath his sunglasses.

I can hardly breathe, hardly imagine what Alex is going through. I'm worried what he'll do to himself.

Several taxi drivers yell at us as Eike drives over the curb and into the bus lane at the airport, skidding to a stop outside the doors. I breathe out a thank-you, hurtling through the automatic doors and into the small foyer.

My eyes land on Alex immediately, going through priority security. He's past the automatic ticket gates. I call him again, watching him turn over his phone and decline. Tears prick my vision. I shout his name, attracting attention from those around us.

He turns to face me. I almost sink to the floor. He's been crying.

Agony lances through my heart. If someone could say *goodbye* with their eyes, he's managing it.

I type out a text.

Ophelia
It wasn't me. It was my account, but it
wasn't me.
I wrote that report before I got to know you.
I deleted it. Someone else posted it.

He looks down at his phone with a neutral expression. He doesn't believe me. He looks so devoid of life, so devoid of hope. I put *us* aside and focus on him.

Ophelia
You can do this, Alex. You're stronger than you think. You're ready.
I see you and I know you, and I know you won't make a mess of this.

Three dots appear above my keyboard.

Alex
If it was anyone, it would've been you.
It was you from the moment we met.

I hiccup a sob. It isn't about the leaked evidence. It's about *him*. It's about the belief that someone could have fixed the darkness inside him.

I look up, dread clawing at my neck. I can't see him anymore.

Ophelia
Please just call me.

Undeliverable.

He's blocked my number.

I stand there, helplessly calling him until long after I've watched the private jet take off. I dial Vincenzo again, my heart breaking. Why won't he just let me speak?

I understand Alex's bitter hatred of the world at that moment. It's a cruel thief that won't let him be mine, won't let me be his. It watched us build a fragile paper house for two delicate hearts and put a match to it all the same.

He's it for me. It sounds rash, but he is. But his shoulders are laden with responsibility that no twenty-three-year-old should bear, and mine are weighted by grief I'll never be able to shake. We've both been fighting for so long, there's no room for healing.

Right person, wrong universe.

My phone pings, and I've never unlocked it faster.

My pulse dulls in my ears, the floor ripples beneath my feet. It's a Jane Austen quote.

Unknown
I was silent, but I was not blind.
You won't bury me so easily.

The attached image is a fuzzy black-and-white photo, but I recognize the scene immediately. Bancroft's broken form kneels before me and Alex in the dark forest, a knife glinting in Alex's hand.

It's exactly what it looks like. It's a prison sentence. It's my chance to get Alex back, swim at nationals, graduate, live a normal, ordinary life, all down the drain. More than that, it's six girls losing yet another father figure.

Ophelia
What do you want from me?

Unknown
Hand yourself over to me, and Alex will
be just fine.

My head swims, ink bleeding in at the edges of my vision. In the middle of the airport, the whole world fades to black.

To be continued...

KEEP READING FOR AN
EXCLUSIVE BONUS CHAPTER

"**O**nly a fucking idiot would drive a Phantom through the Scottish Highlands," I mutter.

I should've bought a Land Rover. The Rolls looks sleek on the busy streets of London, but here amidst the rolling hills and deeply carved glens of the Scottish countryside, I'm longing for four-wheel drive.

"What are you sighing about?" asks Mia, bright and cheery through the speakerphone. In the background, a drawer opens, a spoon clatters into a bowl. It's five in the morning in New York, but my sister couldn't miss the opportunity to "see her big brother through yet another horrific life decision."

"Stupid roads," I mutter, shifting into first gear and continuing down the muddy track. Rain pelts the windshield, the wipers on full power. My headlights do little to combat the dull gloom that settled around the car once I wound my way into Sorrowsong Valley. "And a bad car choice."

"Don't worry, you can always drop out...*again*."

"Shut up, M." This is my second attempt at getting a degree. The first was going well until my mother, deep in the biggest breakdown she'd ever had, called me and begged me to take over her care in place of my father. She told me she was worried he'd kill her, that he'd turn on the girls.

She tried to snatch the words back the next day, but the damage was already done. I packed my career aspirations up alongside my architecture textbooks and Yale rowing gear and headed home that evening.

She was worse than I'd imagined. She's been sick since I left middle school—hell, I think she's been sick since they first fasted her for two days and sent her down a runway at fifteen—but this time wasn't like the others. For the first time, she was scared of my father, flinching at the sound of his voice.

I don't regret leaving Yale. If anything, I'm grateful. Grateful she called me. Grateful I got there before she got hurt and my sisters' childhoods were ruined.

But here I am, doing it all over again, hoping for a better outcome.

Except this time, it's different. Wheels are in motion; a plan is underway. I'm here for *them*. This degree doesn't end with new friendships and a graduation ceremony, but with my father's downfall, the reshaping of Green Aviation, and the freedom of my mother. Failure isn't an option.

Mia crunches a mouthful of cereal into the speaker, making a garbled noise at someone in the background. "Mom wants to talk to you."

"Put her on."

There's muffled shuffling, followed by a shaky breath. I picture her in the darkness of the kitchen in New York, clutching the phone with two frail hands like she does these days. "Hello, sweetheart."

It's impossible to keep the affection out of my voice, and why should I? If her days are numbered, I'll put as much value behind that number as is humanly possible. "Hey, *Maman*."

"Was the drive okay?"

"No traffic, so I can't complain. Did you sleep well? You're seeing Dr. Thomas today, right? Will you ask her to call me after?"

"Alex, this is your chance to finally live your youth. Relax, make friends. I'll be just fine."

She won't be *just fine*, and that's a fact I came to terms with years ago. And I have no intention of relaxing or making friends. If I get distracted by something—*someone*—and something happens to them, I wouldn't be able to live with myself. In, impress Carmichael, out. That's my plan. "I'm going to fly back and visit as soon as the first week is over."

"It's not your responsibility to hold this family together, Alex. I wish you'd see that."

"I do see that," I reassure her. But if I do let go, they'll slip through my fingers and into whatever trap my father has set for them. "I better go, I'm losing signal. I love you, *Maman*. A lot."

"I love you more. Look out for Vincenzo, won't you? I don't trust him not to get himself killed on day one."

No amount of divine intervention will save Vin from his own ridiculous antics, but I agree anyway.

"And…Alex?"

Somehow, the rain gets even harder, my visibility gets worse. "Mmhmm."

"Come back with a girlfriend."

I laugh out loud, disconnecting the call. I don't think I am capable of loving someone else, not until I'm...better. Not until the simplest inhales and exhales aren't the biggest obstacles of my day.

Sorrowsong Castle's tallest spires appear in a gap between two glossy pines, piercing through a low fog. Fucking *finally*. And yet, after two days of driving, it's not a welcome sight. Sorrowsong does not shape its students into admirable people. My father went to Sorrowsong, and his father before that. It's a place to build business connections, to gather blackmail material, to live three glorious years away from the public eye; away from the law.

A text pings through on the dashboard screen. It's Vincenzo.

Vin
Hey bro. Nearly here? How's your mom?
Everything is so fucking old here.
If there are any snacks in your car can
you bring them?

I huff a laugh through my fingers, rubbing my jaw. He's been counting down the days until he can start at Sorrowsong for about five years. His sister is here, too. I think anyone would be excited to come here if they knew they had Belladonna watching over them; she'd punch someone's lights out for looking at Vincenzo funny.

I take a sharp turn in the increasingly narrow track and my GPS announces that I've arrived. The sheet of water on the windshield makes it hard to see, a sharp crack of thunder splintering the relative quiet.

The engine purrs as I accelerate out of the bend, and—*shit. Fuck.* I slam on the horn and the brakes, my seat belt knocking the air from my lungs. A small figure stands in the middle of the road in front of the wide-open gates, turning to face me as if she's got all the time in the world and isn't about to get crushed into the gravel.

I skid to a stop just a hair's breadth away from her miserable form. She makes no effort to move, just closes her eyes. Softly, not tightly, like maybe she'll just rest here for a little nap.

Fucking *idiot*.

I don't know if it's the driving, my guilt for coming here, my anxiety for my sisters back home, but my frustration bubbles over. I've been looking for something to direct my anger at, and here it is; shivering and wide-eyed in a jacket that isn't even waterproof.

The poor conditions don't allow me to get a good glimpse of her, but her hair is a bright shade of copper against the miserable gray backdrop behind us.

Horizontal rain hammers the interior of my car as I lower the window to shout at her. "What in the ever-loving fuck do you think you're doing? Are you *trying* to get killed?"

I expect a flash of hurt, or an angry remark. But instead, she pauses, expression crumpling into a thoughtful frown like she's genuinely considering my question.

It might just be the most relatable thing anyone has ever done.

For the first time, a spark of curiosity pierces the thick, gray blanket of indifference that seems to surround my every waking moment.

Then she opens her mouth, and the reaction I'd anticipated finally comes. "What am *I* doing? What do you think *you're* doing barreling down a narrow lane in fog like this?"

"Exercising my right to drive?" I mutter, quiet enough that I know she won't hear me over the howling wind.

She picks up an overfilled duffel and trudges out of the bright path of my headlights, dropping it at the side of the road like she's actually annoyed by this small series of events. Like *I'm* in the wrong, like she's allowed to stand in the middle of the road and stare aimlessly into the distance, and the drivers of the world have to sit and wait for her to work through whatever emotional turmoil it is that has her auditioning as roadkill.

My route now clear, I should just drive on to the castle.

But I don't.

I'm bored. Have been for days, weeks, months, *years*. Can't remember the last time something spiked my heart rate, piqued my interest. There's nothing about this girl that's inherently interesting; her outfit couldn't be less so. Her bag is a faded shade of charcoal, nothing extraordinary about her height or her shoes or her cheap, rain-soaked jacket.

Yet here I am, creeping forward to get a better look at her.

My phone pings. It's a sound that, nowadays, sends a shard of dread down my spine. A hundred worst-case scenarios flit through my mind. I tug it out of my pocket as I pull the handbrake, reading the text from my therapist and typing a quick reply.

Robert Harwood
Good luck today. I'll call in on your
mother this week.

Alex
Thank you. Let me know how she is. I'm
not sure about her new doctor yet. Talk
tomorrow.

While I'm at it, I tell Vincenzo that I'm not willing to share the
cookies in my glove box.

My phone clatters into the cup holder to my left, and I allow
myself to drink in the woman outside the window for the first time.

She's standing so close I can't see anything above her shoulders,
wearing what my sister Fleur would call a fashion disaster. Her jacket
is eight sizes too big, her skirt hem frayed on top of laddered tights.
Did she get dressed in the dark this morning? Has she lost her hairbrush?

I dip my head lower to see more of her, catching her watching
me with the same curiosity.

The outfit doesn't do her justice.

Something about her has my attention well and truly captivated—
or maybe I've just been alone in a car for too long. She's beautiful,
but not in a way most of the men in my circle would appreciate.
No sharp cheekbones, no neatly applied makeup, no cat-like eyes.
Just a soft sort of beauty; pale brown lashes, a pretty, natural nose
turned red by the cold, and eyes too wide and worried for a place
like Sorrowsong.

I glance out toward the black iron gates—still open—just *begging* me to seal the deal on abandoning my dreams, seducing me
into rotting into my father. I turn my gaze back to the woman to
my right, all chattering teeth and dilated pupils.

She looks terrified, a deer in the headlights.

"Rather die than go in?"

Her tongue darts out to swipe a fat droplet of rain from her pink lower lip, a pale finger removing the strand of hair that has plastered itself there. Something about the action has me gripping the steering wheel tighter.

"Something like that," she replies, watching me warily. She may *look* like she's just come out of the laundry machine, but her voice is soft and sexy, each word buttery in the middle and raspy at the edges. She picks at the reddened skin around her too-bitten fingernails, and though I can't work out if she's about to sprint into the trees around us or ask me for a ride, I think she's too scared to do either.

What is a girl like her doing in a place like this?

Out of pity, I shift into reverse and offer to finish her off. I'm only half joking; if our roles were reversed, I think I'd pick her up on the offer.

This amuses her. Her mouth remains set in the same firm line, but there's a little spark to the cognac color of her eyes that wasn't there before. "Marvelous. If you could just throw me off the drawbridge when you're done."

For the third time in as many minutes, I wonder where this girl has come from.

"I heard the fish needed feeding." I lean over and unlock the passenger door. "Hop in."

Her eyes drop to my watch, to the steering wheel of the Rolls, to the tattoos that spill out from beneath my shirt cuffs. When they coast back to mine, they're full of apprehension, not appreciation. Whatever it is she sees in me is enough to make her pick up her bags and start walking toward the castle.

I peel the car forward to match her slow pace, hampered by her oversized bag. She looks like she might kill me. It's thrilling.

I have this odd sensation—one I haven't felt in a while. Christ, I think I might be having *fun*.

"What's wrong, fish food? Scared of my driving?"

She spins to face me. Oh, she's *mad*. "Is there a reason you're so desperate to get an innocent girl into your car in the middle of nowhere?"

"Innocent." I doubt it. Not if she's here. There's a look in her eye, and I know exactly what it is because I see it every time I lock eyes with my reflection. A burning hatred, a resentment of the world, a complete inability to care about trivial things.

She's grappling for a reason to stay alive, too.

I glance at the time on the dashboard. I'm late, but struggling to care. This girl is more intriguing than whatever *Sorrowsong-is-a-privilege* lecture Carmichael has planned. She stomps around the bonnet, illuminated by the headlights. Her bags are dripping wet, hair stuck to her jacket. *How did she get here? Did she walk the whole way?*

I'm not letting her walk to the castle. She looks about three minutes from hypothermia, two minutes from shitting herself, and one minute from bursting into tears.

And if *I* don't give her a lift, the next person might.

I stop the car, pop the door open, and stride toward her, stretching my aching limbs. The wind is bitter, the raindrops almost painful. She must be freezing.

Her hand darts to her jacket pocket, presumably for a weapon. *Jesus.* I haven't dated in a while. I know I'm rusty with women, but I didn't think I was *stabbed-in-the-first-five-minutes* sort of rusty. My sisters would have a field day with this.

I stop in front of her, lean in a little closer. No heat emanates from her freckled skin, like she's as dead inside as I am. I let my next words caress the spot beneath her ear. A scent that is far too warm and genuine for our surroundings fills my nostrils. Cinnamon and coffee; nothing floral or expensive. "Just out of interest, where would you stab me?"

I hear her breath hitch, watch the line of her shoulders tense. "In the voice box, probably. Seems it'll be the only way to get you to shut up."

I don't know what I was expecting her to say, but it wasn't that. My laugh catches me by surprise, loud and clear in a lull between rumbles of thunder.

Her teeth chatter together on an exhale. It's the final straw. The weight of guilt on my shoulders is big enough already this week. I can't add *letting a creepy ginger girl freeze to death* onto it.

I chuck her bag into the car, which earns me another death glare. "Give that back."

"Get in the car."

"I'll just walk."

Am I... *turned on*? I'm even more out of practice than I thought. "And what does that make me? A glorified luggage service?"

"It makes you a thief."

Fair point.

"I'd rather be a kidnapper," I bite back, sweeping my hand toward the passenger door like a butler.

In the single greatest miracle of our time, she finally gets in the fucking car. I slide into the driver's seat, not missing the whispered *entitled bastard* that slips inside her next inhale.

She kicks wet mud from her boots and onto the pale carpet at her feet. What the hell? *Just* got it cleaned. "What's next? Spit in the glove box?"

Her gaze is heavy, laden with exasperation. "No, shit on the dashboard."

Another laugh slips out, much to my horror. I distract myself from how much fun I'm having by turning on the heater beneath her seat. I switch on the radio, keen to convey an *I'm-not-a-serial-killer* sort of vibe, but it's set to a classical music channel, so that plan goes out the window.

"I just feel like there has to be a middle step there, fish food. Shit on the dashboard is extreme, you could at least…"

"Pee in the cup holder?" she offers, sweetly.

I bite down on a grin. Vincenzo would probably be into that. "Exactly. Everyone is so terribly quick to jump to the extremes these days."

I shift the car into gear, somewhat reluctant to drive. Something feels wrong about ferrying a girl who smells like lazy Sunday mornings into Sorrowsong Castle. She doesn't belong here.

I turn my full attention to her, to the hole in the cuff of her cheap jacket. To the small, thin tote bag at her feet. If I hadn't picked her up, Bill Sikes and Nancy might've. "Are you cosplaying Oliver Twist?"

"Fuck off. Would that make you the Artful Dodger?"

Stroking my ego, Twist. "Clever and charming?"

She scoffs. "No, just irritating."

Clearly a huge fan of hypothermia, she grabs the door handle to leave. I pull the car away to keep her happy, the windscreen wipers doing little to clear the relentless rain. I open my mouth to promise her that I won't murder her, but then decide that's exactly what a murderer would say and promptly shut it again.

We carry on up the lane in slightly awkward silence, the radio crackling from lack of signal. I can see her staring longingly at my sketchbook in the corner of my eye. It's a trapdoor to the endless pit of misery that is my mind. Intricately drawn building plans sit between the pages of chaotic scribbles that anchor me to earth during the most difficult of therapy sessions on the lowest of my days.

"Don't."

"I'm not gonna judge your Mickey Mouse fan art."

My smile isn't so genuine this time. The novelty of her sarcastic attitude is wearing off. "More of a Minnie man myself."

"What *is* in there?"

"Drawings of all my previous victims."

"Divorced, beheaded, died?"

"Then divorced, then beheaded again. With any luck, you just might survive."

She looks like she's swallowed a lemon, eyes wide and wary as she stares out at the world around us. She's oddly charming. I don't think she'll survive the week, but I do find myself rooting for her.

I drum my fingers on the steering wheel, half watching her. If she's wanting me to say something comforting and uplifting, she's chosen the wrong kidnapper. I couldn't be dreading my time at Sorrowsong any more if I tried. A sinking feeling pushes me heavier into my seat, not for what I think I'll encounter here, but what I'll miss at home.

If something happens to my mother, I'm ten hours away. A lot can happen in ten hours.

Beside me, my hostage pulls a cracked phone out of her tote bag, brow furrowed as she blows the water out of the charging port and turns it on. *The police won't help you here*, I want to joke, but it's also true. And I think she knows that already, because she glances at it for half a second and drops it back into the soggy puddle at her feet.

I take a hard right into the staff car park in front of the castle's main structure. It's full, save for one of the chancellor's spaces. *Sorry, Harris.* "You haven't told me your name, fish food."

"And you haven't told me yours."

Fucking hell. I give up on friendly conversation with her and pull off the single greatest reverse bay park in history. She doesn't even look impressed. What a waste. "Alex. My name is Alex."

I unclip my seat belt and shift to face her in the quiet car. The mood shifts slightly, tense to tranquil. It's my first chance to take her in.

Wide, doe eyes blink up at me, a smattering of freckles decorating the pale skin of her cheeks and nose. Her breaths are soft, delicate, like she's waiting for me to say something.

I let my eyes drop. Her skirt sits higher on her thighs now that she's sitting. Her wet shirt molds to her chest in a way I shouldn't even notice. She's athletic, more toned than her outfit would let on. I keep my eyes away from her hair. Mustn't look at the hair.

I've always had a thing for redheads.

Her eyes flick to my forearms, to the swell of my shirt where the top button is undone. God, it's hot in this car. I said I wouldn't entertain any women during my time here, but it's already feeling like a chore. I'm desperate for a distraction, lighting a cigarette even though I've been doing so well at stopping.

I take a long drag, staring out at the gray sky.

Maybe I should try to enjoy my time here. Maybe a little bit of flirting won't hurt. Might pass the time quicker. Might ease the gray cloud. Maybe she'll flirt back. I turn to face her once more. "Maybe Oliver Twist was a *little* harsh."

She yanks her skirt down lower on her thighs, picks up her bag, and, honest-to-God, *runs away from me.*

Fantastic. Never trying that again.

I sink farther into the seat, tipping my head back to blow out a weary breath of smoke. Who *was* that? A hollow sort of emptiness settles in the car; a silence I didn't notice during the other eleven hours of my journey.

In the rearview mirror, I watch her cross the drawbridge like the Grim Reaper himself is nipping at her heels. The second she's out of my sight, the passenger door is yanked open. Vincenzo slides into the car, stealing a cigarette and frowning at the stained carpet beneath his black boots. "Your sisters?"

"No, some weird ginger girl."

His face lights up, a tattooed hand tugging back his hood to reveal a freshly buzzed haircut. "You've got a girl?"

"No, I gave her a ride."

"And? Was she hot? I need all the details, man."

"She ran away from me."

The unlit cigarette falls out of his mouth, chest shaking with laughter. "But was she hot?"

"She was rude."

He grins, all chipped teeth and sparkling blue eyes. "Classic. Everyone wants the mean, hot girl until they're actually mean. Listen," he slaps his palm down on his thigh like a father teaching his son a lesson, "when a hot girl is mean to you, you say thanks. I *love* mean women."

"And that's why you've never made it to a third date."

The flame of his Zippo makes his skin glow orange. "Yeah, but the first two dates are always *great*."

Even if I was interested, I'd need a whole ring binder to keep up with Vincenzo's dating activity. If they reply to his initial hello, he catches feelings. "I'm sure they are."

"Well…if you're not keen, maybe you can introduce me to that ginger girl."

"Absolutely not," I say, before snapping my mouth shut. *What the fuck?* Vincenzo looks like he's just won the lottery. "She's just not your sort of girl. She's scared enough as is," I rush to clarify.

I push open my door and step out into the drizzle before he can reply. A flash of lightning splits the sky into two. It smells like rain, like a damp forest floor. I tip my head back and purge my lungs of coffee and cinnamon, dragging in my first full exhale for what feels like a long time.

Distracted in the first ten minutes. *Not good enough, Alex.*

My life feels like a game of chess against my father, my pieces scattered between Sorrowsong and New York. If I'm to come out on top, I'm going to have to do a whole lot better than this.

ACKNOWLEDGMENTS

TO MR. WOODS, my biggest fan, the best support system, and the reason all of this is possible. I love you.

My parents, for the endless faith in me and all my many career choices. I owe it all to you.

Paisley and Hannah, for helping me shape a messy manuscript into a real book. Your knowledge and your expertise are so valued.

Erin, Tom, Ben, and Doug. I'm sure gift wrapping hundreds of books on my living room floor and covering for me while I write beneath the table at the pub quiz every Monday is above and beyond the call of friendship, but I really appreciate it anyway.

To Daisy, my powerhouse of an agent. You've unlocked doors I never thought I'd walk through, and you've made it look a whole lot easier than I'm sure it is. You're the best of the best!

The biggest of thank-yous to all the other talented agents at PFD who have worked so hard on this book to get it into the hands of more readers.

To Kinza and the wonderful team at Pan Macmillan for taking a chance on Sorrowsong.

To Nicole, Hayley, Sierra, and the incredible Zando-Slowburn team for believing in this book as much as I do.

Somme, for teaching me all I know about authoring and for always being in my corner.

ACKNOWLEDGMENTS

Ellie—we're a dream team! I'll always love working with you.

Rebecca, my idol. I love achieving our dreams together.

Alison, Stef, Manna, Van, Cat, Zarin, Aminah, and Dilan, for all the support that never goes unnoticed.

And last but never ever least, to the readers that picked up this book in all its varying forms. None of this would exist without you being here, and "thank you" doesn't cover it. I'm so lucky to share my stories with you.